The Secret Five
and the
Stunt Nun Legacy

The Secret Five
and the
Stunt Nun Legacy

John Lawrence

Matador
5 Weir Road
Kibworth Beauchamp
Leicester LE8 0LQ, UK
Tel: (+44) 116 279 2299
Fax: (+44) 116 279 2277
Email: books@troubador.co.uk
Web: www.troubador.co.uk/matador

ISBN 978 1848 764 590

British Library Cataloguing in Publication Data.
A catalogue record for this book is available from the British Library.

Typeset in 10.5pt Times New Roman by Troubador Publishing Ltd, Leicester, UK

Matador is an imprint of Troubador Publishing Ltd

Printed in Great Britain by the MPG Books Group, Bodmin and King's Lynn

For my brother, Colin,
who'll now never get to read this book
but who shared the zany world
that was our childhood

Warning:

This book contains mild violence to animals when deemed
appropriate; one or two instances of innocuous swearing;
eighty-eight uses of the word 'suddenly'; three-hundred and
eighty-nine, yes three-hundred and eighty-nine, uses of the
quite irritating qualifier 'quite'; one reference to drug abuse
by a character who should have known better, and three
tasteful references to explicit nudity in order to stoke up the
narrative when all else had failed.

Apathy is the way to happiness. Mental and transcendental tranquillity is only achieved through the joyful celebration of utter mediocrity. Utter mediocrity, if worked at, is the ultimate accomplishment. And then there are all the theories about Did Dog Create Man, and the creation of the universe, going right back to The Big Woof, which always brings me back to the same huge question – why on earth do I have these never-ending bouts of flatulence?

The Thoughts of Whatshisname, 2010

Author's notes

It started as a short story, written for fun, satirising children's books of a certain age. But the characters soon insisted that it became something more hefty.

In the course of writing the book, the intention of parodying elements of the style of Blyton and her contemporaries – the traditionally simple sentence structure, the abundance of the dreaded adverbs such as 'suddenly' and 'carefully', an array of qualifiers such as 'quite' and 'rather', not to mention plot holes the size of Saturn – soon meandered into other styles. (Mr H Pinter, Mr J Joyce, I'm so sorry!) It seemed to become a surreal parody of itself as the satire inflated beyond my original intentions. To sustain this mischievous way of writing, I had to control my mindset as I cast aside rudimentary writing rules while trying to maintain the narrative's Blytonesque anchoring points. And the supposedly one-dimensional 'child' characters began to show signs of a second or even a third dimension, damn them. You can hardly blame them, as they are subject to curmudgeonly authorial commentary and a textual self-awareness – one of them even decides half-way through the book that his character, against my wishes, should wear spectacles. Hmmm.

And, let's face it, these aren't children, I only call them that to upset them – they're young adults, so we can get away with humour that's occasionally a little cheeky, but never intentionally offensive. My parameter was: would it be acceptable for Radio 4? If it was, my internal editor okayed it.

And as for the dog, Whatshisname – he, in particular, deserves a trilogy of his own; he, above all, never lost his sense of purpose; he was the one to lead the narrative in and out of philosophical territory. And he, unlike the four 'children', didn't hide away from the author to complain about their treatment as characters. My only regret is the kangaroo.

If you've never read children's books such as Blyton's, I have two messages: one, your childhood missed a treat; two, I suspect that when you have finished this work, you may well be searching out a Blyton book in an effort to capture the delight of her original style.

Meanwhile, prepare yourself for a mischievous read! Enjoy.

John Lawrence

PART ONE

Chapter One

In which we meet The Secret Five; are forced to listen to Ricky's stream of consciousness oh not again I wish he'd stop; wonder if we've bought the wrong book; blame our parents for encouraging such a style of writing; hear about, but probably don't care about, Uncle Quagmire's strange disappearance.

Whatshisname wasn't thin and wasn't fat. No, that's a lie, he *was* fat. A fat ugly spaniel. As he lay curled up in the front porch of the English country cottage he pondered on the universal question: *do animals think?* He just didn't know. There wasn't enough spare time to think about it, to come up with a convincing conclusion. He sighed and opened one eye. No sign of a super adventure yet, then, thank goodness. Why on earth did they always have to have adventures? And why did they include him in their silly Secret Five club? Maybe if he feigned senility or distemper they'd leave him alone. He sighed again, opened the other eye, and lifted his head to glance at a Persian cat on the lawn. It was lying on its front, casually leafing through a Persian-English phrase book just in case a speaking cat might be needed later in the story.

Whatshisname sniffed the air. Nice! Sweet peas, roses and various other brightly coloured flowers with long and unpronounceable Latin names, most of them ending in -eaeaisa or -dondendadooronron, crowded the garden of the cottage, their scent mingling with his own flatulence which, it seems, had passed through the gates of hell and back before being gently liberated from his generous backside.

He closed his eyes again and sighed, happy to be part of a typical country cottage scene, exactly like you sometimes see on the lid of a very posh tin of biscuits, except for the average contents label, of course. Apart from that, it was typical. It even had a typical village postman, wheeling his squeaky bicycle up the leafy lane. *Squeak,* the bicycle went, *squeak, squeak.* Marvelling at the quality of the ad lib sound effects, the postman rested it against the wall, next to the Best Before Date and the May Contains Nuts label, but it still continued to squeak so he kicked it and it stopped.

The typical village postman carefully looked in his postman's sack and even more carefully took out a letter. He held the envelope up. *To The Secret Five, Guantanamo Cottage* it said. What a surprise! Who'd have thought an envelope could speak! Well, bless his soul and everyone else's too. He smiled, knowing that it might be a very important letter which could start yet another interminable adventure for these four insufferable children and their fat ugly dog. He smiled again, and then another one for luck. He looked at the long long path leading to the cottage door and the dozing dog, shrugged one shoulder, then the other, and tossed the letter over the gate and onto the top of an ecologically-sustainable compost heap.

Satisfied, yet strangely dissatisfied, he adjusted his padded cycling scarf and jumped onto his bicycle. Suddenly he jumped off again, cursing the prankster who had stolen his saddle. Wiping a tear from his eye and re-adjusting his Love Kylie underwear[1], he pushed the now unsqueaky bicycle back up the lane, bemoaning the insignificant part he was contracted to play in the story. As he walked gingerly away he loudly quoted lines from Shakespeare ('Within their alabaster innocent arms, their lips were four red roses on a stalk . . .') and, just in case, from Eastenders ('cor, Mo, that geezer's just fallen down the apples . . .') in the vain hope that he might be called upon to appear later in the story, should the plot

---

[1] *Other ranges of celebrity lacy underwear, usually worn by ladies and rarely by postmen, are also available.*

became desperate enough or the supply of supporting actors suddenly dries up.

Whatshisname watched as the postman disappeared from view. He sighed again. Surely there was a better way of earning bones. Better make a move, they'd wonder where he was, maybe.

Inside the cottage, Betty was slowly waking up after very quickly falling asleep. She ran down to the kitchen in her pink Barbie dressing gown, scratching her bosom, which had appeared almost overnight when she was sound asleep in her bed some years ago. The following morning Betty had asked her embarrassingly flat-chested mother what they were and where they had come from, as they seemed to be a matching pair, almost, but all she got was a mumbled story about The Bosom Fairy and An Unfair Share.

In the kitchen, Betty's Aunt Trinny was carefully toasting and buttering some home-made muffins which had, in truth, been made at someone else's home. Betty's elder brother Daniel, who was over twenty-and-seven-eighths, rather tall and just as serious, was seated at the kitchen table sucking Sugar Puffs up his nose through a straw. This was the first day of their holiday with their aunt, and Daniel was keen to impress. He was also keen to save up enough money for a Ninstation Y-Box Pii 4 games machine. So far he had saved over thirty-one pence, and very soon he would have marginally more. His secret ambition, though, was to buy into an off-shore high-yield tax-diverted bond. Thanks to his casual job as a part-time window mannequin for the local Oxfam shop, buying an on-shore no-yield win-diverted premium bond was far more likely.

It was at that point that Whatshisname came loping into the kitchen, his nose in the air, which is an ideal place for a nose to be if you value your life. Although Whatshisname was, officially, Betty's dog, he was disliked equally by everyone.

'Woof woof woof,' Whatshisname woofed, because he always woofed in threes. Then he began licking and sniffing and snuffling and wagging. Especially wagging, as that was his very *very* favourite. Apart from licking, that is, which took some beating. In fact, whenever Whatshisname sat and thought about it (which he did quite often when searching within his canine consciousness for an idealistic comprehension of morality and truth and his inner doggy-existentialism) when he licked he actually sniffed as well. Indeed, he probably snuffled and wagged at the same time, so all this talk about favourites is a complete waste of your time and mine so let's hear no more about it.

Very soon, all this uninhibited licking and sniffing and snuffling and wagging woke up Ricky and Amy. They were, by birth, and rather painful ones at that, Aunt Trinny's two children, which made them cousins to Daniel and Betty, brother and sister to each other, son and daughter to Aunt Trinny, and grandfather and grandmother to their own future grandchildren in their respective marriages. As annoying young adults (although we shall call them *children*, just to irritate them) they hadn't really given much thought to the rigours of grand-parenting, except for Ricky, who had recently shown an interest in an advert for trousers with an expandable elastic waistband and an integral incontinence trough. He had even built up an impressive collection of stamps. Enough, he thought, to minimise the amount of queuing time at post offices in his old age. Good old Ricky. He was probably going to grow up into an outstandingly sensible adult and utterly boring old fart.

But enough of this pathetic attempt at characterisation. They all knew that it was high time for some gritty dialogue, and Ricky was the first to take up the challenge. 'Hello, everyone,' he said as he and Amy wandered sleepily over to the kitchen table. He was obviously keen to establish himself as a major character at an early stage, but we'll have to see about that, won't we? I mean, all that girly blond hair doesn't help his cause.

'What's for breakfast?' asked Amy in a strangely timorous way, for she was a moist girl of timid disposition and had no redeeming qualities whatsoever except perhaps . . . except perhaps . . . no, definitely no redeeming qualities whatsoever.

'Breakfast? It looks like we've got wholemeal muffins and watered-down rhubarb & turnip flavoured J3O,' replied Betty. 'Do you want some, Amy? And you, Daniel?'

'Hey! What about me?' whined Ricky. There we go again! Ricky often felt a little left out of it all. This was *typical*. No-one ever thought of *his* feelings, those feelings there they go again burning holes in the brain burrowing into my psyche undermining my courage until all I have left yes all I have left is a mouse-like no hamster-like notion of underwhelmingliness what a terrible faddle-fiddle what an utter nuisance je suis oh what a rot I've forgotten how to speak French again . . .

'Ricky!' Betty snapped. With her very own eyes, she glared a reasonably sized glare directly at him.

Ricky jumped. 'Yes?'

'Were you indulging in a stream of consciousness and interior monologue just then?' Betty asked, frowning quietly. 'And were you using the first person tense *and* dubious punctuation? Hmmm? You know we don't allow all that stuff in The Secret Five. It's against our written constitution.'

Of course, Ricky knew he'd been caught out. Maybe if I could bluff my way out of it and crikey that looks very much like a big zit on Betty's nose . . .

'You're doing it again!' Betty squealed.

'What?' queried Amy. 'I didn't notice him doing anything like a stream of . . . a stream of whatever.'

'Consciousness! And *you* wouldn't!' said Betty irritably. 'It's so obvious! His head goes all funny when he does it!'

'I didn't notice anything either,' mumbled Daniel.

'Woof woof woof!' said Whatshisname, who did.

'I can't help it,' whined Ricky. 'I'm quite conscious – so I have some degree of consciousness. And I indulge in the occasional streaming. It's what I do as a character, apparently.'

'Really!' snapped Betty. 'I do hope we don't have to put up with that all the way through the adventure.'

'What adventure?' enquired Amy, quite enquiringly.

'The adventure we are guaranteed to have,' reassured Betty.

'Oh,' said Amy, who was still trying to get to grips with her own character, let alone understand everyone else's, streaming or no streaming.

'All right,' said Betty. 'Ricky, we'll leave it this time, but if there's any more of that stuff, you're out of our guaranteed and spontaneous adventure, okay?'

'Okay,' lied Ricky. Yes, a hamster-like notion of underwhelmingliness what an utter faddle-fiddle . . .

'So, now we've sorted Ricky out, I need to ask,' asked Betty, 'where is Uncle Quagmire?'

'Yes,' said Ricky. 'Where *is* Uncle Quagmire? And, more importantly, why do I always have to call him that? Isn't he married to you, Aunt Trinny? And am I not the fruit of his loin? And why do I not call you *Mummy*? Did not Amy and I emerge through your dilated cervix, attached to your umbilical cord, at some stage?'

Aunt Trinny laughed quietly, but it was far too quiet for the children to hear so let's make her laugh again. Aunt Trinny laughed, a little louder this time. Ricky looked quizzically at her. Amy was bewildered by all the talk about diluted servants and umbrella cords, and the freckles on her nose started to gather together into one big freckly huddle.

'Ricky and Amy, my sweets,' Aunt Trinny said, kindly yet heartlessly, as she ferociously buttered some more muffins. 'When you were both born, Uncle Quagmire and I thought that you calling us Mummy and Daddy would be bowing to certain aspects of the irrational global concept of parenthood in modern society and, although we didn't want to abrogate our childrearing responsibilities, we had to consider the social aspects of care-giving and include a variety of visual, verbal and physical behaviours so that we could engage you both emotionally and successfully manage our interpersonal and intergenerational exchanges.'

'Oh, that's alright then,' chirped Ricky, trying to sneak a peek down Betty's dressing gown.

'And,' Aunt Trinny added, 'we just can't wait to experience empty-nest-syndrome. Bring it on, I say.'

'So,' Amy said, 'thank you for making it all so clear, Aunt Trinny. And it's very comforting to be part of a loving family unit, but where is, erm, Uncle Quagmire?'

'Where indeed, Annabelle,' Aunt Trinny said. 'Sorry, I mean Amy. It is Amy isn't it? Whatever, I'm so glad you've reminded me.' A frown crossed her brow then, rather strangely, crossed back again. 'He went out to buy some Brussels sprouts and some of those new state-of-the-art eco-friendly condoms, and he hasn't come back yet.'

'When was that, dear Aunt Trinny?' Daniel asked, sensibly and incisively.

'About two . . . no, not two . . . it must be three weeks ago,' Aunt Trinny said. 'Now, children, who wants some fried muesli and baked beans?'

'But what if he's had an accident?' whined Ricky. 'Or been kidnapped? Or abducted by aliens and methodically dissected in their mobile experimental laboratory? Or run off with a rather fit blonde lap dancer? Or . . . gosh, did you say fried muesli and baked beans?'

'I think I did,' said Aunt Trinny, uncertainly. 'But help yourselves anyway. You all must be old enough by now to drive mopeds with an engine capacity not exceeding 50cc on UK roads, so you should manage to serve yourself fried muesli and baked beans. I'm just nipping out into the garden to carefully slaughter one of the unsuspecting goats for tonight's dinner.' She looked pensive. 'I'm looking pensive,' she said, 'because I think I'll choose Blodwyn . . . yes, Blodwyn it is then. She's usually the most unsuspecting, what with only three legs now and a painfully inadequate short-term memory.'

Aunt Trinny wandered pensively out of the kitchen, leaving

the four children and their faithful dog Whatshisname to fight over the next line of dialogue.

'Hey,' said Daniel, pleased that he'd got in first. 'Cool! Yo! Rispect! That's hella swag, Uncle Quagmire goin' hooky like tha', fo sho, innit, like, peeps?'

The others stared at him. Amy leaned forward and frowned at Daniel. 'Do you *have* to suddenly talk like that?' She pointed a handy wooden spatula at him.

'Like-a what? I'z well wicked, wooo-man!' Daniel said. 'Random, innit?'

'It's alright, Amy,' Betty said. 'Remember his condition? He tends to go into some form of urban street-talk coma when he gets very nervous or very scared. It was all that stuff about alien abduction and dissection, it started him off. Come on, let's talk about something normal and he'll soon snap out of it.'

The three looked at each other, couldn't think of anything normal to say, so Amy slapped Daniel's face with the spatula.

'Gosh! That was a bit harsh,' Daniel said, holding his cheek.

'Yes, a good slapping works as well,' Betty confirmed.

Satisfied with progress so far, they all sat and tucked into their food, knowing that they needed the sustenance of a good breakfast should things start to happen, which they often would, especially after a good breakfast.

And things did happen, and jolly well right on time too, for when Ricky glanced out of the window he saw the letter that the typical village postman had thrown over the gate several pages ago.

'Look!' he said, pointing with his best finger. 'There's a brand new letter on the compost heap! I'll go and get it, as it might be important and the start of another exciting and spontaneous adventure!' He jumped up, flung open the front door and ran outside to retrieve the letter.

When he came back in again, Amy told him that it might have been a good idea to put on some clothes first, but Ricky was far too busy opening the envelope to listen to a soppy sister.

'It's a letter,' he said, enthusiastically scratching his bottom with the spatula.

Whatshisname sighed. This was a bad sign. This is the way adventures start. Don't they ever learn? Don't read it! *Don't* read it! Please?

'I'm going to read it,' Ricky said.

Whatshisname sank onto the kitchen floor, thinking slippery slopes, wedges, thin ends.

'Who's it from? Show us, do!' said Amy.

The four children gathered around the letter, which was from their dear Uncle Quagmire.

'It's from dear Uncle Quagmire,' said Ricky, with unnecessary predictability.

'What does he want?' asked Amy.

Ricky read the letter, trying his best to paraphrase it in order to avoid accusations of plagiarism. 'It says thanks for gathering around, and he hasn't had an accident or been kidnapped or abducted by aliens and methodically dissected in their mobile experimental laboratory. Nor has he, he says, run off with a rather fit blonde lap dancer yet, although thanks for the suggestion. But he is . . .' Ricky stopped talking.

'Is what?' Amy asked.

'He is . . .' Ricky repeated.

'Is what?' Betty asked.

At this point, Ricky looked up from the letter and at each of the others in turn. His face was ashen, yes, ashen. The others were about to say exactly *how* ashen when, all of a sudden . . .

Chapter Two

In which we experience the first of many irritating Secret Five meetings; the kangaroo doesn't turn up; they all chat and laugh about the doctrines of the sixteenth century Reformation and its effect on religious supremacy in Scandinavia; they meet an insignificant character who is wearing a hat.

'I say,' said Amy crossly. 'That was a really silly place to have a chapter break. Is this how it's going to be?'

'I hope there aren't too many of those!' said Daniel, whose voice had become quite nasal, his nostrils now crammed full of Sugar Puffs. 'But what about the letter, Ricky?'

'He says,' Ricky said, 'that he needs our help and would we like to go and see him. He says that . . . golly! He's been forced into hiding! He's somewhere near here in a village called Stunning Bottom, in a big old spooky house called Greentiles. He says that he chose a big old spooky house rather than a small new unspooky one with a white uPVC conservatory because that's more fitting for our sort of adventure.'

'How very considerate of him,' said Betty. 'I think this calls for an official meeting of The Secret Five.'

'If we must,' Amy moaned.

Whatshisname opened one eye and peeped up at them. This was silly, this relentless urge to have adventures. What *was* it about humans? He closed his eye and released a thimbleful of hell-gas. That might do it.

'Come on everyone,' Betty enthused. 'Let's sit at the table and meet. Officially.'

So they did. They sat down at the table and met, officially, but it must be pointed out that, even if it were unofficial, to an impartial observer it probably wouldn't have looked any different, although it would have significantly changed the meeting's agenda, as the first and most urgent issue to discuss would have been the unnerving presence of that uninvited impartial observer inside their kitchen.

'Okay,' said Betty, who could be a bit bossy at times, as well as being slightly susceptible to an excessive production of earwax. 'Secret Five regulations dictate that we need the password from you all first. Daniel?'

Daniel frowned quite a big frown, the first of several hundred highly irritating frowns. 'I hate passwords,' he moaned. 'Can't we just have a PIN number? Anyway, you *know* me! Why do I always have to say the secret password?'

Betty sighed. 'Because this is a secret club and all secret clubs have secret passwords,' she said. 'We can't risk outsiders and gatecrashers and spies getting into our secret club, can we now?'

Daniel had another frown, slightly bigger than the previous one but with crinkly bits around the edges where his ears were firmly attached to his head. 'But I'm your elder brother! I helped change your nappies and tenderly wiped your dirty bottom with bits of recycled cotton wool, remember? One particular time, I recall . . .'

'Er, thank you, Daniel. That may have been so,' Betty insisted rather insistently. 'But you can never be too sure these days, what with face transplants and all that.'

Daniel twitched. 'Hey! Yo Sis,' he said. 'Yo, random! Diss am well shabby, woo-man. Innit? Like.'

The others groaned. 'Betty, did you have to mention face transplants?' Amy scolded. 'Look what you've done to him now.' She reached out and slapped Daniel with the spatula again. He rubbed his cheek and thanked her.

'Sorry everyone, but we do need passwords,' said Betty relentlessly. 'It's in The Secret Five Constitution, so it would take a convention, hours of vigorous debate, secret ballots, and a special committee to formulate and agree any amendments. And then there's the subsequent ratification process.'

'Or we could just use Tipp-ex?' suggested Ricky.

'That is a reasonable alternative,' said Betty. 'But for now . . . er, Amy, you say the password, then Ricky, then Daniel.'

'But if I say it, then it won't be a secret,' Amy moaned. 'Anyway, I've forgotten it. We change it so often I get confused. We should have it pasted up on the wall.'

Betty huffed, then puffed. Whatshisname, attracted by all the huffing and puffing, stood up. He sidled over to Amy's side.

'Aha!' Amy exclaimed. 'Thank you Whatshisname! He's reminded me of the password! It's *testicle*!'

The others giggled quite a short giggle then stopped because they weren't too sure why they were giggling. Whatshisname lay down again and whimpered, no doubt recalling the surprise outing to the vets when he was but a puppy, in the days before everyone forgot his real name.

'It's *not* testicle!' said Betty. 'You're so stupid! That was the password before the previous password.'

'I thought it was testicle as well,' Daniel said, now quite calm and fully recovered from his bout of street-talk. He snorted out a Sugar Puff at Ricky.

'And me,' said Ricky, picking up the Sugar Puff and popping it into his mouth. 'I thought it was testicle.'

Whatshisname whimpered again, and licked his vacant area. Not only were they planning another adventure, but they just had to keep on and on about *that* fateful day.

'It's ovum!' said Betty. 'Remember?'

They all nodded, paused, looked at each other, then shook their heads.

'Right,' Betty said. 'Amy, what's the password?'

'Ovum,' said Amy.

'Correct. At last!' Betty said.

The other two repeated the secret password then Betty declared the meeting open. 'Now, I vote we go and find Uncle Quagmire,' she said. They all nodded and Betty declared the meeting closed. They stood up and Daniel snorted the rest of the Sugar Puffs at Ricky, who scooped them up and dropped them back into the box.

'Maybe we can all go for a hike to where he is,' suggested Ricky. 'Can we take some food with us, do you think?'

'Ricky!' scolded Betty. 'You're *always* hungry! But it's quite a good idea that is worthy of consideration. Let's take Marmite and rhubarb jam sandwiches! I'll go off and find my John Prescott's Hip and Thigh Diet Cook Book, Volume II, unabridged illustrated pull-out edition, and see what I can rustle up.'

'What about something to eat for Whatshisname?' asked Daniel.

'Woof woof woof,' said Whatshisname, extremely enthusiastically for a dog with his medical history.

'Yes, we simply must take something for Whatshisname,' said Amy. 'How about a big bone that he can chew and chew.'

Whatshisname tried to frown at Amy. Bones? Bones! Dogs' preferred liking for bones is a misconception conceived and perpetuated by humans intent on disposing of their unwanted food scraps. Peanut butter, please! Bones come in at a very poor second to peanut butter!

'Bones, yes! He'll love that! His favourite! But I bagsy carry the sandwiches,' Ricky said.

'Shall we go, then?' asked Amy, rather impatiently.

'Yes, but we'll need to look at a map first,' replied Amy patiently. Then she realised that she'd answered her own question, so she felt rather silly and stood there looking down at her feet in embarrassment.

Ricky went off to put on some clothes, and to go to the toilet for a sneaky stream of consciousness. He returned with The Sunday Sport Concise World Atlas (revised & updated to exclude Cornwall, which had been bitten off by a giant alien). They gathered around to look at the atlas, except for Ricky who was not very good at directions and had gone to clean up the bathroom floor.

Very soon Betty had made their lunch, changed out of her Barbie dressing gown and into jeans and an *I ♥ McFly*[1] a-line v-neck x-factor t-shirt, and they were ready to go.

'Right, we'll take the *little* lanes and *little* paths,' said Daniel, who obviously knew about such things.

So off they set, looking for little lanes and little paths. Whatshisname kept trotting down big lanes and big paths but came back when Daniel cheerily called *Here Boy!* and threw a lump of rock at him. Together they hiked along a riverside path which ran alongside a river, although there was some discussion about whether the river actually ran alongside the path and was therefore, in truth, a pathside river. But after a while the conversation, rather predictably, degenerated into a discussion on the doctrines of the sixteenth century Reformation and its effect on religious supremacy in Scandinavia, so they agreed to set aside the pathside / riverside issue for now, to be fully investigated by Ricky who would present his findings to members at an extraordinary meeting with a buffet lunch included.

But they were now a bit lost, so they stopped walking and gathered round to discuss exactly how lost they might be. The world atlas proved to be a bit confusing to them all.

'Are we here?' asked Daniel, pointing at the map.

'No, silly!' said Amy. 'That's Ethiopia! If we'd have turned right at our gate we would be there, but we turned left, didn't we! Boys! Huh!'

Daniel was a bit upset at Amy's free and easy use of exclamation marks, so he pointed a finger at her.

'Where did you find that?' Amy asked.

'On the path, back there,' Daniel told her, and he put it into his

---

[1] *Other boy bands of supremely dubious talent are available.*

pocket for later, just in case there was an acute finger shortage at some point in the story.

They moved on and then, suddenly, as the path turned left without indicating, they came across a man with a hat.

'Woof woof woof,' said Whatshisname, for no reason whatsoever except to help maintain his status as a key character.

'Let's ask this man with a hat,' said Betty.

'Oh, yes, let's,' said Amy.

Ricky hailed him with his hand. 'Man With A Hat! Is this the way to Stunning Bottom?'

'Aaar,' said the Man With A Hat, nodding his head. His hat nodded too.

'Does that mean yes?' Daniel asked the Man With A Hat.

'Aaar,' the Man With A Hat said.

'Oh, jolly good,' said Daniel.

'Thur be strrraaaange a-goin's on at Stunnin' Bo'um, yunguns. Stay away frum thur,' the Man With A Hat growled.

'Gosh,' said Daniel. 'Really? Truly?'

'What did he say?' asked Betty.

'No idea,' said Daniel. 'Let's ask him again, shall we?'

But the Man With A Hat had gone on his way, eager to exit stage left and resume his day job as an assistant alchemist (which, incidentally, barely funded his acting career so he was now forced to take a part-time job at a call centre, circulating around desks playing Greensleeves on his violin to help soothe the nerves of customers on hold).

'That's queer,' said Amy. 'Why was he only wearing a hat? And why did his donkey have five legs?'

'Why, it's because he's stupid!' said Ricky, and they all laughed except Betty. And Amy and Daniel. And Whatshisname, to whom laughing and panting were so closely allied that he didn't see why he should give the impression that he was panting at the sight of a donkey.

Then Daniel said, 'Wait! Do you know what I'm thinking?'

Chapter Three

In which our pals encounter an unexpected hedge, of all things; Amy, typically, wants to join another story; Whatshisname philosophises about sound and smell; nothing much happens in an extremely short space of time, then the chapter ends a little too abruptly.

'Honestly! I wish he wouldn't do that!' said Amy. 'We need far more warning!'

'Yes!' said Daniel. 'I was just saying . . . erm, what was I saying, before the unexpected chapter break?'

'You said,' said Betty, casting an irritable glance in the direction of the reader who, not for the last time, had been unfairly lumbered with the blame, 'at least I think you said, *do you know what I think?*'

'Oh yes,' Daniel said. 'Right . . . ahem . . . Do you know what I think?'

The others crowded round, closely, there and then, on the riverside path by the pathside river. Daniel lowered his voice. 'I think that he's . . .'

'Why has your voice lowered?' asked Ricky, frowning.

'What?' squeaked Daniel.

'It's lower. Sort of . . . well, lower,' said Ricky.

'Yes,' said Betty. 'I didn't like to mention it, but now you have . . .'

'Look,' said Daniel, quite tetchily, 'I don't control this stuff, you know. Just accept that my voice went lower, okay?'

'Okay,' they all said, glancing at each other, obviously unconvinced. Then they all gathered closer, even closer than they were before, which pleased Ricky as he could sneak a look down Betty's top.

Daniel started again. 'I think that he's . . .'

'What are you doing?' Betty snapped at Ricky.

'Nothing,' replied Ricky, rather too quickly.

'Please listen to me!' whined Daniel.

'Yes you were. You were looking down my top!' Betty snapped back.

'I wasn't!' said Ricky. 'And stop all this snapping!'

'I saw you!' said Betty, unsnappily.

'Erm,' ermed Ricky, 'yes, maybe I did, just a little peek, but I'm at that stage in life. I can't help it . . . or so it seems. And I'm only a young adult, apparently, and have been for years, so it can't be classed as too peculiar, can it now?'

'You two! Can I *please* continue?' Daniel pleaded. 'Could you have this discussion later, much later? Maybe in an appendix?'

'Okay,' Betty said, clasping her palms firmly to her chest. She kept one eye on Ricky and, to be sure, the other eye on Ricky as well. Ricky shrugged, and they gathered closer, even closer than the even closer from before.

'Right! I was saying . . .' Daniel said, and paused, waiting for an interruption, looking around the close group one by one. After a couple of very quiet minutes looking at his friends, with no interruptions on the horizon, Daniel continued.

'I was saying that I think that the man with a donkey might have escaped from the prison which is not far from here and from which people escape sometimes and are usually caught by a group of very clever children with their faithful dog but only after the local village policeman doesn't believe them and they accidentally come across an old spooky house where the rogues are hiding in the hidden cellar with their stolen treasure. That's what I think. Do you?'

'No,' the others said in unison, together.

'Woof woof woof,' agreed Whatshisname.

Daniel looked at them all again. 'Maybe you're right,' he said.

They all stood up straight and continued to walk along the path.

'You were looking more than a bit,' Betty muttered to Ricky. Ricky tried his best to ignore her sharp words but, nevertheless, felt that love was beginning to blossom between himself and Betty, which was a crazy thought when you stop to think about it because he's tremendously ugly and, after all, they are cousins, which might present difficulties in the form of a nursery full of drooling half-wits should they ever get it together and produce an offspring without the precaution of signing up for a course of genetic counselling.

Shaking their heads at all the drivel about drooling half-wits, Betty and Ricky wondered what sort of adventure story they had got themselves into, both of them finding it far too far-fetched to associate half-wits with The Secret Five.

'Er . . .' erred Ricky, scratching the side of his forehead.

'Erm . . .' said Betty, doing the same, but to her own forehead, as scratching Ricky's forehead and saying *erm* would have been downright silly. 'It's probably best to move on, eh? Come on everyone, we need to find this Stunning Bottom.'

They all walked on for a while and then, all of a sudden, they found themselves on a long narrow lane that went somewhere one way and, they thought, somewhere else the other.

Referring carefully to their world atlas, and after a rather heated discussion about which way they should go, they decided to take the direction that was signposted *To Stunning Bottom*. Eventually, after walking for what seemed like quite a long way (although, to be fair, it was nothing compared to the immense distance between Planet Earth and the Andromeda NGC224 Galaxy), Betty started complaining about her feet. To be fair, the others had started to complain about Betty's feet a long time ago. Ricky also started complaining about feeling really hungry, so they stopped and sat down on a bench to eat their sandwiches. But, alas and alack, they found that Ricky had mislaid them somewhere! Clumsy Ricky! He still had the wrapper, though, and they all sat around sniffing it while Whatshisname sat at their feet, chewing the bone that had been thrust under his nose and that he felt under contractual pressure to chew with some fervour.

They sat sniffing and chewing for a while before Daniel suddenly exclaimed, 'What's that?' He pointed with his finger. They all looked at his finger and Amy told him that it was a bogey, but Whatshisname jumped up and licked it off before anyone else could.

'No, that!' said Daniel quite crossly. He was pointing at a hedge with a gap in it.

'It's a gap in a hedge,' said Betty. 'That's a little bit strange.'

They all went over to the gap in the hedge and looked through it. There, through the gap in the hedge, they could see another hedge!

'I don't like this,' said Amy, who obviously didn't like it. 'It's too spooky. I want to join another story.'

Then, without much warning, Whatshisname ran off through the gap in the hedge. 'Woof woof woof,' he barked as he ran, which was a jolly good trick. His ample backside disappeared from view.

'Let's leave him and go. Stupid dog. I never liked him anyway,' said Amy, rather grumpily. 'He was fat and smelled of pineapple and creosote.'

'Look!' said Daniel, ignoring her because he rather liked the heady combination of pineapple and creosote. 'Through the gap in the hedge! If you look carefully through the gap and then through a handy gap in the other hedge, you can see a big spooky house with green tiles! Gosh, it must be Greentiles! What a bit of luck!'

'Erm . . . those tiles aren't green. They're blue,' said Betty, squinting at the blue tiles.

'No, they're green,' said Ricky, staring at the green tiles.

'I think they're blue, too,' said Amy. They all stood there arguing about it for a very long time. Eventually they agreed on a negotiated settlement – the tiles were greenish-blue, although Amy, deep down, preferred bluish-green. Then they secretly and stealthily crept on all fours alongside the hedge, followed by Whatshisname who, having mysteriously re-appeared without any satisfactory explanation and with total disregard for a structured plot progression, padded behind them and was now busy admiring Daniel's firm young buttocks.

Whatshisname had actually been listening from afar to the blue / green argument, and had pondered mournfully about humans and their perception of colour. Although he was a big fan of Galileo, whom he thought was one of the great non-canine thinkers, he had his doubts about the theory that colour and sound only exist in the mind of the observer. Take away the observer, dog or human, and colour and sound don't exist. If a tree falls in a forest and there's no dog there to hear it, does it make a sound? He thought not. And, here's another thought, what if he were in the forest, beneath that tree, and the tree didn't know he was there so it didn't make a sound as it fell, he'd be in mortal danger! But then again, he thought, he'd have to not be there to not hear it, so perhaps his not being there had saved his life! Phew! That was a close one. But, hang on, if he wasn't there, he wouldn't hear it . . . hmmm, this was getting complicated. To be safe, he'd avoid not being in a forest in future, so that he wouldn't not hear a tree falling on him. That seemed like a plan. This perception of the existence of sound and colour is worth more of a ponder, he thought.

He stared up at the tiles. Definitely blue. Definitely. He sat down, looked away and closed his eyes. Of course, the tiles must no longer be blue. Dare he take a peek to check? He turned his head slightly and opened one eye just a fraction. Damn it, they'd turned blue again. He closed the eye and quickly reopened it. Blue again! Those tiles were far too smart for him, he decided. He noticed through the one eye that the children were now all standing and looking strangely at him. He opened the other eye. What's up with them?

'Is he all right?' asked Amy, staring closely at Whatshisname.

Betty frowned. 'He goes like this sometimes. It's as though he's thinking, but that's just not possible. He's only a dog, after all.'

Only a dog! Whatshisname stood and glared at Betty. Only a dog indeed. He'd show them. He lifted his tail and joyfully released a loud burst of hell-gas, adding another olfactory quality to accompany the pineapple and creosote.

'Ugh!' squealed Amy, wrinkling her nose and backing away. 'What a nasty dog!'

Oh *yes*, Whatshisname thought, they got that all right. *That* sound and smell obviously exists. Much more tangible results than the colour experiment. Yesss! He trotted away, wagging his tail in order to spread his joy more widely.

After a bout of wafting and nose wrinkling, the children reached the gate to the house. They stood and read a nameplate on the gate. They gasped a silent yet meaningful gasp. The nameplate said *Greenishbluetiles* and, at the bottom, it said *End of chapter alert*.

'That's good,' said Betty.

'Yes, that's good,' agreed Amy, not really understanding whether it was or not.

'Except it's the wrong house,' Ricky said.

'Oh, bother,' said Betty.

'Oh, bother,' said Daniel, a bit upset that Betty had thought to say it before he did. He was becoming quite grumpy because she was always stealing his best lines.

'Let's go on for a bit,' Ricky suggested. 'We might find a tea shop.'

Unaided, they all started to walk down into the village. But, extremely suddenly, they heard a big roar and a big rumble that shook the very ground under their very feet! Wisely, their very feet stopped walking. Whatshisname ran up to them. He started to whine and whimper. And so did Daniel. Our pals were all terrified! Absolutely terrified!

Chapter Four

In which they discover Greentiles; they meet a weird and highly irritating old woman; they find that their cover has been blown and decide that they should reconsider the suitability of the name The Secret Five; they hear about Uncle Quagmire's secret mission; great, the kettle's boiling.

To be honest, they weren't absolutely terrified at all. In fact, they were quite happy that they had been well prepared for the chapter break. They did, however, whimper a bit when, out of a driveway ahead of them, a big red truck pulled out and drove slowly up the lane towards them. They squeezed themselves against a surprisingly damp dry stone wall as the truck roared and rumbled past them. It had big letters on the side which read *Mysterious Red Truck with Very Suspicious and Evil-Looking Driver.* On the back it read *Am I being driven well? If not, telephone 029880 993123 or stop evil-looking driver and tell him personally.*

'Did you *see* the driver?' asked Betty when it had disappeared out of sight. 'He looked very suspicious and evil if you ask me.'

'Right. What did the driver look like, Betty?' asked Ricky, helpfully.

'Very suspicious and evil,' said Betty. 'And thank you, Ricky.'

'That was spooky, wasn't it?' said Daniel. 'But look! The driveway that the truck came out of. The house at the end of it has *green* tiles and it also looks very spooky and it hasn't got a white uPVC conservatory! You don't think that's where Uncle Quagmire is staying, do you?'

'Good thinking, Daniel. You're not as stupid as we all think you are! Let's go and explore,' said Betty, and they all scampered down the lane then stood in a line at the end of the driveway, looking intently at the house.

'It *has* got green tiles,' said Ricky. 'Shall we go in?'

'Yes, let's,' said Betty.

Blow it, thought Daniel, she's got to a good line first again. He was going to say *yes let's*. This was really getting too much.

Gingerly and secretly they walked backwards up the driveway, so that they wouldn't see anyone who might see them. When they reached the house, they turned and saw a big sign on the door – *NO Vegetarian Fundamentalists, NO Children Seeking An Adventure, NO Tupperware Salesmen (unless those handy cereal dispensers are on offer)*.

They all gasped with intense disappointment, except Whatshisname whose interpretation of intense disappointment had dramatically changed during the surprise outing to the vet's.

'Bother!' exclaimed Ricky. 'Is that the end of our adventure, do you think?'

Whatshisname perked up and willed Betty to say yes. *Please* say yes. Pretty please?

'Why, no!' said Betty quite enthusiastically. 'Let's all go round the back. There might not be a notice on the back door.'

'Splendid idea!' said Daniel, who sometimes felt quite proud of his sister's quick thinking under pressure and her occasional attempts at making macramé plant holders.

So, in single file, they went round the side of the house, as they had to do that to get to the back. Whatshisname trotted and pattered after them, eager to do some trotting and pattering at last, as he had been told that dogs in stories often trot and patter about and he did not want to be seen as a dog that couldn't trot and patter when the situation called for it.

They all reached the back door more or less at the same time. Betty pointed at it. 'Look! There's no notice here! Let's explore! Go on, Ricky, open the door.'

Ricky slowly turned the door knob with one of his free hands and carefully pushed the door open. It creaked and creaked. Then, astonishingly, it creaked some more! They waited patiently, glancing at their wrist watches, until it had stopped all the creaking and, gingerly, almost *too* gingerly, they crept inside. They found themselves in a big spooky hallway with big spooky stairs going up to somewhere or other.

'Well, do you think that we were being *too* gingerly?' Amy whispered to the others. They all nodded their own heads up and down in agreement, but then decided to be slightly less gingerly in future to avoid any more authorial accusations of overgingerliness.

At that moment, or it might have been the moment immediately before, or even after, a figure suddenly appeared in the big spooky hallway! It was a ghostly apparition with a long white robe, ragged grey hair, and skin as grey as the grey of a reasonably grey thing. It seemed to float towards them, making a *oooooh* sound. They all stepped back warily, their faces quite pallid, except for Whatshisname who bravely trotted forward, his tail wagging and his face a fat spaniel colour.

The figure ooooohed again. 'Oooooh! Issa doggay!' it said, and bent down to stroke Whatshisname, who wagged and wagged his tail at the back, and growled and growled at the front, proof positive that he was two written-off small dogs welded together to make one fat one.

'Phew!' said Ricky. 'It's only an old lady.'

And it was indeed only an old lady, a haggish old lady, still with that ragged hair and skin as grey as the grey of the grey thing we mentioned before. But it seemed that she was not pleased at being called an old lady. Not pleased at all.

'Ole lady?' the old lady yelled. 'Ha! I ay chuffed at bin called an ole lady[1]!'

---

[1] *I am not too pleased at being called an elderly lady.*

'I don't think,' muttered Daniel to the others, 'that she's pleased about being called an old lady.'

'Any road up[2], what am yow kids doin' 'ear?' the old lady yelled in some strange Midlands dialect.

The children cowered quite a lot.

'Oy, yow!' the old lady said, pointing at Betty's chest. 'Yes, yow! What am them? Them big boobies? Tek yer eye out, them 'ud. Them cor[3] be real. Blimey, Bab[4]!'

Betty looked down at her chest. In fact, everyone looked at Betty's chest, even Whatshisname, who sat at Betty's feet and looked up at one, then the other, then back again several times, as though he were at a Wimbledon final.

'I can't help it!' Betty said, clutching her hands to her chest. 'Stop looking, everybody!'

'She can't help it!' said Ricky to the old lady. 'Don't look, you're not a member! Leave them alone, she can't help it. Anyway, what sort of silly dialect is that, you old hag?'

'Ole 'ag?' the old hag cried, taking up a position that conveyed minor indignation. 'Oyl 'ave yow know, om fram Doodlay near Wullvramtunn, Black Countary born an' bred, an' oy bin at the Greentoiles Sunset 'ome for The Terminally Biwildered for sum toime, an' no-wun, *no-wun*, 'as ever called me an ole 'ag!'

'Really?' said Ricky, frowning. 'Are you sure? It seems so appropriate. Anyway, I don't really think we can all keep up with your rather silly dialect for long.'

'That's true. Is there any chance you could tone it down a bit?' asked Betty.

The old hag looked pensive, scratching her haggish chin with her haggish finger. 'Oy s'pose . . . I suppose I could drop it if it's too

---

[2] *Anyway. [honest it is!]*

[3] *can't*

[4] *Good gracious, my girl.*

much. I was finding it hard to follow myself. But I was quite looking forward to being mysteriously indecipherable as well.' She looked disappointed. 'All those hours listening to Noddy, wasted! Ha!'

'Noddy?' queried Betty. '*The* Noddy? Toytown and Big Ears Noddy?'

'Ha!' harred the old hag. 'No, silly big-chested girl. Noddy Holder! He's *the* Noddy, stupid child. Remember Slade? Eh? The four piece glam rock combo?' The old hag wiggled her haggish hips. 'Cum on feel the noize!'

The children looked at each other and seriously thought about frowning, or calling for a nurse or two.

'Ha!' the old hag said. 'Wasted on you kids, ain't it? But maybe I could use the dialect occasionally, for dramatic effect, to save wasting it altogether? I could say *bostin!* now and again. Is that all right?'

The children reluctantly agreed, and the old hag once again took up a position that conveyed minor indignation, but this time it was bordering on major. 'Ha!' she said. 'I've never been called an old hag! *Never!* Well, thinking about it, maybe a few times, but *never ever* by a bunch of no-hopers like you lot!'

'No-hopers?' exclaimed Daniel. 'Cheek! I'll have you know that we are the famous Secret Five!'

The old lady, startled, looked at them through her very own haggish eyes, then shrieked a shriek that rang around the hallway, up the stairs, in and out of a handy broom cupboard and back down the stairs again. The children politely waited for it to return. When it did, Ricky was the first to speak.

'What's the matter with her now?' he whispered to the others.

'I think she's mad,' said Betty, a little too loudly.

'Ha! I am not mad,' the old hag said, approaching the children, a haggish finger pointing at them in a seriously haglike way. 'I'm just IMPRESSED.'

Betty nudged Daniel. 'I wish she'd stop talking in capitals. It's so INFURIATING,' she said.

'Well, you just did it,' said Daniel.

'Did I?' Betty frowned.

'Yes, you said INFURIATING,' Daniel said.

'Oh, SORRY,' said Betty.

'You just did it again,' Daniel said. 'Get a grip, Betty!'

Betty furrowed and wrinkled her brow and looked really embarrassed. She thought it best to change the subject. 'Then why are you . . .' she asked the old hag, pausing to ensure that her voice was in lowercase, 'impressed?'

'Why? Because you're *The* Secret Five,' she replied. 'I heard all about you from your dear Uncle Quagmire. What am yow . . . erm, what are you doing here? Are you having another great adventure? Bostin! But where's your kangaroo? Eh?'

'Gosh! How did you . . .' Amy said, stopping mid-sentence and pointing a medium-sized frown at the old hag. 'Kangaroo?'

'You kids must think I'm yampy[5]!' the old hag said.

The children nodded. 'Woof woof woof,' agreed Whatshisname.

'Don't you think I don't know about the kangaroo,' the old hag said. 'I know *all* about you lot and your adventures.'

Whatshisname sighed. He liked this old lady, as she smelled of gammon and freshly-sawn timber. It went well with his pineapple and creosote fragrance. But did she have to encourage all this adventuring?

'You know all about us? But we're The *Secret* Five!' said Ricky. 'We're supposed to be a *secret*! That's the whole idea.'

'Ha!' said the old hag.

'Maybe we should change our name?' suggested Daniel.

The others looked peculiarly at him. The old hag stood there (or, to be precise, just to the right of there) wondering if she had

---

[5] *You must think I am not of sound mind, dear children.*

time to dash off to the toilet while this bit of dialogue took place.

'Change our name? What to?' enquired Ricky.

'Well . . .' said Daniel, quite intelligently, 'I think we'd need an antonym.'

Amy perked up. 'We had an Anthony in our class at school. Will he do?'

'Hmmm . . . an antonym, eh? What about unsecret. Or unconcealed?' suggested Ricky, ignoring his sister's confused look.

'The Unconcealed Five?' said Betty. 'It hasn't got that certain ring to it, has it?'

'Overt?' suggested Daniel.

'The Overt Five,' said Betty, thoughtfully. 'No. It sounds far too French. That'd never do.'

'What about palpable?' suggested Ricky.

They pondered very hard upon *palpable*, then they all agreed that *The Palpable Five* sounded quite stylish, especially in italics.

'But we'll only use it,' said Betty, 'if we find out that The Secret Five is no longer a secret.'

'Shouldn't we have a meeting to decide that?' asked Amy.

'Another meeting?' Daniel groaned. 'This is like déjà vu.'

Ricky pondered. He was sure he'd heard that phrase before.

'Good idea, Amy,' said Betty. 'A meeting. But first we're going to need the password from you all.'

'Ha!' the old hag yelled. 'It's *testicle!*'

Amy jumped up and down. 'Told you so! Told you so!'

Betty glared at Amy, so Amy glared at Ricky who, in turn, glared at Daniel who, having no-one left to glare at, glared down at Whatshisname, who was still behaving as though he was at the Wimbledon final. But then Whatshisname sensed the glare, considered his canine options and turned to glare at the old hag, who had sat down on the stairs while they were glaring and now looked quite relieved that the attention was back on her. She stood up and resumed her old hag expression while pulling a West

Bromwich Albion Football Club bobble hat onto her bobbly grey head.

'Your Uncle Quagmire told me all about you and your funny tricks,' the old hag said, 'so you can stop all that glaring now. You look like morkins[6], you do.'

Betty was a bit put out at being told when and where to glare in this age of human rights for the common people but, nevertheless, she did slowly stop glaring, at her own steady pace, then bravely edged towards the old hag. 'Old hag-like person, where is our Uncle Quagmire?' she demanded in fluent English.

'Woof woof woof!' added Whatshisname in his supporting role.

'Ha!' cackled the old hag. 'Your Uncle Quagmire was hiding here, but now he's gone.' She paused all this irritating cackling to look around her furtively, in a pathetic effort to raise the level of suspense. 'But not before he told me why he was here and all about his secret mission.'

The children gasped.

'Mission?' asked Ricky.

'Secret mission?' asked Amy.

'His secret mission?' asked Daniel.

'All about his secret mission?' asked Betty.

'Woof woof woof woof woof woof?' asked Whatshisname.

'Oh, you're all intrigued now, aren't you?' the old hag said. 'Well, I'm going to tell you, but only if I can join The Secret Five.'

They all gasped again, but this time they gasped separately and in alphabetical order.

'What? You? Join The Secret Five?' exclaimed Ricky.

'Impossible! We'd then be The Secret Six!' said Betty.

'You must admit, a bit of alliteration would be good for marketing,' said Daniel.

---

[6] *You look like silly persons, you do*

'But . . .' began Betty, 'but . . .'

'Yeah,' said Daniel, 'that sort of thing.'

'But . . . The Secret Six?' moaned Betty.

'Actually, wouldn't it be The Palpable Six?' chipped in Amy, showing an uncommon amount of intelligence.

'Ha! If you let me join,' said the old hag, 'I'll tell you all about your Uncle Quagmire and his secret mission.'

The children hummed and hawed, with the emphasis on humming rather than hawing, then Betty went one further and aharred. 'Aha!' she aharred. 'What if we make her an honorary member? Without the privileges.'

'Erm . . . privileges? What sort of privileges?' asked Ricky. 'I didn't know anything about privileges.'

'I will go for that,' said the old hag. 'Ha! I certainly am not much interested in privileges. You can keep your evening with Jennifer Lopez.'

'Jennifer Lopez?' squeaked Ricky. 'An evening? A whole evening? With Jaylo?'

'Yes. You must have missed that particular meeting about privileges, Ricky,' said Betty. 'Now . . .'

'But . . .' said Ricky, looking rather dejected. 'Jaylo!'

'Right,' Betty said swiftly, afraid that Ricky might start his personal investigation into the corrupt and somewhat haphazard distribution of Secret Five privileges. 'Come on, you old hag. Tell us more.'

'Ha! Your Uncle Quagmire had a room here. Go down that corridor,' she said, pointing her haggish finger down a corridor that was conveniently situated between two walls, a ceiling and a floor, 'and it's third on the left, just past the Ovaltine machine.'

'Why aren't you coming then?' enquired Amy. 'Are you scared? Hmmm? Are you a *scaredy-cat*?'

'Ha! No, I'm just going off,' the old hag said, 'to a place where fictional characters am rarely allowed to go. Ooooooh, blimey, got to go!' And she hurried off in some other direction, clutching her nightgown tightly around her two matching old haggish knees.

'She's weird,' said Daniel, watching her scuttle away. 'And fancy trying to include a character with such a stupid dialect in our super adventure! Whatever happened to the Queen's English? Adventure standards are definitely slipping. What's needed is a consumer watchdog.'

'Woof woof woof!' volunteered Whatshisname brightly.

'What, such as Adventure Watch?' suggested Betty.

'Yes,' agreed Daniel. 'That sort of thing. Now, let's all explore down the corridor while she's away.'

Silently, they crept in an orderly creep down the corridor, Betty leading the way, until they reached Uncle Quagmire's door, where they stopped all the orderly creeping. Whatshisname sniffed at the door. Then, for some reason, he began to frantically scrabble and scratch at it. The others watched him for a while until he had scrabbled and scratched a large hole in what, to be honest, was shamefully inept workmanship in terms of door-making.

Betty knelt down carefully and peeked through the hole. 'Gosh! There's something in there!' she breathed.

'What?' Amy asked, in between her own breaths. 'Do tell us, do.'

Chapter Five

In which they learn all about Uncle Quagmire's strange disappearance; we learn that we should never have bought this book, never; we hear about Whatshisname's time system, and meet a posh man with a posh voice who just clutters up the narrative, to be honest; Ricky looks a bit glum.

'It's a floor!' Betty exclaimed.

The others, all things considered, didn't think that such a lacklustre discovery was worth the effort of a gasp, so they just shrugged a private shrug, except Whatshisname who, despite a lifelong yearning to shrug, had never quite mastered the art of shrugging despite secret practice sessions behind the sofa.

Betty stood up and glared at them. This was really testing her leadership skills. 'Judging by all the private shrugging, is anyone remotely interested in the discovery of a floor?' she asked. 'Hmmm? Anyone?'

The others shook their heads except for Whatshisname who was a dog in all senses of the word and didn't see the point in shaking his head unless he was wet.

They had a rather hurried conference (skipping the Powerpoint presentations and the end-of-conference motivational speeches) about whether the presence of a floor was reason enough to explore further. In the end, they took a vote, which resulted in seven to two in favour of entering the room. (Whatshisname lodged a protest vote and there was a lamentable miscount issue.)

Ricky pushed the door open very slowly, trying his best not to be overly ginger, and peeked inside.

'Betty's right,' he confirmed. 'There *is* a floor. And, what is even more interesting, there's a bed standing on it! And what is even more than even more interesting, is that those are Uncle Quagmire's pyjamas on the bed. I can tell, they have those peculiar stains on them, and they are special cordless ones for easier mobility around the house at night.'

They all crowded into the room, looking high and low for any clues that Uncle Quagmire might have left. Then Betty suggested that they looked *between* high and low, and they soon found, on the bedside table, a scrappy piece of paper.

Amy picked it up and stared at it.

'Read it to us, Amy,' Ricky urged. 'Please do.'

Amy frowned a little informal frown.

'What does it say?' asked Betty.

'It says *No milk today*,' Amy said.

Most of the others were extremely intrigued.

'I'm only quite intrigued,' said Ricky, awkwardly.

Just then, on cue, the old hag came bursting through the door.

'Ha! That's much better,' she cackled when she'd finished bursting. 'Takes a bit of pressure off me bladder in case we're not allowed to go for a bit. Now, what do you lot want to know? Eh?'

'Well, very strange old hag,' said Ricky, 'we want to know where our Uncle Quagmire has gone to, but I don't think you'll know.'

The old hag slowly sidled up to Ricky's side. 'Oh, you don't think I will know, eh, Lard Head?' she said. 'Well, Mister Cleverclogs, you shut your cake 'ole[1], as I'll have you know that I know everything there is to know about your Uncle Quagmire, don't you know.'

'Never mind all that! Tell us where he has gone,' demanded Betty in a rather stern voice.

The old hag looked furtively to her left, then furtively to her

---

[1] *do be quiet, there's a good chap.*

right, before furtively speaking. 'He's been kidnapped!' she cackled happily.

'He's been kidnapped?' exclaimed the children. They stood there, waiting, looking shocked and casting sidelong glances upwards and headlong glances downwards.

'What you all waiting for?' the old hag asked, with a confused look on most of her face. 'You all gorra fairce loyk a bulldog chewin' a wasp[2].'

'What? Oh, well, we were rather expecting a chapter break right then,' said Ricky. 'It was an ideal place for one, you see, in the world of popular fiction. A sort of cliffhanger moment.'

The old hag nodded her head in agreement and then joined in with their sidelong glances and waiting. After sidelong glancing and waiting for a minute or so more, they all shrugged a communal shrug and then continued.

'Kidnapped?' the children exclaimed again, but sounding less certain this time.

'You heard, kidnapped!' the old hag said. 'Taken in a big red truck that rumbled and roared away.'

'The big red truck!' exclaimed Daniel.

'Woof woof woof!' said Whatshisname.

'The one that . . .' began Ricky.

'Yes, Ricky, we know,' interrupted Betty. 'But why? And why was Uncle Quagmire here anyway? And what happened to the sprouts and, erm . . .'

'Comidons?' suggested Amy.

The old hag looked quite embarrassed, even by modern old hag standards. 'Ha!' she said. 'I think there might be some sprouts left over. There, you see, on the bedside cabinet.'

Whatshisname padded over to the cabinet and scooped up several sprouts into his mouth.

---

[2] *I've no idea what she said. Make it up.*

'Then what happened to . . .' said Daniel. He stopped speaking as Betty nudged him in his ribs with her elbow, which was conveniently situated in the middle of her arm. Whatshisname trotted over to Daniel and dropped the sprouts at his feet. Daniel quietly frowned and picked them up.

'What Daniel was about to ask,' Betty said, 'is why was our Uncle Quagmire staying here anyway? And what is his very secret mission?'

'Ha!' said the old hag. 'I'll tell you all I know. I'll tell you the whole story, but you must take up positions that convey a sense, like, that you're enthralled and transfixed by my telling of the story, see?'

'Good idea,' said Daniel, rather overenthusiastically. 'I like the idea of being enthralled and transfixed. Tell you what, I'll lie on my side on the bed, with my head supported by my left hand.'

'*I* wanted to do that,' complained Amy. 'Bother! Now I'll just have to sit crossed-legged on the floor looking up at her with a spellbound expression.'

'Okay,' chipped in Ricky, 'then I'm going to stand leaning nonchalantly against the wardrobe with my arms folded, and let my facial expression and the widening of my eyes do all the spellbinding.'

Then Daniel changed his mind about lying on the bed, preferring to stand with his back to the old hag and to turn suddenly every time she said something enthralling, so Betty lay there instead, which suited Ricky as he could see down her top from where he stood.

Meanwhile, Whatshisname had quietly adopted a languid pose under the table in the corner of the room, where he could sniff and lick his vacant area, which was as enthralling as any activity known to dog.

'Right,' said the old hag, her old hag's eyes scanning her eager audience. 'I'll tell you all I know.'

They sat, stood or lay enthralled.

'He's been kidnapped!' the old hag exclaimed.

The children looked at her, then at each other, then back at the old hag.

'And?' prompted Betty.

'And what?' said the old hag.

'And what else?' said Betty.

'That's all I know,' the old hag said. 'Must go. Byeee.'

And with that, she hurried out of the room and down the corridor. Betty jumped up from the bed and went after her.

'Hey!' Betty called. 'You . . . you old hag! Come back! What about our Uncle Quagmire's secret mission?'

The others suddenly appeared at Betty's side.

'Yes, you old hag person, tell us something enthralling!' called Daniel. 'Or else you're out of the Secret . . . Palpable . . . Five? Six? Seven?'

'Woof woof woof,' said Whatshisname in his backup role.

The old hag stopped and turned. Then she realised that she'd turned too far so she turned back, just a little, before speaking. 'I know nothing!' she said. 'NOTHING!'

'She's at it AGAIN!' muttered Betty.

The old hag turned back quite carefully so that she was facing exactly the right way, and scurried off.

'Let's wait a minute, she'll be back,' said Amy.

They all stood and waited for a minute, then for another minute. Whatshisname sat and looked up at them, wondering. To be honest, *a minute* did not make any sense to Whatshisname. After all, his time system did not correlate to the human concept of time, where one second is defined as the duration of 9,192,631,770 periods of the radiation corresponding to the transition between the two hyperfine levels of the ground state of a caesium-133 atom, an atom he thought was particularly over-rated. Instead, Whatshisname's time system was directly correlated to how long it takes to retrieve an average stick thrown by an average human arm in an average park on an average day, from the *Fetch* moment to the *Good Boy* moment. Using this measure, having a wee takes one and a half sticks, eating a pork chop takes eight sticks, and a successful afternoon nap would take at least seven hundred and thirty five sticks.

They had all waited for about ten sticks when they realised that the old hag was not going to come back.

'She's not coming back,' observed Amy. 'Can we all go home now?'

Whatshisname whined in agreement. Surely this adventure was doomed. After all, they had now contaminated the scene of crime, they had failed to draw a chalk figure of a man on the floor, his own fleas were now mixed in with the fleas of the perpetrator – this was a disaster. He knew that they had to create a Secret Five CSI department. But it was too late now. End the adventure!

'No, we can't go home,' said Betty. 'The adventure is only just beginning!'

Whatshisname sighed.

They were standing around, wondering what would happen next, when they were startled to hear a man's posh voice coming from behind them!

'So, children, I am *indeed* what happens next, and I hear that you want to know about your Uncle Quagmire,' the man's posh voice said.

They swung around, and there at the end of the voice stood a medium-sized man with a head of thick hair, but he was quite bald.

'I know all about your Uncle Quagmire's mission,' he said poshly, tucking the head under his arm for later. 'It's amazing what people talk about in their sleep. So, I will gladly tell you everything I know, but only if you let me join your critically-acclaimed Secret Five. That's always been my ambition, second only to the gender realignment by keyhole surgery.'

'Join The Secret Five? Never!' said Amy.

'Never!' said Daniel, but it didn't sound very original.

'Woof woof woof,' said Whatshisname, quite originally.

'Oh all right,' said Betty. 'If it's in the interests of our adventure. But I think that it should be without any of the privileges.'

The medium-sized man pondered for a while, pensively scratching the chin of the head under his arm. 'Hmmm,' he hmmmed poshly. 'I was rather looking forward to the Girls Aloud experience, but if that's what it takes, then so be it.'

'Girls Aloud?' moaned Ricky. 'Did he say *Girls Aloud*? But . . .'

'You missed that meeting as well,' said Betty. 'You really must attend more meetings, Ricky.'

Ricky looked quite glum as the others agreed that the posh medium-sized man could join without privileges.

'Goody goody,' the man said. 'Then gather round me and I'll tell you all about your Uncle Quagmire.' He made quite an effective gather-round motion with his hand.

'Erm, excuse me for asking, sir, but do we need to look enthralled?' enquired Daniel.

'Oh, no no no,' the man said, wasting two potentially useful nos in the process. 'I'm not into all this enthrallment business. But, if you don't mind, before I tell you all this important stuff, we'll have a little break. Is that okay?'

Chapter Six

In which they learn really really useful stuff; they encounter a little old lady in a tea shop; the kangaroo hides in the bushes and thinks, quite foolishly, that we can't see him; we learn the truth, at long last, about how dinosaurs became extinct.

They nodded their heads in agreement (a little too late, it must be said) and then gathered around the man, trying their best not to look too enthralled.

'Well, your dear Uncle Quagmire, as you well know, used to be a government spy . . .' the medium-sized man said.

'I didn't know that!' interrupted Betty. 'Did you, Daniel?'

'No,' said Daniel. 'Did you, Amy and Ricky? After all, you are the fruit of his loins, his off-springs . . . apparently.'

Amy and Ricky exchanged a look. 'No,' said Amy. 'We didn't know he was a government spy! My! Why, all he told us was that he did top secret things for the government, and he used to explain in fine detail how he went undercover in foreign countries and worked top-secretly, using listening devices and extremely cunning disguises, but we never knew he was a spy. Did we, Ricky?'

Ricky nodded his head up and down then realised that he should have shaken it, so he hurriedly shook his head from one side to the other side.

'Yeeesss . . . anyway, enough,' said the posh man, his posh forehead wrinkling all over, as did the forehead of the head under his arm. 'I've got this head to deliver, I'm late and in a bit of a hurry, so please don't interr . . .'

'We won't,' Betty interrupted. 'But shouldn't this be an official meeting of the Secret . . . Palpable . . . Five? Six? Seven? Eight?'

'I say, this is so jolly exciting! My first meeting!' exclaimed the posh man poshly, almost dropping his under-arm head in the excitement of the moment. 'I've always wanted to be in middle management and have meetings every hour of the day! Can I say things like *Let's have some blue sky thinking, team?* Or maybe *Come on, we should all be snorkelling in the same think tank?* Hmmm? Can I?'

The children frowned in unison and ignored his extremely silly request. They chatted about whether an official meeting was absolutely necessary. They came to the conclusion that, under the circumstances, it could be an extraordinary meeting where the password would not be needed, which was a good job because everyone except Betty and Whatshisname were desperately trying to remember it.

'Okay,' okayed the posh man, 'let me just pop this head on the top of the Ovaltine machine, and I'll tell you all about your Uncle Quagmire.'

They stayed gathered around him as he went over to the Ovaltine machine and popped the head on top. Then they listened quite intently as he began to talk to them through his posh mouth.

'Your Uncle Quagmire used to be a spy . . .' he began.

'But we didn't know that,' said Amy.

'Yes, I *know* you didn't know, but you know now, okay?' said the man, rather irritably. 'Now, listen, as I was saying, he used to be a spy but, as you know, he recently became an inventor . . .'

'Gosh, we didn't know that either!' said Amy, and it was quite possible that Ricky agreed with her because he said, 'I agree with Amy.'

'We knew that he made things in his big shed in the garden,' Amy continued. 'Like new designs, new products, that sort of thing, but we didn't know he was an inventor. Did we, Ricky?'

Ricky agreed with Amy again but, for some reason that escaped the children, the man was getting even more irritable. 'Look, kids, listen! He was an inventor!' he shouted. They noticed that he was becoming quite red in the face. He closed his posh eyes and took a posh deep breath before continuing. 'And the government had heard about his latest invention and wanted to use it, and he didn't want them to, so he was forced into hiding right here in Greentiles.'

'Wow!' said Daniel in unrestrained astonishment, but slightly worried that enthrallment might be creeping up on them all, which might severely irritate the irritable posh medium-sized man even more.

The man continued talking. 'It all started when there was a threat to the world, and our government learnt that, if this threat happened, then the world was at risk from it happening, so your Uncle Quagmire has been kidnapped to help prevent it happening. . . erm, can I ask . . . your expressions? Are you all following this?'

To be honest, out of the five, only Whatshisname appeared to be following it, giving a knowing nod of his head in the direction of the man every now and again. The others, far from looking enthralled, were looking positively mystified.

'So,' said Betty, sounding quite important for a girl of her weight/height ratio, 'as I understand it, he's been kidnapped for a reason that is beyond our current comprehension and that of most people.'

'Woof woof woof?' said Whatshisname, glaring hard at Betty.

'That's about the size of it, give or take an inch,' said the man. 'I'm so glad you all understand. Now, where's my head? I must take my leave – or is it take *your* leave, I never know.'

The medium-sized posh man reached up and retrieved the head from the top of the Ovaltine machine. He tucked it under his arm.

'Oh, one more thing,' he said, 'if only to justify my presence in your pathetic little story. Can I say that if you want a really good adventure, and want to know where he was taken to, he's most likely being held captive in a big castle up on Lower Downs. There's something up, something very peculiar indeed, going down up there on Lower Downs, that's for sure. But it's up to you – or is it down to you.'

'We certainly wouldn't say no to a really good adventure,' said Daniel. 'But how far is it to get up to this Lower Downs from here?'

The man and his under-arm head looked quite pensive again. 'It's quite complicated. It depends.'

'Depends on what?' asked Daniel. He instantly regretted his question.

'It depends very much on how you travel,' the posh medium-sized man replied thoughtfully. 'Walking? Well, that would make it a very long way, especially if you stop on the way for a small glass of reduced-sugar lemonade and a honey-glazed ham and organic chive sandwich. Yet if you went by horse and trap, for instance, it would still take you a long time, but not so long as walking, unless it was a very slow old horse, of course, in which case it would certainly be faster to walk alongside and feed it the occasional motivating carrot. But, as an option – and this is where it gets a bit exciting – if you had a Ferrari 612 Scaglietti V12, preferably a red one, then you'd be there in no time, unless you had to stop for petrol, and maybe a tall mug of cappuccino and a roasted vegetable sandwich with pine nuts. It's all so complicated you see. Nothing in this life is straightforward, don't you agree? Anyway, I can't stop here listening to you chatting away all day. I have to go and return this head to its rightful owner.'

And with that, the medium-sized posh man hurried away down the corridor and out of sight. The children all knew that there was a question they should have asked the man, but none of them could think of it.

'Right,' said Betty, turning to the others. 'We need to get this adventure on the road – *any* road – and we need to get ourselves up to Lower Downs. Do you have any really helpful ideas?'

'Well, I'm hungry, so let's go and find a tea shop,' suggested Ricky, really unhelpfully.

Betty glared at him. 'Has anyone *other* than Ricky got any ideas?' she asked.

'Do we still have the world atlas?' asked Amy. 'Where is it?'

'I've got it,' said Daniel. 'I kept it down my trousers.'

Whatshisname sighed and recalled the Shakespearean lines: *Vigilance! For it is the trousers most foul that oft harbour rank-infested detachments.* 'Woof woof woof!' he warned.

Daniel reached down the front of his trousers and pulled out the world atlas, which he offered to Betty. She took it quite gingerly, inspected it, then told them it was safe to gather round. They scoured the pages for Lower Downs.

'It's no good,' Daniel said after a while. 'I'm no good at scouring. Never have been. We need to ask someone the way, urgently. Uncle Quagmire might be in mortal danger of death, and in desperate need of our immediate highly-trained assistance. Maybe Ricky's idea is the best one. The helpful owner of a local teashop would know where this Lower Downs is.'

'He's right,' said Ricky enthusiastically. 'Let's all go and explore.'

And so The Secret Five (founder members only) left Greentiles and started to walk slowly yet urgently in the direction that the road was taking. At one point they were resting on a roadside bench by the side of the road when suddenly, without any warning, nothing happened for a while. Then, in the middle of nothing happening, a strange thing happened. A policeman came riding up on a black policeman's bicycle, but he was white.

'Well, I'm blessed!' he said, drawing to a halt to look at the group of children and their dog. He took off his policeman's helmet, scratched his head, replaced his helmet, then rode on and they never saw him again.

They had just continued walking when Amy exclaimed, 'Look, ahead of us, there's a village. Maybe it has a cosy little teashop with a helpful lady owner who can make us some sandwiches and lend us four bicycles and tell us the way up to Lower Downs.'

'Don't be soppy,' said Daniel, quite hurtfully, but they all hurried their step until they were standing right outside a cosy little teashop. They peered inside. But just as they were starting to question why they had to do all this spontaneous peering, the teashop door opened, and there stood a little old lady with an apron tied neatly around her little old lady's waist.

'Come on in, four lovely children with your doggy,' she said in a little old lady's voice and beckoning them in with her little old lady's arm. 'I'm the helpful lady owner of this cosy little teashop. Would you like me to make you some sandwiches and lend you some bicycles? I'd be quick, as I know you're on an urgent adventure and are probably rushing to rescue somebody in trouble. There's not even time to describe my teashop, although that would have been nice, to give you a sense of place, what with the tired Seventies decor and the musty carpet smell that somewhat overpowers the aroma of burnt toast and festering cheese, made somewhat more pleasant than it sounds by the stiff little silvery vases of dazzlingly gay cut flowers – dahlias, petunias, cornflowers, their faces turned upwards to the sky, shining their vibrancies to all that enter herein, making their welcome known to one and . . .'

'Er, hello! Please stop it,' interrupted Betty. 'This is not Virginia Woolf! We're The Secret Five and such silly talk only muddles us.'

'Sorry,' the little old lady said, brushing her pale and worn fingertips over one of the stiff little vases of dazzlingly gay cut flowers. 'Only it's not very often I get the chance to describe my teashop. Forgive me. Now, children, let's move on to important matters. I suppose you'll be wanting me to join The Secret Five as an honorary member, won't you?'

'Why yes!' exclaimed Amy. 'And how considerate, and what a nice surprise!'

'That would be splendid,' murmured Ricky, rather sullenly. 'But, be warned, *apparently* you'll have to forego all the privileges if you join.'

'Not a problem,' the little old lady said brightly as she sniffed her stiff little armpits in a dazzlingly gay way. 'I can manage without the weekend with the Sugababes thank *you* very much.' And off she shuffled to make their sandwiches out of some recently-fresh bread.

'Sugababes?' bleated Ricky. 'She said a weekend with the Sugababes! But . . . how . . . when . . .'

'You've only yourself to blame,' said Betty. 'I'm going to buy you a diary.'

Ricky sulked, staring at his shoes yet again.

Indeed, the little old lady was just as helpful as she said she was. Very soon, they had packs of sandwiches, some homemade sweets, a bottle of strangely coloured juice, a huge bone for Whatshisname, a brand new bicycle each, and handy laminated directions on how to get up to Lower Downs.

'Thank you very much,' called Betty to the little old lady as they mounted the bicycles outside the teashop. 'Such kindness is rare in these days of anti-social behavioural orders. You certainly give little old ladies a good name.'

'Not at all,' the little old lady said, suddenly becoming quite downcast. 'All this kindness to you is really in memory of my poor dear favourite aunty who, some forty years ago and more, died a brutal and gruesome death at the hands of her ill-tempered husband after she showed kindness to some lovely children and their fat ugly dog who were on an adventure in some distant far-off land.'

'Oh, right,' called Amy, ignoring the blatant foreshadowing. 'Never mind, eh?'

They all waved a cheery goodbye as they rode away from the teashop. The little old lady stood in the doorway waving back at them, wondering what she would tell her little old husband when he found out that she'd given away yet another set of bicycles and most of the week's supper, and that a fat spaniel was now probably gnawing at his much coveted sixty-five-million-year-old rare dinosaur bone from the Mesozoic Period – the very bone, as it happened, that held the much-sought-after reason why the dinosaurs became extinct; the very bone that would have helped scientists discount theories of asteroid strikes, super-volcanoes, climate change and deadly radiation from an exploding supernova, and placed the blame fairly and squarely on the fact that the dinosaurs became so clinically depressed due to all the speculative talk about asteroid strikes, super-volcanoes, climate change and deadly radiation from an exploding supernova that they no longer felt up to any form of procreative activity and, between them, agreed a pact for a worldwide bout of mass dinosaur-suicide on August 10th 64,997,993 BC, a pact that included the crocodiles who, in a rather sneaky move that was unknown to the dinosaurs, had secretly agreed amongst themselves to fake their suicides and then open their greedy crocodile eyes to the mother of all meals.

Anyway, the four children cycled happily along the country lanes in the sunshine, keeping at least one eye out for signs of wild ponies or shy deer so they could say *ah!* and tilt their heads. Whatshisname trotted alongside them, stopping occasionally to sniff something dubious in the hedgerow or about his person, or to gnaw on his bone which, he thought, tasted as though it was a little past its gnaw-by date and hardly worth the effort. He thought that they don't make bones like they used to. No wonder they're a poor second to peanut butter.

After cycling for what seemed like miles and miles, but was in fact miles and miles and miles, they reached a place where they stopped for a rest. Phew! They were really glad of the rest.

After they had been glad for a while they went on their way again, huffing a bit and puffing quite a lot, especially down the hills, which were unbelievably steep as hills go. Eventually, they rounded a bend in the lane and were confronted by a sign!

'Look!' said Betty, dutifully pointing at the sign. 'The signpost for Lower Downs!'

'Yes,' said Daniel as he cycled up to inspect it. 'It says *Really*

Top Secret Government Establishment ahead. All unauthorised authors and their one-dimensional characters please keep out!'

'Bother,' said Ricky. 'Does that mean that we can't go in?'

'Yes,' said Betty rather decisively for someone who doesn't floss her teeth regularly. 'I think that includes us.'

'Oh!' said Daniel.

'Then, this time, do you think it might really be the end of our adventure?' asked Amy.

Yes! thought Whatshisname. *Yes!!*

Chapter Seven

In which Daniel gets a bit irate with the author, which he may live to regret; we'll see, shall we; Whatshisname saves their bacon, or is that the next chapter; anyway, they find an unexpected window to sneak through, and unexpectedly sneak through it.

Unfortunately it wasn't the end of their adventure. To everyone's surprise, except his own, Whatshisname suddenly dropped his bone and grabbed Ricky's sandwiches! He scampered off past the sign, down the lane and up over Lower Downs, until he was out of sight.

'Gosh, he can scamper fast, for his size. I suppose we'd better go after him at some stage,' suggested Betty half-heartedly.

'Must we?' moaned Amy.

'My sandwiches!' cried Ricky in a pathetic girly voice.

'Never mind that. Look over there!' said Daniel, pointing over there somewhere. 'In the direction Whatshisname ran! I can see a castle!'

And indeed, up on the top of Lower Downs, there was a castle sticking up out of the ground. It wasn't a big castle, nor was it a small castle. To be brutally honest it wasn't really a castle, it was just a big old house with tall chimneys but the previous owners had been named Mr and Mrs Castle and since then, to the local folk, it had been known as The Castle's Place and subsequently, over a period of time, shortened to . . .

'Stop it!' cried Daniel loudly, glaring up at the sky. 'Can't you see that you're boring the pants off us?'

The others stared at Daniel very strangely.

'Daniel, who are you shouting at?' asked Amy, looking very hard around her.

'Never mind. Sorry Amy. I've finished shouting now,' said Daniel. Then he pointed a finger upwards and shouted, 'But watch it!' The others glanced up and then give Daniel the benefit of a long stare and a short frown.

'Honestly,' murmured Amy to Daniel. 'Sometimes I do wonder about you. Will you see someone about your mood swings? Promise?'

Daniel didn't answer. He was in one of his moods. But in an effort to progress the plot, they decided to cycle a little closer to the castle. They were soon within spitting distance of the castle gates, and Betty persuaded Ricky that it was a really bad idea to try and prove it. She suggested that they abandon the bicycles and cover them with some handy bracken, just in case.

'Just in case of what?' asked Amy, who was secretly afraid that covering something with handy bracken suggested that, later in the adventure, they would need, very quickly and very urgently, to uncover the something in order to avoid some potentially gruesome fate from a blunt instrument-toting ruffian or a grumpy shotgun-wielding farmer or an alien with six . . .

'Oh for goodness' sake!' said Betty, glaring up at the sky. 'You're right, Daniel. I thought it would be quite difficult to bore the pants off The Secret Five, but he's doing a fine job of it!'

'What? Who? Pants?' squeaked Amy. 'All I asked is *just in case of what*?'

Betty sighed. 'Amy, just in case, that's all,' she said, rather grumpily. 'Trust me on this. Always expect the unexpected.'

They all quickly agreed that *just in case* was a very good reason, so they carefully and obediently hid the bicycles with the handy bracken that had earlier been placed on the hillside by some desperate writer. Then, silently and very secretly, they crept up to the gates of the big old house / castle (trying hard to ignore Whatshisname, who was dashing about outside the gate barking and woofing loudly). They hardly dared breathe, in case the guard heard them and wondered what all the breathing was about. But, as they crept nearer to the gate, they heard a familiar sound! It was a big roar and a big rumble! They dived behind a tree that, unknown to them, had conveniently grown from a seed that fell on that spot eighty-two years ago that very day! What are the chances?

Whatshisname scampered over to huddle with them, thinking it was a hastily-convened official meeting and not wanting to miss it in case the agenda included a vote on another surprise outing to the vets.

'I recognise that sound,' whispered Ricky. 'That roar and rumble.'

'Me too,' whispered Betty. 'Look! It's that big red truck, and it's leaving! The gate is opening for it.'

'Yes, you're right! Let's sneak inside when it's open,' proposed Daniel, quite cleverly for someone of his glove size.

'Yes, let's,' Amy said, unable to think of anything of a more philosophical nature.

The gate opened as the big red truck roared and rumbled up to it. It stopped by the gate. The guard walked over in an extremely guard-like manner to chat to the evil-looking driver. The children strained to hear what was being said but, from where they were hiding, it sounded just like *mwmnfudmbgbo-o-ohha-hamsandwichmmmmomwl*.

'What on earth are they saying?' Amy asked inquisitively.

'I don't know,' said Daniel. 'To me, it sounded something like *mwmnfudmbgbo-o-ohha-hamsandwichmmmmomwl*.'

'Gosh,' said Amy, wondering why she wasn't clever like the others.

'Never mind all that,' said Betty. 'Let's sneak gingerly through the gateway and secretly head for the side of the house! Wait for my secret signal.'

'What's the secret signal?' enquired Daniel.

Betty thought for a while, then said, 'The secret signal will be when I say *go*.'

The others all thought that it was a bit of a boring secret

signal, as secret signals go. Indeed, Daniel was about to suggest having a meeting to democratically decide the secret signal, as it was quite an important aspect of any adventure, but he didn't feel like arguing, so he didn't, thereby allowing yet another opportunity for dramatic conflict to pass. Nevertheless, he made a scribbled mental note to ensure that the deplorable standard of secret signals was to be included on the agenda at the next meeting and then robustly discussed. He had been thinking a lot about introducing more robust discussions to Secret Five meetings. He felt very strongly about such matters as secret signals but, it must be said, in recent times he had felt even more strongly about the fact that his character didn't wear spectacles. It just wasn't right. He would need to address that issue before very long, he knew that. He'd have to choose the right time to raise it, obviously, and not wait until the end of the adventure, when it might be too late for a spectacle request.

'Are you all right, Daniel?' Betty asked, staring curiously at him.

'Hmm,' nodded Daniel, now thinking hard about what type of spectacle frame he'd like. Thin wire frames might make him look even more intelligent.

Betty frowned.

'The signal, Betty?' Amy whispered.

'I do worry about Daniel sometimes,' Betty murmured to Amy.

'Me too,' agreed Amy. 'But I worry about you even more.'

Then, at Betty's boring secret signal, which was a very loud *GO!* they all emerged very carefully from behind the tree and, after sneaking even more very carefully behind the truck, scampered with an almighty scamper towards the house, past where the portcullis would have been if it had been a proper castle and not just named after a couple called Mr and Mrs Castle who used to live there and named their house . . .

'Stop it NOW!' yelled Daniel, halting mid-scamper to glare up at the sky. 'And where's my spectacles?'

'See? He's doing it again!' Amy said to Betty as they scampered on regardless. 'Why's he yelling at the sky? Do you think he's all right?'

'It's probably an alternative to his urban street talk,' suggested Betty. 'I'm not sure which I prefer.'

Daniel, looking decidedly grumpy, sauntered towards the castle / house to join the others. They had all reached the side of the house safely and unobserved, except for Whatshisname who had screeched to a halt when he heard the guard say *ham sandwich.* He was now sitting by the guard, eyelids drooping in a starved-dog / feed-me / aren't I cute pose, and the children could hear the guard talking to him. From where they were huddled it sounded like *mmdghufmmm-o-ah-mmmcreosotemmm-pineapplemmmm-o-poo* but it might have been more like *sodoffstinkydog.*

'Let's leave him there,' suggested Amy. 'We need a token sacrifice in the story anyway.'

'But we can't just desert him,' said Betty. 'He's been our faithful dog through thick and thin. Well, through thick, anyway.'

'Look upon him as a cunning diversion, part of our daring plan,' suggested Daniel, rather cleverly for a boy who doesn't wear spectacles and probably never will.

Amy was about to say how clever Daniel was when suddenly she started. But she finished just as suddenly, so no-one noticed. 'Look!' she said, pointing the index finger of her right hand towards a big window which had been conveniently built into the side of the house. 'There's a big window that's been conveniently built into the side of the house, and it's open!'

'So it is!' agreed Ricky. 'Maybe it's the kitchen window, and maybe there's delicious treacle tarts in there!'

'Don't you think we should be rather cautious?' Betty suggested cautiously. 'After all, this is a top secret government establishment and they might not take too kindly to us creeping around in it.'

'Well,' said Daniel, 'I personally think you're being a bit hasty saying that we should be cautious.'

'I think I agree,' chipped in Amy, cautiously yet confidently.

'Are we going to have a meeting about it?' asked Ricky. 'Because, if so, I'd like several things added to the agenda.'

'Such as?' enquired Daniel, thinking he'd found an ally in his search for robust discussions. Bring on the spectacles!

'Well, the privileges for a start – Jennifer Lopez, The Sugababes, that sort of thing,' said Ricky hopefully.

'Look,' said Betty in her extra-bossy voice. 'We haven't got time for a meeting now, have we? Firstly, that guard might torture and question Whatshisname about the whereabouts of his owners. That we could easily tolerate but, thirdly, our dear Uncle Quagmire's life might be in danger, remember? He'd never forgive us if he died.'

'True,' agreed Amy. 'I'd quite forgotten about all that. You're so clever, Betty. And I dearly wish that I had a shapely bosom like yours.'

'Oh . . . er, thanks,' said Betty. 'Right . . . erm, yes, well, let's all get through that window and see if we can rescue Uncle Quagmire from a death worse than fate!'

Chapter Eight

In which Ricky gets grumpy; more peripheral characters clutter the narrative; Daniel is very irritating, again; Whatshisname saves their bacon, no he really does this time; they all do some corridor creeping and find a door, whoopee doo; the kangaroo gives birth.

Betty gave them all an 'I-told-you-so' look as they all secretly scrambled through the big open window into the next chapter. The four found themselves in a room that looked remarkably like a secret library, with a strange door in one corner and a strange corner in each of the others.

'This room looks remarkably like a secret library,' breathed Amy. Then she breathed *and* frowned as an exasperated gasp came from somewhere above their heads.

'Yes,' said Ricky. 'And look at all those secret books on the secret shelves! Are you thinking what I'm thinking?'

'Two fluffy kittens fast asleep on a pink cushion with a baby tawny owl looking down at them with its head cocked?' asked Amy.

Ricky gave her a strange look, no doubt wondering what utter madness had overtaken his little sister. Two fluffy kittens indeed. He'd been thinking of three, at least.

Fortunately, Betty decided to take charge. 'Open the door in that corner, Ricky, and see where it leads to. Or is it *to where* it leads? Anyone know? Hmmm. I must agendarise the positioning of prepositions sometime. Meanwhile, Ricky, be very careful and somewhat gingerly. Go on! Open it!'

Ricky suddenly looked a bit grumpy, yet again. 'Why me?'

'Why you? Because,' Betty said, 'it appears to be your task, that's all. You're always opening the doors. That's your job . . . apparently. Look upon it as a vocation.'

But Ricky still looked mightily grumpy. 'Can't someone else open it? I always seem to do it a bit too gingerly.'

'I'll do it,' volunteered Daniel, rather bravely for someone who doesn't like surprises or, for that matter, tinned tuna. But he wanted to show how grown up he was. He strode up to the door and gripped the doorknob. Carefully, very slowly, and very bravely, he turned it and made the door open a bit. He pulled it open further, enough to poke his head through the gap. The others stood and watched, all glad that it wasn't their head that was at risk.

Suddenly Daniel slammed the door, yelped, withdrew his head, then slammed it again.

'Someone's coming!' he said in a rather squeaky voice. 'Hide!'

Everyone was truly astonished, Amy being marginally more truly astonished than Betty, although it was a close call.

'Let's hide behind those big open curtains by that big open window!' said Betty. 'Quickly!'

The four children all rushed towards the big window and hurriedly hid behind the big curtains. They were just in time because the door opened and suddenly there were voices in the room! The children were terrified by the sudden voices! No, really, this time they *were* terrified, as there seemed to be two voices, which the children assumed came from two different people (rather than one person talking to himself in two voices, which would have been plain silly). One voice was a gruff-sounding man, the other an ungruff-sounding woman, just to keep it simple.

'Is it done?' said the gruff-sounding man.

'Yes,' said the ungruff-sounding woman. 'He's gone.'

'Good,' said the gruff-sounding man.

I wonder if they're talking about Uncle Quagmire? Betty thought.

I wonder, could they be talking about Uncle Quagmire? Amy thought.

I wonder where the kitchen is, and if there are treacle tarts there? Ricky thought.

Yo, dis am dred, dis am over-dry, man, an' which cool dude is them feds snookin', innit? Daniel thought.

Then they heard the woman's ungruff voice again, although she was now starting to sound slightly less ungruff, which could make it confusing. 'Yes,' she said, 'that Quagmire fellow has gone back, and now we just wait and see what happens.'

It was all the children could do to stop a gasp. Indeed, Daniel made a quite discrete attempt at a gasp, which was one of those silent and deadly ones that are so full of meaning yet, at the same time, devoid of any meaning whatsoever.

'He's gone back to 1964,' the ungruff woman's voice said, rather helpfully, 'thanks to his wonderful invention of . . .' – she paused for effect – 'a *time* machine.'

This time none of the children could suppress a gasp, except Ricky whose mind was set on treacle tarts and who hadn't been paying much attention to the narrative.

'Did you hear something?' the gruff man asked. 'A sort of unsuppressed gasping sound?'

'I did. It came from over there, by the big open window,' said the ungruff woman.

The children froze rigid as they heard the gruff/ungruff couple approach the curtains. They froze slightly more rigid as the couple came and peered out of the window, right by where they were hiding!

'Ah,' said the gruff man as he peered out. 'Nothing to worry about. It's only a fat ugly dog outside the window.'

And it was! It was Whatshisname, who had rather cleverly realised the pickle that his pals were in, and was sitting outside the open window doing an impression of them gasping unsuppressedly. He tilted his head and gave an extra special unsuppressed gasp as the gruff/ungruff couple looked out of the window.

'She's only gasping,' said the ungruff woman.

She! *She!* Whatshisname immediately stopped gasping, mortified at the gender assignment, and seriously considered lifting his leg to show them – then again, maybe he would let it pass, just this once. Honestly, humans! They're supposed to be a dog's best friend!

The couple stepped away from the window. 'Now, so that I know,' the gruff man said, 'and not for any expositional reason, I'd like you to tell me, ungruffly if you will, where this time machine is. Can I see it?'

'It's in the Very Very Secret Room so you can't,' said the ungruff woman. 'And may I say at this point, it's a good job no-one can hear us, as all this is a top secret government secret, you know.'

'I know,' said the man, quietly yet knowingly, but still sounding very gruff.

'I know you know,' said the woman, now sounding slightly gruff enough to not be called an ungruff woman.

But, by now, it had registered with Ricky what the gruff/slightly gruff couple had said about his Uncle Quagmire, and he couldn't stop himself emitting a belated unsuppressed gasp. The couple stopped doing whatever they were doing, looked at each other slightly gruffly, yet inquisitively, then laughed and made some gruff comment about the ugly fat gasping dog. They opened the door and left the room without a hint of an explanation why they had briefly popped into that very room to have a secret conversation that would only serve to prolong this interminable adventure.

But by now The Secret Five knew that this was their call to adventure, the challenge of the first threshold – they were, regrettably, unstoppable. Nothing could prevent the unremitting blitzkrieg of unnecessary weak adverbs, quite superfluous qualifiers, and exclamation marks!!

They waited carefully until the gruff voices had disappeared around at least three bends in the corridor before they dared to emerge! Betty stepped out from behind the big curtains and went over to the big open window. She leaned out. 'Good boy!' she said to Whatshisname, who looked quite pleased at his gender confirmation. 'Come on in. Come on!'

With a bound, head first, Whatshisname leapt through the open window and inside the room. He licked everyone, snuffled a lot, then joined them for a few sticks as they gathered round for an unofficial meeting in the middle of the room.

'Everyone! Did you hear all that about Uncle Quagmire's time machine?' said Amy excitedly.

'Yo!' said Daniel. 'Fo' shizzle ma nizzle. Rispect! Mega so squingy, bro, fo' sho! Innit? Ran-dom!'

'Oh no!' Betty said. 'Poor Daniel! It was the shock of nearly being discovered.'

'Shall I slap him?' asked Amy, rather too enthusiastically.

'No,' said Betty firmly. 'We'll let him calm down a bit, then we can all slap him. First, we have to find this time machine, to see if we can help Uncle Quagmire. Ricky, take a look outside the door.'

Ricky looked quite grumpy yet again. 'Why me?' he squeaked.

'Because Daniel's in shock, and you're a man-boy, so it's your job,' Betty insisted.

Ricky, now looking double grumpy, sidled over to the door.

'And don't sidle!' said Betty.

'I wasn't!' snapped Ricky.

'Betty's right. I think you were sidling a bit,' Amy agreed.

'Yo, Cuz!' said Daniel.

Ricky's grumpiness was multiplying like a rather big multiplying something or other. 'I wouldn't even know *how* to sidle, or what it means, or the etymological origins of the word. And anyway, I'm really hungry so I think I can be excused a *little* sidling . . . if I ever did it . . . which I didn't.'

He frowned, hoping that it didn't count as sidling, and reached for the doorknob. He grasped it and turned it until the door started to open. He yanked it fully open and leapt out into the corridor, thinking that surprise is as good a tactic as any and he'd seen people do it in films so it must be the right thing to do under the circumstances. Anyway, he was hungry and in a hurry.

Fortunately, the corridor was empty. Apart from Ricky, that is. 'All clear,' he called to the others. 'Come on out.'

They followed him into the corridor, which was quite dark and moderately gloomy compared to more, or less, gloomy corridors.

'What shall we do now? Has anyone any ideas?' asked Betty.

'Yo, wagwaan!' said Daniel. 'Hey, aight? Tooooo swag, let's cotch down, let's slurch from de feds, let's . . .'

'Not *you*,' said Betty. 'Has anyone *except* Daniel got any ideas? Honestly, Daniel! We must get you some effective medication for that condition.'

'*Please* can I slap him now?' Amy asked.

'Save it for later,' said Betty, rather sensibly. 'You'll enjoy it all the more. Now, I think we should go find the Very Very Secret Room which that couple accidentally mentioned. It might take some finding, so I think we should all split up.'

'I'd be scared to split up,' said Amy. 'Unless I had Whatshisname to protect me.'

Then she glanced down at Whatshisname and saw that he was very busy enjoying a slow and mournful commemorative lick of his undercarriage region.

'Then again,' Amy said. 'Maybe I'll go with Ricky.'

'I'm hungry,' moaned Ricky. 'And anyway, I want to go with Betty.'

Betty folded her arms across her chest. 'Why me?' she asked.

'Erm . . .' Amy ermed, 'what if we forget the splitting, and all stick together.'

'Good idea,' said Betty. 'Come on! Stick together then follow me! And remember, no sidling!'

'Oh yes, like I'm going to sidle again,' smirked Ricky.

'Ricky!' snapped Betty. 'Was that irony? Hmm? Please tell me it wasn't irony.'

'Ironing?' frowned Ricky.

'Yes, she definitely said ironing,' confirmed Amy.

'No, *irony*,' said Betty. 'You know we don't do *irony*! Get a grip! This isn't Jane Austen! For crying out loud! Next thing, it'll be satire and antiphrasis!'

'Aunty who?' Amy asked. 'Does she do all the ironing then?'

Betty sighed. 'Antiphrasis. Oh, never mind.'

Ricky was still very upset about the sidling / no sidling incident, and now even more upset about the accusation of indiscriminate ironing, but he thought that finding some food was far more important than having another sidling / ironing debate, whatever sidling meant, so he didn't say anything.

Relentlessly, Betty started to creep down the moderately gloomy corridor. Then she stopped and beckoned for the others to follow her, which they did, even Whatshisname, who was keen not to be left out of any corridor creeping activity. As they passed each moderately gloomy doorway they gathered together mid-creep and discussed whether it might be the Very Very Secret Room. The corridors were getting gloomier and gloomier. The children were becoming quite tired with the effort of all this gloomy corridor creeping. Just as Betty was about to suggest an official meeting to discuss whether it was getting too gloomy for effective creeping, she started and stopped.

'Look!' she exclaimed. 'The sign on that door!'

She pointed to a sign on a door and waited patiently for the end-of-chapter exclamation mark to appear!

Chapter Nine

In which Ricky has had just about enough; Old Hag reappears but may, or may not, go into a trance; Whatshisname sniffs; there is a bit of a kerfuffle with a time machine and generally things get moving at long last; maybe the book's not such a bad purchase after all; then again, perhaps it is.

'I'm quitting this story!' squeaked Ricky, quite irritably for someone of his height and hair colour. 'I'm off!'

'Off? Don't be silly, Ricky,' said Betty. 'Why?'

'Why?' Ricky exploded. '*Why?*' he asked again, but this time in italics, which he thought would be much *much* more effective. 'I'll tell you *why*! There goes yet another chapter break without sufficient warning, that's *why*! If I'd known, I could have gone off to the toilet, or gone foraging for treacle tarts, or gone for a smoke . . . no, sorry, delete that last bit . . . but can you see my point? We're being treated as second class characters here! And I'm not standing for it! I'm walking! I'm quitting. For good!'

'What?' said Betty. 'You can't quit! We're The Secret . . . erm, The Palpable Five – or is it Six – in the middle of an exciting adventure! If you quit we'll be The Secret . . . The Palpable Four, or Five, again. We'd need to advertise for another Ricky, and then go through the process of interviewing the candidates. All those CVs! It'd be such a hassle.'

'Tough luck! And yes I *can* quit,' yelled Ricky. 'I've had enough of all this sub-standard treatment *and* Daniel's stupid urban street talk *and* Amy's stupid girlyness *and* being accused of sidling and ironing *and* being called tremendously ugly *and* you let me miss all the stuff about privileges. Jennifer Lopez of all people! And as for you, Betty, I've had enough of your bossiness and your post-adolescent boobs . . . well, actually, I've just had enough of your bossiness, okay? Whatever, I'm off!'

'No, Cuz, dis am dred!' said Daniel. 'Am yo trippin, Cuz? Don' be a fudge, like, innit!'

Betty nodded to Amy, who turned round and slapped Daniel quite hard.

'Ouch,' exclaimed Daniel. 'Hmmm, that's much better. Thank you Amy. Where are we?' He felt his face. Blow! No spectacles yet.

They all watched as Ricky stalked off very grumpily down the moderately gloomy corridor.

'But Ricky!' Betty called, pointing her finger at the door. 'Please stop stalking off very grumpily and come back! This is the room! Right here!'

'But it says *Butler's Bedroom*!' whispered Amy.

'No, above that old faded Victorian sign,' said Betty. 'There! It says *The Very Very Secret Room*. Ricky, come back! Don't you want to rescue your Uncle Quagmire? Let's have a meeting about it, at least! We could arrange an anger management course for you!'

'Oh, no!' called Ricky over his favourite shoulder. 'I'm off, stalking and sidling and ironing out of here. I'm gone. History! Byeeee!' And with that, he disappeared round a moderately gloomy corner and was gone, possibly and hopefully forever[1].

'Isn't this a problem for our adventure?' moaned Amy in a rather soppy voice. 'We're now The Secret Four.'

'Woof woof woof,' said Whatshisname, slightly sorrowfully but really hopeful that the adventure might end here and now due to a significant deficiency in the quota of available adventurers.

'Actually,' said Daniel, now quite recovered after the slapping,

---

[1] *one down, four to go*

'I think we're The Palpable Eight at the moment, if you count Uncle Quagmire and the medium-sized man with the spare head and the Old Hag . . .'

'You mentioned me?' said a voice from behind them. There, at the end of the voice, stood the Old Hag! The children decided to gasp yet again. And well they might, for she had changed out of her long white nightgownie thing and was now clad in an orange and purple Lycra tracksuit, lime-green cardigan, dark glasses perched on her wrinkly old nose and the same old West Bromwich Albion bobble hat on her rather old grey head.

'When? How? Where?' spluttered Amy.

'There she goes again with her spluttering adverbs,' said Old Hag who, as a result of her relentless crusade to become a major character, had now gained capital letters and lost her definite article.

'Where did you come from?' asked Betty. 'And what *are* you wearing?'

'Ha! You think I'm yampy? I followed you!' cackled Old Hag. 'Did you think I wasn't going to take full advantage of my Secret Five membership? Ha! And again I cackle, ha!'

'Ricky!' Amy called down the corridor. 'Come back! We'll let you sidle all you want to!'

'Ha! Rocky's buzzed off, and you've got *me* now!' said Old Hag. 'Anyway, did I overhear you fretting about chapter breaks? Listen, I have the ear of you-know-who, you know, and I can see to all that stuff.' Then she added, a little too furtively, 'I'm old, you know.'

'Ricky!' the three children called. '*Please* come back!'

'Woof woof woof!' called Whatshisname.

But Ricky had gone, disappeared right out of their lives. They stared down the corridor, expecting him to come back, but he didn't. After a while, they stopped all the staring as it was making the inside of their eyes ache. Even though their lifelong pal Ricky had only been gone a few seconds, and absence is supposed to make the heart grow fonder, everyone found that they didn't miss him at all and their super adventure could carry on just as well without him, probably with lower operating costs, thus increasing efficiency which would show itself in greater bottom line profits.

But before Betty could initiate a vigorous fiscal debate, they heard some distant voices. Someone was coming!

'I hear distant voices,' said Betty, quite unnecessarily.

'And me!' whispered Amy. 'Quiet everyone!'

'Woof woof woof,' whispered Whatshisname.

'Let's go into the Very Very Secret Room!' whispered Betty. 'That will get us away from the distant voices. Old Hag, you stay out here and get caught and then ruthlessly tortured. We don't want you messing up our super adventure.'

But Old Hag had other ideas. One was to open up a while-u-wait hairdressing salon for gay or undecided pensioners, if she could get the initial capital outlay, and another was to start up a home collection service of the unwanted dust from vacuum cleaner bags and sell it on to organic muesli manufacturers.

'Ha! But oy knows mower – sorry, I know more about your Uncle Quagmire's secret mission than I let on!' said Old Hag. 'So, I'm coming with you. Dandy, or whatever your name is, go and open the door, and don't make it too gingerly.'

Daniel didn't take too kindly to being called Dandy and having limits set to his level of gingerliness by a colour-blind old hag in a gaudy tracksuit but, after a bit of reluctant shrugging, he carefully yet diligently opened the door and stepped inside. No-one else was in the room! Except, of course, Daniel.

'There's no-one in here . . . except me,' Daniel said, infuriatingly telling us what we already know. 'I did wonder if Uncle Quagmire would still be here.'

Cautiously, they followed him into the Very Very Secret Room. Whatshisname sniffed around the room, as he knew that that sort of behaviour is perfectly acceptable for dogs, but not for humans, although on a literary note he did feel somewhat uncomfortable with two adjacent *thats* and thought that *that that* sounded really silly.

'Ha! There's the time machine!' said Old Hag, uncertainly pointing one of her wavering hag fingers at something in the room. The children looked around. All they could see was a king-sized bed with Queen Anne legs, a wardrobe with Prince Charles legs, an electronic alarm clock showing 1964, and a set of drums complete with cymbals and a handy used earplug rinse bowl. Nothing unusual there, then.

'What?' asked Betty.

'Where?' asked Amy.

'Which?' asked Daniel.

'Woof?' said Whatshisname.

'You really must stop all that stuff,' said Old Hag. 'It's so irritating.'

'Then tell us about the time machine,' demanded Betty. 'Tell us, or we'll withdraw your membership of The Secret Five . . . Four . . . Eight . . . whatever.'

'Ha! You can't!' cackled Old Hag. 'Once a member, always a member. A bit like Reader's Digest and Facebook.'

'Then tell us, where is Uncle Quagmire, Old Hag?' asked Daniel. 'And where is this stupidly impossible time machine?'

Old Hag stepped over to the king-sized bed, which stood uncertainly in the middle of the room. On it, there was a big pink duvet and big pink pillows. Resting on the bed was a single Brussels sprout, which was green.

'Ha!' Old Hag exclaimed. 'I knew it. He's left a clue, see?' She held up the sprout with both hands as though it were an FA trophy, then she pointed at the bed with one of the fingers on one of those hands. 'And this bed is his time machine!'

'The bed?' asked Betty. 'Are you sure?'

'Am I sure?' spat Old Hag, ignoring the No Spitting sign on the wall. 'Ha! Kids! What do you take me for? Eh? Am I sure indeed! He told me all about this stuff. I sit on the bed, shut both of my eyes, then think of the year I want to go to, then it whisks me away there. Just you watch.'

She sat on the bed, the pink of the bedclothes instantly arguing ferociously with the colours of her tracksuit. Then she closed her eyes. The children watched for a while, or it might have been slightly longer, before speaking.

'What is supposed to hap . . .' began Daniel.

'Sssssshhhh!' said Old Hag, opening one eye and pointing it at them. 'If you're patient, like, you'll see what's supposed to hap.'

They waited for another while, a marginally shorter one this time, before daring to speak.

'I don't think it's the bed that's the time machine,' whispered Daniel to the others. 'Look at the alarm clock!'

The others obediently looked at the alarm clock. 'There's a wire running from the alarm clock into the wardrobe!' whispered Betty.

'It's the wardrobe that's the time machine!' whispered Amy.

'Woof woof woof,' whispered Whatshisname.

The children crept carefully to the alarm clock. They saw that it was not an alarm clock at all!

'It's not an alarm clock at all!' confirmed Amy, making commendable use of the copy-and-paste functionality. 'It's a homemade . . . thing.'

And, sure enough, it was indeed a homemade . . . thing.

'Gosh! It's not four minutes past eight o'clock after all!' whispered Betty. 'The 1964 isn't the time, it's a year!'

This, of course, came as no surprise to anyone but the children, who gasped a little but not loudly enough to disturb Old Hag, who appeared to have gone into some sort of trance.

'I'm not in a trance!' spat Old Hag, a little irritably for some reason. 'I'm just concentrating!'

Old Hag was concentrating, apparently.

Carefully, Betty tried hard not to disturb Old Hag's trance as she examined the homemade thing that wasn't an alarm clock.

'I'm not in a trance!!' yelled Old Hag, her eyes still closed as though she were in a trance.

'Look,' whispered Betty, still trying not to disrupt Old Hag's really good impression of a trance. 'There's a switch at the side with a label that reads *Send in Twenty Seconds.*'

'I reckon,' reckoned Daniel in a whispered voice, 'that Uncle Quagmire got into the wardrobe after setting the homemade thing that isn't an alarm clock!'

Just then, Old Hag's eyes jerked open. 'Ha! It worked! I'm back in time!' She looked at the children and Whatshisname.

'What's happening? What year is it, dear children and your fat doggy?' she asked. 'Tell me, has Sandie Shaw won the Eurovision Song Contest yet?'

Betty spoke firmly to her. 'Unfortunately you haven't gone anywhere, Old Hag. You're still here. And who's Sandie Shaw?'

Old Hag looked quite sullen, even by old hag standards, and closed her haggish eyes again. The children glanced at each other. After years of developing a close bonded friendship in which words were often unnecessary for communication and social interaction, that one quick look was enough to tell each other exactly what they had to do in such a situation.

'Erm, what do we have to do?' whispered Amy.

Daniel and Betty shook their heads at Amy's stupidity. 'Tell her, Daniel,' whispered Betty.

Daniel looked at Betty. 'Erm . . .' he said.

'Go on,' whispered Betty, 'tell her.'

'You tell her,' whispered Daniel. 'You're the one who knows about all these things.'

'Why am I always the one?' Betty whispered quite loudly. 'I'm getting fed up of being the one. I'm going to quit!'

'No!' pleaded Amy. 'Please don't leave me with Daniel!'

'Look,' said Daniel, a little upset that Amy wasn't exactly ecstatic at the thought of being left alone with him. 'Let's stop and think about what to do next.'

As they stood there, stopping and thinking about what to do next, occasionally casting a glance in the direction of Old Hag who *definitely* seemed to be in a trance, Whatshisname padded over to the homemade thing that wasn't an alarm clock. He nudged it with his nose and whined a little whine. The children looked at him as he then padded over to the wardrobe and nudged the door with his nose, which was proving to be an excellent part of his anatomy for occasional nudging. Indeed, it was probably the only part of his anatomy made for occasional nudging.

The children looked inquisitively at him, so he sat by the wardrobe, waiting, occasionally nodding his head towards the homemade thing that wasn't an alarm clock, then towards the wardrobe.

'Ah!' said Daniel, eventually.

'Ah!' said Betty, even more eventually.

'What?' said Amy, stupidly.

'I've had an incredibly good idea about what we should do!' said Daniel. 'My incredibly good idea is that we should set that switch on that homemade thing that isn't an alarm clock, then go into the wardrobe and it will send us back in time to help Uncle Quagmire!'

'Exactly,' said Betty.

'Okay,' said Amy.

'Woof woof woof?' said Whatshisname, which meant *ahem, whose idea?*

Daniel reached over to the homemade thing that wasn't an alarm clock and was about to flick its switch when Old Hag suddenly opened her eyes again.

'Ha!' she cackled. 'I overheard you all chatting. Great news, I'm coming with you!'

'I thought you were in a trance,' said Daniel.

'No, Dandy, I *wasn't* in a trance!' Old Hag shouted. 'I was concentrating! Hard!'

'And anyway,' said Amy, 'you said that the bed was Uncle

Quagmire's time machine, and you were wrong!'

'I was close! Anyway, I'm old!' said Old Hag. 'My memory's not what it used to be when I was but a slip of a lad . . . or was it a slip of a lass? See what I mean? But, hold on, I'm sure there's something else I should tell you at this point. Now whatever was it?'

'Go on, girls,' Daniel said. 'Into the wardrobe before Old Hag comes out of her trance!'

'Hey!' yelled Old Hag. She struggled to get off the bed as Betty stepped over to the wardrobe. Betty opened the door a little and peeped inside, then pulled the door open wide. 'It looks just like a normal big wardrobe to me,' she said. 'Except that it's empty and devoid of anything that looks consequential in any way.'

'Right, get in!' said Daniel, enjoying being in charge for a change, even though his spectacles hadn't yet appeared. 'And you, Amy, drag Whatshisname inside with you. Then I'll flick this switch and join you.'

'What about me?' said Old Hag as she fell off the bed, landing with her head tucked between a shapely pair of Queen Anne legs.

'Sorry, Old Hag,' said Daniel in his best apologetic voice. 'The wardrobe's full. We have health and safety considerations to consider. And you'd only be in the way of our super adventure.'

'And it *is* our destiny to rescue Uncle Quagmire,' added Betty as she stepped into the wardrobe. Amy followed her, pulling Whatshisname in by his ears. Old Hag was struggling to get up as Daniel made sure that the display on the homemade thing that wasn't an alarm clock was still set to 1964, then he flicked the switch and hurried into the wardrobe. Even without spectacles, he thought, he'd make a pretty good leader. He slammed the door shut, and they all held their breath!

From inside, they could hear Old Hag banging her scrawny fists on the door and calling, 'I've remembered what it was! There's a chapt . . .'

Chapter Ten

In which there's hardly time to draw a breath; it's over in a flash, and a complete waste of a chapter number; there's a wardrobe and not much other stuff; these chapter preambles just slow down the narrative pace, and that's very irritating; the faithful dog Whatshisname clings fondly to a leg and recalls the good times.

In the wardrobe the children were still holding their breath, thankfully unaware of any sneaky literary divisions, but fully aware of a gentle rocking of the wardrobe from side to side. Amy, unsurprisingly, was very scared and clung to Daniel tightly. Whatshisname was also quite frightened, and wrapped his front paws around Amy's leg, giving him an opportunity to fondly recall old times. The gentle rocking of the wardrobe was accompanied by a piercing high pitched noise, which sounded very much like a scream, very much like a woman screaming, very much like an old woman screaming, very much like . . .

The door burst open and there stood Old Hag, screaming, 'Take me! Take me!'

Daniel was rather aghast at first, as he thought that Old Hag was ready to take full advantage of the Sixties' reputation for its free love and the moral vacuum that existed before Dyson came along, but soon realised that they hadn't gone back in time at all. Old Hag must have stopped the homemade thing that wasn't an alarm clock!

'Take me! You need me!' shouted Old Hag. 'I'm going to go with you. Let me in!'

'You stopped it!' said Amy, frantically trying to shake Whatshisname off her leg. 'That's not fair! You're ruining our adventure! Anyway, there's only room for three persons in here.'

'But I've got a two-for-one voucher!' Old Hag cried, foraging about in her cardigan pocket.

'Oh, let's take her,' said Betty. 'After all, she is a member, and we no longer have Ricky. She can be a poor substitute. Come on in, Old Hag. Hurry!'

'Ha! You won't regret this,' said Old Hag as she clambered in. But it was too late, as they already had.

Daniel went over to reset the homemade thing that wasn't an alarm clock. He flicked the switch and hurried back into the wardrobe. He slammed the door, and they waited and waited. Whatshisname still clung to Amy's leg, sighing and with the merest hint of a smile. Amy clung to Daniel, who also sighed and had the merest hint of a startled frown.

One moment the wardrobe was there, and the next moment – it was still there. And, indeed, the next moment and the moment after that. But apart from all this being still there, absolutely nothing was happening inside the wardrobe – no whirring noises, no spinning through a tunnel-type spinning thing, no computer-graphically-enhanced whirling through time and space with a background of eeee-ooooh-eeeeee-wa-wa-wa-ooooo-eeeeee music.

'This is absolutely horrid. Nothing's happening,' said Amy. 'I expected at least to be whirling through time and space. Do you think the bottom is going to drop out of the wardrobe? Do you?'

PART TWO

Chapter Eleven

In which we meet Uncle Quagmire and immediately regret it; a coach load of peripheral characters make an appearance; stunt nuns are gently introduced into the storyline for some obscure reason; Daniel completely destroys a humdinger of a cliffhanger chapter ending.

Uncle Quagmire was a strange fellow at the best of times and, with a literary flourish, at the worst of times. He was quite an odd-looking fellow for his height, and had a bit of a jolly face. That bit was his nose, which had a jolly shape to it with two matching nostrils. Apart from that, his face was quite sullen looking, but he couldn't see it from where he usually stood so it didn't really matter to him. He was clean-shaven under the little beard on his chin and the little moustache above his top lip, and he had mightily small ears for the size of his head. Altogether he looked like a slightly eccentric scientist, but the children knew that he had a heart of gold, which he kept in a jar in a cupboard under the stairs.

Uncle Quagmire's worries about the first testing of his time machine had proved to be unfounded. His recent failed inventions, to be honest, had given him cause for concern. The inflatable travel dartboard idea had attracted the attention of the authorities after a spot of bother on a BA flight to Dubai, and several experiments with his rocket-powered mousetrap had repeatedly caused damage to the village church's ancient stained glass window, which now incorporated several spread-eagled-mouse-shaped holes in the sacred depiction of the Last Supper, one of them missing Judas Iscariot's pint of shandy by a whisker.

But his prototype time machine had worked spectacularly! Just twenty-one minutes ago he had landed safely, with a bit of a bump, on a swath of small flowers which looked quite out of place in a large flower bed in the middle of 1964 Salzburg.

'My goodness!' he had muttered to himself, looking around in slight wonderment. 'It worked! My time machine actually worked! Assuming this is 1964, of course. How splendacious!'

People had stared at him as though he'd just dropped out of the sky! He'd stood up and had marvelled at his own ingenuity. But he knew that all the spontaneous marvelling must be curbed, for he had an important mission, and that mission was top-secret, so he couldn't tell a soul about it. Except, that is, a coach party of swarthy men and their even swarthier wives that he'd met as he was brushing the crushed flowers off his clothes. They had stopped to ask the way to somewhere or other. During his explanation on how to get to somewhere or other he inadvertently told them all about his secret mission.

'Bother!' he said, after a few minutes of studious attention by the group of swarthy yet attentive people. 'I'm not supposed to tell anyone all this secret stuff.'

'That's quite all right,' one swarthy man at the back shouted. 'You have to bear in mind, good fellow, that we are all Italians from a nearby place called Italy, and we don't speak or understand any English whatsoever, as sure as day follows night. Not a single word. We didn't comprehend a bloomin' word, and that's no lie, so you have no worries on that count, chum.'

'He's dead right,' his swarthy Italian wife added. 'Every man-jack of us didn't understand any of that stuff you just said, but we're tickled pink that you've told us the way to somewhere or other, and explained all about your secret mission, pal.'

'Phew!' said Uncle Quagmire, wiping his own brow with one of his free hands. 'I was almost compromisated then. I really appreciate your swarthy honesty.'

'It's been a sheer pleasure,' yet another swarthy man said, before leading his swarthy coach party off stage-left. Uncle Quagmire walked away, knowing exactly what his mission instructions were, and exactly where he was supposed to go next.

But just as he was walking away and wondering where he was supposed to go next, he heard a series of whooshing and thudding noises that sounded like three children, a dog and an old hag landing on a Salzburg flower bed!

'Ouch!' cried Amy. 'That hurt!'

'Not as much as it hurt me. You landed on me!' said Daniel. That made them all laugh, except Whatshisname, who was incapable of laughing due to the structure of the canine neural circuits, and who always experienced a great deal of trouble responding to the punch lines of jokes unless accompanied by a proffered Good Boy biscuit.

'Look! There's Uncle Quagmire!' exclaimed Betty, pointing her finger accurately at Uncle Quagmire.

'And so it is!' said Amy, quite excitedly. 'And still as badly-dressed as ever!'

Whatshisname scampered happily over to Uncle Quagmire and joyfully bit his left ankle rather firmly. Their relationship had certainly seen better times, many sticks ago. Understandably, those better times were before the unfortunate bouncing-dog experiment involving the home-made trebuchet, the over-zealous trampoline and the ill-fated queue of people at the bus stop.

The children ran over to Uncle Quagmire, leaving Old Hag floundering on the flower bed.

'Oy! Wait for me!' she yelled. 'I'm old, you know!'

'Uncle Quagmire!' cried Amy in quite a girly way. 'We didn't know what had happened to you! Old Hag told us you were on a secret mission.'

'Yes, I certainly am,' said Uncle Quagmire, 'but as it's so secret I'd probably have to kill you with my bare hands if I told you about it.'

'That's okay,' said Amy. 'Tell us all about it, please do!'

'Later,' said Uncle Quagmire. 'Where's the other one . . . erm, the boy, you know the one, always hungry – quite ugly – ah yes, Ricky, that's his name.'

'He left us,' said Daniel, fairly responsibly and just as seriously. 'He said he was being treated badly and stormed off. Old Hag here has taken his place.'

'Oh bother, not her!' Uncle Quagmire said. 'She's old, you know.'

They all turned and watched as Old Hag raised herself out of the flower bed. 'Ha!' she cried as she eventually scuttled over to them. 'So, this is 1964, is it?'

'1964?' gasped Betty. 'Gosh and wow! But where are we? Is this Stoke-on-Trent?'

'No, silly girl,' said Uncle Quagmire, having a private chuckle at Betty's expense. 'This is like Stoke-on-Trent but it's more like Salzburg.'

'The one near Brisbane?' asked Daniel. 'Golly, how exciting!'

Uncle Quagmire had yet another private chuckle, with the reassuring thought that two private chuckles in the space of a few seconds was really going some.

'No,' he said. 'This Salzburg is near Austria, which is closely joined by land to several other neighbouring countries.'

'Gosh!' said Daniel, ever eager to expand his woefully inadequate knowledge about European geography and, surreptitiously, the history of lace making in the East Midlands.

'I tell you what,' said Uncle Quagmire, keen to maintain the narrative pace. 'All this fantasterful time-travelling has made me quite thirsty. How about finding a shop that dispenses drinks and we'll chat all about it over a scrumlicious cup of whatever they sell in these times.'

'Good idea!' said Betty, enthusiastically. 'It's a shame Ricky isn't here to enjoy it, isn't it?'

'Woof woof WOOF!!!!' barked Whatshisname for no reason whatsoever except, perhaps, as a subconscious motivation derived from anthropological customs, or because Uncle Quagmire had trodden 'accidentally' on his paw.

Happily, they all walked or, in the case of Whatshisname,

limped, to an Austrian outdoor café in a four-sided outdoor square, where they all sat down and ordered lemon and lime cordial and ginger cake, which were freely available in Salzburg in 1964, were they not?

'So, tell us all about this secret mission,' said Daniel. 'And the reason why you were kidnapped.'

'I know it all!' interrupted Old Hag, who had trailed behind them and was now making herself quite comfortable at their table. 'Ask me! Ask me!'

'Okay,' said Betty, with a hint of a firm but tranquil shrug. 'Tell us if you must.'

'Well,' said Old Hag, 'your Uncle Quagmire is on a secret mission and he was forced to make use of his time machine to come here and save the world by stopping a stunt nun from getting preggers . . .' Quite suddenly she stopped talking and looked around her. 'Where are we, Quaggy? Is this Loughborough? Where am the nuns?'

'No, it's not Loughborough, silly Old Hag. We're in Salzburg, near Austria,' said Uncle Quagmire knowingly and almost reassuringly.

'Are you sure it's not the one near Brisbane, Uncle Quagmire?' asked Daniel.

'Stunt nun?' enquired Betty.

'Preggers?' asked Amy. 'What does that mean?'

'Woof woof woof,' moaned Whatshisname, licking his paw.

'I thought you said you was going to Loughborough,' said Old Hag. 'I'm sure that you said . . .'

'Anyway,' interrupted Uncle Quagmire, 'as I was saying, children, I was kidnapped and made to . . .'

'Go back to nineteen sixty four!' said Old Hag.

'Look!' said Uncle Quagmire to Old Hag, quite irritably for a man of his shoe size. 'It's *my* story and there are people out there waiting to know all about this, okay? Don't you have to do something, go somewhere? Go off to the toilet or something like that?'

'Oh blimey, ta very much, I knew there was something I had to do,' mumbled Old Hag, as she scrambled off her chair and scurried away, bravely followed by Whatshisname who had been desperate to go since chapter six.

'Right,' said Uncle Quagmire, 'now she's gone, gather round the table and I'll explain.'

'Yes, let's!' said Amy, gathering round a little too quickly and making herself dizzy.

'Well children, thanks for gathering round so obediently. Now, my very secret mission is to stop a stunt nun from getting pregnant . . .' started Uncle Quagmire.

'What's a stunt nun?' asked Amy, rather unnecessarily.

'You don't know? Hmmm. I'll come to that later,' said Uncle Quagmire. 'Now, you know that I used to work for the government, secretly, undercover . . .'

'Gosh! A bit like our Secret Five!' said Amy.

'Yes, if you like . . .' he went on, 'except for the kangaroo, of course. Well, as you probably know, I retired on a rather generocious final-salary retired-undercover-spy graduated occupational pension – the value of which, by the way, can go up or down – after the unfortunate incident with the royal-corgi-cam in the Queen's private bathroom. But then they learnt about my latest invention . . .'

'Your time machine!' said Betty.

'Quite,' said Uncle Quagmire, quite quietly. 'So they asked me to do one more job for them, and I refused.'

'Ha! He refused!' cackled Old Hag, adjusting the gusset of her tracksuit bottoms as she reappeared and hoisted herself onto a chair.

'Shush!' shushed Daniel. 'Let him finish. It might become mildly interesting.'

'In the end,' Uncle Quagmire continued, 'I went into hiding at Greentiles but they found me and kidnapped me so that they could send me here to . . .'

At that point Old Hag started waving her arms around and yelled, 'Chapter break! Chapter break!'

'What?' exclaimed Uncle Quagmire, glaring a very effective glare at Old Hag.

'Oh, it's all right,' said Betty. 'She's got inside information about chapter breaks. There's obviously one due.'

'Oh,' said Uncle Quagmire. 'In that case, I'll pause on a mini cliffhanger, shall I?'

The children thought that was a good idea, and said so. 'That's a good idea,' they all said, quite unsurprisingly.

'So,' said Uncle Quagmire, 'they secretly told me that a certain criminal mastermind is being very nasty indeed and is about to threatenise the civilised world with . . .' He paused, to rack up the tension and to maximise the dramatic effect, '*worldwide mass destruction!*'

'Worldwide mass destruction?' exclaimed Daniel. 'Golly, that's quite serious, isn't it? Now, anyone fancy another glass of lemon and lime cordial?'

'Er, yes,' said Uncle Quagmire. 'But you've now completely destroyed the *worldwide mass destruction* cliffhanger chapter ending!'

'Oh, sorry,' said Daniel meekly.

They all sat looking at each other, quietly sipping their cordials, which tasted quite nice.

Chapter Twelve

In which we learn of a highly dangerous mission; a shadowy group is mentioned, very briefly; Betty explains about fallopian tubes, which is quite interesting, everything else considered; Old Hag slumps onto a handy wall; the reader ponders upon the wisdom of impulse book purchases.

'I am *really* sorry,' said Daniel, even more meekly than his previous meekly. 'I think I ruined the end-of-chapter cliffhanger.'

'Ha! You should be sorry, Dando!' cackled Old Hag. 'Don't know you're born, you kids don't. Come to think of it, you haven't been born yet, have you?'

The children each raised both of their eyebrows and looked quizzically at Old Hag. Given her choice of clothes, who can blame them. Whatshisname, who had sneaked back into the chapter while Old Hag was busy cackling, tried his best to look quizzical but failed quite miserably. Looking quizzical had never been his strong point, his time on the vet's table during the surprise outing being the closest he had come to raising an eyebrow or two.

'Anyway,' said Uncle Quagmire, bravely carrying on despite the digressive narrative, 'they told me that the only way to preventicate this certain criminal mastermind from destroying or dominating the civilised world is to . . .'

Uncle Quagmire paused melodramatically. The children were deeply impressed by his use of dramatic effect and histrionic verbal dexterity, but in truth it was because he had a lump of ginger cake stuck in his throat. He coughed, and bits of cake splattered out, having a dramatic effect on the face of Whatshisname, who tried frantically to lick them off. Uncle Quagmire retrieved the bits of cake, popped them back into his mouth, and continued almost exactly from where he had left off: 'is to go back in time and, through fair means or foul, to stop him from being born!'

The children gasped a huge gasp, as they hadn't gasped for a while and one had built up inside them. Old Hag, not wanting to be left out of any Secret Five activity, also decided to gasp, but she wasn't so good at it, having missed out on all the training, and it sounded more like an amateur wheeze than a highly-trained gasp.

'Go back? time? fair? foul? stop? born?' said Betty, in a daze and unable to say prepositions or conjunctives.

'Yes, Betty,' said Uncle Quagmire. 'You're right when you say go back time fair foul stop born, for that is my mission in a very small and concise nutshell, if nutshells come that small and concise these days, that is. It'll be highly dangerous, no doubt, and very highly risky, but now I'm here I'll do what I have to do to save the world, and more if necessary. You children are very naughty indeed and shouldn't have followed me here. But as you're here, the mission for you, should you choose to accept it, is simple but too highly dangerous. And far too highly risky.'

'I knew I should have left the story at the beginning,' mumbled Amy. 'I don't like the sound of anything that's too highly risky. I wanted to be in an adventure where we discover buried treasure and easily outwit a gang of clumsy escaped convicts.'

'I understand your fears, Ann . . . Angela . . . erm, Amy?' Uncle Quagmire said. 'I wouldn't want to lose you to a hideously prolonged death. After all, you've always been like a daughter to me.'

'I am your daughter,' Amy reminded him.

Uncle Quagmire stared at her. 'Oh . . . okay. But, despite that, I still wouldn't want to lose you.'

'Don't be so silly, Amy,' said Daniel in a real man's voice. 'We'll be all right. Maybe. Anyway, Uncle Quagmire, I have some questions.'

And indeed, Daniel had some questions, because someone

who shall remain nameless had slipped a list of important questions into his hand while everyone's attention was elsewhere. 'Question Number One,' he said, consulting the piece of paper, 'is about stunt nuns – what exactly is a stunt nun?'

'Oh, I'm sorry,' Uncle Quagmire said. 'I thought everyone knew.'

'I know, I know, I know!' yelled Old Hag, waving her arm in the air like a classroom swot. Uncle Quagmire slapped her.

'Right, let me explain,' he said, firmly yet diligently. 'In this very city at this very moment some Hollywood people are filming a very spectavagant film, and it's got lots of nuns in it. One of those nuns must do dangerous things, like running quite quickly down a green grassy hillside, so she'll need a running stunt nun double. You see?'

'Oh,' said one of the children[1].

'Question Two,' said Daniel quite relentlessly referring to his list. 'What has the stunt nun got to do with the man who is threatening to destroy or dominate the world?'

'Good question,' said Uncle Quagmire, and Daniel felt quite proud of his question, although it wasn't him that thought of the question, was it now?

Uncle Quagmire beckoned them to gather round closely, which they already were, so they first tried to ungather a bit so they could gather round again.

'The stunt nun, Clarissa Claghorn, is staying near here in the Hotel Bristol,' said Uncle Quagmire, 'which is the sister hotel to the Hotel Salzburg in Bristol. Coincidentally, there is also a Hotel Bristol in Bristol, but that's neither here nor there – unless you are staying there, of course, in which case you'd have to know whether it's here or there otherwise you'd never find your way back to it,

---

[1] *Pick one, it's your choice.*

and your luggage would be lost forever, together with the fluffy bathrobe and the rather fetching shower cap you intended to steal. Anyway, children, I do wish you'd stop digressatering, for it is here in Salzburg at the Hotel Bristol that she first meets and . . . and, erm, becomes very friendly with an American tourist named Bartle de Lylow.'

'Oh,' said Amy meaningfully.

'And,' continued Uncle Quagmire, 'in that weekend they first meet and, erm, um, become overly friendly. Their overly friendship results in the sudden conception of Sampson de Lylow, the man that heads a shadowy group who call themselves *The Shadowy Group*, and he is the very man who is threatening the very securitiness of mankind with his shadowy threats of destroying the world as we know it by starting a new master race and re-populating the world with perfect subjects, and who, amongst other things, will exterminate all smirking patronising television chefs and those authors who insist on writing very long sentences that go on and on for ever and ever and then seem to stop in mid. This man, dear children, is so utterly evil that he fully deserves to be made to sit on the naughty step for quite a long time. Anyway, I cannot tell you any more about his shadowy threat as it would give substance to the narrative and ruin your little adventure. Suffice it to say that my secret mission is to stop that conception so that Sampson de Lylow will never be born!'

Amy raised one of her hands into the air around her head. 'Can I ask something?' she said, obviously very keen to ask a penetrating and incisive question.

'Hang on, is it on my list of official penetrating and incisive questions?' asked Daniel, waving the piece of paper at her.

'I don't know,' said Amy. 'I'll try it. It's this – what does conception mean?'

'Erm . . .' said Daniel, checking his list. 'No, it's not on the list! So I'm not sure if that's allowed.'

But Betty was suddenly very eager to share her thorough

knowledge of all things gynaecological with her cousin Amy. 'Conception, Amy,' she said quite loudly and steadfastly, 'is where the man's spermatozoa, after ejaculation, enters the woman's cervix, some of which then enter the fallopian tube, where the nuclei of an individual sperm will enthusiastically fuse with the ovum's nucleus to form something called the zygote.'

'Oh,' said Amy, keen to be identified as a major character but still very much in the dark, both about the mechanics of conception and the reason why they had to stop this Bartle man and Clarissa woman getting together to stop a baby happening.

Uncle Quagmire looked strangely at Betty for a while, then for a while longer, before speaking. 'Er,' he erred, thoroughly wrinkling his very own brow. 'O-kay. Very, erm, edifying. Now, can I say that, although I think that you're all very nauchievous for following me here, and the secret mission will be highly very dangerous and highly very risky, I suppose I could use you all as disposable pawns in my secret mission to stop this, er, enthusiastic sperm fusing business.'

Disposable pawns! Gosh! The children suddenly felt quite important! And, even though some of them, would you believe, weren't at all sure what it all meant, they felt quite excited at the thought of stopping a conception.

Just then, without any consideration whatsoever for the mechanics of plot progression, two things happened. One, Whatshisname barked an excited 'woof woof woof' but everyone ignored him except for one lady passer-by who poked him quite sharply with her pointy umbrella as she passed. And two, Daniel decided that this was an opportune time to raise the burning issue of his character wearing spectacles.

'I'd like to wear spectacles!' he said, to prove the point.

'What?' Betty spluttered, ignoring the fact that it's hard, if not impossible, to splutter one short word.

The others looked strangely at Daniel, who hadn't ever openly voiced a desire to wear spectacles.

'I said,' he said, 'I'd like to be a character that wears

spectacles. Wire framed ones. Varifocals, preferably. That'd be good. Ones with an anti-reflective coating.'

'But,' butted Amy, 'you've got this far in the story without wearing glasses! Do you actually need them to see with?'

'I don't think so,' Daniel said. He put down his drink and squinted at the others to see if that made any difference to his vision. It didn't.

'It's only attention seeking if you ask me,' mumbled Amy.

'It's not!' said Daniel, glad of the attention. 'It's just that I'd like the opportunity to suck the curly end of the side bit that rests around the ear when I'm thinking hard about some difficult aspect of the adventure. I can also point the curly bit at someone when I'm making a valid point.'

'Ah! Sounds reasonable to me,' offered Uncle Quagmire. 'If not a little late. Go ahead then, Daniel. Wear spectacles from here on. Now, where were we?'

Daniel sucked on the curly end of his spectacle arm and put on a ponderous look.

Whatshisname sighed. He was always on the lookout for an iconic moment in the history of The Secret Five, and that definitely wasn't it.

'I think you were talking about stopping a concession,' said Amy, glancing at Daniel's spectacles and wondering whether to request some for herself.

'So, what is the plan, Uncle Quagmire?' asked Daniel, proudly slipping on his spectacles and pushing them up the bridge of his nose. They felt *really* good.

'Well,' said Uncle Quagmire, 'today is the day when Clarissa and Bartle meet and . . . and . . .'

'Can I ask why do you keep doing that?' asked Amy. 'All that dot dot dot stuff?'

Uncle Quagmire smiled a knowing smile. 'Oh how much you have to learn, strange child. It's lit-speak for me being uncertain, not wanting to say the words, or a literary pause.'

'Oh, gosh!' Amy said. 'How very interesting!'

'As I was saying . . .' Uncle Quagmire continued in a rather grown-up manner, 'according to Sampson de Lylow's autobiography *My Plan Is To Dominate The World* – which, incidentally, is ghost-written by himself – very soon is the time when his parents Clarissa and Bartle meet while they are touring a big castle not far from here. Then they have dinner, and later on the, erm, conception takes place, so the strategic and daring plan is to stop them from getting together in the first place.'

The children seemed utterly confused by it all, but Daniel managed to suggest something which sounded quite sensible. 'Why don't we just kidnap this Bartle fellow?'

Betty was keen to join in all the suggesting. 'Or kidnap Clarissa?'

'I don't think kidnapping is a good idea, children,' Uncle Quagmire said. 'I think the besterest way is to keep them apart.'

'Or kidnap both of them and keep them in the same room!' said Amy, rather stupidly.

'Woof woof woof,' said Whatshisname wearily.

'What about me?' piped up Old Hag.

'What about you?' asked Daniel.

'Can't I suggest someone to kidnap?' she said.

'Oh, if you must,' said Daniel bravely. 'As you're an honorary member of The Secret Five.'

'Right,' she said in her best old hag voice. 'How about us kidnapping *you*, Quaggy? Ay? Ay?'

'What? Kidnap me?' exclaimed Uncle Quagmire, his jolly nose twitching quite uncontrollably. 'I've already been kidnapped once in this adventure! Twice would be downright clumsy. Anyway, why me?'

'Ha! Because *they* won't be expecting it,' Old Hag said. 'Always surprise your enemy, that's what they all said in the war. Do the unexpected. I'm old, you know.'

'Look,' said Uncle Quagmire. 'No kidnapping, okay? Not

Clarissa, not Bartle. And especially not me! It would make the plot structure far too complifficult for everyone.'

'What about the dog, then?' cackled Old Hag. 'Ha! She looks as if a bit of kidnapping might do her some good. Bostin' idea, don't you think? Ay?'

Everyone ignored her, except Whatshisname who whimpered and nuzzled up against Betty's leg for comfort.

'Right, enough of all this loose talk!' said Uncle Quagmire, quite firmly for a man with tremendously thin knees. 'Gather round again for my undeniably good propoggestion. I propoggest that now we go to the castle which, apparently, is not far from here, where some of us befriend Clarissa and some of us befriend Bartle, and we keep them apart at this critical time.'

'Good plan!' said Daniel.

'Really good plan!' said Betty, striving for originality.

'Really *really* good plan,' agreed Amy, inventively.

'Woooof,' said Whatshisname, who was now sitting with his ears pricked, which must have been painful but nothing compared to having his testicles whipped away without a by-your-leave.

'Good!' said Uncle Quagmire. 'Let's finish off our ginger cake, pay the bill, and go and explore!'

They all sat, quietly finishing off their ginger cake and trying desperately to think of some useful dialogue which would give value to the plot, which they couldn't, so they didn't. Then, after a long and heated discussion and an equally long and heated silence with the Austrian waitress about the forthcoming Euro currency and the lamentable failings of the Common Agricultural Policy, they strolled off purposefully in several directions.

'Where are you going?' called Uncle Quagmire from his direction.

'This way,' yelled Daniel from his direction.

'I'm this way,' yelled Amy from yet another direction. 'And so is Betty.'

'Ha!' yelled Old Hag from her direction.

'Woof woof woof,' said Whatshisname in a muffled bark. He was sitting quite gloomily where they had left him with the bill in his mouth and the waitress standing over him with her hand outstretched, waiting to be paid.

'Come this way, everyone,' called Amy. 'Here there's a sign that says *To The Castle.*'

'Good idea,' said Betty. 'Amy's not often wrong about such things.'

They all started to walk in Amy's chosen direction. The sun shone all the while but it was now very, very cloudy so they couldn't see it shining at all. They continued on their way, chatting and laughing, but not usually at the same time. They walked and walked until the castle came looming into view. To be fair, it had always been in view, as the café in the outdoor square was right alongside the castle, so it had actually been very secretly and quietly looming all the time.

They all stopped all the walking and walking to look up at the quietly looming castle. 'Gosh! This is a *real* castle!' said Daniel excitedly, yet with a hint of desolation. 'It's nothing like his pathetic pretend castle back in chapter seven, is it? How that one got into the story I'll never know. This one's got those corbels and bastions and bulwarks and segmental ramps and hard sticky-up things at the top! Gosh again!'

They all followed Daniel up to the castle walls, but found that they could walk no further without actually going inside.

'Let's go inside,' Daniel suggested. 'But here's a secret suggestion. What about leaving Old Hag out here to keep watch.'

'Good idea!' said Betty.

'What?' Old Hag cackled. 'Stay outside and miss all the inside fun? Ha! You must be joking. I want to witness your missionary zeal!'

'Actually,' said Uncle Quagmire, quite sternly. 'It *is* a jolly good idea. Old Hag, stay here with the faithful dog Whatshisname and keep watch.'

'Why me?' said Old Hag.

'Woof?' said Whatshisname.

'What for?' Old Hag asked.

'Woof woof?' said Whatshisname.

'I'm not staying here with this blasted mongrel!' said Old Hag.

'Woof woof woof!!!' said Whatshisname.

'She stinks of creosote and pineapple,' said Old Hag.

'Woof woof woof woof woof WOOF!' said Whatshisname.

'Yes, yow do!' said Old Hag to Whatshisname. 'Dow yow argue! Look, the shock 'as med moy goo back ter me dialect now!'

'Woof woof?' said Whatshisname. 'Woof woof woof wooooooof?'

'It dow not!' Old Hag snapped at Whatshisname. 'It ay loike that, yow mungrel! Be noice ter moy!'

'No, Old Hag!' pleaded Betty. '*Anything* but the dialect! Please! Look, what if you stay here alone and Whatshisname comes with us?'

Whatshisname looked relieved at the latest and most sensible suggestion, and wagged his tail quite quickly from side to side and back again.

'So warramoy s'posed ter do ear?' asked Old Hag.

'For a start, do as Betty says and please *please* drop the dialect,' said Daniel. 'And in answer to your question, you can keep watch.'

'What for?' asked Old Hag.

'For . . .' began Daniel, 'well, for things that might ruin our adventure, that's what for.'

'Such as?' asked Old Hag.

'I don't know, do I?' said Daniel, looking to the others for support.

'If you're in our secret club,' said Betty quite helpfully, 'then you should do whatever needs to be done in the name of adventure, and watching for something that might ruin our adventure is an essential part of every adventure. It's our calling, see?'

The children murmured several quiet yet meaningful murmurs in agreement. Old Hag looked even more bewildered than usual, worried that her privilegeless membership of the club was at risk. She slumped down on a handy wall, ideal for slumping on.

'Oh, all right,' she murmured sullenly. 'But I'd have thought we'd have a meeting before making these decisions. Some democracy this has turned out to be. Ha! and pa! I gorra royt cob on now![2]'

'Okay!' said Uncle Quagmire, ignoring the sullen murmurs and the right cobs. 'That's decided. Let's go inside and find out about the tours.'

And so they trooped into the castle, leaving Old Hag slumped forlornly on the wall murmuring to herself in her Black Country dialect and struggling to understand a word of it. But little did the children know that Old Hag was secretly hatching a secret plan that would threaten their great big adventure! Notably, she had recently abandoned both of her other pathetic smaller plans in favour of this one big threatening new plan! In fact, understandably, she was now becoming so confused about which plan she was supposed to be secretly hatching that she wished she had invested in a Personal Digital Assistant with two gigabytes of random access memory and a wireless interface, or the services of a part time secretary named Joanne, preferably without an interface, wireless or not, but with some degree of accessible memory.

This planning was downright complicated. It wasn't so much about working with the germ of an idea, and by golly Old Hag had more than enough germs, it was the implementation that mattered. She knew that you can lead a horse to water but you can't make it windsurf. All she needed now was a horse and a sturdy surfboard, just in case her theory proved to be wrong.

Ha! Those children, if that's what they really were, wouldn't know what had hit them!

---

[2] *I am jolly well not in a good mood.*

Chapter Thirteen

In which we meet a badly-researched 1964 Austrian man; The Secret Five benefit from their close-surveillance training; Betty has an idea; Amy doesn't; our pals find themselves in a predicament; Daniel can't hack it and should never have been in the story in the first place; the kangaroo enjoys the experience of a hop-on role.

The three children, closely followed by Whatshisname and Uncle Quagmire, made their way inside the big castle which, they noted with some surprise, seemed as big on the inside as it was on the outside. They reached a big door with really big knobs on and a small notice written in Austrian.

'Blow!' said Betty. 'It's in Austrian!'

'Gosh!' said Amy. 'I never thought there were other languages in the world besides English and Latin.'

'Nor did I,' said Daniel, peering through his spectacles at the notice. 'How very strange!'

Just then, they heard a man's voice behind them, slightly to the left. 'Can I help you three childs?' it said in a kind of English. 'Although I am Austrian by nature, I speak all sorts of languages quite fluidly and I am willing to help you in your cosy wosy little adventure, as you're the world-famous Secret Five whose fame goes before you and a little to the side.'

They all turned to see a middle-aged man dressed in whatever clothes a Salzburg man wore in 1964.

'That's good!' said Amy. 'I didn't know we were *that* famous.'

'Oh, *everyone* knows about you,' the man said, waving his Austrian arm around him to indicate everyone. 'Everyone,' he repeated for dramatic effect. 'Even across borders and in another time.' He nodded in the direction of Uncle Quagmire. 'And we all know deeply about your Uncle Quagmire as well. And the kangaroo, of course. Lovely. But enough of this tiresome bantam. How may I be of some helpful?'

'Well,' Daniel said, feeling quite faint from all the sudden fame, 'we're actually on an adventure and need to join a tour so that . . . oops!'

Phew! Daniel stopped himself from revealing their very secret mission just in time!

'What Daniel was about to say,' said Amy, 'was that we need to join a tour so that we can stop a con . . .' Golly! Amy stopped herself from talking just in time!

'Woof woo . . .' said Whatshisname, happily joining in all the truncation.

'What Daniel was about to say,' said Betty, 'was that we need to join a tour so that we can stop a conception taking place and save the w . . .'

'Erm, don't listen to them,' Uncle Quagmire interrupted in a rather grown up way for someone with no tonsils. 'It's just an adventure they're on, that's all, and they are really stupid children beneath their sophisticated veneer. Have fun with them, won't you.' And with that, Uncle Quagmire stalked off, leaving the children to sort out all this mess by themselves.

'Well, childs, it seems that you might need help to get on top of your secret missionary, and you have come to the right Austrian for such helpfulness,' said the right helpful Austrian. 'I will helpfully help you, but lonely if I can join The Secret Five.' He leaned towards Daniel. 'Nice spectaculars!' he whispered.

Daniel frowned, then pushed his spectacles up the bridge of his nose and smiled. He liked this man.

'Not *another* member!' said Amy. 'At this rate we'll have to do another production run on the badges.'

'Maybe he can join us as an honorary member?' sighed Betty. 'Sort of a European wing. After all, this could be our big chance to pioneer globalisation. Shall we have a meeting to decide?'

'We've no time!' urged Daniel. 'We have to do those secret things we have to do, and do them rather quickly!'

'But I can help!' the right helpful Austrian said. 'Let me and my extended familiar join. *Please?*'

'Is that with or without the privileges?' enquired Betty.

'Erm,' ermed the man. 'Without, I think. I have no time for the week's holiday with Kylie, that's for sure. Whoever she might be. Now, if it was Cilla, oooh, chook, that'd be very differential.'

Despite not having a clue who Cilla was, Betty was certainly grateful that Ricky wasn't there to hear about the Kylie privilege, which had taken ages to arrange, what with all the Secret Five commitments. And they all thought that yet another request to join the secret organisation was taking it a bit too far, with or without privileges. But after a brief informal meeting (in which passwords and secret signs were strictly voluntary) they agreed that the right helpful Austrian and his immediate family could join for a limited trial period of twenty-eight days, full refund guaranteed.

'That's good. Right,' said the right helpful Austrian, 'you are in need to join a tower? Well, I am your man. I am the tower guide for today, tomorrow and the day before yesterday. And as you are members of the British harm of my secret European club, you can join the tower for free, and what is more, at no cost.'

'Wow!' said Daniel.

'There's my group of towerists over there,' said the right helpful Austrian, pointing to a group of tourists over there. 'Come on, follow me, three childs and your fateful fat spanner.'

The three childs and their fateful fat spanner followed him, but then stopped quite suddenly and quite urgently when they saw that Uncle Quagmire was now amongst the group of tourists and behaving rather oddly, even by his standards.

'Look,' said Betty spontaneously. 'Uncle Quagmire is amongst the group of tourists over there!'

'And he's pointing at someone!' said Amy. 'I wonder if it's Clarissa!'

And indeed, Uncle Quagmire was standing behind a lady, pointing at her with his finger above her head.

'She doesn't look much like a stunt nun,' all the children thought very quietly to themselves.

'   ,' Whatshisname thought to himself even more quietly, as he'd recently suspected that, in fact, animals don't actually think.

The lady was dressed in what could be described as normal everyday clothes, but won't be, for she was wearing a very posh short-sleeved green flowery cotton frock that hung from her two shoulders and reached down past the both of her knees at the same time. She looked quite pretty for a stunt nun, not having the knobbly elbows that we normally associate with the dreadful side effects of that demanding and dangerous profession.

The children watched as Uncle Quagmire wandered over to a man who was standing on his own feet nearby. The man was bald, and quite thin from the waist down, yet very fat elsewhere, and he was dressed in a pair of tourist's shorts and a tourist's shirt. Uncle Quagmire pointed at the man from above his bald head. Instantly the children knew exactly what to do.

'That must be Bartle de Lylow, the conceptor!' said Betty. 'I know what to do! We'll join the group!'

But as she said it, Whatshisname trotted off and stood by the man whose name must have been Bartle de Lylow. That very man bent down to stroke Whatshisname's head! Whatshisname looked at the children and winked, as if to say, 'I can wink, you know!'

'Let's go and say hello to Mr Bartle,' suggested Betty. 'Come on!'

The children carefully hurried over to the man. Betty grabbed Whatshisname by his tail and dragged him away. 'Sorry,' she said. 'He's very friendly.'

'Yeah, I can see that, kid,' said the man. 'And very ugly as well, it must be said. But I do like the heady aroma of creosote, so it's okay, I guess.'

Whatshisname sat down and, for a couple of sticks, waited for the mention of pineapple but none came. In truth, he was quite disappointed because, if he had to choose between the two fragrances, pineapple would win paws down.

'Can we join you in the group?' asked Betty.

'Of course you can,' said the man. 'I will now introduce myself for clarity purposes. My name's Bartle de Lylow. I'm an American tourist, from America, on vacation here in 1964 Salzburg, near Austria.'

'Yes, we k . . .' said Amy, but stopped when she realised that she would seem really stupid if she continued, but not as stupid as stopping speaking on the silent 'k' in *know*.

It was then that the children noticed that Uncle Quagmire was busy talking to Clarissa!

'Look,' said Amy. 'Uncle Quagmire's talking to Clarissa!'

'We know that!' said Betty. 'Pay attention, Amy!'

Amy frowned a rather girly frown. But behind the frown she had noticed that the guide was now leading the group down some stairs that, she deduced, went downstairs somewhere. She was about to say something very incisive indeed but didn't want to be forced to frown again, and couldn't think of anything to say, so she didn't.

'This is the way to the dungeons, towerists,' the guide called loudly in his best guide voice. 'Follow me, everyone, including the three childs and their painfully ugly spanner who are all busy on a secret missionary to savour the world.'

The three children and Whatshisname, keen to savour the world, followed the guide and the tour group. They each kept an eye on Bartle as they toured the dungeons, making a total of four eyes in all, which was well within The Secret Five procedural guidelines for this type of low-level close surveillance.

The dungeons were really dingy, dull, dark, dank, dreary,

dingy (again), and quite horrid. They discussed at some length how deeply depressing it must have been for the prisoners not to be able to see the cerulean spread of the sky, the yew tree and her spire, the flowers that with one rosy gleam covered a thousand leagues and seemed to set the hills on fire, and the neighbouring convent's outdoor shower block with its rather dilapidated and ineffective screening.

Suddenly, out of the blue, Betty had a truly marketable idea! 'What if we lock Bartle in a cell? They've all got bolts on the outside!'

'Good idea, Betty!' said Amy.

'Hmmm,' hmmmed Daniel thoughtfully. 'I admire your out-of-the-blue idea, but how on earth will we get him in there?'

'Good question,' Betty said. 'Here's a plan. You all go into one of the cells and make some very strange noises. Then I'll persuade and entice Bartle to investigate the strange noises in the cell and you'll all rush out and we'll bolt the door with him inside!'

'Why can't I do the enticing?' asked Amy sulkily.

'Or me?' said Daniel strangely.

'Woof woof woof?' said Whatshisname.

'Look,' Betty insisted, 'I'll do the enticing this time, and you can take it in turns next time.'

'Good plan,' said Daniel.

Whatshisname looked quite forlorn because he hadn't done any serious enticing since – well, a long time, obviously.

After the group had passed the cell doors, Amy, Daniel and Whatshisname obediently sneaked into the cell, and Betty went over to talk enticingly to Bartle.

'Excuse me, Mr Bartle, sir,' she said in a disappointingly unenticing way. 'I heard some strange noises coming from one of those cells back there, and thought that you look like a brave and very strong man, and might want to investigate.'

'Me? Brave and very strong?' Bartle snorted. 'Huh! Lily-livered, spineless, pusillanimous and pathetically feeble I'd agree on, but brave and very strong? No way! Get lost, kid.'

'But . . .' butted Betty.

'Anyway,' Bartle went on, 'I'm also lustful, lecherous and prurient, and there's a rather tasty broad over there in that posh short-sleeved green flowery cotton frock that I've got my lecherous eyes fixed upon. At the moment she's talking to that scruffy bearded mad scientist guy with mightily small ears, but I fancy taking her out to dinner later and, if all goes well, enticing her into my bed for some serious unprotected canoodling tonight. Is she in for a rare treat? The answer to that is *yessir*!'

'No sir, you can't!' said Betty, tugging at his shirt. 'Please, Mr Bartle! It sounded so scary in there. Someone might need help. Desperately. You could be a hero! An all-American hero! Just like, er, Forest Gump, or George W. Bush!'

Bartle frowned for a few seconds, then sighed quite a big sigh for a man with his taste in shorts. 'Okay,' he said. 'Just this once, pesky kid. Where is it?'

Betty led him to the cell and stood outside the door. From inside, there was a curious whining sound, which sounded just like a dog having his ears enthusiastically pinched by two eager children.

'You're right. What a strange noise! Almost inhuman!' said Bartle. Quite carefully and not very bravely he pushed open the door with his fingers. 'I can't see anything in there, kid,' he said. 'It's too darned dingy, dull, dark, dank, dreary, dingy . . . again.' He sighed and turned to Betty. 'Do I have to say all this stuff?'

Betty shrugged. 'I'm afraid so.'

He shook his head and continued. 'It's dingy and dark, and it's even more scary in there than you said. I'll, erm, yes, that's it, I'll go and find some matches or a handy torch.'

And with that, he walked away!

'No, Mr Bartle!' Betty shouted. 'Come back! Your country needs you!'

'Won't be long,' Bartle called back. 'Don't wait up.'

'Bother!' said Betty, knowing that he wouldn't be back, as he was such a grumpy man. She stepped inside the dark cell, where she could just about see Daniel and Amy. They appeared to be pinching Whatshisname's ears.

'Where is he?' Daniel asked.

'What?' yelled Betty.

'I said,' Daniel shouted, 'where is he? Shut up Whatshisname!'

'Yes, where's he gone?' Amy yelled.

'Yowmmmmouchmmm,' Whatshisname howled[1].

'He's gone,' yelled Betty. She pointed to Whatshisname. 'You can stop pinching his ears now.'

'What?' yelled Amy.

'Huh?' yelled Daniel.

'I said,' shouted Betty, 'that you can stop pinching his ears now!'

'Oh,' said Daniel, releasing their faithful dog's ears. 'Okay.'

'Wooooof,' croaked Whatshisname.

Just then, with the four of them inside the dark cell, they heard hurried footsteps outside. 'I hear hurried footsteps outside,' said Amy, in an ingratiating effort to prove that she'd been paying attention this time. 'I think someone's coming! How mysterious!'

'I wonder if it's . . .' Daniel said.

'Ha!' said a voice from outside the cell. 'Wonder no more, Dandy! Got you!'

Instantly, at that very instant, the door slammed shut and they heard the bolting sound of the bolt being bolted!

'Got you!' cackled the voice again, just in case anyone had missed it the first time. 'Ha! Rot in there, why don't you?'

'That's Old Hag's voice!' said Betty. She started banging on the door with a handy fist. 'Let us out!'

---

[1] *Animals were definitely harmed in the making of this book.*

'Ha! Never! Never in a million years!' cackled Old Hag through the door. 'Well, maybe not never. Maybe later. Ha! Later in a million years!'

'Please!' begged Amy. 'It's so dark, dingy, dull, dark, dank . . .'

'Amy!' pleaded Betty. 'Enough!'

'Okay, sorry,' Amy said. 'It's just dark in here. But let us out! Our dog smells horrid!'

'Woof woof woof,' agreed Whatshisname.

Daniel decided to be a man about this and stand up for his inalienable bespectacled rights. 'Old Hag! I *demand* and *insist* that you let us out this *instant*!' he said insistently, and with a flurry of italics to reinforce his demands.

'Ha! Shut up Dandy!' Old Hag shouted in a cackly way.

'Yo, fo' sho, innit,' said Daniel, and he began to cry.

'This is just what you interfering children deserve!' shouted Old Hag through the cell door. 'I'm going now, to complete my very own secret mission and my significant part in this clever plot. Ha! You didn't know about my secret mission, did you? Well, it's a secret, so there.'

Betty pressed her ear to the door and listened for precisely twelve seconds. 'She's gone!' she said to the others. 'To complete her own secret mission! What did she mean, part of a clever plot?'

'Ha! I'm still here, brats!' shouted Old Hag. 'And I'm not going away until the end of the chapter!'

'She's really milking this,' whispered Amy.

'What do you want with us, Old Hag?' called Betty. 'We're just a group of harmless children and their faithful dog seeking an adventure, never afraid to explore places where less brave children would never go, fearlessly righting wrongs and wronging rights.'

'Is that what we do?' whispered Amy. 'Gosh!'

'Haven't you read our mission statement, Amy?' Betty said, frowning hard in her direction. 'Shame on you. Those are our core values and – oh, do stop crying, Daniel!'

Daniel removed his spectacles and wiped his eyes with the

back of his own left hand. 'Dwabi, woo-man, Ah-m stout! Rispect! No chicky blurbing, innit?'

'Oh no,' said Betty. 'He's gone as well. Slap him, Amy.'

'Hey sis, cuz!' said Daniel. 'Ah-m hella Goody-Two, das me! Ah-m rockin' an' strolling! I ain't moked, innit! Any roadway, chowlee! Less get off our keisters an' do dis thang 'cos I do'n wanna circle the drain . . . Nah wot I mean?'

Amy slapped him really hard. Daniel reeled back, then reeled forwards again. 'Amy! Don't do that! You're making me reel backwards and forwards!' he squeaked, tears rolling down his cheeks and into a handy gutter, from where they would eventually reach the sea and fascinate a small shoal of inquisitive fish. 'And we could all jolly well die in here,' he added. 'From starvation or malnutrition, or even rising damp! Don't you understand, we could DIE!'

And he was right! They could all DIE in there if someone didn't find a way out!

Chapter Fourteen

In which Whatshisname ponders the meaning of life; there's a lot of tapping and groping; they all long to find a secret tunnel; Daniel hurts his foot; shame; they hear a noise; this is desperate stuff; we start to wonder about Waterstone's exchange policy.

'No, Daniel, you're wrong! We couldn't DIE,' said Amy brightly. 'We're far too important to the story to DIE. By the way, I really do enjoy slapping you. It's quite satisfying, therapeutic, and I do wonder if I should seek counselling about it.'

But she was right, both about the counselling and the fact that they were far too important to the story. We would not have reached this far without them.[1] And maybe things weren't so bad after all because, through the gloom and darkness, Betty spotted a notice on the wall. 'Look! A notice on the wall!' she said, as predictable as ever.

Daniel immediately stopped the silly crying, put his spectacles back on and looked at the wall. They all went over to the notice, except for Whatshisname, who sat down and hung his head. The spontaneous and relentless ear pinching and the strangely capitalised word DIE had given him cause to reflect once again on the meaning of life. Indeed, was it all worth it, this dog's life? He sighed. He knew that The Secret Five was a staunchly secular organisation, yet lately he'd been pondering not only on the Do Animals Think? quandary (a question that had no ready answer, he

---

[1] *Although it's worth considering giving it a go.*

suspected) but specifically on the question Does Dog Exist? He'd been thinking a lot more about the possibility that he, Whatshisname, only exists in the minds of humans because they can see and, evidently, smell him. It's that colour / no colour thing again. Remove all observers, with their noses, and he doesn't exist. Hmmm. That's worth more of an extended ponder sometime. And here's a thought, he thought – did Man create Dog when he stepped out of his cave and looked at the sunlight glinting off the clutter of bones lying on the ground, and did Man One say to Man Two, 'Ugg, Man Two, we must find a way of recycling all those bones, so what about us creating an animal that chews them to pulp and is quite servile to boot, ugg.' That might have been it! Dog was created by Man as part of his early recycling imperatives.

Or, hang on, was Man created by Dog? First there was Dog? If so, he thought, clearly Dog didn't create Man in his own image, that wouldn't have made any sense – Crufts would be a nightmare, trying to tell owners from entries. Judging the Obedience World Cup and, indeed, the Heelwork To Music event would be a mighty challenge for the panel – whose heels do they scrutinise? A tweed-skirted florist from Cheltenham could scoop the Best In Breed prize. No, he thought, thank Dog that Man wasn't like Dog. I mean, look at them now. They know they could DIE in the dungeon and all they're interested in is a stupid notice on a wall. Dog help them. He sighed again and tried to lick his sore ears. Dog should have been created with longer tongues, that's for sure.

'Golly!' said Betty as she read the notice on the wall. 'It says, in fifteen languages, *There is probably no secret switch or secret tunnel hidden in this dungeon cell.*'

'Bother!' said Amy, summing up all her thoughts in one incisive word.

'Woof woof woof,' said Whatshisname, taking a break from trying to stretch his tongue.

'Well, I reckon there is a secret tunnel,' reckoned Daniel, who was sometimes jolly good at reckoning. 'I reckon – again – that there's a big loose secret brick in the wall that lifts out and reveals a secret switch. There always is. Adventures wouldn't be adventures without hidden secret switches.'

'He's right,' said Betty. 'Come on! Let's tap the walls and see.'

They groped around and tapped the walls of the dark and dank cell for a loose brick, having organised their tapping and groping so that they didn't tap and grope the same part of the wall, which would have been a real waste of a tap and a grope. All of a sudden Amy squealed, 'I think I've found the big loose secret brick! Over here!'

The others rushed over to Squealing Amy and had a grope.

'She's right,' confirmed Betty. 'This big brick is loose!'

Whatshisname sensed the excitement and gave up trying to lick his ears. He padded over to the others and was a little dismayed that he had missed out on all the groping. Daniel pushed and pulled at the big loose brick until it came away from the wall and fell on his foot.

'Is there a lever inside the hole?' Amy asked.

'Ouch!' said Daniel. 'Aaaaaagh! My foot!'

'I don't think so,' said Betty, feeling around in the hole.

'Owwww!' said Daniel, his spectacles steaming up with all the agony.

'Is there a switch then?' asked Amy, brightly.

'Aaaaagh!' moaned Daniel. 'I feel quite faint!'

'There might be a switch in there somewhere,' said Betty.

'Woof woof woof,' agreed Whatshisname, standing on his back legs and peering into the hole.

'Ow! Do you think it's broken?' asked Daniel, sinking down onto the floor and clutching his foot, which had instantly swollen up to one and a half times the size of a normal human size 7 foot, making it a size 10½ and potentially rather awkward for any future shoe shopping if he ever wanted to buy a matching pair.

'No. There's nothing in here,' said Betty. 'Just a hole with another brick at the back.'

'Is that back brick loose then?' asked Amy.

'I feel really faint now,' said Daniel, really faintly.

'No, the back brick is quite firm,' said Betty enthusiastically. 'So, let's tap and grope around some more. Daniel, you take that wall at the back.'

'But . . .' moaned Daniel.

'And Amy,' said Betty, 'you take the wall by the door.'

Daniel struggled to his foot. Gingerly, cautiously, he tried to put some weight onto the size 10½ foot, and realised that he had made a huge song and dance about nothing. He was a man after all! A damaged foot shouldn't distract him from his mission, nor should it clutter the narrative. Too late, but he just had to be brave. Mind you, he was still irritated by their overwhelming lack of concern, so he decided that he'd join the second phase of mass groping and, as a protest, he wouldn't tap. At all. That would show them!

They all continued their groping and/or tapping until they realised, suddenly, that the notice on the wall was right. There was probably no secret switch or secret tunnel!

'Blow,' said Betty, quite unhappily.

'I agree,' agreed Amy.

'Woof woof woof,' said Whatshisname, sinking onto the floor. It was about time for a nap anyway. His ears still burned from all the pinching and his brain hurt from all the philosophical pondering.

They were all quite dejected and very irritated at the lack of foresight of the eleventh century architects, quality engineers, project managers and brickies. Betty and Amy sat down gloomily on the cell's stone floor. Daniel sat on a big wooden square that was set into the middle of the cell floor. It had a big metal ring attached to it, just like a handle.

'I can't believe that we're trapped in here,' Daniel said. 'A dungeon cell without any means of escape.' He started to fiddle with the big metal ring on the floor.

'Neither can I,' said Amy. 'It's *so* unfair.'

'Maybe you're right,' said Betty quite unhappily. 'Maybe we *are* going to DIE in here after all.'

'We all need to talk,' said Daniel. 'Talking is good. I think we should have a meeting to decide what to do and to brainstorm some ideas. Run them through the wringer, shred the unworkable ones and gilt-frame the workable ones and scrutinise them for positive threads and negative threads then follow them through until we're left with a cost-effective solution. That usually works. After all, The Secret Five has always been proud of its listening culture.'

'Er, sorry?' said Amy. 'What did you say? I wasn't really listening.'

'I said . . .' started Daniel.

'Hey, I tell you what,' said Betty, standing up. 'I've just thought of what we should do. I think we should have a meeting to decide what to do and to brainstorm some ideas. Run them through the wringer. That usually works.'

'Good idea, Betty!' said Amy.

'Woof woof woof!' agreed Whatshisname.

'So,' said Betty, 'I declare this meeting open. Password please, Daniel.'

'What? I don't know. I've forgotten,' sulked Daniel, whisking off his spectacles. He sucked the curly end that rests on an ear. 'Is it still testicle?'

Betty sighed quite a big sigh, by modern standards. 'Honestly, Daniel, you haven't been the same since you decided you had to wear spectacles. And no, it's *not* testicle. Will you please stop sucking your spectacles, and stop playing with that big metal ring in the floor!'

Daniel obediently stopped playing with the big metal ring in the floor, the one that looked like *a handle*. He cleaned the spectacle lenses on his sleeve.

'Look,' said Betty quite firmly. 'If you can't remember the password, then give me the secret sign.'

'I didn't think we had agreed a secret sign,' said Amy.

'Nor me,' said Daniel dolefully. 'The last one you suggested was total rubbish.'

'Of course we have agreed a secret sign!' confirmed Betty. 'Any self-respecting children's secret club has an agreed secret sign.'

'Then what is it?' asked Daniel. 'Hmmm? I bet you don't know.'

'I can't *tell* you, can I?' said Betty. 'Then it wouldn't be a secret, would it?'

Daniel was now quite depressed, not to mention confused. He put his spectacles back on and started to fiddle with the big metal ring in the floor, *the one that looked like a handle.*

'Can't we just have a meeting without secret passwords and secret signs?' Amy suggested.

'What's the point of that?' asked Betty, sitting down again. 'Daniel! Please stop playing with that big metal ring in the floor.'

'Why?' said Daniel, pulling up the big metal ring and then dropping it so that it thudded with a loud echoing thud against the big wooden square in the floor.

'Because it's not ours and you might break it!' said Betty.

Daniel again stopped playing with the big metal ring in the floor, THE ONE THAT LOOKED LIKE A HANDLE.

'Thank you, Daniel,' said Betty. 'Now, what if we have a meeting to agree a new password and the secret sign, then have a secondary meeting to decide how to get us out of this cell that was built without a secret door.'

Daniel and Amy agreed, and they were about to start the meeting when Betty suddenly said, 'Daniel! What's that you're sitting on?'

Daniel looked down at the big wooden square in the floor. 'A big wooden square in the floor,' he said, quite accurately.

'Is it warmer to sit on?' Betty asked. 'Because this stone floor is making my lower region quite chilly and Aunt Trinny always warns us of the inherent danger of such things. She says it causes hammer, erm, hammer something.'

'I think it must be warmer,' said Daniel, 'although there seems to be quite a draught around the edges, blowing up from somewhere.'

He moved over so that the two girls and Whatshisname could also sit on the big wooden square in the floor. They sat and became even more quite depressed about their predicament, about there being no obvious means of escape. Betty started to play with the big metal ring in the floor, *THE ONE THAT LOOKED LIKE A HANDLE*.

Irritatingly, they sat there for approximately two hours ten minutes (or, for Whatshisname, seven hundred and eighty five sticks) although to them it only seemed like a day or so. To kill time, they took the opportunity to chat about this and that, which actually didn't take them very long because, as indicative pronouns, *this* and *that* weren't very interesting words. Not compared to postpositive adjectives or subordinating conjunctions, anyway.

Suddenly, without warning, they heard what sounded like a noise outside the door. Actually, it was slightly more than a noise, it was a voice!

'Are you in there?' the slightly noisy voice said.

The children stood up, astonished, and froze! They could, of course, have stayed sitting on the floor to freeze, but freezing is much more effective in an upright position, according to leading scientists[2].

But, putting revolutionary theories of astonished freezing aside, who could this be, asking if they were in there? And how did the voice know that anyone was in there in the first place? This was indeed a mystery!

---

[2] *See Appendix I : Twenty-First Century Cryogenic Theories Relating to the Anatomical Attitude in Modern Man.*

Chapter Fifteen

In which they are in danger of being rescued from their predicament; there's a bit of careless talk about a spy in their midst; a colour prejudice issue rears its ugly head but then goes away so don't worry too much about it; a cute tabby kitten causes a global catastrophe.

'What was that?' Amy asked. 'Did you hear something?'

'I think that was someone outside the door saying *are you in there*,' said Daniel, who was now highly experienced in listening.

Whatshisname trotted over to the door and started to scratch and paw at it. He whimpered, just a little, for he recognised a mystery voice when he heard one.

'Hello,' called the mystery voice. 'Are you in there?'

'What shall we do?' whispered Daniel uncertainly.

'Ask who it is,' suggested Amy. 'Go on, Betty.'

'Okay,' whispered Betty. She pressed her face up against the door and asked, 'Who is it?'

'It's me!' said the voice.

Betty turned to the others. 'It said *it's me*,' she whispered.

'Ask it again,' suggested Daniel.

'You ask it this time,' whispered Betty.

Daniel did so, trying not to sound too needy.

'It's me, Ricky!' replied the voice.

'It says *it's me, Ricky*,' whispered Daniel to the others.

'It can't be Ricky!' whispered Amy. 'It's 1964, and he hasn't been born yet, apparently.'

'She's right,' said Betty, quite amazed at Amy's sudden and uncharacteristic flash of cleverness.

They gasped as they heard the sound of a bolt being unbolted.

Slowly, yet compassionately, the door creaked open! There stood Ricky, dressed in an Austrian outfit which consisted of lederhosen, a baggy shirt in a sort of green curtain material and a silly Austrian hat. The three children and Whatshisname stepped back in a moderate display of acute amazement.

'It *is* Ricky!' said Amy. 'Gosh! What *are* you wearing? Crikey! Are those your own knees?'

'They are,' confirmed Ricky, waggling his own knees to prove it. 'And the shorts, for sheer comfort, are of a breathable fabric.'

Amy stared at the shorts. She listened really hard. She came to the conclusion that Ricky was fibbing big-time, as she couldn't hear them breathing.

'Wait!' said Betty. 'How do we know that it is actually Ricky? What with face transplants and all that. He could be anyone.'

'But I'm not anyone!' said Ricky, who really was Ricky and not anyone.

'Hmmm,' said Betty, 'if you are indeed Ricky, give us the secret sign.'

'Secret sign?' squeaked Ricky. 'I didn't even know we had agreed on a secret sign.'

'Then it is him!' said Amy excitedly to the others. She turned to Ricky. 'We've been trapped in here for ages! How did you get here?'

'Never mind that,' said Ricky, quite firmly and urgently. 'I've really missed you two, you know.'

'There's four of us,' insisted Amy, frowning hard at his sudden inability to count properly.

'Erm . . . yes, four, of course,' agreed Ricky, quickly averting his gaze from Betty's chest. 'Now, we must go and find this Bartle fellow and save the world!'

'Woof woof woof!' agreed Whatshisname.

'How do you know about all that?' asked Daniel.

'It's quite a long story,' said Ricky.

'Don't bother then,' said Betty.

'Well, since you ask, I sort of found myself whooshed away here to 1964,' said Ricky relentlessly. 'I landed on top of a swarthy Italian tourist, and when I explained about The Secret Five, he said that he and all his friends were honorary members and he told me all about Uncle Quagmire and his secret mission.' Suddenly, he stopped talking and glanced inside the dungeon cell.

'Isn't that a secret trapdoor in the floor?' he said. 'It probably leads to a secret tunnel and freedom.'

The others turned and looked at the big wooden square in the floor with a big metal ring that looked like a handle. Daniel stamped his foot and looked upwards. 'Well,' he said, quite upset. 'This is typical! You'd have thought that *somebody* would have told us.'

Betty and Amy stamped their feet in agreement. In fact they stamped their feet so hard that it *really* hurt, so it serves them right.

'Come on!' urged Ricky. 'Hurry up, I'm jolly hungry! Oh, nice spectacles Daniel. They almost suit you. You look, erm, what's the word?'

'Intelligent?' Daniel suggested.

'No, that's not it,' Ricky said, and turned on his very own heels.

They followed Ricky as he hurried away to find the nearest castle teashop. But, much sooner than anyone expected, they came across the right helpful Austrian guide, who was standing outside the castle gift shop with a swarming group of Italian tourists. They were having a lively informed discussion about the children's secret mission.

'Blow me down if it ain't them Secret Five kids again!' said one particularly swarthy non-English-speaking Italian tourist. 'You're all looking as bright as buttons!'

'Ah,' the right helpful Austrian guide said, turning to the children. 'I wondered where you all were, childs and your spanner. We were just discussing your charming inaptitude. What is the current position of your missionary?'

'Please sir,' said Betty. 'Our mission is going quite slowly, but thank you for asking. Right now, our friend here has a condition and needs a teashop, urgently.'

The right helpful Austrian smiled a medium-sized smile and shrugged both his shoulders. 'Alas,' he alassed. 'Today the castle teashop is closed for training porpoises. I hope this does not upset your inconvenience too much.'

The children were all a little intrigued about the training but could wait until the appendix at the end to be enlightened. They didn't want anything as trivial as the exploitation of endangered sea-life to ruin their adventure at this stage.

Betty decided to take charge once again. She thanked the right helpful Austrian and said a fond yet indifferent farewell. Then, quite carefully, she told Ricky that his hunger would just have to wait. 'We have to find Clarissa the stunt nun, urgently and confidently!'

So the children strode urgently and confidently to the castle exit, Ricky's breathable fabric swish-swishing as he walked. Whatshisname trotting alongside them almost as confidently. Indeed, if it had to be measured, for whatever reason, it was probably about ninety-two per cent as confidently, give or take a bit.

Much to their surprise, they were cheered out of the castle by the massed swarmed group of swarthy Italian tourists, who yelled, 'Go get 'em, Secret Five!' and 'Stop that bloomin' conception and save the world, Secret Five!' It was very encouraging, all this secret support.

But, as they left the castle, Betty stopped quite suddenly, as though she was thinking. Whatshisname stopped trotting, and sat down for a few sticks to wait to hear why she had stopped so suddenly.

'Sorry to stop so suddenly, everyone, but what I don't understand,' Betty said, 'amongst the millions of other things I don't understand, is how Ricky knew we were in that cell. That's quite a mystery, isn't it? And how exactly did he follow us here to Salzburg? And why did he decide to return to the adventure?'

'Yes,' agreed Daniel, frowning behind his spectacles in Ricky's general direction. 'Now you mention it, it is strange.'

'Yes,' agreed Amy, frowning deeply and directly at Ricky. 'Very strange indeed.'

'Woof woof woof,' said Whatshisname, trying unsuccessfully to frown deeply and directly at Ricky.

'Well,' Ricky said, 'I decided that, in the spirit of everlasting friendship, and realising that I hadn't actually had enough of Betty's bossiness, *etcetera*, I had to find you and rescue you, so I found the time machine in the Very Very Secret Room, worked out how to work it, worked it, then somehow landed here in Salzburg, you see.'

Betty stood close to Ricky, which he didn't mind at all. She stared hard at him. 'How *very* convenient,' she said in a strangely menacing voice.

Ricky looked quizzically at her. 'What do you mean?' he asked. 'And why the strangely menacing voice?'

'Because it's extremely strange, and just as menacing, how you changed your mind and found us,' said Betty. 'How did you know we were at this very castle, eh? Isn't it strange, Amy and Daniel?'

'Woof woof woof?' said Whatshisname, who also thought it particularly strange but was a bit miffed that no-one had asked him for his opinion.

'Now you mention it,' said Amy, copying Betty's strange but menacing voice and staring at Ricky with her own strange and menacing eyes, 'it is very strange, isn't it?'

Daniel joined in all the mass menace. 'Strange,' he said. He removed his spectacles, sucked the curly bit that rests on the ear, leaned forwards and stared quite hard at Ricky. 'You don't think he's switched sides, do you, everyone? Hmmm? Do you think he's turned?' Daniel put his spectacles back on and stared harder. 'He looks a bit uncomfortable if you ask me. And he's sweating a bit as well.'

Ricky's face flushed. 'Of course I look uncomfortable!' he admitted. 'You're surrounding me and all staring at me! And I'm always sweating! I'm a really sweaty person. You should know that.' He wiped his hand across his brow, causing a drop of sweat to fall onto the cobbled street and into a gutter. Eventually that same drop of sweat would draw the attention of, and cause further bewilderment to, the fascinated shoal of inquisitive fish in the sea.

'He's right,' said Amy. 'He has always been sweaty. I can vouch for his sweatiness. I remember when . . .'

'Amy!' snapped Ricky.

Amy frowned. 'I was going to tell them about that time many years ago when all the sweat just . . .'

'No! It's *not* important!' said Ricky. 'What *is* important is that I'm on your side!'

'We can't be sure, though,' said Betty. 'How do we know?'

'He might have been got at,' suggested Daniel. 'He's a double agent, I reckon. What if he's in the pay of The Shadowy Group, waiting to scuttle our daring plan in favour of his own secret daring plan. Perhaps we should interrogate him.'

'Didn't we once have a super training session on torture and interrogation techniques?' said Amy. 'Remember?'

'Oh yes,' said Betty. 'Ricky missed that meeting, but I suppose that would be an advantage for us. Mind you, it was a real shame about Aunt Trinny's favourite parrot, but it should have talked. Maybe we can practice the same techniques on Ricky but without the leg waxing kit. He does look uncomfortable, doesn't he? Look at his eyes. They're sweating as well.'

'What do you expect?' moaned Ricky, pathetically wiping the tears from his eyes and trying to edge away from the others. 'I'm loyal to the cause, honestly! Don't torture and interrogate me, please! I can't stand pain or the sight of blood, especially my own. How can I prove that I'm still on your side?'

Amy looked at Betty, who looked at Daniel, who looked down at Whatshisname, who had by now lost interest in all this talk of interrogation and was now far too busy licking the desolate area of his undercarriage to waste a look on anyone.

'I tell you what, let's give this some thought,' suggested Betty.

'Yes let's,' agreed Amy.

Daniel nodded his head and scratched his chin in thought. Amy also scratched her chin in thought, although she wasn't sure what she was supposed to think about at such short notice and why chin-scratching helped in any way at all. Whatshisname stopped all the licking and looked up at his chums as they stood silently in thought. There were times when they were way beyond his comprehension but, nevertheless, he scratched his chin in sympathy, knowing that a useful side effect would be to dislodge a few unwary fleas.

'Maybe this is not the time or place,' Betty suggested. 'Should we each keep an eye on him? Watch out for unusual behaviour, secret coded signals being passed to secret contacts, that sort of thing?'

'What?' exclaimed Ricky in a startled squeaky voice.

'Or shall we just believe him?' suggested Daniel.

'Yes, that sounds like a good option,' said Amy who was, as ever, keen to give her support to any unworkable compromise.

'Good,' said Betty. 'Then I declare this meeting closed.'

'Er, can I just say,' said Ricky, 'that you never declared it open.'

'He's right, you didn't,' agreed Amy.

'See, he's already trying to divide us!' said Daniel. 'Typical *agent provocateur* behaviour, if you ask me. I now think we should re-consider the intensive interrogation option.'

'But . . .' butted Ricky, looking really panicky, 'this is so silly! You're always picking on me!' He frowned and looked thoughtfully at his shoes. 'Is it because I'm black?'

'Huh?' said Betty, wide-eyed, her brain trying hard to process this new piece of information.

'I said is it because I'm black?' he repeated, still shoe-gazing.

'But . . .' said Amy, staring at Ricky, her white brother.

'Erm . . .' said Daniel.

'Woof woof woof?' said Whatshisname.

'Ricky,' said Betty, 'I'm not sure how to say this, but, um, you're not actually black. Not in the black sense.'

'You're at it again! You're mocking me!' moaned Ricky. 'You're all *so* colour prejudiced! It's institutionalised racism, that's what it is! I'm going to write to The President!'

'Ricky,' said Betty. 'Honestly, you aren't black. At all.'

Ricky lifted his head and looked at the others one by one. He frowned again. 'Aren't I?' he asked. 'Are you sure? Not even metaphorically?'

'Betty's quite right,' confirmed Daniel. 'You're white . . . well, pinkish. Sort of freckly pinkish white with a hint of waxen. Just like the rest of us. If anyone is black, by rights it should be me.'

'That's true,' said Ricky. 'I do understand and am in awe of your street-talk, after all. But, if you're all right, and I'm not even slightly or metaphorically black, then I suppose I feel a bit disappointed.'

Betty was truly lost for words for a few moments, and kept on glancing at Ricky in case he suddenly started to turn black. Then she thought it best to take control again. 'Ricky – and everyone, of whatever creed and colour – we really have no time for all this. Maybe we can talk about Ricky's doubtful allegiance and his apparent colour problem later on? But for now, we have to find Clarissa!'

'Sounds like a good idea,' said Ricky. 'It'll take my mind off the disappointment. But what I didn't mention is why I'm dressed like this, in this green swirly patterned curtain material.'

'I did wonder,' said Amy. 'It's not exactly *you*, is it?'

'I will tell you,' said Ricky, 'even though you've all been quite nasty to me. I met a kindly man – who, incidentally, doesn't care about the colour of my skin – and he's making a big film here about a nun who sings quite a lot and he asked me to be an extra in the film, so I had to . . .'

'Never mind that,' interrupted Betty. 'It all sounds quite boring. I just want to know how you found us.'

'Old Hag told me,' Ricky blurted out.

'Old Hag!' exclaimed Betty. 'She's the one who locked us in that dungeon cell!'

'I know,' said Ricky. 'She boasted about it. So I stole her West Brom bobble hat and made her tell me where you were, otherwise the hat would get relegated, again. She told me, then went off with the Bartle fellow on her own very secret mission.'

'Went off with Mr Bartle?' said Amy. 'Is that good news for our adventure?'

'Erm, I'm not sure,' said Daniel uncertainly.

'She said she was going to find Uncle Quagmire and Clarissa,' said Ricky, 'and that Clarissa must get together with Bartle. She said she would stop Uncle Quagmire stopping them from getting together!'

'If Ricky is telling the truth, which we don't know for sure because he's a bit sulky and his loyalty is suspect,' said Betty, 'that means . . . erm . . .'

'Absolutely right!' agreed Daniel. 'And so . . .'

'I'm not sulky!' said Ricky, sulkily.

'Hang on,' whimpered Amy, equally sulkily. 'That means what, Betty?'

Betty was suddenly irritated by Amy's whimpering and endless stupidity. 'You can be so endlessly stupid and unbelievably silly sometimes. It means that, erm, um, it means that we now have to find Old Hag and stop her stopping Uncle Quagmire from stopping them getting together. So, what are you waiting for? Let's go!'

Without any significant hesitation, the children and

Whatshisname all scampered off into the distance towards the Hotel Bristol[1].

Now, outside the castle, it all went very quiet. Very quiet indeed.

Very quiet.

Due to the fact that there were now no visible characters to provide an acceptable end-of-chapter cliffhanger, and there was no action whatsoever (apart, that is, from a rather cute and inquisitive tabby kitten which had wandered into view, and cliffhangers that involve wandering tabby kittens are never that enthralling) this left no option than to end the chapter right here.

Which would have been fine, had the cute little tabby kitten not inquisitively pawed a spring-loaded inhumane mouse trap that had been placed just outside the castle gate in order to capture inhumane mice. The trap snapped shut and the cute little kitten yowled and mewed, then scrabbled around desperately trying to shake it off. The yowling attracted the attention of a kindly old man across the street. The kindly old man, whose hundredth birthday was tomorrow, threw his precious shopping to one side and hobbled towards the kitten, but was accidentally and spectacularly killed by a speeding limousine. On the back seat of the limousine were a top government minister and his overly-attentive mistress, a lady who looked remarkably like the postman from chapter one, in a rather fetching cerise skirt and frilly pink blouse. They were both questioned by the ambitious and incorruptible policeman who suddenly appeared at the scene along with many curious and upstanding bystanders. This resulted in the beginning of a long period of government sleaze allegations and expenses scandals, denials and resignations, a dramatic fall in the

_____

[1] *the one in Salzburg rather than the one in Bristol.*

sale of duck houses, and eventually the downfall of the government itself, which in turn prompted the exposure of corruption in many other European countries' governments and, thereafter, the mass resignation of politicians the world over, in a global war on sleaze.

But apart from the rather cute and inquisitive tabby kitten wandering into view, it was all very quiet indeed.

Chapter Sixteen

In which they all get a bit motivated and do some crouching; Whatshisname gains a nice collar; they meet a kindly man called Bob who may or may not want to join The Secret Five; Ricky becomes aghast and slightly agog; they meet Clarissa the stunt nun; other stuff happens, but not all at once.

They were all very excited about this new phase of their adventure as they hurried towards the Hotel Bristol in Salzburg, near Austria. But, it has to be reported, Amy and Ricky were definitely still sulking beneath all the excitement.

'I'm *not* sulking, you know,' Amy whispered to Ricky.

'Nor am I,' whispered Ricky. 'Actually, I'm both excited and, at the same time, rather fed up. Tell you what, shall you and I start another Secret Five? The New Improved Secret Five. With added zest, but without the others? We could recruit.'

Another Secret Five? Amy wasn't sure. She did feel some comfort in belonging. Belonging mattered. And she hadn't yet completed her training and certainly hadn't achieved as much as the others. For instance, she'd never managed a stream of consciousness. Never. Isn't it sad when you think about it never never ever have I had a stream of consciousness after all this time oh I do miss my hamster gordon and his little ways oh and my word they're all looking at me strangely as though I'm not all there what's that noise I wonder if I can sneak back to the dungeon I felt safe there oh why are they looking at me oh those lovely dark eyes of daniel's I wonder if I'll ever find a boy I like before I get all saggy oh oh is that a bit of girly wind oh oh oh that's not very good maybe they'll not notice oooh is this a stream oh how scrummy a stream of cons. . .

'Amy?' Betty said.

'Yes?' Amy squeaked.

'Are you . . . were you . . .' Betty said, frowning.

'No, not ever, ever,' Amy snapped. 'Ever. Anyway, I can't.'

'Hmmm, yes, I can believe that,' Betty agreed.

They hurried onwards. The hotel was in sight. Amy suddenly felt good. Really good. Another tick in the box. (Actually, the first tick in the box.) Maybe The Original Secret Five wasn't all that bad. She'd try and persuade Ricky that a breakaway group wasn't a good idea. She felt surprisingly confident and boldly led the others to the front of the big hotel.

'Everyone!' she boldly said, in an effort to motivate the restless troops. 'Let's crouch here, underneath the hotel restaurant window!' This is it! The new Amy, full of motivation, confident, self-assured, cool, assertive.

And the others obeyed! They dutifully crouched under the hotel restaurant window, making full use of the well-practiced covert surveillance techniques which were a fundamental part of Secret Five basic training. Whatshisname also crouched, although to an untrained onlooker it might have looked as though he was napping for a few sticks.

'Amy,' said Betty, 'you're probably the most dispensable and minimally gifted of us all, so you peek in through the window.'

'Why? Why me?' Amy moaned, instantly losing her motivation, confidence, self-assuredness, coolness and assertiveness. In fact, the only discernable *ness* she now had left was mellowness, and Secret Five adventure tactics had no prerequisite for mellowness.

'Why do we have to have all this *why why why why why*?' Betty moaned. 'It's so irritating. Why do you do it? Hmmm? Why? Why?'

'Just take a look, Amy,' encouraged Daniel. 'It'd be easier for us all to do as Betty says.'

Amy frowned in protest which, sadly, went unnoticed. She

uncrouched a little, and took a discernibly mellow peek through the window.

'I can see Mr Bartle,' she said, 'with Old Hag at a table, eating and talking. No, wait . . . they're just eating now . . . no, now they're just talking . . . they're eating again . . . talking . . . eating. . . eating *and* talking . . .'

'We get it, Amy,' said Betty. 'Can you see Uncle Quagmire at all?'

'Oooh, yes! He's just come into the restaurant! With that stunt nun Clarissa,' Amy gasped. 'He hasn't seen Old Hag and Bartle yet. We ought to have an on-site meeting so that we can agree a good plan.'

'Hang on a moment! *I'm* the one who is supposed to call meetings,' said Betty, rather irritably.

'Why can't I?' asked Amy, even more rather irritably. She so yearned to be assertive again. 'Why is it always you?'

'Why me?' said Betty. 'I'll tell you why me! Because I'm the one who's been on the distance-learning training courses all about meetings! You must take into account that I have the necessary skill base that allows me to call meetings, cancel meetings, take meetings, facilitate meetings . . . end meetings . . . erm, order the meeting's biscuits . . . and instantly recognise every species of wetland plant native to Britain.'

'It'd be good if you could add to that list *remind Ricky about meetings*,' Ricky muttered. 'Girls Aloud! *Girls Aloud!*'

'You didn't hear about the Holiday With Kylie privilege,' Amy whispered.

'Kylie?' Ricky groaned. '*The* Kylie? Holiday? When? How?'

'Thanks Amy,' Betty said through heavily-gritted teeth. 'Thank you very much.'

'My pleasure,' said Amy brightly. That had done her confidence no harm at all. 'Now, about Uncle Quagmire and Clarissa. If we're not going to have an on-site meeting, I think it's safe for you all to look at them now.'

Betty, Daniel and an even grumpier Ricky immediately stopped all the crouching and edged up cautiously to take a look inside the restaurant. Uncle Quagmire glanced at them and waved. Clarissa the stunt nun turned and waved at them as well. The children waved back.

'This covert surveillance is working well, but maybe one of us could go in,' suggested Betty. 'We should warn Uncle Quagmire that Old Hag is mysteriously being a danger to his secret mission.'

'What if we send in Whatshisname with a note on his collar,' said Ricky. He'd decided to prove to the others that he was faithful to the cause, whatever that was.

'Good idea, Ricky!' said Betty. 'Anyone got any paper?'

'No,' the others said.

'Anyone got a pencil?' Betty asked.

'No,' the others said.

'Whatshisname hasn't got a collar,' observed Amy.

They were all quiet for a while.

'Anyone got any other ideas?' asked Betty, eventually.

'No,' the others said.

'Woof woof woof woof woof woof,' said Whatshisname, which meant 'Please Miss, I have a plan! If only I had the physical arrangement of the human glottis and larynx, and could therefore master the vocal abilities of homo sapiens, I could tell you all about it!'

'So, nobody has a plan,' said Betty.

'Woof! Woof! Woof!' said Whatshisname.

They all crouched down under the window again and started to sulk, a bit like spoiled children. Exactly like spoiled children, in fact. But just then, without any significant warning, they heard a voice. 'Hello, children!' it said. They looked up and there was Uncle Quagmire following his voice out of the restaurant. 'I must have overheard you asking about paper and pencil,' he said, 'so I've brought you some.'

'Gosh!' said Amy, taking the paper and pencil from Uncle Quagmire. 'Thanks!'

'No problem,' said Uncle Quagmire as he went back inside the restaurant.

'That was lucky!' said Betty. 'Right, what shall we write on the note?'

They chatted about what to write, and eventually decided on *Thank you very much for the paper and pencil, Uncle Quagmire. Beware Old Hag because . . .*

They would have liked to write more, but the piece of paper was only one-sided and quite small, and the pencil was quite long. To make matters worse, it was an HB pencil.

'Now, we could have put it under Whatshisname's collar but he hasn't got one,' said Betty. 'What shall we do? Any ideas? Anyone? Will our adventure stop here, for the want of a dog collar?'

Just then, luckily for the children's adventure, an Austrian street trader suddenly appeared in the story, carrying a big tray full of dog collars of various colours and sizes.

'Look!' said Ricky, pointing. 'An Austrian street trader with a big tray full of dog collars of various colours and sizes! Let's go and buy one.'

This was his big chance for heroism! Ricky stood up and went over to the street trader, who looked remarkably like the postman from chapter one. With the money Ricky had mysteriously gained as a short-term high-interest loan from a passing impoverished author, he bought a size extra-large and brought it back to where their faithful dog was faithfully cowering. He fastened it around Whatshisname's neck.

'Gosh! Doesn't he look good with a collar?' Amy said.

'Yes,' agreed Betty. 'It's a shame it's very pink and very fluffy with lots of sequins, but look, this note fits under it very well. Well done Ricky.'

'Woooooof,' said Whatshisname, now quite gloomy because, yet again, events had conspired against his mission to establish his true doggy sexuality to the world.

Betty pulled at Whatshisname's collar and urged, 'Go find Uncle Quagmire! Go find, boy!'

'Woof woof woof,' barked Whatshisname, quickly translating *gofe hind* into Classic Doggish, and slightly happier now that someone in authority had again recognised his true gender. He trotted bravely into the restaurant. The children watched as he trotted equally bravely up to Uncle Quagmire's table, at which point he stopped all the brave trotting. They saw Uncle Quagmire smile and kick out at Whatshisname, who backed away to a safe distance. Then the children saw Old Hag, from where she sat at the other side of the restaurant, wave a piece of peanut butter sandwich in the air! Whatshisname padded over to her and snatched it from her hand. Old Hag whipped away the note from his collar! They watched as she opened it up and read it. Quite slowly and quite deliberately, she ripped it up there and then in front of their very eyes and their very noses. She glared at the children's eyes and noses, then smiled an Old Hag smile.

'Oh no!' said Daniel. 'If I'm not mistaken, this looks very much like a plot reversal!'

The children watched in horror as Old Hag and Bartle talked a bit, then they both stood up and went over to Uncle Quagmire and Clarissa's table.

'Oh no!' said Daniel. 'And now a threat to the resolution!'

Uncle Quagmire looked quite aghast that Bartle was about to talk to Clarissa, but not as aghast as Whatshisname, who had just realised what he had done through his liking for peanut butter sandwiches! Because of him the world would be threatened! He hung his head. This was dreadful! Whatshisname's Peanut Butter Sandwiches would surely go down in history alongside Hitler's Savoury Pancakes, Stalin's Spaghetti Hoops, Saddam Hussein's Pot Noodles and Napoleon's Spicy Bean Burgers! Maybe he could bluff it out. Maybe he couldn't. Bluffing wasn't one of his strengths. Indeed, come to think of it, he didn't know exactly what his strengths were. Maybe he didn't have any! Other than knowing his weaknesses, that is. That was a strength, for sure. Or was it? Maybe knowing your weaknesses was not actually a strength but another weakness? The fluffy pink collar could be classed as a major weakness, that's for sure. Ho hum. Maybe Jean-Paul Sartre was right after all, we are each in charge of defining our own lives. I like peanut butter, therefore I am, Whatshisname thought. And what about an empirical worldview? Then again, what about it? Oh, this was all *so* depressing. Was canine depression curable? Probably not. It was even more depressing, knowing that his depression had no known cure. Peanut butter sandwiches had a lot to answer for. Or was it a lot to answer *to*? Oh, it was all so much more depressing, all this not knowing. All dogs, by nature, desire to know. Maybe he should have been Pavlov's dog. He fancied a psychic secretion now and again. Preferably peanut butter flavoured. He sighed and scratched his ear, dislodging a squadron of fleas, each of which had been happily defining their own lives up to that point, and were now condemned to be free to have an empirical worldview of their very own. Until the next unsuspecting host came trotting along, that is.

Whatshisname looked up. The others were staring at him. Maybe it was the collar. Best make a move. Ears dragging on the ground, he skulked out of the restaurant to join them, putting on his extra-special apologetic and depressed look, thinking Sartre thoughts, not yet realising the imminent danger he was in from a vengeful backlash. But just then, thankfully, before they could do any permanent damage to their faithful dog (such as ripping out his heart and liver and feeding it to him as an extra-special treat), Daniel had a great idea.

'Oh, yes, right, well, here's my great idea,' Daniel said. 'Erm, what if we just walk in and ask Bartle to step outside for a moment and then kidnap him?'

'And *that's* your great idea?' Betty asked, rather nastily.

'Well, to be honest,' Daniel said, 'I didn't think it was that great, but, well, you know.' He pointed his finger up at the sky.

'Ah, I know what you mean,' said Betty, rather less nastily.

Just then, yet another featureless one-dimensional character appeared on the scene, to ruin what, apparently, was a less-than-great idea.

'Hi again, Ricky!' said the yet another featureless one-dimensional character as he approached. 'I'm the kindly man who is making a movie, but probably known to you Limeys as a film. Bor-ing! Anyway, the *moo-vie* is about nuns – gee, kid, that outfit does suit you.'

Ricky greeted the man cheerily. 'Why, hello again,' he said politely. 'At this stage, I should really ask if we can be of any help. Can we?'

'Well,' said the man, taking a big breath for what would be quite a long sentence, 'if you remember, when we last met I said to you that you'd be perfect for a little part as an extra in the sentimental yet artful crowd-pleaser of a magical movie that we're making here in Salzburg so I came to find you to ask you if you are ready to start filming right now not far from here.'

'Gosh, yes!' said Ricky, quite eagerly for a boy of his extremely common blood group.

The others were intrigued. 'I'm intrigued,' Betty confirmed. 'And so are the others. Tell us, please do, sir!'

'Sir? Well, for a start,' the man said, 'you can call me Bob.'

'Sir Bob?' said Amy.

'No, just Bob,' said the man. 'It's short for . . . hmmm, I've forgotten. Never mind.' He stood looking at them one by one. 'Ricky's job will be as a stunt double for one of the children in the film, but I've just had an idea! Would you *all* be interested in being stunt doubles? You'll have to hang from some trees for a minute. We can't risk the nice actor children getting hurt, you see. They're too precious. Whereas you . . .'

'No way!' said Betty. 'We are on a very important mission, and the future well-being of mankind relies on us! We are too busy adventuring, sorry.'

'It's good rates of pay,' said Ricky.

'We'll do it!' yelled Daniel, eager to garnish his funds for a Ninstation Y-Box Pii 4, which, of course, hadn't even been invented in 1964.

'Woof woof woof,' said Whatshisname, hardly pausing in his frantic effort to scratch off his fluffy pink collar.

'Daniel!' scolded Betty. 'Shush. Be still.' Then she turned to Bob. 'Don't listen to him, Mr Bob. It's his spectacles, they're having an effect on his judgment. Our secret mission is far too important to appear in a film. And there's still three hundred and thirty five . . . no, three hundred and thirty seven exclamation marks to go!! So, there's no way we can do it. For one thing, I suppose that we would all have to wear clothes made from that rather interesting curtain material, just like Ricky is wearing?'

'I'm afraid so,' said Bob.

'Then we'll do it,' said Betty. 'Where do you want us? This is my best side.' She tapped her left cheek.

'Excuse me, can I respectfully suggest,' Amy respectfully suggested to Betty, 'that you propose a Secret Five meeting about all this?'

'Hey!' said Bob. 'Now you mention it, can *I* join The Secret Five? I spoke to several of your affiliated members of your provisional European wing about it and they're all quite excited about all the privileges, despite looking very foreign and swarthy. And I have heard all about your very secret mission. Do you know, one day I'm gonna have to make a movie about you all.'

'That'll be nice,' said Amy.

'Yeah,' said Bob. 'The Secret Five is one of the known unknowns, greatly respected worldwide.'

'Known unknowns?' Betty said, frowning quite a big frown for someone with her taste in cheeses.

Bob nodded. 'Yeah, as opposed to unknown knowns which, frankly, we know little about compared to the known knowns.'

'Erm, do you *all* talk like this in America?' Betty asked.

'I reckon so,' Bob said, 'as far as I know, anyway. Who knows. That's one of the unknown unknowns. Now, about this membership.'

Ricky was about to start a serious discussion on the subject of membership privileges, but Betty interrupted him before he could speak, so it hardly counts as an interruption, does it now?

'Here's a great idea,' she whispered to the others. 'Gather round in a huddle so that I can tell you all about it.'

'Is this a meeting?' asked Bob. 'Hey, I could be the guest speaker!'

'Sorry, Mr Bob,' Betty said. 'Rules dictate that this has to be a very private meeting.'

Bob nodded his head and stepped back respectfully so that the very private meeting could take place. The children and Whatshisname gathered round in a huddle.

'This had better be a *proper* great idea and worth a huddle,' whispered Amy. 'To be honest, I was rather disappointed with the last great idea.'

'This one is guaranteed to be great,' Betty whispered. 'It's this – what if we agree to do this stunting for Bob, but first ask him to go and get Clarissa the stunt nun from the restaurant, so she can come with us, on her own! Then we'd be taking her away from Bartle!'

'Wow! That is one great idea!' said Daniel. 'Simple. But great.'

'Thank you, Daniel,' said Betty. 'Ricky, you go and ask him.'

'Why me?' moaned Ricky.

'Again, why must we always have this *why me* argument?' chided Betty. 'Other children's secret clubs don't continually argue about who does what and when, do they? Now, go and sidle over to him and ask!'

Ricky was aghast and, to be brutally frank, slightly agog. He'd never been chided before. 'Hold on,' he said. 'Chiding I can take, but the last time I sidled – accidentally, it must be said – you all jolly well lampooned me for it! So why should I sidle now? Hmmm?'

'He's right,' said Amy. 'We were a bit harsh on his involuntary sidling.'

'I don't recall any lampooning, though,' added Daniel.

'Okay,' said Betty. 'No sidling. Just edge up to him and ask.'

Edging seemed to be perfectly acceptable to Ricky, so he did. 'Please, Mr Bob,' Ricky said, after he had edged just far enough. 'In that restaurant is a lady called Clarissa. She's a stunt nun in your film. If you persuade her to come with us, and away from danger, then we'll all do this job for you.'

The man smiled quite a big smile for his size of mouth, then nodded his head. 'Of course. Anything to assist your pathetic little adventure. And then she can help you do your stunting. Just wait here.'

They resumed their crouching position outside the restaurant and watched through the window as Bob went inside. Within barely the amount of time that light takes to cross a rather busy road during rush hour in Cheadle, Bob and Clarissa were heading out of the restaurant, but not before Clarissa had kissed Uncle Quagmire full on the lips for a full three and a half seconds.

'Did you see that?' gasped Amy, unable to believe what she had seen with her very own eyes.

'I did,' said Ricky. 'I've never seen Aunt Trinny kiss him like that! Have you?'

'Well,' said Amy, 'I did catch them holding hands once. Remember?'

'Yes, of course!' said Ricky. 'That was when she fell down that unexpected well in that field and Uncle Quagmire rescued her. That was so exciting!'

Amy nodded her head knowingly, yet unknowingly. Before they could enter into a discussion about the finer detail of inter-parental fondness, Bob and Clarissa approached the children at regular walking pace.

'This is Clarissa,' said Bob. 'She's stunting for me in scenes which are considered too dangerous for many highly paid actresses.'

'Pleased to meet you,' said Clarissa the stunt nun, shaking their hands one by one. She even shook Whatshisname's paw! The dog's tail wagged and wagged just over eighteen to the dozen. 'Nice pink collar, doggy! Good girl,' she said to Whatshisname. She turned to the children, leaving Whatshisname to growl quietly and frantically tear again at his fluffy pink collar.

'I've heard such a lot about you from your Uncle Quagmire,' Clarissa said. 'What a lovely handsome fellow he is.' She sighed a big sigh and the children frowned a big frown. 'And that Bartle de Lylow! Such a nice man. Very handsome indeed, for an American.' She glanced back into the restaurant, where Uncle Quagmire was busy arguing with Old Hag. Bartle looked very perplexed by all these comings and goings, especially the goings. Clarissa caught his eye and waved. She was really good at all the waving.

The children panicked! They had to fend off a plot reversal, and fast!

'Please,' urged Betty, grabbing Clarissa's arm. 'Quickly! We all need to go with Bob to do our stunting!'

'Yes,' Bob said, beckoning them with a free arm. 'Let's go, and get these children filmed hanging from trees, and then they can get on with their adventure. I'm so excited at being a member of The Secret Five! I'm so happy! The only thing that might upset me now is a chapt . . .'

Chapter Seventeen

In which the author gets a little peeved; Old Hag gets tripped up by a posh nun; our pals sit on a grassy hillside and almost sing a bit; Ricky tries yet again to complain about the treatment of their characters; he's walking a fine line; the kangaroo, unseen, peeks around a corner.

'Gee, what a bummer, was that really necessary?' moaned an irritated Bob as they all boarded a little private bus that was to take them to the filming location. 'There's always someone who likes to spoil things, ain't there?'

'We're used to it by now,' said Betty. 'But tell us what we have to do, Mr Bob, please do.'

And so, on their way to the film location, Bob patiently explained all about their task, which was for them to change into some green swirly curtain-material clothes and then hang upside down from trees over a lakeside lane.

'But we knew all that already,' moaned Daniel. 'What a waste!'

'Ah,' said Bob, 'but wait, there's something else. You also have to wave and yell at an old car as it goes by, under the trees.'

The children were pathetically easy to please, and excitedly told him that they were quite good at yelling and waving at old cars, and were extremely excited and eager to change into their curtain costumes to perform their rather daring stunt over the lakeside lane, and for it to be enthusiastically described in precise detail, covering several pages, to show exactly what brave stunt children they were.

But all too soon, before we know it, in the space of an ellipsis . . . the children had done their silly stunting, changed out of their sillier costumes, and had then been paid handsomely for their efforts. Very handsomely indeed. In comparison, more erudite and hard-working creative people often go unpaid for their efforts. Efforts which are probably far more important, artistically and literally, and far more skilful. As a result, it means that it is not really possible for the children's stunt work to be described here in detail, which is a shame but hey, that's life.

'Well!' mumbled Betty to the others. 'What a miserable . . .'

'Ssshhhh! I wouldn't say anything,' whispered Daniel. 'You know that *he* can be a bit touchy and sometimes seek revenge.'

'Who?' asked Amy, as she counted her money.

'Never mind,' said Daniel, squirreling the wad of notes into his pocket, not realising that the Austrian Schilling of 1964 would be delightfully obsolete by the time they got themselves back to the twenty-first century. Shame.

'They can always watch our bit on the DVD!' whispered Betty. 'That'll show him! If they look carefully, they'll see Whatshisname up a tree as well!'

'Please, who's *him*?' pleaded Amy. 'And what's a VDV?'

Whatshisname stood there and wondered what Pavlov's dog would have made of this lot. How would he have dealt with their mental meanderings? Salivated over them, probably. He must try that some time. Whatshisname was having second thoughts about his Dog Created Man theory. Surely not. Unless Dog had the blueprint the wrong way up. That might explain it. He uttered an involuntary sigh, released an eggcupful of hell-gas and sank down on the grass for a jolly good nap.

Betty suddenly gasped quite a good gasp. 'Bother!' she said. 'Over there, coming this way! It's Old Hag, and she's with Mr Bartle!'

'Crikey, what are they doing here?' said Ricky.

Old Hag looked very pleased with herself, in an old hag way. 'Aha!' she aharred as she approached them, dragging Mr Bartle by the hand. 'I saw you silly well-paid children hanging from those trees and waving at that old car.'

'Good,' Daniel said, glancing skywards. 'I'm glad someone did.'

'Indeed, ha!' Old Hag cackled, pointing a random finger in their direction. 'You were all rubbish. Couldn't hang from trees for toffee. It'll be cut out, as sure as eggs is . . . erm . . .'

'Eggs?' offered Betty.

'Yes, eggs,' agreed Old Hag. 'Now, I have to tell you this, as I *do* love to tell secrets. All this is part of my very own secret mission, which is a secret, so there! Enough said. Now, where's Clarissa the stunt nun? Eh? This handsome bald American gentleman would like to see her.'

Bartle stood there and, understandably, looked confused by it all.

'Ricky, tell her we don't know where Clarissa is,' whispered Betty.

'Why can't you tell her yourself?' moaned Ricky. 'Here we go again, expecting me to do all sorts of stuff, like opening doors, or telling people things. I could easily leave again, you know!'

'I'll tell her,' volunteered Daniel. 'I'm very good at telling.' He turned to Old Hag and said, firmly yet softly, 'We don't know.'

'Ha!' cackled Old Hag, dragging Bartle by the hand. 'I don't believe you! Come on, Bartle. Let's go and find the lovely Clarissa and you two can chat a bit. Then you've got some serious canoodling to do.'

'What's canoodling?' whispered Amy to Betty as they watched Old Hag and Bartle scurry away.

'It's the bit that comes before conception, or so I hear,' said Betty knowingly.

'Oh,' said Amy, thinking very hard inside her head. 'Remind me again what conception is?'

'No time for that now!' cried Daniel. 'There's an Old Hag to catch! Look! She's seen Clarissa! Come on!'

This was becoming exciting! No, really it was!! Thrusting his way through a needless outbreak of exclamation marks, Daniel hared after Old Hag, who was dragging poor Bartle along at quite a pace. But just then, or round about then, something else happened! A posh lady, dressed in a nun's outfit with a guitar around her neck, leapt out in front of Old Hag, tripped her up, and sent her flying to the ground! Off came Old Hag's West Brom bobble hat as she tumbled headlong into some quite long Austrian grass, just avoiding flattening the sole specimen of an unknown sub-variety of edelweiss, and so preserving the extraordinary and unique flower for future generations.

Bartle took one look at Old Hag sprawled on the ground (or it might have been two looks without a gap between), frowned all over his head, then ran as fast as he could up the lane back to town. He looked very scared indeed, and very bald. Old Hag struggled to her feet and searched frantically for her precious bobble hat in the long grass, trampling to death the sole specimen of that unknown sub-variety of edelweiss in the process.

When they saw her struggling and searching, how the children laughed![1]

The posh nun with the guitar wandered over to the children. 'Well I never!' she said, although she had, so that was a whopper. 'I thought so! Bob told me you were here, but I didn't believe him. You're The Secret Five! Super-duper! I've heard all about you and your adventures! You are definitely one of my favourite things, apart from whiskers on kittens, of course.'

The children didn't know what to make of this nun with curlers in her hair under her wimple.

'I believe that we don't know what to make of you,' said Betty, 'but thank you for leaping out and stopping Old Hag from going about her devious task.'

---

[1] *See Appendix II: How We Laugh: The Behavioural, Cognitive and Emotional Processes Scientifically Explored.*

'Think nothing of it,' said the posh nun. 'Which you probably won't anyway. I could see that you needed help in your little adventure.'

'Are you a stunt nun as well?' asked Amy, quite stupidly.

The posh nun laughed but it was only a semi-posh laugh as she was off-duty. 'You're a lamb, my dear, but no,' she said. 'That's just Clarissa, who does all the dangerous things for me, like running down hillsides, climbing trees, dancing around fountains, and tasting my food in case one of my numerous enemies tries to poison me.'

'Oh,' said Amy, who always managed to say the right thing at the right time.

'But please *please* tell me all about your adventures,' said the posh nun. 'Come over here on this grassy hillside. Sit around me and we'll all look very enthralled. Let's start at the very beginning.'

The children and Whatshisname all thought that was a very good place to start. They were also very pleased that they had been invited to sit around and look enthralled, as they hadn't done that for some considerable time. They sat themselves down on the grassy hillside and told the posh nun all about their adventures, carefully omitting the one where they had unintentionally slaughtered a genial tramp and intentionally buried his remains. When they explained about Clarissa, Bartle, the devious Old Hag and the fantastically impossible time travel, the posh nun nodded her head and understood completely. She wished them well, and began to tune her guitar so she could play them some jolly ditty about bright copper mittens and warm woollen kettles, a song, she told them, that was a work-in-progress.

But just then she stopped, looked, stopped looking, looked again, then said, 'Isn't that Clarissa, down there by those typical Austrian trees? Talking to someone bald who looks rather like your friend Bartle?'

They all looked and, sure enough, down there by the trees, there was Clarissa talking to someone who looked like Bartle! Old

Hag was standing by them, trying to pull them closer together and struggling to put on her bobble hat.

'Oh no!' exclaimed Betty. 'Not only does he look like Bartle, it *is* him!'

'Woof woof woof,' said Whatshisname, who was becoming worried that his part was slipping away.

The children all jumped up, ready to spring into immediate action. 'Sorry! We are ready to spring into immediate action and must go and run after them,' said Betty to the posh nun. 'But thank you so much for enthralling us.'

'Erm, is that it?' the posh nun asked, an overly-posh frown appearing on her posh nun's forehead. 'I'm quite sure I'm contracted to do more than this, you know.'

'Sorry about that,' Betty said. 'Maybe you can appear in the next adventure. We'll have a quiet word. For now, you can sing a little song as we run away if you like.'

'Oh, well,' the posh nun said. 'Then I don't feel so bad. I suppose that will have to do.' She cleared her throat. 'Doe . . .' she sang.

And that was enough to drive the children away. 'Come on, run, before we're caught up in the sheer magic and sugary sentiment of the song!' urged Daniel. 'We must stop Clarissa and Bartle from . . . conceptualising! And, look! They've both got handy bicycles! If we're not careful, we're going to lose them as they pedal off down the lane and round the corner!'

The five of them scampered towards Clarissa and Bartle but, as they got nearer, Old Hag saw them! Waving her skinny arms about, she made the pair jump quickly onto their bicycles and, before very long, as predicted, the children had lost them as the two pedalled off down the lane and round the corner. Old Hag tottered after them.

'Blow!' said Amy.

'I was going to say *blow*!' moaned Ricky, frowning such a huge frown that, if he had been wearing spectacles, they would surely have fallen off and been trampled underfoot by a passer-by who, to be honest, should have been more careful and watched where he was walking.

'Does he have to do all that?' moaned Daniel.

'What? Who?' asked Amy.

'I mean,' said Daniel. 'Here we are, about to experience a failed mission, and all he can think of is Ricky's frowning and moaning, and a fictitious clumsy passer-by!'

Ricky was looking more sullen by the minute. 'That is positively the last time I frown and moan!' he moaned, frowning. 'And this seems a good opportunity to speak my mind about our treatment. Firstly, I'm fed up of . . .'

Chapter Eighteen

In which they meet a kindly old Austrian lady in yet another teashop; Heidi the three-legged lamb is mentioned; a hotel receptionist successfully consults her guest book; Whatshisname has to feint a faint and then nibbles at a buttock or two.

'See? *That* is the very reason why I left the story before!' said Ricky, indignantly. 'It's quite unacceptable, and I haven't eaten anything of note for at least forty pages! I'm going to quit again!'

'Ricky!' pleaded Betty. 'Please stay.' She placed a hand – her own hand – on Ricky's shoulder. 'I tell you what, Ricky, as a concession I'll let you sneak a peek down my top when I'm not looking. And I think I'm falling in love with you a bit, and probably couldn't go on without you. Or maybe not. But if you go, I go!'

'What? Okay!' agreed Ricky rather too quickly. 'Then perhaps, given those circumstances – especially the concessionary sneaky peek – I'll consider staying.'

'Never mind all that!' said Daniel, taking control as if he were a bespectacled adult. 'We have to catch them! They're heading for town, probably back to the hotel where they'll soon start some unsupervised unprotected canoodling. We need to be fast!'

'Yes!' said Ricky excitedly. 'Just like a Rapid Response Team!'

'Exactly!' said Daniel.

'Right,' said Betty, 'let's first find a teashop for Ricky to have something to eat, then we'll find some rapid response bicycles and follow them!'

'Good idea!' said Amy.

They started to walk quickly towards town, stopping on the way to help a man and a lady with a puncture on one of their bicycles. Eventually, Amy spotted an Austrian teashop. 'Look!' she said, pointing with her best pointing finger. 'A teashop for Ricky!'

'Yes!' said Ricky eagerly. 'And a friendly little old Austrian lady in a pinafore standing waiting for us! This is just like home! I wonder if she'll have some bicycles for us to borrow.'

Still wondering, they stepped inside the teashop, where the little old Austrian lady in a pinafore gave them a cheery Austrian welcome.

'You m ust be Th e Sec ret Fiv e!' she said, cheerily welcoming them in perfect broken English. 'I'v e hea rd all ab out y ou from my n iece in En glan d.'

'Oh, gosh!' said Daniel. 'Whereabouts in En glan d does your n iece live?'

'Y ou wou ldn't kno w he r,' said the little old Austrian lady in a pinafore. 'Sh e run s a teas hop nea r Lower Dow ns. Her husba nd ha s a very val uable collec tion of ve ry old fossilis ed bo nes of whi ch he is v ery proud. They're h is pr ide and j oy, but he ha s a bit of a tem per, just l ike my o wn dear hu sband, ble ss h is cur sed s oul. I fe ar that my ni ece's life will e nd in a rath er gr uesome fash ion somet ime in the dis tant f ut ure.'

'Woof woof woof,' Whatshisname said, quite happily.

'Never mind, eh?' said Betty. 'Now, have you any tasty sultana scones, zesty carrot cordial and some bicycles to help us on our way?'

'Of cou rse, m y dea rs,' the little old Austrian lady in a pinafore said. 'C ome on in! Y ou all lo ok as th ou gh you ne ed some fo od ins ide y ou. Espec ial ly the ug ly b oy.'

Ricky looked at Daniel sympathetically and Daniel looked at Ricky sympathetically. They followed the girls and Whatshisname into the shop, where the little old Austrian lady in a pinafore made them a lip-smacking tea. She also gave Whatshisname a nice big leg of lamb to chew on with relish, which made him choke a little bit, but that doesn't really matter, does it now?

Very soon the children were cycling quite steadily into town, on quite steady bicycles provided by the little old Austrian lady in a pinafore. She had cheerily waved them off from her doorstep, wondering what her little old Austrian husband would say about the loss of another brand new set of bicycles and the depleted state of his favourite lamb, Heidi, a lamb that meant more to him than life itself and which he had recently entered into the forthcoming Annual Salzburg, Bletchley & District Stocky-Hooved Horned Mammal Show, in which he had an excellent chance of retaining both the prestigious Best Working Juvenile Fully-Limbed Sheep Award and the Ultimate Agility (Burning Hoops & Hot Bed of Coals) Supreme Woolly Four-Legged Champion Award sponsored by Snuffit Fire Extinguishers Inc.

Blissfully unaware of anything, as usual, the children raced into town on their very urgent mission. Whatshisname half-trotted, half-scampered, half-ran alongside them in a deceptively faithful way. They all felt very important and serious, considering their bank balance, which was now quite healthy thanks to the spot of paid stunting work. But we don't want to dwell too long on that, do we, otherwise some people, such as lowly-paid authors, might get a bit miffed by the utter injustice of it all, and want to seek retribution.

Eventually they reached the hotel without being run over and badly squashed by a fully-laden runaway truck, conveniently placed in the narrative, which only just missed them as it careered out of a side road, killing a benevolent greengrocer and a priest who had been chatting about plans for a substantial fundraising event for local orphans.

Anyway, they carefully threw their bicycles to the ground and raced into the hotel's reception. It was a huge big reception, with lots of quite posh shiny bits and carpet everywhere, except on the ceiling, walls and windows.

Betty bravely went up to the lady behind the reception desk.

'Quickly!' she said quickly. 'We have to save the world! We have to find Clarissa the stunt nun and Mr Bartle de Lylow! Have you seen them?'

'I certainly have,' replied the lady behind the reception desk, consulting her reception desk book. 'Stunt nun, Room 405, it says here, in quite nice writing with a beautifully crafted R. The fastest way is to take the lift up to the ninth floor, then the stairs back down to the fourth floor. And good luck, Secret Five!'

'Okay!' urged Ricky, sneaking an authorised peek down Betty's top. 'Let's go!'

They raced to the lift and stood in front of the doors, waiting. Then Daniel pressed the button and they waited some more. Meanwhile, Whatshisname had found the stairs and was already waiting patiently for them on the fourth floor.

Eventually the children reached the fourth floor and were walking carefully towards Room 405 when, quite suddenly, Daniel said, 'Stop!'

They stopped, and what a blow! They saw Old Hag standing guard outside Room 405!

'Bother!' said Betty. 'She's standing guard outside Room 405! I knew we shouldn't have stopped at that teashop. It's a habit we must break, although we do appear to give tremendous and long-lasting pleasure to the little old lady owners, it must be said.'

'What shall we do now?' said Amy. 'Bartle and Clarissa must be in there.'

'I think a meeting is called for,' suggested Daniel. 'So that we can decide what to do.'

'No!' said Ricky, quite fiercely for a boy with a hint of athlete's foot. 'No more meetings! I'm sick of meetings, they make me really grumpy, so I don't think we should have any more! Ever! And certainly no privileges.'

Amy was shocked! 'But Ricky,' she said shockingly, 'if we don't have meetings, how else can we decide what we're going to do?'

'I tell you what I'm going to do,' said Betty, firmly taking charge. 'I'm going to somehow get Whatshisname to distract her, then burst into the room using this master key that I just found in my hand.'

'Wow!' said the others, together, quite astonished at how utterly firm she could be when the moment calls for utter firmness.

'Woof?' said Whatshisname, quite lost for words.

'Then I don't think we need a meeting at all,' said Daniel.

'Good,' snapped Ricky.

'I'm not so sure,' said Amy, 'that I like this loss of our egalitarian rights. But carry on. We'll take a vote at the next meeting on whether we want to lose our democratic mandate.'

'Now,' said Betty, 'how can we get Whatshisname to distract Old Hag?'

'What about,' suggested Amy, 'if he walks past her and then pretends to pass out? For some strange and inexplicable reason, Old Hag likes him, and she'll leave her post to go and attend to him.'

'Good idea!' said Betty.

'Woof woof woof?' said Whatshisname.

'Right, boy,' said Amy to Whatshisname, pointing down the corridor towards Old Hag. 'Go faint!'

Whatshisname looked at Amy quite seriously, yet quite inquisitively, as he tried to translate *gofe aynt* into Classic Doggish. *Gofe aynt* . . . hmmm . . .

'Go, boy!' said Daniel, also pointing down the corridor. 'Go faint!'

Whatshisname looked at Daniel quite inquisitively, yet quite seriously. G*ofe aynt? Nope, me no understand.* Then he looked down the corridor and saw Old Hag by Room 405. A friend!

'Woof woof woof!' he said, and bounded down the corridor. Old Hag turned to see what all the bounding and woofing was about. Whatshisname leapt up at her, she fell backwards and, with quite a resounding thump, hit her head on the very wall that was holding the very ceiling up! She lay quite still as Whatshisname stood looking down at her for a moment, pondering his next move. He looked back up the corridor to where the children stood. *Ah! Go faint!* Right! He fell over in a pretend faint on top of Old Hag.

The children looked at each other. 'Do you think he's really fainted?' asked Amy.

'He's not *that* clever!' said Betty. 'Come on! Before Old Hag wakes up.'

They scampered down the corridor and stopped by the pile of bodies outside Room 405. Whatshisname opened one eye to see what was happening. Happy that his fainting ruse had worked, he stood up, shook himself, then waited for a big Thank You hug from his pals, which never came.

'I'm going to unlock the door,' whispered Betty, tiptoeing over Old Hag, the master key in her hand. The other children and Whatshisname tiptoed after her until they were all standing pressed against the door. Betty slipped the key into the lock and turned it.

'Go on, Daniel, open the door,' she whispered. 'It's your job!'

Daniel pushed the door open quite gingerly, quite carefully, and quite suddenly they all fell into the bedroom and landed in a heap on the floor! How they would have laughed if they could have seen themselves, which they could, of course, but not from an audience perspective. They all managed to stand up and were forced to gasp at what they saw before them! There, lying on a big double bed, her stunt nun's outfit by her side, was Clarissa! She looked really happy yet really sad. She also looked really naked. And, lying on his front by her side, eyes shut tight, was Bartle! He also looked really naked.

'Why, hello children!' said Clarissa. 'What a nice surprise! This is Bartle de Lylow. Isn't he handsome? And very nice, but . . .'

'Very nice butt?' squeaked Betty.

'No, he's very nice, *but* he tries a little too hard to be a caring lover,' said Clarissa, a stunt-frown audaciously crossing her brow.

The children didn't know what to say or where to look. And, while we're on the subject of their woeful inadequacies, nor did they know how to write remotely acceptable poetry in trochaic tetrameter or cook a dolcelatte and watercress soufflé.

'Sorry!' said Betty, quite apologetically, proving that she did indeed know what to say after all. 'We were just . . . just passing?'

She started to back out of the room. The others took the hint and started to back out as well, except Whatshisname who bounded onto the bed and began to lick and nibble at Bartle's buttocks.

'Come boy!' said Betty. Bartle opened his eyes and looked up, quite startled for a man of his age. Whatshisname, realising that he should have been backing out of the room and not licking and nibbling an American tourist's bare buttock, jumped off the bed and happily joined in with all the backing out.

When they were all satisfied that they were fully backed out, Betty quietly closed the door behind them. Just as quietly they stepped over Old Hag and stood in the corridor, shocked, waiting for someone to speak first. Nobody did, which was a bit unfortunate because some speech marks were ready and waiting.

' '

'Woof woof woof,' said Whatshisname after a few moments, a marvellously reliable dog, for sure.

'Well, does this mean that our adventure is over?' asked Daniel, eventually.

'I think it does,' said Ricky. 'This was all for nothing. All those exclamation marks wasted!!'

Whatshisname looked up at them, willing them to call the whole thing off. Maybe this time . . .

'I don't understand,' wailed Amy, in a sort of pathetic not-understanding way, quite thrown by the sight of people without any clothes on. 'Why was . . . what was . . . how come . . .'

'I know exactly what you mean,' said Daniel, solemnly. 'It's over.'

'Woof woof woof,' said Whatshisname, feeling a mixture of elation due to the prospect that he might be able to get his head down for a few thousand sticks, and despondency that Sampson de Lylow's shadowy ideals, now a real possibility, had made no mention of endless supplies of meaty chunks for all fat spaniels.

Standing there in the corridor, the others looked at Betty for guidance. But her face had turned quite pale, her cheeks the colour of Dulux Tropical Cornplaster silk emulsion[1]. And when they saw

---

[1] *Other brands and colours of silk emulsion with immensely harebrained names are available*

the glum and gloomy look on her face they knew that a literary device in the form of a central crisis had taken place! They badly needed a break!

Chapter Nineteen

In which Uncle Quagmire reads extracts from Sampson's autobiography; pay attention as you'll be tested on it later; Whatshisname reflects on Kafka's tortured life and Tesco's current offers; The Secret Five get a bit miffed about something really trivial.

'Let's face it,' Betty said. 'Chapter breaks don't help our adventure one bit. They slow things down, we've just lost valuable seconds!'

Whatshisname sighed and hung his head. Looks like she's still in adventure mode, then. Get over it, *let it go!*

'Come on!' Betty said urgently. 'We need to find Uncle Quagmire because, pitifully, he's the closest thing we've got to a mentor.'

Resisting the urge to give Old Hag a gentle kicking, they all raced up the stairs to the ninth floor and pressed the button for the lift down to the ground floor. As they waited, Amy asked, 'Is our adventure over, then?'

'Well, Amy,' said Daniel as the lift doors opened and they all carefully stepped inside, 'think about it.' He removed his spectacles and sucked the curly bit that rests on an ear. 'We haven't actually stopped the conception, we haven't rescued Uncle Quagmire, Ricky might have turned, and we haven't got ourselves back to 2010.'

'Gosh,' said Amy. 'I hadn't thought of all that.'

'I haven't turned!' moaned Ricky, grumpily turning away from Daniel. 'And I hate those stupid glasses!'

'Now now, boys!' said Betty. 'And I know you're hankering for some spectacles like Daniel's, Ricky, so don't be so silly.'

Ricky perked up at the mention of the word hankering. Hankering. *Hankering*. Yes, he liked that word. He would use it in casual conversation as soon as the right moment presented itself. Han-ker-ing. Hmmm.

Betty was keen to get things moving. 'Come on, everyone, we'll have to find Uncle Quagmire and ask him how we get back and if we can rescue the situation. Let's wait in the hotel's reception, shall we? He's sure to wander through very soon, if I'm not mistaken.'

Safely in the reception, they waited and waited, which made Ricky quite grumpy because it had been ages since he last ate anything of any substance and the others kept on glancing at him suspiciously, waiting for him to give secret signals to secret accomplices. Whatshisname was also quite grumpy, as he still had the taste of Bartle's buttocks on his long shiny tongue, and was desperate to lick something more savoury, like his own backside, so he did.

Suddenly, and extremely predictably, Uncle Quagmire wandered through the hotel reception. He had a book under one of his arms, probably his left one.

'Hello,' he said, unable to think of a less boring expression of greeting. 'I was wondering where I'd got to. Or maybe I was wondering where you'd got to. Anyway, never mind, I've finished wondering now. There you all are. I've been trying to find Clarissa, to explain all about the danger of canoodling with Bartle.'

The children looked quite glum and quite mournful.

'What's the matter?' Uncle Quagmire asked. 'I've rarely seen you all looking so glumful. Not since the day your very favourite pet hamster let me down big time in my daring experiment with the turbocharged hamster wheel.'

'It's Clarissa and Bartle. We think it's too late,' said Daniel.

'Yes, they're upstairs,' said Betty.

'On the bed,' added Ricky. 'Together. Looking happy. And tired. Might be a sign of something, or other.'

'Woof woof woof,' said Whatshisname, woefully.

'But . . .' said Amy.

'Oh dear,' moaned Uncle Quagmire, sinking down into a handy armchair. 'Oh dear oh dear.'

'But . . .' said Amy again.

'It does look as though you've failed miserably. Mediocrity has always been your forte. However . . .' said Uncle Quagmire. He stopped, and the children all thought that he was thinking, as his little ears were wiggling and waggling, a sure sign of thinking. They watched him for a while.

'Are you thinking?' asked Ricky, eventually.

'I certainly am,' said Uncle Quagmire.

'Erm . . . shall we just stand here while you think?' asked Betty.

'Shush!' said Uncle Quagmire. 'I'm thinking.'

So the children just stood there, thinking, while Uncle Quagmire was thinking. Whatshisname had finished all his licking and looked up at them, keen to know what they were all doing, standing there. He had never felt comfortable with the concept of thinking, and had always thought that it was overrated compared to not thinking. Anyway, there was all the debate about the notion that animals may not think, and that muddied the polemics a little, and he couldn't cope with muddy polemics.

'Woof woof woof?' he whispered, but they all shushed him so he just stood there, trying not to think, looking up at them. He really wasn't quite sure if they were all thinking or not thinking. It was hard to tell, but his money was on not thinking. Then he thought that he'd better start thinking again, quickly but discreetly, just like the great thinkers used to do in times of crisis and, come to think of it, at all other times as well. Gently, he started thinking, then lifted his tail and quickly passed a discrete amount of hell-gas.

Uncle Quagmire glanced suspiciously at Whatshisname and wrinkled his nose. He turned to the children. 'Now, it might surprise you but I've been thinking. Listen to me. You'll have to crowd around me for this, because it could get quite complicated, especially for you Amy.'

The children crowded around Uncle Quagmire's armchair, as did several inquisitive hotel guests who happened to be passing and wondered what all the crowding was about. One of them looked very much like the typical village postman from chapter one, standing proudly in his lederhosen with his hands on his very own hips.

'What I've been thinking is . . .' began Uncle Quagmire.

'Hang on,' said Daniel, looking around him. 'Who are all these people?'

'Oh, don't worry, apparently they're just several inquisitive hotel guests,' reassured Uncle Quagmire.

'Sorry,' said Daniel. 'I wasn't paying attention. Carry on.'

'Thank you,' said Uncle Quagmire. 'Now, from what you've said, the modern world is still not safe from the terrible evilness that is Sampson de Lylow. I've been thinking very hard indeed, as you know, and I have a stunning brand new plan that will save the world.'

The children gasped, and so did the several inquisitive hotel guests.

'What do you mean, brand new plan?' asked an inquisitive lady hotel guest.

'It's . . .' said Uncle Quagmire.

'Erm, excuse me!' said Daniel, looking up, seemingly into thin air. 'Why did that dialogue go to *her*? Hmmm?'

The others looked at Daniel as if he were quite mad. 'He's doing it again,' whispered Amy to Betty.

'Ignore him,' suggested Betty. 'He has rather a strained relationship with you-know-who.'

'Who?' asked Amy.

'You know!' said Betty. 'You-know-who!'

'Oh,' said Amy, and looked up, bewildered, into the same bit of thin air that Daniel had looked up into.

'Anyway,' said Daniel sternly, 'I demand to say *What do you mean, brand new plan?*'

'Go on then,' said Betty. 'And hurry up!'

'Okay!' said Daniel. 'Here goes. What do you mean, brand new plan?'

Daniel glanced up into the thin air and smirked a little winning smirk, unaware that revenge is a dish best served hot enough to burn the roof of his mouth quite badly when the opportunity next arises.

'Well,' said Uncle Quagmire, flicking through the book, 'I've found something interascinating in Sampson de Lylow's autobiography *My Plan Is To Dominate The World*, available at all good booksellers, and subsequently The Works, in forty-six years from now. My new plan means that you children will have to travel forward to 1980. And I can't come with you.'

'1980?' gasped an inquisitive man hotel guest. 'Isn't that when Sebastian Coe will win the 1500 metres at the Moscow Olympics in an amazing 3 minutes 38.4 seconds?'

'Look!' Daniel yelled into thin air. 'Enough!' Then he frowned a knowing frown. 'A*ha*! How does *he* know that? Hmmm? Getting too clever for your boots, now, aren't you?' He prodded a finger into the air. 'Caught you out!'

The others edged away from Daniel. Betty, being a caring sister, took the precaution of kicking his shin before she edged away. 'Honestly, Daniel!' she scolded. 'If it isn't your stupid urban street talk, it's all this talking to you-know-who! You've got to get a grip. You're supposed to set an example to a younger sibling!'

'But . . .' said Daniel, rubbing his shin.

'Children!' snapped Uncle Quagmire. 'Enough! Pay attention instantly!'

Heavily influenced by all the snapping, they instantly paid attention. Uncle Quagmire held up the book at page 125 and said, 'Let me read something from page 125 to you, then you'll understand. Or, from bitter experience, you may not.'

'This is so exciting!' exclaimed another inquisitive hotel guest. Daniel glared at him, then decided that his best strategy would be to look quite grumpy for a while.

'You know,' said Uncle Quagmire, 'that Sampson de Lylow wrote in his autobiography that he was conceived in Salzburg and that his mother is Clarissa and his father was a fellow named Bartle, whom you've already met.'

Amy started to ask a question but Uncle Quagmire held up his hand to stop her. 'Amy! Shush! Defer your incisive questioning, and let me read what he wrote about an incident that happened to him in 1980. Now, just to warn you, he writes in a rather modernist style, with a surfeit of temporal juxtapositions and parenthetical statements, which I'm sure you children will notice straight away. Nevertheless, Sampson writes: *Until that fateful day in 1980, which I am about to relate, the sun shone on my life as the sun shines on a waiting nocturnal flower in the desert or on a colourful humming bird in the light-trimmed foliage of a jungle treetop . . .*'

Uncle Quagmire paused. 'I forgot to mention that the writing is not only modernist in its style but it's downright crass as well. Personally I prefer Blyton at her best. But I shall continue, as he goes on – *and on that day a vast cloud from an indifferent world came and blotted the sun [silencing my natural humanity and kindness] which emptied my agreeable soul to make room for the person I am today, an idealist, a man driven into the arms of the Devil himself, a man whose conscience is heavy with the deeds that I feel obliged to perpetrate against the evils of Mankind and against the seemingly endless buy-one-get-one-free offers on shower-gel at Tesco . . .*'

There were murmurings amongst the inquisitive hotel guests, and a couple of them disappeared in search of the nearest Tesco store. The children, however, looked positively bewildered, yet again. Whatshisname sat nodding his head, obviously deeply moved by the emotional narrative, the Kafkaesque evocation of a world in which personal viewpoints often fail, and the complex ontological notion that Chappie Variety 10-Pouch Packs might be on a BOGOF offer at Tesco as well.

Uncle Quagmire went on: '*It all seems so inconsequential now. So, so absurd. So deeply absurd. How foolish I was . . .*'

'Excuse me, Uncle Quagmire, but is that *you* talking, or are you still reading?' asked Ricky.

'I'm reading!' snapped Uncle Quagmire, quite irritably, before continuing reading: '*How foolish I was . . .*'

'I don't think he *is* reading it,' whispered Ricky to Betty.

Uncle Quagmire slammed the book down onto his lap, making the children frown quite suddenly and, as a side effect, making himself wince.

'Look,' he squeaked, wiping a tear from his eye, 'to make it easier, I tell you what. I'll summapsulate what Sampson says in words you can *all* understand. Okay?'

They all thought that was a good idea, except one inquisitive lady hotel guest who said she wanted Uncle Quagmire to read on, as she was quite taken with the way in which the narrative conveyed a sense of spiritual crisis caused by a failure of conventional values and the way that Uncle Quagmire sucked on his moustache at every punctuation mark.

'Sampson de Lylow,' continued Uncle Quagmire, 'was a normal teenager until 1980. He was troubled, impetuous, dissolute, self-indulgent . . .'

'Is that what *we're* like?' asked Amy.

Uncle Quagmire ignored her and continued. '. . . not to mention headstrong, wayward, hedonistic . . .'

'It certainly sounds like us,' said Betty.

'And then something happened,' said Uncle Quagmire, relentlessly. 'He was the subject of a rejection at school, a rejection so cruel and heartless that it turned him into the man he became instead of the man who . . . erm, the man who . . . he didn't become.'

Amy looked very confused. 'Are you sure you don't want to go back to reading it from the book?' she asked.

Uncle Quagmire ignored her and continued talking. 'It was the final straw for Sampson de Lylow. After years of being humiliated and teased mercilessly about his mightily small ears . . .'

'Just like yours!' exclaimed Amy. 'What a coincidence!'

'. . . he had the chance,' Uncle Quagmire continued, 'to make a name for himself on stage. Admittedly it was in a school play but, for the first time in his life, he would be applauded as a soloist in a boy band. Before he could accomplish his castanet solo, however, he was banished from the band and the chance to shine was suddenly whisked away from him in an extremely humiliating and even more extremely public manner.'

'Gosh!' said Daniel, unable to think of anything deeply profound to say.

'Indeed. So your mission, Secret Five, is to go to that school in 1980 and stop that utter humiliation,' Uncle Quagmire said with a serious expression on some parts of his face.

'But why can't you come with us?' asked Amy.

Uncle Quagmire smiled, then stopped smiling, making it quite a short smile as smiles go. 'Because,' he said, 'you will need to mingle with the schoolchildren, and I'd look silly trying to do that, wouldn't I? What with my knobbly knees and my disarmingly attractive facial hair.'

'Excuse me, I have a question,' said one of the several inquisitive hotel guests, raising his hand.

Daniel looked quite upset. 'So do I!' he said, waving his arm in the air. 'It's . . . erm . . . erm . . .'

'My question is,' continued the hotel guest after waiting a while for Daniel to stop erming, 'how do the children and their wretch of a dog get to 1980?'

'That's it!' said Daniel. '*That* was my question! I should have asked that!'

'Good question,' said Uncle Quagmire. 'Potentially an excelteresting question, Mr. Inquisitive Hotel Guest. In reply, that's not a problem as long as we've got some Brussels sprouts, something like a wardrobe for a portal, and something like a digital alarm clock.'

The hotel guests were very confused at the mention of digital alarm clocks. The children were also confused, as they didn't realise that sprouts were a fundamental component in time travel.

'I didn't realise that sprouts are a fundamental component in time travel,' said good old reliable Betty.

'Woof woof woof,' said Whatshisname, who did. He also realised their low carbon footprint advantages.

'Tell me,' said Uncle Quagmire, 'when you travelled back to 1964, did you have some Brussels sprouts on your person?'

'Why yes!' said Betty. 'Daniel had some. He pocketed them at Greentiles. I saw him!'

'I was saving them for Ricky,' explained Daniel. 'In case he got hungry at a later stage in the story.'

'And I had some in my pocket as well,' added Ricky. 'I was saving them . . . for me.'

'Well, there you are,' said Uncle Quagmire. 'Time travel can only work with sprouts in the equation, you see. It's the sulforaphane and the dithiolthiones that react with the glucosinolates to overcome the quantum object's timeline resistance. But, silly me, everyone knows that, I suppose.'

The children looked at each other. They were about to say that actually they didn't know that when Bartle de Lylow came wandering through the reception, heading for the exit. He walked slowly and looked tired yet disenchanted in an enchanting sort of way. His bald head looked quite dishevelled.

'There goes Mr Bartle!' whispered Amy.

'Shall I go after him and ask him how the conception went?' whispered Betty.

'Good idea!' said one of the inquisitive hotel guests eagerly.

'No,' said Uncle Quagmire quite firmly. 'It's not a good idea at all. I'll go upstairs and question Clarissa about it, to make sure we're on the right track. I think she trusts me and doesn't mind my hand accivertantly brushing her stunt nun's shapely knee. If deemed necessary, that is.'

'And she thinks that you're quite handsome!' said Amy.

Uncle Quagmire looked stunned, then he looked quite pleased, then he looked pleasantly stunned. He ran his fingertips over his moustache and straightened some of his hairs. 'My my,' he said, 'I don't know about that.'

'No, nor did we,' said the children.

'But what do we do while you're talking with Clarissa?' asked Daniel.

'I want you to find an enclosed space that will act as a portal,' said Uncle Quagmire. 'And a digital clock. Impossible to find in these times, I know, but just do your best. It's only critical. Fail and you will probably die. Failure is not in my vocabulary.'

'Erm . . .' said Ricky.

'And, before you erm some more,' Uncle Quagmire said, 'evidently it is. But you know what I mean.'

'Woof woof woof?' said Whatshisname, who didn't.

Uncle Quagmire stood up and straightened his tie. He handed Ricky a sheet of paper. 'These are the instructions for setting up the clock. Use this knowledge wisely, young ones. You may want to look at them later or, just in case an unforeseen event happens, a bit earlier than later. So, I'll see you back here in ten, er, let's say twenty minutes. No, make it thirty. And I'll then tell you if you have to go to 1980.' He walked towards the lift, pausing only to adjust his nostril hairs in a mirror. The inquisitive hotel guests began to drift away in quite small but manageable drifts, leaving The Secret Five to discuss what to do next.

'So,' said Ricky, 'it seems that we need to find a portal. Urgently! Very urgently!'

The others all nodded and murmured agreement.

'Anyone got any idea what a portal is?' Ricky added. 'I haven't. Shall we find somewhere to eat first?'

'No time for that!' said Betty. 'It's portal time. Let's split up and find something like a wardrobe that will serve as a portal.'

'Tell me,' said Daniel to Betty, 'are you the only one of us who knows what a portal actually is?'

'Woof woof woof!!!' said Whatshisname indignantly.

'Don't be rude!' said Amy. 'Of course we know. It's another name for a wardrobe. Silly boy!'

'She could be right,' said Ricky. 'Do you know, sometimes I think Amy is much cleverer than she looks.'

'Huh?' said Amy.

'Let's spring into action!' urged Betty. 'Daniel and Ricky, you go find a handy portal. Amy and I will search for something like a digital clock.'

'What about me?' asked an inquisitive pale lady who had missed the cue for all the drifting away.

'What *about* you?' asked Daniel, rather firmly yet quite limply.

'Well,' said the pale lady, 'I wondered if I could help you find your portal and something that looks like a digital clock.'

The children looked at each other for about two seconds longer than was necessary. Then Betty spoke.

'I don't want to be rude,' she said, 'but we are The Secret Five at the critical phase of an important adventure. We are highly motivated and highly trained in this sort of thing, and I'm not sure that you are allowed to help us.'

'I don't know why *he* does this to us,' moaned Daniel, jabbing his thumb skywards. 'We're continually being interrupted by complete strangers who want to join our adventure and probably join our secret club as well.'

'Nonsense!' the pale lady said. 'But if you don't want to hear about the wardrobe in my room . . .'

'Wardrobe?' said Amy. 'In your room?'

'Yes,' said the inquisitive pale lady. 'But I'm afraid that the digital display alarm clock doesn't get invented until sometime in the future, so you're out of luck. You'll have to stay here, in 1964. What a laugh!'

All of a sudden, Betty became quite grumpy, grumpier than she had ever been before, so grumpy that you could almost hear the sound of someone's typing slowing down uncertainly. She spoke in a really grumpy voice to the others.

'I'm getting fed up of this. I can fully understand why you walked off, Ricky. Chapter breaks and all that I can put up with, just about, but plot holes are something else. Is there some place we can all go and have a quiet chat without you-know-who listening? Without the dog?'

'Over there!' said Daniel, pointing to a handy sidebar nearby. 'Let's go in there and talk privately!'

'Yes, let's!' agreed Amy, frowning.

Chapter Twenty

In which several troublesome things happen, and Ricky regrets the lack of HobNobs.

They all trooped off to the sidebar, leaving the inquisitive pale lady standing there with Whatshisname. Suddenly he felt quite alone and dejected without his chums.

'Hello!' said the lady, bending down to stroke Whatshisname's head. 'You're a lovely fellow, aren't you?'

'Woof woof woof!' said Whatshisname, pleased at being called a fellow, given previous misguided assumptions about his gender.

'I tell you what!' said the inquisitive pale lady. 'While they're away, why don't I go and sit over there on that comfy chair, alongside their sidebar, and you can sit by me and we can chat.'

'Woof woof woof!' said

'Okay, we can talk in here,' said Daniel, 'without him listening and being regularly punctuated by exclamation marks. We can be ourselves. God, this is so tiring.'

'You're right,' said Betty. 'We can talk in here like adults. Anyone else uneasy with all this crap?'

'Me,' said Amy. 'It feels so tiresome and dreary being a one dimensional anodyne protagonist and having to say stuff like "yes, let's".'

'Too bloody right!' Ricky said. 'And, what gets me is the regular use of these simple adjectives, qualifiers, adverbs, and basic linguistic structure.'

'Although I notice,' Daniel said, 'that sometimes you're actually given dialogue with a particularly literary register, Betty.'

Whatshisname. He followed her and sat down at her feet. He peeked over her shoulder to see inside the sidebar, but couldn't see anything except a haze of italics, so he gazed up at her, his eyes considerably full of dole. To be honest, this could turn out to be his worst nightmare, apart from the trebuchet incident – what on earth were his pals talking about? Not vets, surely?

Never mind, he had this nice inquisitive lady for company. He only wished that he had the power of speech, then he could tell her all about Nixie digital clocks.

'You are really nice,' the inquisitive lady sighed. 'Just like my old doggy.'

She stroked Whatshisname's head. He sighed and began to relax a bit.

'Yes, I remember my old doggy, bless her, looking up at me as I drove the knife in. Such pitiful eyes. She made no sound as she died, just a little gurgle. When you think

'You're just jealous. But it's refreshing when it happens, that's for sure,' she said, 'although I crave for dramatic irony and the odd metaphor.'

'So, do we just carry on? What do you think, Betty?' Ricky asked.

'We have no choice.'

'Betty's right,' agreed Amy. 'We do have to. God, let's get it over with. I can't wait for a good bonk when we get out of here.'

They laughed. 'That's what I like about Amy,' Daniel said. 'She always lets her art show through.'

'But this is crazy!' said Ricky. 'I can't do this. I have a third dimension that's bursting to break out.'

'Just stick with it for now,' suggested Betty.

'Exactly,' said Daniel. 'But to be honest, that dog gets on my nerves. The suggestion that it knows more than we do is ridiculous.'

'I'll agree with that,' said Ricky. 'But can I make a point? We have no plotted means of getting back to the present day.

about it, if only she'd made no sound in life, then I'd have had no reason to have killed her – where are you going? Come back! Nice doggy!'

But Whatshisname had gone! He had shot off and was now busy cowering behind the reception desk.

The inquisitive lady shrugged, then slipped the penknife back into her pocket. She waited for the children to finish in the sidebar, and thought this was taking far longer than she'd expected. She started to worry that her meagre part in the story might become even more meagre by the time they'd finished.

More worrying to her was that she might not have enough meaningful narrative to fill the space alongside the sidebar. But, happily for her and for everyone, it worked out just fine.

We can't just walk out, as we'd be stuck in 1964, and I have other contracts. I'm due to play the young Leopold Bloom in Ulysses The Prequel soon.'

'So what do we do?' asked Amy.

'Well, we can't all leave now,' said Betty.

'And I can't live in 1964 Salzburg forever, for God's sake,' said Daniel. 'This is a plot hole that I can't see a way out of. How do we get out of 1964? No digital alarm clocks, you see. It's yet another plot cock-up. Just like all these 1964 people who know we exist! Crazy!'

'Maybe,' suggested Betty, 'we should quiz this Uncle Quagmire character about it. He seems to know about this sort of stuff.'

'Then we'll do that,' said Ricky.

'And be nice to the dog,' said Amy. 'She's probably as upset as all of us.'

'Isn't she a he?' asked Betty.

Amy shrugged. 'No idea.'

'Let's go and do as Betty says,' said Ricky, 'and quiz this Quagmire character.'

'Okay, let's go,' said Daniel. 'The quicker we get on with Act III, the quicker we'll be out of here.'

'Yes, let's go,' said Amy.

'Hello!' the inquisitive pale dog-murdering lady said as the four children came back from the sidebar. 'Did you enjoy your little meeting?'

'Meeting? What meeting?' said Ricky, looking genuinely confused. 'Where's Whatshisname?'

The dog-murdering pale inquisitive lady frowned. 'I don't know. I was just explaining all about my tendency to kill defenceless animals for the flimsiest of reasons and he took off somewhere. Can I help you look for him? *Please?*'

'No, we'll look later,' said Daniel who was, deep down, not that mortified about losing Whatshisname.

'Yes, we have to go and find Uncle Quagmire, quite urgently,' said Betty, feeling very important all of a sudden.

'Oh dear, don't you want to use my wardrobe?' the pale lady asked inquisitively.

'Not just yet, thanks,' said Betty. She beckoned the others towards the lift. 'But we'll be back soon, I believe.'

Leaving the pale inquisitive dog-murdering lady standing there fingering her knife and looking even more pale and inquisitive, the children quickly made their secret way up to the ninth floor then scampered down the stairs to the fourth floor. But when they reached the room, they saw that Whatshisname had mysteriously reached there before them! He looked very relieved to see them, or at least as very relieved as dogs can look with their somewhat rigid facial structure.

'Gosh! Where's Old Hag?' asked Amy. And gosh indeed, as Old Hag was no longer lying there unconscious. She had completely disappeared!

'This is worrying!' said Amy, worryingly.

'I trust that she's not somewhere else, thoroughly spoiling our thrilling adventure again,' moaned Ricky.

'Never mind her,' urged Betty. 'Shall we knock this time? Or just burst in again? You know what happened the last time we decided to burst.'

'I definitely think we should knock quite politely,' said Amy. 'I'm really not too keen on all this bodily nakedness. I still haven't fully recovered from seeing Ricky in chapter one. I meant to ask, Ricky, what was that tiny wrinkly . . .'

'Sssh, Amy!' Betty shushed. She knocked gently and compassionately on the door. Then the four children and Whatshisname pressed their favourite ears against the door, listening very very hard indeed. They could hear voices, the creaking of a bed, and the sound of a pair of man's trousers being put on rather hurriedly! They didn't know what to do! Secret Five training had never covered how to react to bed creaking and hurried trousers!

'What shall we do?' whispered Daniel.

'I suggest we should wait,' suggested Ricky. 'I thought I heard someone opening one of those little packets of HobNobs that you get on the tray by the kettle in the room.'

But, just then, suddenly, yet tenderly, and with a surfeit of irritating, and totally unnecessary, commas, the door opened, wide! There stood Uncle Quagmire! And there was no sign of a HobNob in his hands!

'Oh, it's *you*,' he said perceptively. 'Yes . . . well . . . I was just, er, questioning Clarissa about . . . about . . . well, it's all very inconclusive.'

Ricky peered around Uncle Quagmire, trying to see if there were indeed any HobNobs or, as he was desperate, custard creams going spare. The others, meanwhile, were all wondering why Uncle Quagmire's trousers were on back to front, and they were about to ask that very question when they heard Clarissa's voice from inside the room.

'Quaggy! Where are you?' she called. 'I'm getting quite cold!'

'Children,' said Uncle Quagmire in a strangely quiet voice. 'I'm trying to . . . erm, to mend the, er, radiator for Clarissa? Yes, that's it. So here's a good plan – just *go away* and I'll see you down in the hotel reception. Won't be long.'

'But, Uncle Quagmire, we need to ask you something,' said Ricky. 'Firstly about the peculiar behaviour of your trousers, secondly about the digital alarm clock. It hasn't been invented yet, so we can't get back. Isn't there another way to time travel? What about Euro Tunnel? Or a no-frills airline?'

'Quaggy!' called Clarissa. 'Come back to . . .'

'Not now!' yelled Uncle Quagmire over his shoulder. 'The *children* are here!'

'B-b-b-but . . .' stuttered Amy.

'Never mind all that butting and stuttering,' said Uncle Quagmire, quite irritably. 'In answer to your incisive question, Richard . . . I mean Ricky, I forgot to mention, there is something called a Nixie clock . . .'

'Woof woof woof,' said Whatshisname wearily.

'. . . that was a sort of forerunner of the digital clock in the Fifties.' Uncle Quagmire stopped talking and glanced down at his trousers. He suddenly realised that his trousers were on back-to-front! 'Oh, erm, yes, I can explain. Time travel does have a strange effectation on our attire – sometimes – so do watch out for any sudden clothing re-positioning, won't you. Anyway, you all go and wait in the nearest available hotel reception for me, there's good children, and then we can all gather round and do a planosal for the rest of the adventure. Now, I must go and finish this . . . radiator maintenance and, er, the intensive questioning of Clarissa. As I say, so far, it's all very inconclusive and unproductive. Apart from the . . . oh, never mind. Byeeee!'

And, on the third *e* in *byeeee*, he slammed the door in their faces!

'Well!' exclaimed Amy in a muffled voice, her face now pressed firmly to the door. 'What a rude man! If he wasn't a blood relative I'd be so upset by his utter rudeness.'

'I agree,' agreed Betty, 'with whatever you just said. But what was that about a clock? Isn't that what we want?'

Daniel removed his spectacles. 'Listen,' he said, pointing the curly bit at the others and trying unsuccessfully to look and sound remotely intelligent. 'You heard what he said. It's all very inconclusive. There's probably no need for us to go to 1980. Don't you think we should all decide to accept defeat and go back – or is it forwards – to 2010, mid-adventure? It would be so much easier for us all.'

'But his maladjusted trousers! And all this radiator repairing? I don't understand!' Amy moaned.

'I think this all means,' said Ricky, 'that we will have failed in our heroic adventure, and surely that can never *ever* happen?'

'Woof woof woof,' said Whatshisname, hopefully.

'Hmmm. Why not?' said Daniel, sucking the end of his spectacles' curly bit. 'Surely there are times when failed heroes like us have to take it easy?'

'Shall we go and wait in the reception?' suggested Amy. 'It sounds as though Uncle Quagmire will be a while, what with all that strange radiator fixing and intensive questioning. And do watch out for all that clothing repositioning, won't you?' She looked down and inspected her own clothing. They all looked fine, so far.

When they eventually made their way back down to the reception there was no sign of the inquisitive dog-murdering pale lady. Whatshisname took the opportunity to be very glad indeed. He sighed with relief. He could relax again!

'She's gone. That's a good job,' said Ricky. 'She'd only have asked to join our secret club.'

'Hello!' said the dog-murdering inquisitive pale lady's voice from behind them. 'Are you still interested in using my wardrobe? Oh, your sacrificial doggy is back!'

The children turned in surprise. Whatshisname, his gladness short-lived, skulked behind Ricky and growled a meaningful growl. His second line of defence would be a burst of noxious hell-gas.

'Oh, hello!' said Betty. 'Yes, we do have a small problem. We need a special sort of clock, apparently. It's called a Nixie clock.'

'Well,' said the lady, looking past Ricky to glare at Whatshisname. 'Isn't it just your lucky day! I have in my room something that looks a bit like a digital alarm clock. It's a Nixie clock complete with microcontroller and voltage-regulator. What a strange coincidence! I take it everywhere with me.'

The children were delighted! The pale lady said that she had planned to keep it for a few years in case someone eventually came up with an online auction website on which she could make a small fortune for Fifties memorabilia and be frequently targeted by online fraudsters from Bulgaria due to the lack of a robust firewall, but she thought that the children's cause was a worthwhile one so she would let them have it for free. 'As long as I can join The Secret Five,' she added. 'And commandeer the dog for my own perverse entertainment.'

Whatshisname growled again, and Ricky stamped his very own foot. 'I knew it!' he said. 'Didn't we say this would happen?' He turned inquisitively to the pale dog-murdering lady. 'I'm in favour of the dog commandeering, in fact I'd encourage it, but can I ask, is this membership with or without privileges?'

The pale lady pondered the question. 'Well,' she said, 'hmmm, yes . . . with, I think.'

'We have no choice,' said Betty. 'We have to go back to 1980. Or is it forward?'

'I think we should start to make people swear an oath of allegiance or something,' said Ricky, quite glumly. 'We're letting in people without any terms and conditions, and don't know if they're going to be loyal and trustworthy. That can't be good for future loyalty and trustworthiness.'

The others all thought that was a valid point, especially as they still doubted Ricky's loyalty and trustworthiness, so they huddled together and discussed whether the pale lady with a wardrobe looked like a potentially trustworthy member of their elite club and how they could test her loyalty. But then Betty pointed out that, very soon, if the adventure went well, they would be back in 2010 and the lady, as she looked so very pale, will have quietly died years ago, and there were no constitutional procedures for granting posthumous Secret Five membership, so they might as well let her in and make use of her Nixie clock.

'Good plan!' said Ricky. 'Which one of us is going to tell her that she's going to quietly die very soon? Can I? Let me! Please!'

'Woof woof woof!' volunteered Whatshisname eagerly.

'We don't have to tell her that,' said Betty, quite sensibly. 'We just say that she's got temporary membership but advise her to make full use of the privileges soon because she hasn't got much time left.'

Of course, when they told the pale lady, she was quite understanding, and yet still inquisitive and pale. She was also quite disappointed when they said that she couldn't have Whatshisname as they may need a nourishing ready meal later in the story, should they all get marooned on a lifeboat mid-ocean for weeks on end while searching for a strange and mysterious island where there was probably some treasure that had been buried in a stout and sturdy wooden box.

'I'm quite understanding of your executive decisions,' the pale lady said, 'and slightly interested in the bit of narrative about the buried treasure, which has the potential to sound terribly exciting, if you like that sort of thing, and don't mind the story suddenly shooting off in a completely different, irrelevant and illogical direction. But for now, whenever you're ready, go and help yourself to my wardrobe and my clock. Here's my room key. I gave the other one to someone else, so this is proving to be a very popular pastime indeed.'

'Popular?' asked Betty, frowning an important frown. 'Someone else?'

'Why, yes!' said the pale lady. 'Only a few minutes ago, an old lady with a West Bromwich Albion bobble hat went up to use the wardrobe and the clock. She said she was a fully paid-up member of The Secret Five, and not to mention it to you as it would be a nice surprise. But for the sake of this particular adventure, and to help fill this ever-growing plot hole, I have. So there.'

'Oh, blow!' exclaimed Daniel. 'What did she say she was going to do?'

'She didn't,' said the pale lady inquisitively. 'But she did seem to be in a bit of a hurry.'

'Gosh, do you think she overheard what Uncle Quagmire was saying?' Amy asked.

'Well, I did notice her lurking secretively and making copious notes,' the pale inquisitive lady said, 'while your Uncle Quagmire was telling you all about that Sampson de Lylow rogue.'

The children were horrified at all the secret lurking and copious notes! Old Hag had overheard their secret plans to go to 1980 and stop Sampson de Lylow being driven into the arms of the devil himself! This called for some sort of urgent action! Ricky, in a burst of urgency that was unknown where food was not involved, took charge. 'Hurry up!' he urged, grabbing the key from the pale lady. 'We have to get to that room to stop Old Hag!'

But they were stopped in their tracks by Amy. 'Look!' she said, pointing. 'Uncle Quagmire has left Sampson's autobiography! It's on that chair.'

And, sure enough, there on a chair was the book!

'Let's take it with us,' suggested Betty. 'You never know when we'll need it.'

Daniel grabbed the book and stuffed it down the front of his trousers, suspecting that it might be important to the story at some stage. They all said goodbye to the pale inquisitive lady and hurried upstairs to her room. Whatshisname bounded after them. It was ages since he had been involved in any sort of bounding activity and it made him feel good, especially to be able to get some distance between the pale dog-murdering lady and him.

'This is my room,' the pale lady said as they reached her room.

'Er, sorry, I thought we'd all said goodbye to you in the reception,' whispered Daniel.

'Woof woof woof!' agreed Whatshisname.

'Oh,' whispered the pale lady. 'My mistake. I'll go then, shall I?'

They all nodded their heads and the pale lady hurried away from the narrative, again. Daniel glanced up into thin air and shook his head in disbelief. Then, quickly, they let themselves into the pale inquisitive lady's room. There, in a pale corner of the room, stood a wardrobe! But, to their utter dismay, there was no sign of Old Hag.

'There's no sign of Old Hag,' confirmed Ricky. 'But look! On the bedside cabinet. A contraption! She must have already gone to 1980!'

And, sure enough, on the bedside cabinet, was a clock-like contraption! It was a wooden box with a dial and big red digital numbers, and looked quite a lot like a clock.

Feeling important for a change, Ricky opened up the sheet of paper that Uncle Quagmire had given them. They all gathered very closely around him as he followed the detailed instructions. Carefully, he rigged up the clock and the wardrobe. Unfortunately, due to the fact that they were gathered very closely around him, no-one else could see exactly how all the up-rigging was done. So, damn it, it has to remain a mystery to all except the children and Whatshisname.

'All secretly and carefully done,' said Ricky, standing back and admiring his work. 'I did have a few problems with the tensile modulator and the economy-mode regulator toggle switch but, apart from that, it's all quite easy really. All it needs now is to set the year and we're done.'

'Well done, Ricky. Let's get into the portal wardrobe,' suggested Amy. She opened the wardrobe door and peeked inside.

'I'll now set the year,' Ricky volunteered. 'I'm good at setting years.'

'Oh, all right,' said Daniel, slightly grumpily. He was thinking that his role as alpha male was slipping away, not realising that he himself was closer to a delta or epsilon male. But Daniel thought that Ricky was definitely a born beta male and should know his place when it comes to doing stuff like this. 'And hurry up, won't you, Ricky?' he grumped.

Amy, Betty and Daniel headed for the wardrobe as Ricky set about setting the clock to 1980. But Whatshisname was growling, the hackles on the back of his neck standing up out of respect.

'What's up, boy?' asked Ricky.

'Ha!' a voice said. They looked to where the voice seemed to be coming from, and suddenly realised that it was from the bed! At first they all thought it was a talking bed, but soon they realised that Old Hag was hiding under the bedclothes!

She struggled to untangle herself and get to the wardrobe. 'I'm coming with you!' she yelled, then fell flat on her face on the floor. 'Ouch! Wait! I bet you've got some sprouts! Wait for me! Ha! I have my own secret mission to attend to!'

'Stop her!' Betty yelled.

With no thought for his own safety, Whatshisname grabbed the leg of Old Hag's trousers and pulled and pulled, giving Ricky time to hurriedly finish setting the clock and climb into the wardrobe. To their dismay, Old Hag clambered in after him, dragging a growling Whatshisname, who was still attached to her trouser leg.

'Get her out!' Amy yelled. 'I don't like these plot reversals!'

Ricky, who was slightly strong for a boy of his spineless character, and Amy, who wasn't, grabbed hold of Old Hag. Carefully, yet brutally, they dragged her out of the wardrobe.

'Ricky! Amy! Whatshisname!' shouted Betty. 'Come back in! Quickly!'

Whatshisname, thinking Betty had shouted *I've got a ham sandwich! With pickle!* let go of Old Hag and jumped into the wardrobe! Meanwhile, Ricky and Amy held on very firmly to her as she struggled and wriggled.

'Catch us up later!' shouted Betty. She slammed the wardrobe door just as a strange and unearthly whirring sound began to happen. Betty, Daniel and Whatshisname were on their way to 1980!

Or so they thought!

Chapter Twenty One

In which even more troublesome things happen; Old Hag has a fine reason to chuckle; the chapter ends on a bit of a cliffhanger; so that's what you call it; yes.

In the bedroom, Old Hag suddenly stopped struggling.

'Why have you suddenly stopped struggling?' asked Amy. 'Is there something we should know?'

'It's a trick!' said Ricky. 'She's an awfully devious old hag. Keep struggling with her, even though she's not struggling herself!'

'Ha!' said Old Hag, struggling to stop them struggling. 'You're right, Ricko, I am rather devious and proud of it! I'd have already gone to 1980 and settled this mission if I'd have had some Brussels sprouts! But, silly children, take a look at the time-travel clock! Ha! and ha! again! Look at it!! I'm so unbelievably happy that I could have a crack at the world record for the number of exclamation marks in one paragraph!!!'

They stopped all the unnecessary struggling and looked at the time-travel clock on the bedside cabinet.

'Does that say what I think it says?' asked Amy.

'I don't know,' said Ricky, letting go of Old Hag. 'What do *you* think it says?'

'It looks like 1880,' said Amy, quite confused.

'Ha!' said Old Hag gleefully. 'You've sent them to the wrong century! What a laugh! I'm so utterly gleeful!'

Amy and Ricky stared at the numbers on the clock, then at each other, then back to the numbers on the clock. Old Hag stood examining her fingernails as they did all the staring. Eventually, fed up of staring, Ricky spoke. 'Er . . .' he said.

Old Hag chuckled. '*Er?* Is that all you can say? *Er?* They've gone backwards to 1880 and all you can think of is *er*? Ha! Silly children. My mission is becoming easier by the hour. This stopping you from saving the world is a doddle, it really is.'

'But . . .' said Amy.

'Erm . . .' said Ricky.

'While you're standing there, butting and erming,' cackled Old Hag, 'I'm off to find Bartle. I want to make sure he'll do the necessary with Clarissa the stunt nun. I'm going to see that they're happy ever after and that she is soon big with stunt child. Ha! Take your time, *losers*!' She made an L sign with her finger and thumb and waved it around in front of Amy.

'Erm . . .' said Amy.

'But . . .' said Ricky.

Old Hag hurried out of the room, chuckling to herself, which has been proved to be the most effective way to chuckle. Amy and Ricky both examined the clock, just in case it was a typo. But no, it still read 1880.

'How did that happen?' Amy asked. 'Gosh! Did you make a mistake, Ricky?'

Ricky hung his head in shame. He shuffled over to the wardrobe and peeked inside. It was empty, apart from a faint aroma of creosote and pineapple. He sank down on the edge of the bed.

'I don't know what to do,' he said, quite mournfully. 'They'll be trapped in 1880. They'll need a digital alarm clock to get back. And it's all my fault.'

'That's true,' Amy said, brightly. 'I'm quite happy to blame you totally for their loss. I'm all for a blame culture in The Secret Five.'

'I feel like hankering,' Ricky said.

'What?'

'I said I feel like *hankering*,' Ricky said. He was glad of the opportunity to use the word at last. 'Do you have one?'

'One what?' Amy was confused.

'A hanky,' Ricky said.

'No! And I've no idea what you're on about, Ricky,' Amy snapped. 'Sometimes, honestly! Pull yourself together and just accept the fact that you've probably killed the other three. Now, shall we go and find Uncle Quagmire to explain what's happened? Do you think he's finished questioning Clarissa and mending her radiator by now?'

Ricky wondered how he could have made such a silly mistake. Then he had a thought. He shot to his feet and looked up into thin air. He looked quite stern! Oh oh.

'What's up there?' enquired Amy, looking up at exactly the same bit of thin air. 'Daniel's always looking up there. I don't understand.'

'It's *him*, you know,' he murmured. 'I'd have been all right without *him*. He never lets me eat when I feel hungry, and he always makes me look *so* pathetic and mediocre and spineless.'

'Who?' said Amy, who was a zealous defender of mediocrity. 'Ricky, you really do behave strangely sometimes. I'm wondering if I'm safe being left here with you. Let's go and find Uncle Quagmire before I become too worried to continue the adventure.'

Ricky gritted his teeth in the direction of the thin air, not a very effective gesture, but it made him happy, so we'll let it go for now.

And off they went in search of Uncle Quagmire. He would know exactly what to do, and they both had the luxury of several chapters to think how they could save the world and rescue their pals!

PART THREE

Chapter Twenty Two

In which we meet a strange man; there's a pathetic bit of a brooklet of consciousness which is quite confusing goodness knows why it's there I do need a haircut oh yes I do; they discover that they are not where they are supposed to be; the kangaroo, typically, stays very quiet indeed.

'Gosh!' exclaimed Daniel as he landed with a big thump in the middle of a strange churchyard. 'Is it 1980? This is exciting, isn't it, Betty?'

But there was no reply! Daniel looked around him. No Betty, no Whatshisname! He removed his spectacles and tried looking around him again. Still no Betty! Still no Whatshisname!

'Gosh!' he exclaimed again, but louder. 'This is exciting, ISN'T IT BETTY?'

No reply again! What a waste of capitals. He slipped his spectacles on. They felt good, reassuring. But he was alone and that wasn't good. To add to his aloneness, it started to rain as he hunched up against a cold grey gravestone. A crow began to caw at him from the top of the yew trees that surrounded the churchyard. 'Caw, caw,' it cawed, as if it were laughing at him, which it was, as crows have an excellent sense of humour due to their tendency to bump into each other at night.

Quietly, very quietly, he wondered if Betty was somewhere else. Maybe she had landed in another chapter! This was awful, awful, awful. She might be lost forever! What a terrible thought! And Ricky and Amy, where were they? They would also be somewhere else, and probably incapable of saving the world! Worryingly, he was now The Palpable One and would have to save the world on his own. He did *not* fancy the idea of that. He just didn't feel up to it, no, no, not up to it at all. He sat for quite a while, sitting, wondering, sitting, wondering, feeling in his pockets for anything that might help, anything. Yes, some sprouts he had so must chew sprouts would that help help it might help funny old life I certainly need to trim my toenails that's what I need to do yes that's what I will do as soon as I can maybe I'll just trim every other toenail for a change I hate the smell of rain I wonder if I can ever be a gentleman farmer when I'm grown up maybe I might look into it when I feel up to it but not now I don't like being alone like this still all this being alone at least gives me the chance to indulge in a bit of stream of consciousness just like Ricky does only a bit better then again it's hardly a stream I suppose maybe more like a streamlet of consciousness or no perhaps a creek of consciousness or no not a creek how about a rill or beck or gill or yes more like a brook or even a brooklet yes that was it a brooklet of consciousness.

But, glory be, the sudden onset of a brooklet of consciousness faded away as quickly as it had begun, and he was back to being treated as a third-person with punctuation and without any insight into his pathetic fragmentary thoughts whatsoever.

Just then, Daniel the Third Person suddenly heard a scampering noise and saw a flash of pink collar!

'Whatshisname!' Daniel exclaimed in a rather girly voice. His favourite dog had appeared at his side! Daniel got to his feet and patted Whatshisname's head. Daniel was, for the first time in his life, really glad to see him. They were now The Palpable Two – himself and this fat ugly dog with a fluffy pink collar. Together, with their combined resources, they could save the world! How, he hadn't a clue.

'Where's Betty?' Daniel asked, not really expecting an answer that didn't include the word *woof*.

'Woof woof woof!' said Whatshisname.

'I'm over here!' called Betty from over here.

He looked up and saw Betty as she came scurrying down the

path between the gravestones. He was really pleased to see her, and told her so. 'I'm really pleased to see you,' he said. 'And I *love* the scurry!'

'We landed over there and . . .' Betty stopped, then looked hard at Daniel. She frowned. 'Daniel, can I ask something? While you've been here on your own, all alone, have you been indulging in some interior monologue? Bordering on a stream of consciousness maybe? Please tell me you haven't.'

Daniel blushed and looked down at his feet. 'I might have. If Ricky can do it then so can I! Anyway, I couldn't help it, it just came over me. I'm rarely left alone and I felt the need, that's all. And I enjoyed it, so there. Nothing wrong with enjoying something, is there? Hmmm?'

'I suppose not,' she sighed. 'It's very un-Secret Five, and against our written constitution. Boys! Huh! To be honest, I prefer your silly street-talk. Now, listen, I need to tell you at this stage that I landed over there, by that funny looking man.' She pointed over there at a funny looking man who was standing sheltering in the entrance to the church. He was certainly dressed rather peculiarly, in a long black coat and black top hat and black gloves. Black was obviously the new black. And so was grey, because he had a big grey beard on his chin, with big bushy whiskers to match. He was leaning on a walking cane and looking up at the sky.

'He's dressed really strangely,' said Betty. 'Is that what they wore in 1980, do you think? He asked me if we'd fallen from a balloon. Let's go and talk to him. He might know where Sampson's school is. Come on, hurry!'

'But shouldn't we wait around here for the others?' asked Daniel.

'There's no time,' said Betty. 'It's up to you and me to save the world! We need to find Sampson's school!'

'Woof woof woof?' said Whatshisname. Bravely, and eager to help, he trotted after them as they went up to the strange man.

Maybe saving the world wasn't a bad idea after all. He, Whatshisname, could be a hero. His name could resound in mythology as the Great Dog Benefactor of Mankind! He could be the Re-creator of the World! And yet his name might be an issue. *Whatshisname* doesn't sound mythical or romantic in the slightest. Not like Prometheus, or Zeus, or Persephone. The Great Dog Benefactor Whatshisname? Hmmm. Now he'd completely lost interest in saving the world. He paused on the path. What to do? Hold on, in the grass down there, is that a maturing doggy poo? He trotted over and lowered his head and, by necessity, his nose. He sniffed. It was! This was more like it. He sniffed again, inhaling deeply, taking in the essence of . . . Labrador maybe? At the moment, there were more important things than saving the world and becoming The Great Dog Benefactor. That could wait. Yes, definitely Labrador. *Sniff.* Their silly adventure and the strange man could also wait. This – *sniiiiiiff* – was much more important.

'Well, I'm blessed, there are now *two* Urchins!' said the strange man as Betty and Daniel approached him. ''Twas a great surprise to see the girl appear so. You are obviously not fowls of the air, especially that sniffing dog over there – nice collar, by the way – but I could not for the life of me see one of those confounded dirigibles that you must have fallen from. Are you hurt?'

'We're okay,' said Daniel.

'Oh-kay?' said the man, frowning deeply. 'What in heaven's name does *oh-kay* mean?'

'It means we're . . . okay,' said Betty, 'but without an aitch. And we didn't fall from a balloon. We travelled in a time machine. It's a very reliable form of transport, we find, unaffected by leaves on the line and congestion charges.'

'Well, I never,' said the man, who had obviously forgotten that he had. 'I've travelled on those highly life-threatening Iron Horse railways, but never in a time machine. What is the world coming to, yea verily. Before we know it there will be hybrid horseless carriages with catalytic converters. Anyway, young lady Urchin, can I just say that, with infant mortality the way it is, and the inclemency of the weather, you coming out without your woollen vest and your elbow-length gloves is asking for a dose of scarlet fever or even the pox. Would I not wish upon you such a tragedy. That curious dog, yes, but not you. And what or whom is this McFly on your strange blouse? A Scottish poet, by any chance?'

Daniel and Betty glanced a short economical glance at each other and frowned.

'Are you all right?' Betty asked the man.

'I am,' said the alright man. 'And I am also concerned for your health, young lady, as I would for any daughter of mine. If I had one, that is. Impotency is a terrible curse, believe me. But your clothing doth seem uncommonly unseemly, that is all.'

Daniel nodded. 'Do you know,' he said, 'as a caring brother, I've been worrying a lot about her unseemliness as well.'

Betty clasped her arms to her chest. 'Just leave them out of it,' she said, quite moodily. 'Look, I'm of voting age *plus some*, and well old enough for a McFly T-shirt, and we're on an important mission to save the world, and all you can think of is my . . . my . . .'

'Bosom?' said Daniel, helpfully.

The man staggered backwards, almost losing his top hat in the process of the stagger. He managed to stop himself mid-stagger, and staggered forwards again.

'Children!' he said. 'Is it the righteous thing where you come from, for a child to address someone so forthrightly? This is the talk of raggedy children and ruffians! I beseech you, as the Moral Shepherd of this parish's flock, I will not tolerate such behaviour! And you should only spoke when you're speaken to! Where are your parents or guardians? I must have words with them about you. All this vulgar workhouse talk is most unbecoming. Of course, I blame our monarch, that Queen Victoria, for this degradation of morals.'

'Quee . . . ?' said Daniel.

'Vict . . . ?' said Betty.

'Woof woof wo . . . ?' said Whatshisname, who had rejoined them after his short but joyful sensory encounter with the Labrador poo.

'Excuse me,' said Betty. 'But don't you mean Queen Elizabeth?'

The man looked quite aghast. 'Do you learn nothing at week-school?' he asked. 'Queen Elizabeth was our monarch some, er, three hundred years ago, give or take! Nice ankles, by all accounts. No, our queen is Victoria. The *hussy!*'

Betty frowned and looked around her. The houses around the churchyard, with their mullioned windows and decorative bargeboards, all looked really old but really new at the same time, and she was slightly bewildered when a horse and trap came clip-clopping and trap-trapping along the lane the other side of the churchyard wall.

'Erm . . .' ermed Betty. 'If I may speak, sir? The Revivalist Architectural features on those houses and the clip-clopping and trap-trapping do worry me just a little. Tell me, is this really nineteen-eighty?'

The strange man looked aghast yet again, but then his aghastness cleverly turned into a rather quizzical expression. '*Nineteen*-eighty? This is *Eighteen*-eighty, my girl. I must speak to your parents about your schooling, and the need for extra Arithmetic lessons, yea verily.'

'Eighteen-eighty!' Betty stammered and spluttered, so it sounded more like 'ay-ay-huh-tin-tin-ay-ay-huh-splut-tee-tee-huh?' She was utterly shocked! They had been time-machined to the wrong year!

But we knew that didn't we? So, as a mini-cliffhanger, it's somewhat lacking, if not total rubbish, and one wonders if her utter shock might have been avoided if she had been paying more attention, for goodness' sake.

Chapter Twenty Three

In which sulforaphanes, dithiolthiones and glucosinolates are again mentioned, of course; there is some impromptu smiling; an apple makes a guest appearance; the sighting of a familiar house is interrupted by an unexpected chapter break.

The strange man frowned silently at Betty's outburst, the authorial whining, and the unnerving experience of being flung headlong into a new chapter without warning. He pointed his silent frown at Daniel so that he wouldn't feel left out.

Betty leaned towards Daniel. 'Erm, Daniel,' she whispered, 'I think we need an urgent meeting.'

'A meeting?' Daniel whispered back. 'With just the two of us?'

'Woof woof woof?' whispered Whatshisname.

'He said it's *eighteen*-eighty,' Betty said in a whispery voice. 'Apparently, we're in the nineteenth century, and we've lost Ricky and Amy who might be stranded forever in Salzburg, near Austria, in another time. I think that's enough reason for an extraordinarily-convened meeting, don't you?'

'I suppose so,' said Daniel in a mournful yet pathetic whisper. 'But I am a bit hungry now. I think I've caught something from Ricky. Some wasting disease. Can you ask him if there's anything to nibble around here?'

Betty spoke to the man. 'Excuse me, kindly sir, but we think that we are quite seriously lost, and we need to have a private meeting of our secret club, *and* we have to find a nineteenth century teashop quite urgently. My brother here has developed a condition that appears to run in the family, you see.'

The man seemed quite taken aback. 'My word!' he said. He leant forward towards them, so it was difficult to continue being taken aback. 'This secret club, is it open to new members? And what do you call it, dear strange children?'

'It's The Secret Five,' said Daniel. 'Highly exclusive, very secret. Although to be honest, at the last count we are probably up to The Secret Five Hundred by now.'

'Aaaah,' aaaahed the man knowingly. 'Highly exclusive, very secret? Rather like my very own secret club, The Fraternal Order of Puritan Sadists. Do you want to know our secret FOPS password? And I can demonstrate our secret FOPS handshake if you so desire. It doesn't hurt. Much.'

Eagerly, he began to remove a glove.

Betty and Daniel said they'd rather not, under the circumstances, and carefully tried to explain that they'd arrived in the wrong year and had he a portal and a digital alarm clock that he might lend to them.

'Stop all this nonsensical talk!' boomed the man. 'I cannot tolerate you two lost Urchins running loose and roaming the lanes of my parish frightening my pathetic flock with all this tittle-tattle about porters! Come! You need shelter and warmth and lots of porridge, if I am not mistaken. The vicarage these days is out of Victorian bounds for Mere Urchins unless accompanied by an adult of sane mind, so I will take you along to The Big House. Perhaps Mrs Wells the Housekeeper can do something with you until you are both well enough to walk.'

''But we can walk, look!' said Daniel, demonstrating how he could walk on the spot. The strange man frowned at Daniel's even stranger behaviour and shook his head firmly from side to side.

'You are obviously delirious,' the man said. 'And quite ugly, too. Come. Follow me. This can be my Good Turn, then I am done for this week, apart from a bit of symbolic pastoral care.' And with that, he strode off down the path and towards the lane.

Betty and Daniel looked at each other, then at Whatshisname, who shrugged an attempted shrug that seemed to say, 'I don't know what to do either so stop looking at me and while you're at it get this stupid pink fluffy collar from around my neck'.

As their options were quite limited, Betty suggested to Daniel that they had a mobile meeting while they followed the strange man in the top hat, who was now waving his walking cane in the air in an effort to encourage them onwards.

'Hurry, Urchins,' he called. 'And the curious deformed animal. This way.'

'Right,' said Betty to Daniel as they followed the man, 'let's go along with it. They might have a handy portal up at this Big House. We've got the Brussels sprouts, so all we'd need then is a digital alarm clock and we're done.'

'Woof woof woof?' said Whatshisname.

Suddenly, Daniel stopped walking and started to rummage deep in his pockets.

'What's the matter now?' asked Betty. 'What are you doing, Daniel? Boys, honestly! There's no time for that now!'

'I'm only rummaging deep in my pockets. I don't think I've got any sprouts left,' he moaned. 'I must have eaten them all while I sat on that gravestone. Waiting for you!'

'You ate all the sprouts?' exclaimed Betty. 'I don't believe *you*, Daniel! It's bad enough Ricky eating everything in sight without you getting in on the act! Are you sure that you're not just intensely jealous of his character's traits? Isn't it enough to have been given spectacles? Hmmm?'

Daniel looked embarrassed. 'Don't blame me!' he whispered. 'It's out of my control!'

Betty shook her head in disbelief. 'You're always blaming You-Know-Who. Despite that, you're so tiresome! Without those sprouts, where are we going to get the sulforaphanes, dithiolthiones and glucosinolates which, apparently, overcome the quantum object's timeline resistance and help us get back home?'

Daniel still looked embarrassed, and Betty was lost for words.

'Really, Daniel!' she scolded.

Again she was lost for words.

'Can't you be trusted with anything?'

'I thought you were lost for words,' observed Daniel.

'I am supposed to be!' she snapped. 'In fact, I have never *ever* been so lost for words . . . *ever!* And, to illustrate that fact, I'm now going to be sullen and silent for a while, if you don't mind. Boys!'

Sullenly and silently, lost for words, they followed the strange man. At one point, Daniel stopped to pick up an apple that had fallen from an apple tree that overhung the lane, but he didn't offer Betty a bite as she had been so nasty to him. That would teach her.

Eventually they rounded a convenient bend in the lane, where the strange man stopped and pointed ahead with his walking cane.

'Children, or whatever you are, do you see that house with the chimneys? It almost looks like a castle, does it not? That is where the Squire lives. Mrs Wells is his housekeeper and maid and does other menial skivvying duties. They often take in random Urchins off the street. Lord only knows what becomes of them after that.'

Betty and Daniel stopped alongside the strange man.

'It's stopped raining,' said Daniel.

Betty looked at him. 'Well?' she said. 'So what?'

Daniel shrugged. 'I just thought I'd say it. People have to know.'

'That's true,' said Betty. 'I would have said it in a more subtle way, more sub-textual. But well done for thinking of it.'

Daniel smiled at Betty, who smiled back. They were pals again. Whatshisname looked up at them both and tried desperately to join in all the smiling activities, but it could easily have been mistaken for a severe bout of canine indigestion.

Then, after all the impromptu smiling, they stood and looked at the house. Suddenly, unexpectedly, it seemed very familiar indeed.

'Gosh! It looks very much like the house that Uncle Quagmire was brought to when he was kidnapped,' Betty said.

'I think it might be,' agreed Daniel. 'But it looks newer, somehow.'

'Of course it's newer!' said Betty. 'It's over a hundred years ago, isn't it?'

'A hundred years?' scoffed the strange man. 'What are you talking about? It was built quite recently, with help of funds from the Penny Arcade Commission.'

'What a coincidence!' Daniel said. 'The time machine bringing us back to the same place.'

'Woof woof woof,' said Whatshisname wearily.

Betty sighed. 'Do think, Daniel! You don't consider the bigger picture, do you? It's not really a coincidence. With budgets so tight these days, he's saving money by re-using the same set and location, you see.'

'Woof woof woof!' said Whatshisname, which meant 'that's what I said! Give me some credit!'

'I never thought of that,' said Daniel. 'You are so clever, Betty.'

'In fact,' said Betty. 'If you hadn't pointed out the fact that it was the same house, we might have got away with it.'

'Children!' snapped the strange man, waving his walking cane. 'I must get you to safety before you die of consumption. Hurry!'

As they followed the man through the gateway they remembered how, earlier that day (which, incidentally, was proving to be a very long one), it had been the entrance to a top secret government establishment, and they had had to sneak behind the big red truck that roared and rumbled.

The strange man stopped walking. 'Ah!' he said. He looked worried and even more strange.

'What?' said Betty, feeling that she knew what was coming.

'I feel that another one of those confounded breaks is almost upon us,' he said perceptively. 'They are so tiresome, don't you think, Urchins?'

Chapter Twenty Four

In which we meet a thirteen-year-old boy; we sense a nagging feeling of interminability and want this story to end right now; but hey, things are looking up, as canine taxidermy is mentioned, fleetingly; a chamber pot issue rears its fairly ugly head; Daniel is brutally murdered in his bed.

'Yes,' said Betty. 'They are. And sometimes absolutely pointless.'

'Quite. Ah, look, see there?' said the strange man, pointing his Victorian antique cane at a Victorian antique boy sitting on a doorstep. 'That looks uncommonly like Mrs Wells' boy sitting there. Perchance he must be visiting her. He is thirteen, if you are at all interested in that fact.'

They weren't at all interested but, carefully, they approached the thirteen-year-old boy on the doorstep. He was eating a sandwich rather heartily. The strange man pointed his walking cane at the boy as they approached. 'Herbert! Is your mother inside the Big House?'

The boy stood up. To be honest, he did look a lot like a Herbert. He was dressed in three-quarter-length trousers on his four-quarter-length legs, a brown peaked cap, a velvety jacket, and a white shirt with a big stiff collar around his big stiff neck. 'No, Mr Parson sir,' he said. 'Mama is out shopping for food for the Master's larder. But she will return very soon, I expect.'

'Then listen, young Herbert,' said the man quite sternly. 'Fix your attention on what I say, as I have to go back home and attend to my confounded bunions before they spontaneously ignite. When your mother gets back tell her that the Parson says that she has to look after these two Urchins, to give them some porridge and hot peas, and a cold bath every day until they are strong enough to play unaided at Strip Hopscotch in the lane. As for the wretched dog, well, maybe she could be stuffed as a trophy for the Drawing Room.'

Whatshisname looked quite glum at the thought, and his mournful eyes began to water a little as he tried to imagine exactly how the stuffing might be accomplished. He decided to sit quite still to prove that he could be a motionless dog without being subject to the stuffing process.

The Parson herded them towards the boy. 'There you are then, and please do not thank me, as it would only cause me to feign much embarrassment and I would have to give a lengthy speech about Duty and Moral Obligation. Now, Urchins, wait here with young Herbert until his mother returns, otherwise I will have you put into the workhouse with all the other ne'er-do-wells!'

The Parson turned and hurried away, anxious to get safely indoors before any more Urchins fell unannounced from the heavens, and to avoid the acute discomfort of another sudden chapter break.

The thirteen-year-old boy sank back down onto the step. Whatshisname had noted the sandwich in his hand. He recognised a begging opportunity when he saw one, so he cast aside any thoughts of getting stuffed and trotted up to Herbert. Daniel did the same, and they both sat staring at the boy, their heads cocked, their noses a few inches from the boy's face, both willing him to hand over the sandwich.

'Hello dog,' the boy said. 'And hello strangely-dressed boy and girl. Which one of you smells of creosote and pineapple?'

'It's him,' said Daniel, hurriedly pointing at Whatshisname.

'Woooooof,' Whatshisname said, quite weakly and pathetically.

'It's a *him*?' queried the boy, looking rather curiously at Whatshisname. 'Really? Nice collar, anyway.'

'Are you Herbert?' Betty asked the boy.

Herbert nodded his head. 'I think so. They all call me Bertie, but I don't know why.' He looked up at Betty. 'You look quite unseemly for a mere girl,' he said. 'Where is your woollen vest, and why aren't you sewing or playing a piano or making lacy doily things for the parlour?'

Betty scowled back at him politely but made a mental note to find out more about doilies in case they might be useful for some of the more audacious Secret Five exploits.

'I'm Daniel,' said Daniel to Bertie. 'The scowling girl is Betty. And she does look unseemly, doesn't she? But she's family, so leave her alone. You hurt my family, you hurt me.'

Bertie looked warily at him.

'To be honest, I seem to have developed a family wasting condition,' moaned Daniel. 'It's food-related and . . .' He stopped talking as Bertie wolfed down the rest of his sandwich as quickly as he could.

'Never mind, eh?' mumbled Bertie through a mouthful of sandwich. Whatshisname snuffled around in the gravel for crumbs, and Daniel thought of doing the same.

'We should wait for Mama downstairs in the scullery,' Bertie suggested. He stood up and opened the door. 'Follow me,' he said, leading them inside the Big House, which was, not surprisingly, a typical Victorian Big House.

'Mama will return soon,' Herbert bravely predicted as they went down some steps into the scullery. 'But please make yourself at home on some typically Victorian scullery furniture and then explain why you are dressed in all this futuristic attire, and why your dog is wearing *that* collar. I'm going to be a draper's apprentice, eventually, so I know all about clothes and collars, you see. And I am also quite gifted. Apparently.'

They wrinkled their noses as they entered the scullery, as it smelled strongly of gutted fish and steaming clothes. In one corner was a great big sink which, coincidentally, had several corners of its own. A big tin bath hung facing the wall. Daniel assumed that there was no water in it.

Whatshisname bravely flopped down at Betty's feet as they sat around the long scullery table. Daniel and Betty explained very carefully about The Secret Five, stunt nuns, and how they had travelled back in time. Herbert was quite enthralled, in a Victorian sort of way, and made lots of notes in a Victorian notebook. But, just as he was becoming slightly more than quite enthralled, his mother returned, dragging a huge dead pig behind her. As she stepped into the scullery she was dressed in a long dark dress with a frilly white collar, which presumably she had been dressed in before stepping into the scullery.

'Gosh!' said Betty loudly. 'Is that a typically Victorian cloak you're wearing?'

'Oh yes, my dear,' said Mrs Wells. 'Fancy forgetting to mention that! Now, judging by his somewhat frenzied and detailed description of this young lady's attire, I assume that you are the time-travelling Urchins and their faithful dog that the Parson just mentioned to me in the lane, to save us going through the excruciating agony of the *and who are you?* dialogue.'

'We are indeed,' said Daniel, very politely. 'But first things first – do you have any food, by any chance? I have recently contracted a food-related condition from my family, you see. I need a regular infusion of jam tarts and that sort of thing.'

Mrs Wells laughed quite a short laugh for a woman of her height. 'I do have some food,' she said. 'After all, this is a scullery. But you understand that it is commonly understood in these Victorian times that jam weakens a child's moral fibre, so it will just be bread and Dutch marge, with some sherbet on hot peas to follow.'

'Oh, Mama!' moaned Bertie. 'Can we first go outside and play Funerals? It is not very often I make new friends, and I usually have to be the cortege *and* the Parson *and* the mourners *and* the body all at the same time, which can be so tiring. It is quite exciting having new friends to play with.'

His mother became quite stern. 'Now I'm quite stern . . .

apparently!' she said. 'For one thing, Bertie my lad, where are your grammatical sensibilities? New friends to play with indeed! You should know that a preposition is something you should never end a sentence with. A writer you will never make, that I am certain of. And another thing, you are *not* going out this time of day, oh my dear Lord no! I have a Housemaid's reputation to consider. And I did not breast feed you with my own nutritious milk until you were eight-years-old just for you to go off and die of Excitement or Exhaustion while playing outside. I want you fit enough to fight and die a heroic but gruesome death for the British Empire. Besides, it is time for your cold bath and for you to clean out my chamber pot, young Bertie. It has been building up for some three days now.'

'Oh, Mama!' cried Bertie. 'Very nice monologue, can I say, but *please* do not make me do such things. If only Father were here.'

'Don't dare speak of him,' scolded Mrs Wells. 'If it weren't for his wretched fixation with cricket, we would be together still, I declare. And 'tis because of his lack of money management skills that I find myself in this skivvying Predicament.'

'But Mama!' said Bertie. 'I was about to ask these strange children if I could join their Secret Five secret club. I could write all about it one day and make you pots and pots of money! Enough so that you do not have to work your fingers and thumbs to the marrow being a housemaid here at Squire Humphrey de Lylow's house.'

'Woof woof woof!' said Whatshisname, sitting up and suddenly becoming quite animated for a trainee stuffed dog.

'Daniel?' said Betty, in a grown-up manner. 'Bertie can join our secret club, can't he?'

'Woof!' said Whatshisname. He nudged Betty with his nose.

Daniel looked quite sullen. 'Must we invite *everyone* to join?' he mumbled to Betty. 'I'm rapidly losing count of how many members we have.'

'Woof woof!!' said Whatshisname, nudging Betty's leg a bit harder.

'Stop nudging my leg a bit harder, Whatshisname!' scolded Betty. She turned to Daniel. 'Daniel, it's in our interest for him to join. We might well need his help to . . .' She paused.

'Why have you paused?' Daniel whispered. 'Is this yet another dramatic device?'

'Woof?' said Whatshisname.

'I paused because I thought Bertie mentioned the name *de Lylow*,' Betty said.

'Woof,' sighed Whatshisname.

'I did,' said Bertie. 'The de Lylows own this Big House. Can I join The Secret Five? Please? I'll let you be the corpse when we play Funerals in the lane. You don't *have* to be embalmed, it's your choice.'

'But *de Lylow*! Surely not,' said Betty. 'It can't be. Daniel, have you still got Sampson's autobiography?'

Daniel reached a hand down his trousers and pulled out the book. Mrs Wells looked truly aghast, as she knew that Storage Of Books Within The Crotch Area was a criminal offence punishable by a very stiff fine indeed.

'Here it is!' Daniel said, not noticing Mrs Wells' aghastness. Betty cautiously took the book, put it down on the table in front of her, and started to scan through the first chapter. Suddenly she stopped, shrieked, then pointed to something on a page. She frowned at Daniel, blew the page, then continued to scan the chapter until she found what she was looking for.

'Here!' she exclaimed. 'It says on page twelve that his great-great-grandfather was Squire Humphrey de Lylow!'

'Gosh!' said Daniel. Then he frowned. 'Who?'

Mrs Wells stopped whatever she was doing at the time and, instead of doing it, began to talk. 'What's this nonsense?' she asked. 'Squire Humphrey de Lylow is a *young* man, not yet thirty-two-and-a-half years of age, so how can he be a great-great-grandfather?' She laughed. 'Unless you really are time-travellers, of course! Which would be plain ridiculous. No-one has yet thought of such a thing and it really is scientifically impossible.'

'But Mama!' exclaimed Bertie. 'Of course they are time-travellers! Would not a dog in this state have been sent off to a convalescent home in Weston Super Mare in Victorian times?'

'Herbert George Wells!' scolded Mrs Wells. 'Don't vex me so! Stop all this talk about time travel. You do fill your head with such nonsense. It will never get you anywhere!'

'Sorry, Mama,' said Bertie, who had just had a sudden urge to write about these time travellers, but now realised that he would have to keep yet another of his urges a deep dark secret from his mother.

Betty was now truly engrossed in the book.

'We don't have to stop another conception, do we?' Daniel asked her. 'It was all so tiring and confusing.'

'Shush! I'm truly engrossed in the book,' said Betty thoughtfully. 'And no, I don't think we do. It says here that he emigrated to America in 1880 to start a new life, after a disastrous fire at his mansion ruined him whilst he was away in London.' She looked at Mrs Wells. 'Please Mrs Wells, has he had a disastrous fire yet?'

'Disastrous fire indeed!' said Mrs Wells. 'Impossible! Squire de Lylow has all sorts of Precautions here at the House. He employs one Person for each Candle that burns, and they have to watch to make sure it does not cause such a disastrous fire. Do you know, now you mention it, I started here as a Candle Watcher, but was soon promoted to Chief Wood-Louse Catcher before being demoted to Under Chief Housemaid. I never got over that. Anyway, the Candles are lovely when they burn brightly, and the gentle glow of the incandescent lights in the shards of silver seem to gleam in the bubbles that sparkle in our tumblers.'

'Hmmm, good stuff, Mama!' murmured Herbert, scribbling something in his note book and secretly wondering what the word *stuff* actually meant.

'And another thing,' Mrs Wells said. 'The Squire has had Paraffin Lamps installed in the Best Rooms, and they are as safe as safe can be, compared to . . . compared to . . . erm, not having any Paraffin Lamps.'

Betty and Daniel weren't at all convinced about the Candle Watchers, and Very Confused about the use of All The Capitals. Betty didn't know whether to show Mrs Wells the autobiography to prove that there really was going to be a fire that would cause the Squire to emigrate to America but, before she could decide, Mrs Wells' dialogue continued remorselessly.

'Now,' she said, firmly yet softly. 'I am going to prepare a nice cold bath for you dear Children. I suppose I should use the old tin bath that's hanging on the wall now it has been mentioned as a prop, but I am sure the Squire will not mind me using his Special Bathing Facilities while he is away in London. Get completely undressed, all of you, and I will be back down quicker than you can say compassion fatigue.'

Betty was quite shocked. 'I'm not taking my clothes off in front of anyone, especially in front of *boys*!'

'Oh, please do!' pleaded Bertie. 'I am earnestly seeking ways of destroying my self-respect and every little helps.'

'I will!' Daniel said in a strangely eager tone.

'Er . . .' said Bertie.

'Woof woof woof?' said Whatshisname.

Just then, much to Daniel's disappointment, they heard a commotion from upstairs. 'What's that commotion from upstairs?' Mrs Wells said. 'My my, if I'm not greatly mistaken, it sounds like the voice of Samuel Landscape, the fairly local Policeman.'

The commotion seemed to be coming nearer and nearer! Whatshisname growled, then barked such a loud bark that it frightened all the dogs in the room. He ran under the table and cowered.

'Why, it *is* you, Samuel,' said Mrs Wells, as a tall Victorian Policeman dressed in a tall Victorian Policeman's uniform appeared in the doorway. 'And what brings you here at such a reasonable hour? It's not about the pig's entrails again, is it? I made sure I tied them up very tightly before transportation up the lane, that I did. I know how much it upsets Vera the Nervous Victorian Vegetarian.'

'No,' said the tall Policeman in a loud Policeman's voice as he entered the scullery, ducking his head and the top part of his shoulders so that he could get safely through the doorway. 'It is certainly not the matter of the pig's entrails that brings me here, Mrs Wells.'

Then he espied Betty and Daniel, who both thought that the tall Policeman looked really frightening, as well as being really rather tall.

'Well well well Mrs Wells,' he said. 'What have we here? Are these the two Urchins that the Parson has told me about?'

'Indeed they probably are,' replied Mrs Wells. 'I was just going to bathe them and scrub all their little nooks and crannies.'

'Actually,' said Betty, suddenly standing up. 'We're not Urchins at all. We're really . . .'

But the Policeman held up his Policeman's hand to stop Betty talking. 'The narrative dictates that you stop talking,' he ordered. 'Sit back down on that Victorian scullery chair, girl Urchin.'

He walked up to the table and glared a long long glare at Betty. 'Not only,' he said in a rather official Policeman's voice, 'is she as unseemly as the Parson tried desperately to describe, nearly causing him a heart attack when he got to the bit about – well, never mind that – not only is she unseemly, but she's got the cheek of the Devil himself, answering a Proper Grown Up like that.'

Betty thought it wise to sit down again as the Policeman circled the table, which took quite a long time because it was a very long oblong table, not really designed for circling. When he eventually returned to the children he looked quite exhausted.

'Right,' he said, reaching all the way up and wiping the sweat from his tall Policeman's brow. 'And what's your name, boy Urchin with spectacles?'

'Sir, they call me Daniel,' said Daniel.

'Good. And what do *I* call you?' asked the Policeman.

'Erm, Daniel?' said Daniel.

'Well, Ermdaniel,' said the Policeman, reaching out his Policeman's hand and grabbing Ermdaniel's ear. 'You're quite a young villain, by the looks and feel of you, despite the fancy spectacles. You're nicked!'

'Ouch,' said Ermdaniel. 'What do you mean *nicked*?'

'I have no idea. I am so sorry,' said the Policeman, looking quite embarrassed at his unexplained use of twentieth century television police-talk. 'Ahem . . . I meant, by the Powers invested in me by, erm, whosoever gives me these Powers – and, by the way, pays me a Pittance for the vital work I do for the Victorian Community – I put you very much under arrest, Ermdaniel, boy Urchin!'

Chapter Twenty Five

In which something happens to Daniel (who wasn't, you may have noticed, murdered at all); Whatshisname cowers a bit, which is typical; the chapter, thankfully, finishes quite quickly but not before Daniel kills Betty in a fit of pique.

Betty gasped loudly when the Policeman put Daniel under arrest, as it came as quite a shock! It also shocked Whatshisname under the table, who released a loud gasp as well! The Policeman looked a little unnerved by the under-table gasping.

He looked around him suspiciously while he held tightly onto Daniel's ear, then bent down to examine the source of the under-table gasping. 'Bless me!' he exclaimed. 'Is there a Freak Circus in Town? What a strange creature!'

Whatshisname whimpered and pressed himself up against Betty's legs.

'The boy is under arrest?' Mrs Wells said. 'Samuel Landscape, I'm ashamed of you! Why arrest him? He looks such a harmless boy. Ugly, yes, but harmless.'

'It is my Official Duty, Mrs Wells, that it is. And while I am at it,' the Policeman said, pointing at Betty, 'I also arrest *you*! Stand up, so I can grab your ear and make you go *ouch* as well. In answer to your penetrating question, Mrs Wells, the boy Urchin was seen consuming a stolen apple in a lane without a licence.'

'A lane without a licence?' enquired Betty.

'Hmmm . . . just a syntactical issue,' said the Policeman, shaking his head.

'Ouch! Cool it, dude!' shouted Daniel. 'Anyway, it was lying on the ground!'

'The apple or the lane?' Betty asked.

'And the girl Urchin,' said the Policemen, 'is arrested for Annoying the Inhabitants by Virtue of Improper Dress without a Licence. And Aiding and Abetting the Theft of an Apple. And any other Bye Law I can think of, including Owning an Animal with an Offensive Collar.'

'Ouch!' said Betty.

'Woof woof woof?' said Whatshisname.

'I wouldn't be surprised if the Magistrate ordered you both to have a Jolly Good Whipping, followed by standing in a corner while naming the parts of a daffodil in alphabetical order, then some hard labour for a month before being sent to Reformatory School for a year or two,' sneered the Policeman in an official yet informal manner.

'But we are contracted to save the world, dude!' exclaimed Daniel, who was becoming quite nervous and dangerously close to a bout of street-talk. 'It's going to be in the hands of a criminally-minded evil mega-criminal, and we're the only ones who can stop it! Apart from Amy and Ricky, that is. All we need are Brussels sprouts and a portal to get to 1980. Innit!'

'And a digital alarm clock,' added Betty, casting a glance at her brother.

'Ah ha!' ahhaed the Policeman. 'Amy and Ricky, eh? There are *more* Urchins? I can see that promotion to Proper Constable coming my way very soon! Where are they hiding?'

Bertie had been sitting down all this time, quietly making notes in his Victorian note book, but now he thought it was time that he helped his new friends. 'Please Constable,' he said. 'These two children are indeed very important people, and belong to a *very* secret club! I believe that I was just about to become a member as well. They say they are time travellers who come all the way from . . .' He paused and looked at Betty. 'When do you come from?'

Betty tried to wrench her ear away from the Policeman's

grasp, but he gripped it even harder. 'Ouch!' she cried again. 'We came all the way from the twenty-first century! Let me go!'

'Ah-ha!' ahhaed the Policeman. 'Secret Membership of a *Very* Secret Club? That's breaking another Bye Law, I'll be bound. As is Fraudulently Claiming to be a Time Traveller without a Licence.'

'We'll let you join The Secret Five,' offered Betty, 'if you let us go!'

'Yet another crime!' said the Policeman, squeezing her ear even harder. 'Failing to Bribe a Policeman will be added to the list of charges, I fancy. If only I had a free hand to make a note of all this in my note book.'

'I've already done that,' said Bertie, scribbling away in his own Victorian note book.

The Policeman dragged Betty and Daniel towards the stairs. Whatshisname bravely peeked out from under the table and decided to take drastic action there and then! He leapt out and grabbed the leg of the Policeman's trousers, pulling and pulling until the Policeman said, 'Please stop it, doggy.' Instantly, and without any thought for his own safety, Whatshisname let go and crawled back under the table to do some serious cowering. As he cowered, he recalled Roosevelt's assertion that the only thing we have to fear is fear itself – what a joke! It was painfully obvious to him that Franklin D hadn't seen the size of this Victorian Policeman's boots. Whatshisname plumped for working out his own salvation with fear and trembling. To support his campaign for survival, he promptly decided to hold an extraordinary and unilateral meeting of The Secret Five there and then. Quick as a flash, using his Emergency Power of Mandate and some flexible proxy voting, he voted by two votes to one (with one abstention) to stay under the table for at least four hundred sticks.

The Policeman led Betty and Daniel by their very own ears up the stairs, all the way out of the Big House, down the lane and back into the village. Villagers came out of their typical Victorian houses to stare at them with their typical Victorian eyes. Betty could hear the Tut-Tutting and *Good Gracious* and *Are Those Real?* as they passed the onlookers. One of them looked rather like the postman in chapter one, looking decidedly pleased with himself in his Victorian costume and hamming it up with fervour as he jeered them on their way to the courthouse.

On the way, the Policeman gruffly informed the children that the Magistrate, a rather fierce and grumpy old man by all accounts, was in court today. He was doing something strange called Petty Sessions, so in all probability there would be a classic miscarriage of justice – they would be found guilty without appeal, then imprisoned with a good stiff sentence.

Now the two children were in real trouble! They were stranded deep in 1880 with no-one to help them! No-one at all![1]

---

[1] *That's the plan, anyway.*

Chapter Twenty Six

In which we meet a Magistrate; the Policeman finds cause to laugh a bit; bad news for Whatshisname at long last; a character witness is urgently needed but unlikely to be found at such short notice; shame.

Betty and Daniel, behind our very backs, had been led by their ears into a small gloomy Victorian courtroom. They had been dragged by the tall Policeman into the dock, where they now stood side by side, one of their ears glowing red. Both children looked quite worried! Betty was worried about Whatshisname, Ricky, Amy, Uncle Quagmire, Aunt Trinny, Bertie, McFly's ongoing popularity, the future of the world, and whether Daniel would lapse into his stupid street-talk coma again, but not necessarily in that order. Daniel was also worried, although, as usual, he couldn't quite pin down exactly what he was worried about so he stood no chance of sorting them into any semblance of order.

In the gloom of the courtroom the children found it hard to make out the glum look on the grim faces of the spectators, but they both thought that they looked very much like the people who had jeered them on the way to court (including the postman from chapter one) and, strangely, very much like the swarthy Italian tourists from 1964 Salzburg[1].

As they waited for the fierce and grumpy Magistrate to enter, Betty told Daniel that things could be much worse, to which Daniel quietly pointed out that they were stuck in 1880 without

---

[1] *It's encouraging, as enthusiastic and reliable extras are hard to come by these days.*

any means of returning home, he had no idea of the parts of a daffodil, they were due to be whipped to within an inch of their lives for some menial misdemeanour then dressed in a suit with arrows on and imprisoned for a very long time with only bread and water for nourishment and sanitary arrangements that would be a thousand times worse than a rampaging outbreak of severe diarrhoea on a wet weekend at the Glastonbury Festival, so how could it possibly get worse?

'Let's be a bit more positive, shall we?' she whispered as the grumpy-looking old Magistrate entered the courtroom. 'In the true spirit of The Secret Five, something will happen. It always does. We won't be left to rot. We're too important, remember? And courtroom scenes such as these always end up with the protagonists being released then being mobbed and feted by the press on the steps outside the courtroom. Trust me on this.'

Daniel wasn't convinced, firstly because he didn't know what a protagonist was, and thought it sounded quite painful, and secondly because he'd seen the utter grumpiness of the Magistrate, who had sat himself down and was now glaring very firmly in the direction of the children. 'Quiet in the dock!' he bellowed. 'And stop lolling while I'm bellowing! Yes, you Urchins! No Urchin lolls in *my* Sessions, despite the fact that they are petty!'

The old Magistrate then pointed his bellow at the Policeman. 'Constable Landscape, I believe it was you who, with complete disregard for your own safety and Well Being, did arrest these two Urchins. Please describe the offences with which these Ragamuffins are charged.'

The Policeman stood up and bowed to the Magistrate.

'Well, Mr Magistrate, sir,' he said. 'The boy is charged with Stealing and Consuming an Apple without a Licence. And the girl – well, where do I start? Annoying the Inhabitants and Palpitating a Parson by Virtue of Improper Dress, Aiding and Abetting the Theft of an Apple . . .'

The Magistrate suddenly looked less grumpy. 'All hanging

offences, in my book!' he chuckled. 'Oh yes, it is surely my lucky day!'

'And there's more,' continued the Policeman. 'Owning an Animal with an Offensive Collar. Belonging to a Very Secret Society without a Very Secret Society Licence . . .'

The old Magistrate glared at Betty. 'Enough! I can see immediately,' he said, 'that the Improper Dress violation is proven, and I hope our Parson recovers his Well Being very soon. Tell me, why do you wear a man's trousers, girl Urchin? Very tight trousers at that. And a strumpet's blouse.'

'They're jeans!' exclaimed Betty. 'And a tee shirt!'

'I'll have you address me as sir!' boomed the Magistrate. 'And what utter mumbo jumbo you talk! *Jeans* indeed. And as for this secret society, tell me about it, boy Urchin. Or is it a secret?'

Daniel leaned forward. 'Sire, we're proud to be known as . . .' – he paused for dramatic effect – 'The Secret Five!'

The Policeman laughed quite an official laugh for a Constable. The laugh from the other people in the courtroom was raucous yet unofficial. The old Magistrate frowned and waited for the laughter to fade. He looked at Betty, then at Daniel, then back to Betty. 'What is Education coming to these days? Do you not do Arithmetic in week school? You two are five? What does this mean?'

'Sir,' said Betty. 'Two of the others are back – or is it forward – in the twentieth century. The other one is a mere dog who was quite cleverly pretending to cower under a table but is now probably launching a daring rescue attempt and will burst through that very door at any second and carry us off with barely a thought for his own safety.'

A general murmur murmured around the courtroom and out of a handy window. Everyone turned their heads to stare at that very door, waiting for Whatshisname to daringly burst into the room and carry off the two children with barely a thought for his own safety.

After a few minutes of waiting and murmuring, some people began to imagine, quite correctly, that Whatshisname was still cowering under a table somewhere, and that bursting into courtrooms and carrying off two children with barely a thought for his own safety was extremely low on his agenda for the day compared to licking his bottom.

The Magistrate grunted, then hammered his trained Magistrate's fist on the desk, which quivered and shook quite a lot.

'Enough!' he bellowed. 'And I do not know what you were all waiting for, as I believe that the mere dog will soon be in the safe hands of a typical Victorian Taxidermist. In his imminently inert state, methinks, thoughts of a daring rescue attempt are quite fanciful.'

The children looked at each other. 'That sounds bad news for Whatshisname,' whispered Daniel. 'And yet, it might be an improvement. I suppose we could take it in turns to carry him about. And we could always consider a wheel at each corner.'

'But he's been my faithful doggy!' said Betty. 'I owe it to him . . . I think. We need to launch our own daring rescue attempt, to attempt to rescue him daringly!'

'How?' moaned Daniel.

'I'll think of something,' she replied, and began to think very hard inside her head.

'Hush!' boomed the Magistrate. 'Enough of all this hard thinking. And, may I say, where else can you think if not inside the head!' He glanced up at the ceiling and sighed. 'Now, Urchins, let's get down to business. Do you two have any character witnesses? If not, I'll get straight to the bit I enjoy, the hanging verdict. Where on earth did I leave my little black cap?'

The children were stunned and quite worried, especially Daniel who looked even closer to sliding into a bout of street-talk.

'Please, sir,' pleaded Betty. 'Two things. First, we need to be excused for a while, as we have to launch a daring rescue attempt, which probably won't take too long. Secondly, we're obviously both stunned and quite worried that we have no character witnesses. Not one. All our friends are in 2010, you see. Or 1964. Or 1980.'

The people in the courtroom laughed another unofficial laugh. The Magistrate frowned importantly at the children. 'You keep mentioning this preposterous notion of time travel,' he boomed. 'Is not it a fact of imagination? Can you prove it? For instance, Urchins, can you tell me things about the future? Hmmm?'

'Well, sir . . .' Betty said, trying to remember her history lessons, 'in the future there will be such things as . . . such things as . . .' She turned to Daniel. 'How many world wars have there been since 1880?'

Daniel smiled a silly smile and shrugged a big shrug with his very own shoulders. 'Hey,' he said. 'Sha up! Don' be a noobee! Mos'def a deuce, siso'mine! Innit?'

The Magistrate leaned forward and squinted at Daniel. 'Is the boy speaking in tongues?' he enquired. 'Shall I call for the Parson?'

Betty was about to slap Daniel but thought that Slapping a Boy without a Licence might be added to the growing list of crimes, so she didn't.

'Please, sir,' she said. 'He's frightened, that's all. His vocabulary becomes utterly strange when he's scared, you see. Maybe you can say something to unscare him, sir. Or I could slap him. Personally I prefer the slapping but it's your choice. Take a moment.'

Chapter Twenty Seven

In which the postman wears a pink bonnet; there is a brief exchange regarding aspects of pension planning, which everyone should consider from an early age in these days of economic uncertainty; a terrible thing happens, but not until much later, probably in another chapter.

The Magistrate looked slightly unsettled by the sudden and unannounced chapter break. 'Stay calm!' he boomed at the spectators, who looked as though they might panic and stampede at any moment. 'It is, apparently, merely something called a chapter break. Constable Landscape warned me about them. He fears that the Urchins might use them as a cover to escape. Watch them both very closely indeed, Constable.'

The Constable leaned forward and glared very closely indeed at the children as the Magistrate continued his booming. 'I think the people should decide about the slapping of the boy!' he announced, in a rare fit of democracy. He looked around at the Victorian people in the courtroom. All of them looked very eager to take part in the proceedings. 'Those in favour of a hearty slapping, say *aye*!' the Magistrate boomed.

Now, it might be recalled that revenge is a dish best served hot enough to burn the roof of a mouth quite badly when the opportunity next arises. Grudges are shameful, to be avoided, but unfortunately the people in the court responded to the Magistrate's request in a big way. 'Aye!' they all shouted. The postman from chapter one ayed particularly loudly in his relentless but futile search for stardom.

The Magistrate held up his hand to stop the loud ayeing and pointed a fierce glare at Betty, at the same time raising his substantial Victorian eyebrows as if to say *what are you waiting for?*

Betty shrugged.

'Sorry again, Daniel,' she murmured. 'This has to be the last time, surely, so I'll try to make it very special.' Then she slapped him really hard!

'Ouch!' he moaned, holding a hand to his rather red cheek which now matched his rather red ear. The people in the court cheered loudly! Hurrah! They threw their caps and bonnets high into the air! Hurrah again!

After a few more minutes, during which the people clamoured and mingled and bartered to try and recover their caps and bonnets, some quite unsuccessfully it seemed, the Magistrate called them to order. The postman, a rather fetching pink bonnet perched on his head, looked particularly pleased with his new headgear.

'Now,' said the Magistrate. 'Where were we? Ah, yes. You were going to tell me things about the future to prove that you are indeed time travellers. Well?'

Daniel rubbed his cheek and looked quite sulky.

'I don't know anything about world wars,' Betty said. 'That sort of thing isn't something we are supposed to know, as it would really ruin our adventures. But we did hear that some men flew to the moon.'

The people in the courtroom sniggered and tittered. Betty heard muttering of *fanciful talk* and *talking through her bottom*.

Daniel, despite his utter grumpiness, thought that he would try to help his sister. 'Sire!' he shouted above the tittering and sniggering. 'I've remembered something from the future! I do know that they lay sleeping policemen across the roads to slow down traffic, because Uncle Quagmire is always complaining about them and drives as fast as he can over them!'

Constable Landscape gasped a huge gasp then fainted in a big heap on the floor, which managed to break his fall. Several concerned people gathered round and started to kick him.

'Stop this Victorian courtroom fiasco!' boomed the Magistrate. 'Constable Landscape, I demand that you awaken and recover from your fainting fit at once, otherwise I will make you a Ward of Court. Awaken! For we will need you for some penetrating dialogue very soon, I fear.'

Daniel looked at Betty for inspiration as Constable Landscape struggled to his feet, vowing never to fall asleep again in case he was carried off somewhere for horizontal traffic-control duties. Daniel sensed that Betty was having trouble thinking of something that might impress the Magistrate. He had to think fast!

'Podcasts!' he exclaimed.

The Magistrate frowned. His frown spread quickly around the courtroom and back again like a trapped Mexican wave.

Daniel quite cleverly sensed the wave and realised that he had to think of something else. 'Blogs?' he offered hopefully.

Betty kicked his ankle.

'Blogs?' the Magistrate repeated, and frowned an even bigger frown. 'Are these podcasts and blogs undergarments of some kind? Can't you think of something of greater importance to mankind?'

'Erm . . . Twitter?' Daniel said. 'Or Eminem?'

The Magistrate appeared to be becoming rather more grumpy than normal. 'Bah! If you cannot think of something really impressive, Urchin Number One, I will have no option but to . . .'

'SERPS!' Daniel interrupted, suddenly remembering a time when Uncle Quagmire talked to him at some considerable length about the urgent need for pension planning from the age of three.

Betty turned and pointed quite a big glare at Daniel. 'Serps? Silly boy!' she scolded. 'How is a social disease of the twentieth century going to help us out of this predicament?'

'Yes,' added the Magistrate. 'I agree. What is this *serps*? Is it highly contagious?'

'Sire, it's State Earnings-Related Pension Scheme,' Daniel replied, quite eagerly for a boy facing the death penalty, or worse. 'It's to provide employed people with additional pension, but they can contract out of SERPS if they have a PEP or an occupational pension, apparently. It's really only for Wrinklies and Crumblies. I'm not too sure about all the small print, though. And it might have all changed since I was three.'

'Wrinklies and Crumblies?' asked the Magistrate. 'This is very confusing. What are those, pray?'

'Sir, they're very *very* old people,' said Betty, quite enthusiastically joining the SERPS debate. 'You know . . . queue busters . . . stair-lift pilots . . . shredded-wheat-face . . . old people, a bit like yourself.'

'What?' the Magistrate boomed. 'All the insolence does not help your cause, Urchin Number Two, and makes me boom a lot. And, boy Urchin, is this your way of proving that you are from another time? Perps and seps and twittle indeed! At this rate I will increase the sentence with a jolly good ticking-off before the hanging!'

'Please, sir,' pleaded Betty. 'Ignore him. He's just not very clever.'

Betty suddenly and quite dramatically remembered Sampson's autobiography. She turned to Daniel. 'Daniel,' she whispered. 'I've had an idea that must rate amongst the top ten best ever Secret Five ideas! Why don't we show him Sampson's autobiography?'

'Good idea!' said Daniel. He plunged his hand down his trousers.

The people in the courtroom gasped! 'Clerk of the court,' boomed the Magistrate. 'Note that the boy is feeling about within his trousers, will you? Stop that at once! Or I will add Unauthorised Licentious Behaviour without a Licence to the list of charges!'

Daniel stopped that at once.

'Why have you stopped?' Betty said.

'I've lost it!' Daniel moaned. 'It must have been when we were dragged here! And, to be honest, I don't want unauthorised lice . . . or whatever he said, added to the list of charges, do I? I just want to go home!'

'Hush at once, raggedy Urchins! Let us get back to my perfectly reasonable request for a character witness,' said the Magistrate. 'If you have not brought one along with you, is there anyone in the courtroom that you have seen before?'

Daniel and Betty looked very carefully around the room. 'The policeman?' offered Daniel, adding 'Ouch' as Betty kicked his ankle again.

'Good!' said the Magistrate. 'Constable Landscape! Good to see you have been obliging enough to recover from your fainting fit in order to partake in some meaningful dialogue. Can you vouch for the characters of these two cheeky lying thieving Urchins?'

'Well,' said the Policeman, leaning forward in eager anticipation of his moment in the spotlight, 'much as it grieves me to say so, for they have been a part of my life for over three chapters now, and it would hurt me so to see them whipped enthusiastically and then incarcerated for years or hung by the neck until fairly dead, but there comes a time when you have to protect the Victorian Public and tell the truth about such unruly Urchins. I only wish that those ASBOs were available . . .'

'But he's a Policeman!' shouted Betty. 'It was him who arrested us! This isn't British justice at its very best, is it now?'

The Magistrate banged his trained fist on the desk again, and was becoming rather red in the face. But then, very suddenly and quite inexplicably, the doors flew open wide! The people in the courtroom were so astonished that some of them raised one or both of their eyebrows. Everyone turned their heads to see a figure standing in the doorway!

'It's Whatshisname!' shouted Daniel. 'At last! He's come to rescue us!'

'No it's not!' said Betty. 'Silly boy. Can you smell creosote or pineapple? Can you? Hmmm? No! It's the figure of a man, standing silhouetted in the courtroom doorway!'

'Nice imagery, Betty,' whispered Daniel. 'Who is it?'

'Wait!' the figure of a man said in a rather stern man's voice. 'Enough of this interminable courtroom scene! *I'll* be a character witness for these two dear harmless inept children. Now, where do I need to stand for maximum dramatic effect?'

Betty and Daniel were transfixed! They stared at the figure of a man. They might now be saved from their ghastly fate!

But who was the figure? And where had he come from? And why was he stark naked?

PART FOUR

Chapter Twenty Eight

In which our heroes meet yet another peripheral character but this one has severe dandruff; Amy and Ricky are close to saving the world; or maybe not; there is mention of a four-in-a-bed romp but don't get too excited; that may be George Michael hiding behind the kangaroo; no, for legal purposes, it's definitely not.

'Honestly, Amy!' moaned Ricky. 'Do you have to keep landing on top of me?'

'I couldn't help it!' squeaked Amy. 'I don't have any control over it, do I? It's the sprouts and the wardrobe that have the control, apparently. And will you stop doing that to me! You're fondling my buttocks! Again! I'm your sister!'

'I'm *not* fondling, I'm just trying to get you off me!' said Ricky. 'But, I must admit, you are jolly well firm-bodied and I did feel a strangely erotic sense of eroticism which, I think, must be totally out of character and not wise for a brother-sister relationship, surely.'

Amy struggled to her feet on the school's lush lawn where they had landed. She was quite red in the face! 'What silly talk! Just get up off the lush lawn,' she ordered, with very little ill-feeling and even less understanding of the word *eroticism*.

Ricky struggled to his feet and looked about him. 'Where are we? I'm hungry.'

'Hopefully we're in 1980!' Amy snapped. 'Remember? We made sure the Nixie clock was set to the right year this time and then we asked Uncle Quagmire to keep Old Hag away from our wardrobe when we time-travelled.' She paused uncertainly then lowered her voice. 'Is that enough backstory?'

Ricky nodded his head twice. He was still quite embarrassed at the strange sense of eroticism which, interestingly, seemed to be stronger than his usual uncontrollable sense of hunger.

Amy looked carefully around her. 'It looks very much like a school,' she observed. 'Sort of big, with big windows and a big roof to keep the small pupils quite dry. How exciting! I haven't been in one of these for ages!'

'Hopefully, this is Sampson's school, the Stanley Gibbons School for the Fairly Gifted,' Ricky said.

Just then, without warning, a first floor window clattered open and a man's head and shoulders poked out, causing an outbreak of scattered showers of dandruff onto the shrubbery below. 'Hey, you two pupils!' the man called. 'What were you doing there, lying on the grass? Were you indulging in a congress? Did I miss a concrescence?'

Amy frowned and looked quite confused. She wasn't used to such language and so many syllables in one sentence. She turned to Ricky, who looked just as quite confused. He was also perplexed at all the talk of a concrescence on the lawn. He looked around for a statue.

'Please sir,' Amy called to the head and shoulders of the man. 'We weren't doing anything naughty like . . .' She tried desperately to remember the correct terminology. '. . . like canoodling, if that's what you meant. We've only just arrived from 1964, you see. We're looking for someone called Sampson de Lylow so that we can stop him from becoming evil and then we will have saved the world.'

The man didn't look too convinced. 'I'm not too convinced,' he called. 'And I probably don't look as though I am either. Now, shoulders back, stand upright, and get inside before I start to take my duties as headmaster very seriously for a change. And if I find, when examining the photographs I took of you very secretly with my six-point-two-million-pixel digital camera, that you were up to no good then it's the high jump for you. Or the shot put, as we're quite short of participants in that particular discipline in the Inter-School Underperformers' Olympics.'

'Please, sir,' called Ricky. 'Two things before you go. One, did you know that your severe dandruff can easily be cured by use of a good shampoo containing selenium sulphide, eating plenty of Vitamin B6, and a strict hair-washing regime where you avoid hairdryers? And two, do you actually know where we could find the boy called Sampson? We are, as my surprisingly firm-bodied sister suggested, The Secret Five on a mission to save the world from his future evilness, you see. We need to stop his utter humiliation.'

But, without warning, the man disappeared, slamming the window behind him. Then, just as suddenly, the window opened again and there were the man's head and shoulders and further localised showers of dandruff.

'So sorry,' he called. 'How foolish of me. An immediate correction is needed, before I get the letters flooding in. This is 1980, of course, and the digital camera doesn't get properly invented until about seven years from now. I did, in fact, mean my Penron 35mm single lens reflex camera with its 100mm coated Sigtax lens with macro capability. Now, please carry on.'

'Excuse me, don't go, sir at the window,' Amy called. 'We are at the right school, aren't we? The one that Sampson de Lylow was at in 1980?'

'I can't be expected to know everyone by name!' yelled the man at the window. 'It's difficult enough trying to remember the name of my wife and my two secret lovers. I know one is called Simon, but the others? Hmmm, I'll need to think about that. Anyway, why not pop along to the Big Hall. Most of the . . . what do you call them . . . you know, little people . . . children, that's it, they'll be in there.' And, with that, he slammed the window and disappeared yet again, hopefully forever unless the story demands a four-in-a-bed romp.

Amy stamped her foot, critically wounding a rather unfortunate but rare lawn weevil in the process. 'I really don't want to be in this story!' she said, quite sulkily for a girl of her woefully inadequate shoe size. 'He was horrid. There are so many rude characters in this adventure. We never ever meet *really* nice people, apart from little old ladies in their tea shops.'

Ricky crowded around her as best he could. 'Come on, old thing,' he said. 'Let me give you a reassuring platonic hug. And did you mention tea shops?'

'Ricky!' Amy shrieked. 'We have no time for, er, plutonic hugging or stupid tea shops! Don't you have any sense of responsibility for the future of mankind? Come on, we must find Sampson.'

And, with that, she set off quickly and determinedly towards the school entrance.

'Amy!' called Ricky. 'Come back!'

But Amy had disappeared, as predicted, into the school entrance, and Ricky was left pondering his options. Should he wait here for her to come back, maybe nursing the rare weevil back to health while he waited? Or was he brave enough to follow her and help to save the world?

Probably not, actually.

Just then, rather unexpectedly, Ricky looked upwards and scowled a big scowl at nothing in particular. 'Oh yeah?' he said. 'Not brave enough, eh? I'll show you!'

He set off towards the entrance. He looked quite determined, for a change.

Inside the school, Amy hurried and scurried down a corridor, hoping that she was hurrying and scurrying in the right direction. She stopped. Up until the use of the verb gerund *hoping* she was sure it was the right direction. Now she wasn't so sure.

But then, right on time, she heard a boy's voice say something of extreme importance.

'Can I help you?'

She turned to face the boy's voice, which came from the direction of a boy who had a lot of brown hair on his head and a really handsome tanned face. Both of Amy's knees went all wobbly, fortunately for her stability at the very same time.

'Hi! I'm George,' he said, holding out his tanned hand. 'How are your wobbly knees?'

'G-g-g-gosh!' s-s-s-s-stammered Amy as she s-s-s-slipped her hand into his and let him sh-sh-sh-shake it. This might be, at long last, an indication of the emergence of her latent sexuality. 'Hello George,' she said, gazing into his big eyes. 'I'm looking for the right direction for . . . we're . . . I'm . . . erm . . . looking for Sampson. G-g-g-gosh!'

'Why?' George asked incisively, letting go of her hand.

Quite suddenly Ricky appeared at her side. He looked determined, and took the opportunity to glare firmly at George. 'Ah, my darling sister, whom I will protect until my dying day,' he said. He put his arm around his trophy sister. 'Found you at last!'

Amy scowled hard at Ricky, pushed his arm off her shoulders and kicked out at his shins.

Ricky rubbed his shin, scowled back at Amy with a bigger and more robust scowl, then stood bravely in front of her, his arms folded, facing George. 'Ahem! Let me politely explain who we are, as we must seem awfully mysterious to you. We are the forward spearhead contingent of The Secret Five and can't stop to talk – *or to flirt* – or to give away the secret purpose of our secret mission apart from the fact that we're travelling through time to try and save the world from the grip of an evil mega-monster and that we have two friends and their dog with a pink fluffy collar all stuck back in 1880 and who are probably lost forever but hey that's life. And, before you ask, boy stranger, you're far too good looking to join our intensely secret club. I'm so sorry. Is all that quite clear? Now, where's Sampson de Lylow? And a handy tea shop.'

Amy was rooted to the spot, thanks to some carelessly discarded chewing gum. She peered over Ricky's shoulder. 'Let George join us if he asks,' she whispered to Ricky. 'Please?'

'Oh, of course I'll join,' George said, flashing his whiter-than-white teeth at them. 'And I think I can help. If you're looking for

Sampson, I can help find him, I'm your man. Yeah.' He wiggled his hips and ran his fingers silently through his own hair, as it would have been very forward of him to run them silently through someone else's hair. 'Sampson's probably getting ready and doing some last minute rehearsing for the musical that we're performing very soon. God knows he needs to.'

Ricky leaned forwards towards George. 'Er, can I say something?' he whispered. 'We can't mention God. If you don't mind. Our Secret Five world is predominantly secular and godless, you see.'

'Oh, sorry, I didn't realise,' said George, apologetically wiggling his hips again.

'A musical?' said Amy, trying desperately to pick up the narrative pace a little.

'Yeah,' said George. 'The school is performing a special musical version of *The Birthday Party.*'

'Nick Cave's Birthday Party?' said Ricky, rather too cleverly for someone of his taste in breakfast cereals. 'Wow! They are definitely the darkest of the post-punk bands, creating bleak and raucous soundscapes that are an ideal backdrop for Nick Cave's dark and profound lyrics about religious perversity and extreme violence! Wow again! I love their rockabilly licks, their hellacious feedback and their unremitting pace and base rhythm! So, can I come and watch it? I also like Whitney Houston, by the way.'

George looked very strangely at Ricky. 'Whitney who?'

'No, Hou*ston*,' said Ricky.

'Oh. Well, you're welcome to come along,' George said, quite patiently. 'But it's actually Harold Pinter's play *The Birthday Party*, and not Nick Cave's band. We've rewritten it as a musical version, specially for tonight. Yeah.'

Suddenly he spun round on his heels and ended up pointing one of his fingers in their direction and sort of looking at them under his eyebrows in a mysterious way.

'Yeah, you see,' he continued, 'I have considerable talent and wrote a song specially for it, to counteract the abundant mystification and the menacing claustrophobia of Pinter's neurotic world. It's called *Wake Me Up Before You Go, Goldberg*. But I may have to tighten up the lyrics a bit.' He leaned forward, close to Ricky. 'By the way, you do have *very* good skin. Do you moisturise? And has anyone told you that you have really nice eyes?'

Amy stepped in front of Ricky. 'What about mine?' she asked, pointing to her eyes one by one and trying to pout but only succeeding with her top lip.

'Oh behave!' Ricky said, pushing Amy aside quite roughly. 'We're on a secret mission, so stop sulking. George, thanks a lot for the compliment about my skin and eyes, I quite like yours too, as skin and eyes go, and you have made me feel good about myself, and again I feel a strange sense of . . . erm, never mind. But we need to find Sampson, urgently. Apparently, he's supposed to be humiliatingly ejected from a band very soon, and we have to stop it happening.'

George looked quizzically at them, perhaps still thinking about the utter silliness of disturbing lyrics about extreme violence and religious perversity. Then he told them to follow him, that he would lead them to Sampson as long as he could definitely join The Secret Five, with a copious amount of privileges.

Ricky and Amy hastily agreed that he could join their provisional wing, but with severely restricted copious privileges.

'Cool! That'll do me. The play is in the Big Hall,' George said as he led them along the long grey school corridor. 'It's been hard work. We have had to rehearse hard, man. It's the only way to get it right.'

Ricky agreed. 'If you're gonna do it, do it right. Right?' he said to George, who stopped, turned and looked quite curiously at him for a while before walking on.

As they reached the Big Hall, another boy suddenly came up to George, adding to the confusing clutter of peripheral characters.

'Yeah, this is Andrew,' George told them. He introduced Amy and Ricky to Andrew, which was really quite astonishing as he hadn't yet been told their names, but it might have been a gift that certain people possess.

Amy's knees began to tremble again. 'G-g-g-gosh!' she s-s-s-s-said. She was surprised that all boys weren't ugly, and that she'd now met two boys who put the boom-boom into her heart. She felt like telling them that. Maybe later. First she'd need a recap on what conception and canoodling were all about, and which one came first. If only Betty was here and not stuck in some Victorian courtroom threatened with hanging, she thought, although some people might wonder how she knew about Betty's predicament, and those people just need to relax a bit.

As she shook Andrew's hand, she noticed his *big* eyes! She wanted to lick them! Slurp slurp! To roll them round in her mouth!

'Amy! Yeuk!' said Ricky, wrinkling his nose. 'Get a grip!'

'Erm, that was only a silent thought,' said Amy.

'Oh, sorry,' Ricky murmured, looking down at his shoes.

'We need to find Sampson, Andrew,' Amy said. 'He's about to be ejected from some band and utterly humiliated.'

'That'll be our band,' Andrew said. 'And we'll be doing the humiliating, yeah.'

'*Your* band?' Ricky said, raising both of his eyebrows together.

'Yeah, I was gonna tell you,' George said. 'Andrew and me and Sampson. One day we'll be famous, yeah. But one of us is holding us back and Andrew thinks it's Sampson. So we're gonna sack and humiliate him. We no longer think a castanet player is hip in *Bash!*, do we Andrew?'

'Bash?' Amy enquired.

'No, *Bash!*,' George said. 'In italics, and with an exclamation mark, not a question mark. We did try a question mark but it didn't work. It made us look indecisive. But do you like our group's name? Sampson thought of it. Maybe we can change it when he's gone. Come on, follow me into the hall. Let me take you to the very place where Sampson will be sacked and humiliated.'

Amy nudged Ricky as George grabbed the doorknob. 'You have to tell them not to humiliate Sampson!' she whispered.

Ricky suddenly felt quite important and very serious. 'Gosh!

It's been a while since I took on any responsibility and didn't moan about it,' he said, beaming. 'I'll do it!'

Ricky then stood up straight and used his very best voice as he told Andrew and George not to sack Sampson. 'No!' he said, very forcefully for a boy with his DNA. 'You can't sack Sampson! Please!'

'But he's useless!' Andrew said. 'Give us one good reason why we shouldn't sack him.'

'Because,' Ricky said, 'it means that, if you do, he'll turn evil, and eventually seek world domination through evil means. And, more importantly, I quite like castanet music. I used to play them myself when I was but a small child. I gave it up when I was four years old. It was disturbing the gerbil.'

'Cool!' said George. 'Get on down! We'll keep him then, shall we Andrew?'

'What!' said Ricky. 'Just like that! You'll not sack and humiliate him? You've changed your mind? It's *that* easy to be persuasive?'

'Yup,' said Andrew. '*That* easy.'

'But we want a challenge!' said Ricky. 'Where's the setbacks and reversals and bits of the adventure where we give up hope and can't go on, only to pick ourselves up and carry on regardless of adversity?'

'Mmmm, quite,' said Andrew. 'Sorry we've ruined the structural elements of your adventure, but Amy is such a babe! She makes the sun shine brighter than Doris Day, she does. We'd do anything for her, wouldn't we George?'

George looked unsure, although the bit about Doris Day had caught his attention. Amy's cheeks flushed bright red, resembling the colour of a freshly-squashed grey squirrel's[1] pool of blood in the middle of a rather busy A-road just outside Skipton.

'Gosh!' she said in a meaningless way, yet somehow full of

---

[1] *Other out-of-control rodents are available.*

meaning. She turned to Ricky. 'Ricky, if this means that our adventure is really over, apart from getting home that is, have I got time to learn something about canoodling?'

Ricky looked quite confused and worried! He was worried firstly that Betty and Daniel were wasting their time in 1880 (although he would have given his right arm to be invited to their forthcoming celebration banquet, which of course he didn't know about and even if he did, and had been invited, losing his right arm would have made the efficient handling of the best silverware quite a challenge) and, secondly, that their part of the adventure was not really worth the paper it was printed on (and yet, if it were recycled paper or paper from a sustainable source, then it would be much less of a waste). He was also worried that Amy was becoming a bit of a tart and it was his duty, as a caring brother, to stop her from sliding deep into degradation so early in life.

'No time for that, Amy,' he said. 'The performance starts soon. I can hear the audience drifting into the next chapter.'

'I can't hear anything,' George complained.

'Nor me,' said Andrew.

'Can't you?' said Amy. 'We can.'

Chapter Twenty Nine

In which we get all Pinteresque, as if Blytonesque wasn't challenging enough; we definitely regret ever picking this book up; good job it was discounted; oh, it wasn't; anyway, moving swiftly on, Sampson plays his castanet solo and then something else happens but more slowly this time.

'Oh yes,' said George, as he heard the drifting audience. 'I can hear them now.'

'You get used to these things after a while,' Amy said. 'Now, let's talk about how to canoodle . . .'

'Amy!' scolded Ricky. 'We must cease all this sexual awakening!'

'Look, we've got to go and get ready,' said George, very eager to change the subject. 'Are you two gonna go in and watch the performance? That'd be really cool, man. Yeah!'

As Ricky and Amy had never actually seen a play before, they jumped at the chance. 'Very good,' said Andrew. 'Mind you, I don't know how the performance will go. We've got a stand-in playing the part of Lulu. How she'll cope with playing the tin drum while singing Boom Bang-a-Bang I don't know. And she's a bit old, *and* has been refusing to take off her West Brom FC bobble hat on stage.'

Ricky and Amy were aghast, bordering on agog! They were also utterly speechless!

'I'm utterly speechless!' said Ricky.

'And so am I!' agreed Amy. 'Really *really* speechless! Do you think it's *her*? Do you Ricky? Hmm? Do you?'

Ricky was about to ask Andrew what the old lady looked like, but the boys had already disappeared. He turned to Amy.

'Tell me,' he said, 'when Uncle Quagmire told us he'd take care of Old Hag, do you think he actually did it?'

Amy looked quite puzzled, as usual. 'I don't know,' she whined.

'You don't know?'

'I don't know.'

'You look quite puzzled.'

'I do?'

'Yes, quite puzzled.'

'Oh.'

'It's irrefutable.'

'Irrefutable?'

'Yes, irrefutable.'

'Oh.'

'You were not a success, Amy.'

'Was I not?' *(Vacant look)*

'No, Amy.' *(Engaged look)*

'I had mislaid my glasses.'

'Don't lie. You don't wear glasses.' *(very long meaningful pause)* 'You're sweating.'

'I'm sweating?'

'Yes, you're sweating.'

'I was the belle of that ball.'

'You were.'

'Erm, hold on, what are we doing, Ricky?'

'I've no idea, Amy,' Ricky said, giving a great big shrug that seemed to go on for a long time. He pointed upwards. 'You-Know-Who gets carried away sometimes. He's into all that Pinteresque stuff, it seems.'

'You-Know-Who?' Amy asked. She looked up at the ceiling, frowned, then shook her head. 'Sometimes I can't keep up with it all,' she muttered. 'Weren't we talking about the sudden threat of a plot reversal, with the chance of Old Hag beating us to it?'

Ricky looked aghast, but with much less agogness this time. 'Of course!' he said. 'But what can we do?'

'What if we have a meeting?' Amy suggested. 'We haven't had one of those for ages.'

Ricky shook his head. 'Neither of us is equipped to call and facilitate meetings!' he moaned. 'It's inadequate succession planning, if you ask me.'

Amy didn't ask him.

'I said . . .' Ricky said.

'I know what you said,' said Amy. 'You said . . . erm . . . you said *inaccurate session planning, if you ask me*. I just chose not to ask you. And I don't see why we shouldn't have a meeting to get us out of this hole you've got us into. Boys! I tell you what, I'll make the decision this time. We'll go inside the Big Hall and join the audience, so we can see what happens and maybe experience the spectacular outcome of our wonderful adventure. Then we can go home and sleep. Can we take George home with us? Can we? Pleeeeease?'

Ricky tutted gently and pushed open the door. The two of them went through into the Big Hall. They were really surprised, as there were lots and lots of people!

'Gosh!' said Amy. 'I didn't realise that there were so many other people in the world! Did you?'

Ricky said that he did, but he'd heard that most other people weren't really that interesting. Not compared to them, anyway.

They found two empty seats on the end of the front row, and sat down and waited. When all the members of the audience had taken their seats and the volume of sweetie wrapper rustling was acceptably high, the curtains opened and the performance began. From the start, the play was a daring spectacle for the school to perform. It opened with a cornflakes advert and a lengthy confessional dialogue that had a rampaging vitality and a bouncing-ball talkalonga screen so that everyone could join in. The audience was soon experiencing a spiritual liberation through the powerful conflicting emotions and the liberal distribution of bags of Jelly Tots from the stage. Then the three members of *Bash!* came onto the stage to a tumultuous silence. Andrew and George clutched their guitars and waved to the audience in true rock star fashion before launching into their song. Amy noticed that Andrew had no strings on his guitar, but he enthusiastically plucked at thin air and made guitar sounds with his mouth.

Then, with breathtaking timidity, Sampson started his castanet solo. Both Amy and Ricky couldn't help but stare. He was quite an odd-looking boy for his height, and had mightily small ears for the size of his head. He certainly didn't look like a criminal mastermind who, as a career move, would want to dominate the world. Indeed, at times, he was having problems dominating his castanets, which kept flying out of his hands and clattering to the floor. He could easily have been mistaken for a blind castanet juggler.

Suddenly, given a subtle entrance cue from the prompter ('Are you deaf? It's your entrance, you old biddy!') the character Lulu entered from stage left, carrying a pack of cheese sandwiches. Amy and Ricky wanted desperately to gasp! It was indeed Old Hag, direct from her performance in 1964 Salzburg! She was dressed in a schoolgirl's outfit and her West Brom FC bobble hat.

'It *is* Old Hag!' whispered Amy.

'I can see that!' whispered Ricky. 'How on earth . . . ? Yeuk! That short skirt, it's disgusting! I feel sick! And what are all those blue squiggly lines on her legs.'

'I believe people catch them from being old,' whispered Amy. 'I think they're called various veins. But I don't understand how she and her various veins beat us here. It's not fair to our adventure!'

Ricky shushed her. 'Shush! Let's listen to the play. I've never seen a play before. Are they acting? It all seems so *real*.'

Several members of the audience, who didn't like all the shushing and whispering, shushed Ricky and whispered to each other how disgusting it was to go to a play and have people shushing and whispering all the time. Amy was also a bit put out by Ricky's shushing, and sank into her seat. She decided to keep a wary eye, or two, on Old Hag, using techniques that the highly informative Secret Five Intensive Surveillance Training Module had taught her, such as not falling asleep. This was, she knew, a highly important stakeout. Carefully she watched as the play continued.

| Meg: | I really want to play at something! |
| Goldberg: | Something? |

No-one speaks for fifteen seconds, just to embarrass the audience.

| Lulu: | What sort of something? |

Another long pause, as though the actors have forgotten their lines.

| Meg: | Any something. |
| Lulu: | Ha! I know! *(Pause)* Let's play sacking the castanet player! |

The members of the audience gasped in unison! They whispered amongst themselves and then shushed each other. Ricky looked at Amy in horror, then Amy looked at Ricky in horror. On stage, *Bash!* looked as though they would have liked a quick gasp as well. Old Hag, a.k.a. Lulu, appeared to be enjoying it, although the girl playing Meg looked very confused.

Meg:	Er . . . um . . . sack . . . the castanet player?
Lulu:	*(waving arm about)* Ha! Yes! He's worthless! Tell us, George and Andrew, is he any good? Tell us!
George:	Well, actually . . . no.
Andrew:	Er . . . I agree. He's pretty worthless.

Lulu: Then SACK HIM! Ha!

Lulu turns to the audience and encourages them to clap and chant.

        (clapping) Come on! Sack Sampson! Sack Sampson! Sack Sampson! Sack Sampson! Sack Sampson! Sack Sampson!

Led by Old Hag, the audience began to clap and chant. Ricky thought seriously about standing up and bravely stopping the utter madness, but found himself clapping and chanting as well! Plays were jolly good fun after all! He was beginning to enjoy himself!

'What *are* you doing?' Amy shouted at Ricky. 'Remember our super adventure? He will dominate the world if we're not totally effective! We were doing so well!'

'This is fun, Amy!' yelled Ricky. 'Come on, join in! Sack Sampson! Sack Sampson!'

Amy felt really grumpy. She looked up at Sampson on the stage. His face was red! He looked as if he was about to cry.

Sampson: Ah-guh . . . Ah-guh . . . eeeh-gag . . . gah . . . gah.

Amy leaned closer to Ricky and asked, 'What's he saying?'

Ricky stopped clapping and shrugged. 'I think he's having a fit and is about to turn into an evil mega-monster, due to the utter humiliation that we haven't been able to stop.'

'Good analysis,' said Amy. 'But stand up and take charge! You're the man . . . boy . . . whatever you are.'

Ricky suddenly felt quite important again. 'Yes! Yes I will!' he said. He stood up and, at the top of his very own voice, shouted, 'Stop! STOP!'

The audience immediately stopped clapping and chanting. Ricky felt quite powerful for a boy with his meagre talents.

Old Hag came shuffling to the front of the stage. 'Ha!' she

cackled, pointing a haggish finger at Ricky. 'Ricko! It's you! And you've failed in your secret mission! See how Sampson is turning! Look! Ha! I've beaten The Secret Five! Rejoice!'

'NO!' shouted Ricky in very stern capital letters. 'George, Andrew, you mustn't sack him! You need a castanet player to offset the effective pathos of the bass guitar and the precise intervallic construction of the chords!'

Amy was momentarily quite proud of Ricky, and looked up adoringly at what she still thought of as just an ugly stupid brother.

'That's true, yeah!' said Andrew from the stage. 'We *do* need a castanet player in the band.'

'What about Ricko!' shouted Old Hag, pointing at Ricky. 'He can play. He has rhythm. Not much else, but ha! who cares?'

'Great idea!' agreed George. 'He did say he could play. Cool! Come on up, man!' He turned and pointed to Sampson. 'And *you* can go. Leave the stage immediately, utterly humiliated and utterly embarrassed.'

'What?' cried Ricky.

'He said,' said Amy, rather helpfully, 'and you can go, leave the stage immediately, utterly humiliated and utterly embarrassed.'

Ricky couldn't believe his ears, eyes, nose or, while we're at it, that old wives tale about wearing a dried body of a frog in a silk bag around the neck in order to avert fits.

Quite suddenly, Sampson threw his castanets to the floor! 'You bastards!' he called. 'Especially YOU!' He pointed a small finger and a big glare at Ricky, who cringed with fright.

Amy nudged Ricky. 'Stop cringing with fright!' she said. 'And what does *bastard* mean? Can he say that? I don't think he can. It sounds quite rude.'

Ricky shook his head. 'Erm, Sampson,' he called. 'Can you call us all something else, please. We don't actually have that sort of language where we come from, you see. It's not in the constitution.'

'Sorry!' Sampson said. 'How about scamp?'

'Better,' said Ricky, after getting the nod from Amy.

Sampson retrieved his castanets, repositioned himself on stage, and threw them to the floor again. 'You scamp!' he yelled, again pointing at Ricky with his finger. '*You* have humiliated and disgraced me!' He skulked to the side of the stage. 'I'm really upset!' he said. 'I'm now going to skulk right off, and probably turn very evil. Very evil indeed!'

'Ha! That's my boy!' shouted Old Hag. 'The world needs more evility!'

'Thank you, Mummy,' said Sampson, strangely yet tenderly. 'I don't know why you are quite suddenly looking so old, but you're right. The world *needs* evility. And once I've had enough practice I might even try to dominate that very world!'

The audience applauded and cheered and called *oh no you won't*, as they thought it was all part of the play. Sampson obviously thought they were cheering his utter humiliation so he stormed off the stage, pausing only to glare an even bigger glare at Ricky.

'Right, he's gone,' George called down to Ricky. 'Come on up! Your castanets await you.'

Ricky looked quite confused. 'Erm, did *I* cause Sampson to turn evil just then?' he asked Amy.

Amy joined in with all the glaring at Ricky.

'Ricky!' Andrew called, walking to the edge of the stage and holding out his hand. 'Come on! You're in a band!'

'In a band? Cool!' said Ricky, instantly forgetting the calamity he had thrust upon the future world. He quickly clambered up onto the stage and grabbed the castanets. 'This is so cool! One minute I'm sitting in the audience, minding my own adventure, the next, WHAM! I'm in a band!'

George and Andrew raised their eyebrows at each other, not for the first or last time. Old Hag scuttled over to Ricky with her various veins and patted him on the back.

In the audience, Amy looked on in utmost amazement. She was also very bewildered! Not only had Sampson called Old Hag

Mummy, but he had turned evil after all their efforts, and their failure to stop his evilness was because Ricky could play the castanets and had taken his place in *Bash!*! The future of the world was again threatened! She wondered whether Betty, Daniel and Whatshisname would be able to save the world from where they were, or if they had been killed in a rather gruesome fashion by a surprise visit from a naked knife-wielding madman in a Victorian courthouse while the judge and several onlookers looked on helplessly! Although her wonderings were only a shot in the dark, only time and a turn of a page or two would tell if it were true!

PART FIVE

Chapter Thirty

In which Bertie needs consoling and suffers from Puberty; Daniel and Betty make an amazing discovery; well, maybe not that amazing; oh no?; no; oh, do you want to make anything of it?; now boys; there is a hint of intertextuality from HG Wells' books, but it may pass you by in your rush to get to the last page and put an end to this torture.

In the scullery of The Big House Whatshisname had waited patiently for many sticks while Betty and Daniel were in court. Under the table he was biding his time, ready to spring into action when the moment came to launch his daring rescue plan. He had bided the time by making sure that he licked himself sparkly clean. To be honest, time biding wasn't something that was of tremendously high importance to him. He suspected that canine history was littered with famous dogs that had bided their time and then ended up regretting it. He tried to think of famous dogs, apart from Pavlov's dog and Lassie, and couldn't, no matter how hard he tried to think. The knowledge gap made him feel inadequate. If only he had completed that MA in Modern Canine History at the red brick kennels. He sighed and carried on licking his bottom.

He reckoned that he had waited about five hundred and ninety sticks when he heard a commotion heading his way down the stairs. And he could hear voices! He paused mid-lick.

'Well, children,' a lady's voice said. 'It is so nice to have you back again. I was just in the kitchen deep frying some unfortunate dead pig's giblets, eyes and toenails. Come on, make yourselves comfortable in the scullery again. Your dog with her fluffy pink collar is still cowering under the table, if I am not sorely mistaken, as the aroma of creosote and pineapple still lingers.'

Her pink collar*! Cowering!* Whatshisname thought very quietly to himself: *I'll have you know I'm coiled like a spring, ready to launch my daring rescue attempt when the time is right!*

'Yes,' said the lady's voice as the lady's voice's face peeked under the table. 'She's still cowering.'

Then another peeking face appeared. It was Betty! Whatshisname sprang out, desperately disappointed that his rescue attempt would have to be put on ice for now, but so excited to see Betty that he licked and licked her face with the very same tongue that he had licked and licked his whiffy backside just a few seconds earlier. Lucky old Betty!

Then Whatshisname noticed that Daniel was also standing there! And, a little to the left of there, was Uncle Quagmire, dressed in a hastily-borrowed black suit and standing cautiously by the big scullery sink in the corner. Happily, his tail wagging and wagging, Whatshisname trotted over to Uncle Quagmire and joyfully sank his teeth into his ankle quite sharply. Uncle Quagmire kicked him.

Bertie, who had been lurking nearby all the time, scribbling notes in his Victorian note book, spoke to his mother. 'Mama,' he said, 'tell them about the surprise banquet! Please do!'

Mrs Wells smiled quite a big smile for such a small Victorian woman. 'If it will not slow down the narrative pace any more than it is already, it is a very good idea to tell them, young Bertie,' she agreed. She turned quite slowly to face the children but spoke quickly. 'We have prepared a handsome banquet to celebrate your successful release from custodial custody and your acquittal on all charges except Admitting Owning a Kangaroo without Due Regard for the Neighbours, for which you received the fittingly lenient sentence of a Suspended Apology. Now, I have planned that we will eat in the Squire's Dining Room and I have taken the liberty to invite a few special guests in your honour.'

'Gosh!' said Betty, suddenly overflowing with verbal extravagance.

'I've never had a banquet held in my honour before,' said Daniel. 'Will there be voluptuous serving wenches with . . .'

'No,' interrupted Mrs Wells quite firmly. 'And you, young man, should partake of a cold bath before you eat.'

'Can I sit by Betty?' Bertie enquired eagerly.

'Only if you all sit in alphabetical order,' his mother replied. 'And that's not very likely, is it now, unless I am made to change my mind and happen to suggest it later on.'

Then Uncle Quagmire stepped forward, very keen to take part in the narrative. 'Well well, Mrs Wells,' he said, 'I've heard all about your kindaciousness . . .'

'Kindaciousness?' asked Bertie.

'Yes,' confirmed Uncle Quagmire, frowning. 'Kindaciousness.'

'I like it!' said Bertie, strangely. He scribbled something in his note book.

Then Uncle Quagmire continued exactly where he left off – '. . . to these pathetic children and their horrid fat dog. You might have been mightily surprised at seeing me here, so I had better summarapsulate what has happened. Just for your benefit, of course.'

Bertie licked his pencil and scribbled some more.

'Of course,' Mrs Wells said, sidling up to Uncle Quagmire. 'Uncle Quagmire, tell us all what happened, please do. The story needs you at this time.'

'Well, erm,' Uncle Quagmire said, 'to be honest, I've never been very good at expositions and backstories.'

'Shall I do it then?' asked Betty eagerly, raising her hand. 'Let me! Oooh, I just *love* doing backstories!'

Uncle Quagmire looked quite relieved, but not as relieved as he was recently when he managed to travel urgently, with the Nixie digital clock, on his rescue mission from 1964 Salzburg to 1880 after hearing from Ricky and Amy all about what had happened with the wrong year then appearing rather dramatically and surprisingly naked in the doorway of the courtroom and causing an uproar by loudly and quite sternly demanding some immediate emergency clothes and the even more immediate release of Daniel and Betty and after a lot of arguing eventually persuading the grumpy old Magistrate that they were just two harmless insipid children from the twenty-first century who were merely trying to save the world from an evil mega-monster's grip (and yes he would gladly try to explain how SERPS operated but bodcasts and plogs were somewhat beyond him) before being hurrahed out of the courtroom and leading the two children through the throngs of cheering people which included the postman from chapter one who was particularly vocal in his mock-Victorian celebration but who still felt some degree of niggling discomfort from the bicycle saddle removal incident.

'Hang *on*!' squeaked Betty. 'I mean . . . what *is* the point of me explaining it all now?' She stamped her right foot in a severe fit of disgust, then turned to Daniel. 'I know now why Ricky walked off in chapter nine. Honestly!'

'Shall we walk off?' Daniel asked. 'I'm jolly well up for it if you are.'

'Ooooh, may I walk off with you?' enquired Mrs Wells.

'Woof woof woof?' said Whatshisname enthusiastically.

'Hold on everyone!' said Uncle Quagmire, very sternly. 'No walking off! Let me give you a grown-up perspectangle on this. You told me about the Squire and the fire, and it all sounds a bit dire, I fear. If you two walk out now, who's going to stop the disaster of the Squire's fire and save the world from the evil that is Sampson de Lylow? Only The Secret Five are trained to do that sort of thing, so I stand no chance of saving any world, do I? Especially with my dodgy knees.'

Daniel glanced at Betty, and Betty glanced at Daniel, until it was difficult to know who was glancing at whom. Whatshisname turned his head to look around for someone to glance at, couldn't find anyone, so he tried very hard to glance at himself.

'And,' continued Uncle Quagmire, ignoring all the mass

glancing, 'if my perfect judgment is correct yet again, Ricky and Amy won't have had much luck in 1980 with stopping Sampson from becoming evil. They will probably have experienced some major obstacle which will have a dramatic effect on how things have turned out. So we can't rely on them. As usual.'

Daniel leaned a little towards Uncle Quagmire. 'They are your own children, dear Uncle Quagmire,' he reminded him.

Uncle Quagmire looked slightly confused, but continued relentlessly. 'And there's no chance of *that* dog being able to do anything of importance to save mankind, is there? Not with a pink fluffy collar like that. And can someone tell me why he has quite suddenly gone cross-eyed?'

'Woof woof woof!!!' said Whatshisname.

'So you two children are going to have to stay here until the Squire's fire is quenchinguished,' said Uncle Quagmire. 'I will stay for a while, just to experience the Victorian way of life for a moment or two, and to be on hand for any sudden reversal in fortunes or the unexpected appearance of comely maids or Eccles Cakes.'

'Yes,' said Bertie. 'I'd really prefer it if you could all stay, as I have become quite attached to you.' He wandered over and stood by Betty. 'Especially you, Betty.' He lowered his voice a little. 'I was wondering if you would consider assisting me in my quest for a joyful adolescence.'

Betty looked shocked at his little lowered voice, and really quite embarrassed! She didn't know what to say!

'Really!' she said. 'I don't know what to say. Except . . . *you men are all the same! Leave me alone and if you dare mention my ample bosom I promise I will tear your testicles off with my bare teeth!*'

Bertie stepped back, quite alarmed! He glared at his feet a bit, then stamped off up the stairs. Daniel looked aghast, and began to blink a lot with his eyelids. Betty seemed to be even more embarrassed by her own sudden outburst, which went against all the formal Secret Five etiquette training. There was a long silence in the scullery as everyone looked at each other's feet, waiting for someone to say something of importance.

Whatshisname had reacted badly at the mention of tearing testicles off with bare teeth. He had tried to wipe the tears from his eyes with his paw without much success, but he decided that he would be the one to break the embarrassed silence. Good old reliable Whatshisname! 'Woof woof woof?' he said.

Everyone looked quite relieved. Mrs Wells seemed a little concerned about her son. 'Why don't you two children go and console young Bertie. He will, I surmise, be up in the Butler's bedroom. The Butler is away on an intensive Victorian Butlering Self-Improvement, Butler's Body Language and Presentation Skills course, so Bertie uses that room in which to mope, sulk, meditate, and play with himself. Now, Uncle Quagmire, if you please, you stay and help me unknot these pig's giblets.'

Betty and Daniel, with Whatshisname trotting behind them, made their way up the stairs. 'This is so exciting,' said Daniel as they found their way along a short, yet surprisingly long, moderately gloomy corridor. 'I've never been in a butler's bedroom before.'

'I'm glad to hear that, Daniel,' said Betty. As they walked down the corridor, it was becoming gloomier and gloomier.

'This all feels quite familiar,' said Daniel. 'Very strange indeed.'

Betty suddenly stopped and glared at Daniel. Whatshisname sat down at her feet and looked up at her. 'I told you, Daniel, didn't I?' Betty said. 'It's all about re-using locations, so stop pointing these things out! You're ruining the story.' She turned on her very own heels and hurried away down the moderately gloomy corridor. Whatshisname got up and pattered after her, followed by a rather glum Daniel.

'Look!' she called, having stopped by a door. 'It says *Butler's Bedroom*.'

Daniel sauntered up and stood by her side. 'But isn't this the room where . . .'

'Stop spoiling it!' scolded Betty. 'There's people out there who . . .'

'But . . .' began Daniel.

'And stop beginning!' said Betty. 'Nothing you can begin to say will be of any importance! Let's go inside and talk to Bertie.'

'But Betty,' said Daniel, 'if we were in this very room in this very house in the twenty-first century, it means it didn't burn down at all!'

'I told you . . .' Betty began to say as she reached for the doorknob.

'Now *you're* beginning,' observed Daniel, frowning.

Betty turned to face Daniel and his frown. 'Er . . . say all that again,' she said, her own brow wrinkling into what could only be described as a rather big matching frown.

Daniel's expression quickly went from slightly intelligent to very confused. He really felt like sucking the end of the curly bit of his spectacles, but didn't. 'I think I said,' he said, 'that if we were in *this* room in *this* house in the twenty-first century, it means . . . erm . . . that . . . erm, it didn't burn down after all?'

Betty stared at Daniel. She then stared at the door. 'So . . .' she began hesitantly.

Whatshisname looked up at her, wide-eyed, waiting for the elusive moment when some sort of realisation would emerge.

'So . . .' she began again.

Daniel shrugged. He had lost it now. 'Don't ask me,' he said. 'I've no idea what I meant.'

Whatshisname slumped down onto the floor. He decided to wait while they thought it through. Epiphanies were hard to come by these days, so he might as well make himself comfortable for a few sticks.

'So . . .' Daniel began.

'Yes, so . . .' Betty said.

They stood there for quite a while, until Daniel's frown disappeared behind his ears. 'Yes!' he said. 'If this room and this house are still the same room and house, then . . . then . . .'

'Yes?' urged Betty.

Whatshisname yawned and passed a thimbleful of noxious hell-gas.

'Then,' said Daniel, 'the house didn't burn down!'

Whatshisname sighed and looked up at them.

Betty looked at Daniel, and her own big frown also disappeared behind her own ears. 'Then we can go home? And does this mean that Sampson isn't threatening the world now?'

Daniel had lost it again. 'I don't know,' he moaned. 'Why can't we be given some degree of intelligence? Is it too much to ask?'

Whatshisname sighed yet again and settled his head down.

'I think this door is the very same door!' said Betty, studying the very same door. 'So that means . . . that means that there was no fire!'

Daniel's face lit up, which was quite a good trick but not advisable under the circumstances. 'So the Squire didn't emigrate!' he said. 'So Bartle and Clarissa didn't do the conception thing! And Sampson doesn't exist! We can go home then! We've done it! We've saved the world!'

Betty nodded her head fairly slowly. 'I think so.'

'And what is more important is that I thought of it first!' Daniel said. 'It's all quite exciting and will look absolutely brilliant on my CV, should I ever want to join our competitors.'

'Saving the world wasn't much of an effort, it must be said,' said Betty. 'We didn't exactly have to outwit a gang of ruffians after getting tied up and left to rot in a dirty barn until rescued by our faithful dog, did we?'

'Woof woof woof?' Whatshisname said.

'But we can go home now?' asked Daniel.

'I suppose so,' Betty said, frowning ever so slightly. 'But only after the celebration meal. It would be quite rude to miss that, wouldn't it, as all historical epics need one. And we do have to sort out some Brussels sprouts and a portal and the digital clock. And we had better see if Bertie is all right. I feel awful about not giving him a hand with his quest for a joyful adolescence.'

Daniel opened his mouth to say something when the Butler's Bedroom door opened a little, and there was Bertie's peering face!

'I thought it was you,' his peering face said. 'I could sense all the frowning and I could smell the heady aroma of creosote and pineapple.' He looked sheepishly at Betty. 'Can I apologise for my forwardness in a moment of sheer madness down in the scullery. It was merely the crystallisation of all my unbearable mounting puberty. And I was touched by your countenance, the sheer unadulterated beauty of your lips half-open and almost misty in their pallid quivering, and your eyes full of futurity, and of course your ample bosoms which compel an unendurable excitement . . .'

'Er, *hello*!' interrupted Daniel. 'Could we talk about something else, please? What *is* the matter with everyone? What have the standards and principles of The Secret Five come to?'

'Sorry, Daniel,' said Bertie, opening the door wide. 'I am being quite feeble. Come on in. But did you like my turn of phrase? Not bad for a Victorian middle-class child, eh? Do you think I would make an author? That is what I would like to be, I think. Perhaps I should apply for the position of the Founding Father of Science Fiction. It would be much more exciting than silly old drapery.'

Daniel, understandably, was unsure of what exactly an author did, apart from forcing people to do things they didn't want to do, and silly old drapery sounded a little odd for a boy's hobby, but he nodded his head in agreement as it was much easier than shaking it.

'I think we are supposed to take you to the Dining Room for the banquet,' said Betty as they stepped into the bedroom. 'But we have just made a discovery that means . . .' She stopped, unsure if she should share their discovery.

Bertie frowned quite a good frown, a result of several recent hours of practice, but not quite up to Secret Five standard, as his whole face all the way down to his chin seemed to get puckered. Betty and Daniel decided that they would never frown again if that's what it looked like, and as a result they thought that they could hear distant cheering.

'You can tell me,' Bertie said. 'I'm a member, remember? You share your exciting discovery with me and I'll share mine with you. Oh, by the way, forgive the rather strange lighting in here, and excuse the blatant foreshadowing, but the Squire is experimenting with these new Paraffin Lamps.'

'Gosh!' exclaimed Daniel. 'They look quite dangerous.'

'Yes,' agreed Betty, sighing.

Meanwhile, Whatshisname, without a by-your-leave, had sneaked into the Butler's Bedroom. He sniffed around the room. It was slightly unnerving for him to pick up his own scent four hundred million sticks in the future, and then he began to ponder deeply on whether it was a sign that was meant to point him in the direction of the true meaning of canine life, or whether it was just a sign that he needed a jolly good bath. Either way, he knew deep down that this moment was merely a blip in the course of the cosmos. He'd wondered lately about such things – creation, dualism, reincarnation, distemper. Indeed, he suspected that he was a re-embodiment of the respected thinker Zenan of Athens, as he embraced the same ancient philosophy that apathy is the way to happiness, and that mental and transcendental tranquillity is only achieved through the joyful celebration of utter mediocrity. Utter mediocrity, if worked at, is the ultimate accomplishment, he knew that, of course. He had also pondered hard on the theories of the creation of the universe, going right back to The Big Woof, which always brought him back to the same big question – why on Earth did he have these never-ending bouts of flatulence? There it goes again! Oops! He tried his very best to look blameless as he sank down onto the carpet and closed his eyes.

Bertie, meanwhile, was becoming enthralled at the children's story of time travel. He asked them all sorts of questions about the twentieth century, most of which they couldn't answer. 'So, have men landed on the moon?' he asked, wrinkling his nose and glancing at Whatshisname as the transcendental fragrance wafted over him.

'We think so,' said Betty uncertainly. 'It's not something we are supposed to know, really, but we think they did.'

'I think they landed in some kind of contraption,' said Daniel. 'I sneaked a look at a picture of it in a magazine. It looked jolly well like a sort of round and metal thing. I think.'

'And is there social chaos?' Bertie asked as he scribbled something in his note book.

Betty and Daniel looked at each other and shrugged. 'We don't really know,' said Daniel.

'I did hear someone on the radio,' said Betty helpfully, 'talking about social chaos, so maybe there is and we don't know it.'

'I do not know what *ray-dio* means, or even how to spell it, obviously, but I will assume that there is plenty of social chaos,' said Bertie quite firmly. He scribbled something else in his Victorian notebook.

Just then, thank goodness, they were interrupted by Mrs Wells calling to them. 'Weird time-travelling children and their ugly fat dog,' she called. 'The guests have arrived. Come along and eat before infant mortality strikes. Your watercress and pig's trotter soup will be congealing.'

'We had all better go to the Dining Room,' said Bertie. 'I fear that her guests might become rather agitated if we are late. If my estimates are correct, we will need to pass through a chapter break to reach there. This is so exciting! My first chapter break! I must make a note of how it goes!'

Chapter Thirty One

In which Whatshisname meets a new friend; we meet another Mrs Wells, no relation; yes, it is very confusing; we learn about the Canine Alphabet; invasive medical procedures are mentioned; is this chapter far too long? probably, so pour that glass of wine before you start; Betty accidentally slaughters several other characters.

To be honest, young Bertie Wells was quite disappointed with the chapter break experience. He expected something more of a literary epiphany, of which a chapter break fell far short. He knew he could do better, and no doubt would.

Daniel and Betty followed Bertie into the Dining Room. 'Gosh!' exclaimed Betty excitedly. 'I can see why it has capital letters now!' Daniel was also quite excited but couldn't be bothered to exclaim. He looked at the large round mahogany table, the impressive marble fireplace and the stuffed black poodle sitting upright on the hearth. He watched as Whatshisname trotted gingerly over to the poodle and sniffed around it.

The poodle had an indescribable taint of death about it, which reminded Whatshisname of Victor Hugo's intensely fresh writing in which he suggested that *nous sommes tous condamnés à mort avec des sursis indéfinis*, although, to be fair, Whatshisname did initially mistake the indescribable taint for lavender mothballs. He sat down and looked the poodle straight in the eyes. In an effort to establish himself as the dominant member of the pack, he drew himself to his full width and said, 'Woof woof woof!' rather firmly. The black poodle didn't move a muscle, a sign that either Whatshisname's dominance had been quickly and overwhelmingly established, or the poodle's muscles had been unceremoniously ripped from its body and replaced with Victorian cotton wool soaked in black treacle.

Meanwhile, Daniel and Betty were busy looking around them, but taking care not to look too busy. 'There's lots of candles in here,' whispered Betty to Daniel. 'Do you *really* think the danger of a fire is over?'

'Of course,' reassured Daniel, secretly hoping to help set up another literary foreshadowing and therefore cement his place as a major character should a trilogy be on the cards.

Just then, Betty started. 'Oh, no! I've started!' she said. 'And all because that awful grumpy Magistrate is standing over there! Look!'

And Betty was right! The awful grumpy Magistrate was indeed standing over there! And he was talking to the Parson and the Policeman! Standing near them were a stern-looking gentlemen, who was smoking a big cigar, and an old lady, who wasn't. The stern-looking gentleman's dapper appearance, his expensive cigar, and his shiny silver watch chain suggested that he was of immensely good breeding, but the finger up his nose suggested that he was not.

'Yo!' said Daniel for no reason whatsoever.

But before the children had time to arrange an extraordinary meeting to decide what to do next, Mrs Wells scuttled into the room with a tray full of soup bowls. 'Sorry for the scuttling,' she said. 'It was totally out of my control. Now, sit yourselves down in strict alphabetical order, then I will introduce the children to the stern-looking gentlemen with a cigar and the old lady who is without a cigar. After that, I will take my leave and attend to the main course before all the pig's blood boils away to nothing. Your Uncle Quagmire may or may not join us as soon as he has finished his verbal intercourse with Alice the mysterious maid, recovered from his cocaine-fuelled frenzy, and then completed his long-overdue ablutions.'

'Yo, minty!' said Daniel. 'I'z could slide off and cut sling load summink fierce meself! Random! Innit!'

Betty turned to look at Daniel, who was now murmuring and staring at the ceiling. Not only did she not understand exactly where Uncle Quagmire was and what he was doing, and was confused by the mention of yet another Victorian character, Alice, but she realised that Daniel was now extremely nervous at seeing all these people. She feared the worst! 'I fear the worst,' she whispered to Bertie.

'Cosmic cataclysm?' whispered Bertie excitedly. 'Mass social disorder? A world of abominable desolation where the sun has lost its energy? An incessant array of talentless boy bands?'

Betty scowled. 'No,' she snapped back rather too snappily. 'It's more serious. Daniel's slipping into a street-talk coma again. I must have a quiet word with him about it, or slap him seriously hard.'

'Attention everyone,' called Mrs Wells before Betty could indulge in some serious slapping or quiet wording. 'I now realise – and, after all, someone has to – that you cannot sort yourselves into alphabetical order and sit down until I name these new characters. Children, there are quite a lot of characters in this scene, so pay much attention, if you will be so kind. You already know the grumpy Magistrate, the Policeman and the Parson.' She pointed at the stern-looking gentleman. 'This new male character, this stern-looking gentleman, a man of forbidding aspect to be sure, is Mr Ramekin. He is an off-duty Victorian Child Brain Doctor, reasonable rates assured, indifferent bedside manner guaranteed at all times, and quite a dish if you ask me. But, between you and me, empirical sciences, especially this new-fangled science of inner conscious experience, confuse me greatly and get right up my typical Victorian nose, so they do.'

Mr Ramekin frowned a learned yet silly frown at Mrs Wells, then nodded grimly at the children. He continued to pick his nose quite energetically. 'I like to call myself a *Psychologist*. I've no idea what psychology is, yet, but I understand that the Germans are very keen to export it and I just want to be ahead of my time.'

He examined the end of his finger for the results of his intensive nostril drilling and licked his lips in anticipation.

'Oh no!' whispered Betty. 'A child psychologist! Daniel, I should sneak out now if I were you.'

'And this old woman,' called Mrs Wells, pointing to the old woman who was dressed in a typically Victorian long black dress and a shawl, 'who, may I confirm, is dressed in a typically Victorian long black dress and a shawl, is Mrs Wells. She's not related, just a friend of the family. She's old and always keen to partake of a free meal.'

'Ah!' cackled the older Mrs Wells, her wrinkly old face wrinkling at them all. 'That's no lie, 'tis sure that I do, / through bell-swarmèd bird-charmèd branches of yew.'

Betty and Daniel were quite astounded!

'Yo, Sis,' said Daniel, waving a hand about like a demented rapper. 'Dis am nuts and a half, f'sho! A versemonger, innit? Minty! Cool!'

Bertie leaned towards Betty, his pen in his hand. 'I don't think I'll make notes about Daniel, if you don't mind,' he said. 'And shouldn't it be *elder* Mrs Wells?'

Betty shrugged both her shoulders but, in truth, she was intrigued by the appearance of another Mrs Wells. 'Excuse me everyone,' she said, raising her hand in an intriguing manner. 'Can I say that we now have *two* Mrs Wells. It's bad enough with Betty and Bertie, now it's even more confusing for everyone. And why does *that* Mrs Wells,' – she pointed at Mrs Wells' old and unrelated friend of the family – 'talk like that? And why does she sound a bit like Old Hag? Hmmm?'

Everyone started to murmur to each other about the poor standard of characterisation, except Whatshisname of course, who was still trying to outstare the stuffed poodle and desperately attempting to recall his early training, in particular the chapter of *Canine Behaviour for Dummies* that gave helpful hints on Dominance Over Inanimate Objects.

'Cease all this murmuring!' boomed the Magistrate quite suddenly. 'It is very similar to being back in petty sessions, except I do not have the benefit of being able to despatch you all to the gallows for Unlicenced Murmuring. God knows, if it were not for the appearance fee I would not be here. Now, far from being eager to agree with such an unseemly Urchin, I declare that I would also like to know why *that* Mrs Wells talks in that silly way.' He pointed his best Magistrate's finger at the older Mrs Wells.

'Yea verily,' said the Parson, 'and so would I.'

'Ah,' cackled Older Mrs Wells, pointing her own finger at the Magistrate. 'For 'tis men that fall lightly upon their words, / that mock their breath 'til 'ere the . . . 'ere the . . . erm, birds?'

'Cool beans!' sniggered Daniel. 'Jus' snag tha' wicked versifying, Vickies!'

'Please!' said Mrs Wells the Younger. 'Older Mrs Wells is on a short holiday here with us, so your forbearance is requested. She is Poet-in-Residence at the local workhouse, the Ian McMillan of our time, that I do know for sure.'

'Wait a Victorian moment!' Constable Landscape said. He stepped forward and brandished his Policeman's truncheon at Older Mrs Wells. 'I now recognise you as the Local Workhouse Poet-in-Residence! Haven't I arrested you several times for Aggravated Behaviour?'

'Ah!' said Older Mrs Wells, quite bravely wrinkling her face at the Policeman. She then spoke in one of those intensely irritating poets' voices that is supposed to convey angst and torment but usually sounds as though they have some sort of uncontrollable bowel-tightening condition only brought on by stanzas of limping iambics and Terza Rima. 'My innocence is broad, like a wingèd blade, / 'til the breath of time has passed its best, / 'til the fickle quenching spirit of maid, / Hath shadowed my eternal beating . . . er, beating . . . er . . .'

She raised her eyebrows and looked around for inspiration.

'Hmmm, how about *breast*?' suggested the Parson.

'Breast?' queried Betty. 'Just one?'

'For now,' confirmed the Parson. 'It rhymes with best, you see.'

Constable Landscape stepped forward again and seemed quite keen to establish his Policeman's authority. 'I have quite a lot of Policeman's authority building up,' he said, 'and would ask you to stop all this talk of, um, those things, if you please. Now, Mrs Wells?'

'Yes,' said both Mrs Wells together.

'See!' said Betty. 'I told you that it would be too confusing.'

'Hush, Urchin,' boomed the Magistrate. 'Let the well-meaning but incompetent constable have his say. Then we can all eat, or go and enjoy a damn good hanging.'

Constable Landscape stepped forward yet again, but then had to step backwards as he had stepped forward so many times in the narrative that he was now almost out of the room. He stopped stepping backwards and reached out to grab Older Mrs Wells by one of her free arms. He cleared his Policeman's throat and spoke. 'Older Mrs Wells, I hereby arrest you for Aggravated Arson.'

'Arson?' gasped everyone except the Policeman, Older Mrs Wells, Whatshisname and the stuffed black poodle.

'Wooooof?' breathed Whatshisname, still staring intently at the black poodle and not wanting to be left out of any mass gasping.

'Yes, Arson, of the Aggravated kind!' said Constable Landscape. 'You have a record of criminal tendencies to set fire to things without sufficient warning and without a Proper Licence and, while we are at it, to greatly overuse alliteration and internal rhymes in your poetic works. I want to make these Victorian streets safe for Victorians to walk down – or up – at night, and for readers of Victorian poetry to feel unintimidated by a surfeit of aural effects.'

'Gah! Cool!' said Daniel, still overawed by the mass of characters crammed into one scene. 'Scoot de mean bitch off t'clink, baconman!'

The Psychologist looked at Daniel with an interested yet semi-professional expression.

'Aha!' cackled Older Mrs Wells as she wrenched herself free from the Policeman's grip. She looked across the room at Betty. 'Any chance of me doing a dramatic monologue at this stage?' she asked.

'Why ask me?' asked Betty.

'Because you probably have the ear of the author, that's why!' snapped Older Mrs Wells.

Betty thought for a moment, then said, wisely, 'No. No monologue. Dramatic or otherwise. Sorry.'

Older Mrs Wells shrugged her shoulders in a poetic manner.

'Very interesting,' said the Psychologist, studying Betty with his Psychologist's eyes and relieved to be allocated some dialogue at last. 'By the way,' he added, glancing at Whatshisname, 'I do amateur taxidermy on the side. The poodle is my work. Good, do you not think? A matching pair would certainly be quite something. I could leave the pink collar on, as dispensation. I could also reposition some of her surplus fat, or make a puppy or two out of it. A family group, if you will.'

'Woof woof woof!!!' said Whatshisname, his eyes still fixed on the poodle.

Mrs Wells the Younger had placed a bowl of soup at each of the place settings and a big bone on the floor for Whatshisname. She was eager to have everyone seated around the Squire's large ornate dining table.

'I'm eager,' she said with a sigh, 'and it's about time too, to have everyone seated around the Squire's large ornate dining table. In strict alphabetical order, if you please.'

'I think,' the Magistrate said, 'we should let Older Mrs Wells join us and eat, before being arrested and tried and hung by the neck until quite dead. Let her enjoy this splendid celebration banquet, which every good epic historical novel should have, then you can do what you like with her, Constable Landscape.'

There was a murmur of agreement amongst the gathered characters. The next few minutes were spent sorting out where everyone was seated. Bertie and Betty were sure that, alphabetically, they were sitting next to each other until Older Mrs Wells told them her first name was Bessie. Further confusion was caused by the fact that the Magistrate and the Psychologist, quite remarkably, had exactly the same names – Dugdale Algernon Quintin Neckrash.

Someone then suggested that everyone should sit in alphabetical order according to their occupation. This, however, caused problems with Betty, Daniel and Bertie, as they were all Children (although Daniel and Betty were sub-categorised as Urchins), so they had to go back to the original idea. After some discussion, the problem was solved by the Psychologist sitting on the Magistrate's lap.

During all this time, Whatshisname had completed the task of establishing dominance over the stuffed black poodle. He looked on, totally enthralled by this aspect of human behaviour, as everyone sorted themselves out alphabetically. Quietly and quite secretly, he thanked his lucky stars for the numerical advantage of the Official Canine Alphabet, which consisted of only eleven letters: s, i, t, a, y, f, e, tch, w, oo, f. For the life of him he could not think of any reason for needing any more than that.

Eventually, after all the exhausting pondering, he trotted over to the table and flopped down at Betty's feet, where he decided to doze for a few sticks while everyone noisily sipped their pig's blood and watercress soup.

'Tell everyone about your time travel,' Bertie suggested to Betty and Daniel.

'Yo,' said Daniel. 'Iz fully sick! It's absofrickinlutely gah! Innit!'

'Is he of right mind?' asked Mr Ramekin the Psychologist from his position on the Magistrate's lap. He studied Daniel over his Victorian spectacles, which he had suddenly acquired through a literary loophole. 'Or is he from some far flung country?' He put

down his soup spoon and leaned forwards towards Daniel. 'D o
y o u u n d e r   s t a n d m e , Ch i l d ?' he said slowly.

'He is *quite* English and perfectly normal – almost – thank
you Mr Ramekin, sir,' said Betty, in defence of her brother. 'It's
just that when he gets very nervous he sometimes talks like that.
It's all these people, you're scaring him. Usually we just slap him
and he recovers.'

'Of course. I remember now. Slapping is a good idea,' said the
Magistrate, pushing the Psychologist aside. He rubbed his hands
together eagerly, which was quite a dangerous thing to do given
the incendiary risks. 'Allow me.'

'Gentlemen!' admonished Mrs Wells the Younger as she came
back into the room bearing a large silver dish on which rested a
dead pig's head with a banana in its mouth. 'I would ask you all to
respect the Squire's house, and to respect these two poor time
travellers who have travelled wide and far in order to save their
modern world. Or so they say.'

'Yo, woo-man,' said Daniel. 'I'z well amped, chocca wid
dubble-yoo-emm-dee, no sheet, innit.'

Encouraged by all the creative talk, Older Mrs Wells stood up
and started waving a hand in an intensely arty fashion. 'Yea, tho'
they melt our molten hearts, / Apart from thy holy soul do I depart,
/ And crush the crumbling cradle . . .'

'*Please* can I arrest her now? She could accidentally fall down
the stairs?' pleaded Constable Landscape.

The Parson said grace, which consisted of thanking the Lord
for giving them their daily bread, while slipping in a quick plea for
added strength to withstand the temptations of the flesh and the
revolutionary *What The Butler Saw* machine in the vestry. As they
all tucked into their quite lovely meal, accompanied by several
bottles of pre-blessed red wine which the Parson had borrowed
from the church, the Psychologist seemed very keen to ask the
children about time travel. 'Do you have any proof that you are
indeed Time Travellers?' he enquired.

'Bah! I've already asked them for proof,' scowled the Magistrate. 'All I got was talk of Eminems.'

'Whatever!' said Daniel and he gulped a mouthful of wine from his glass. 'Eminem is sick and a half! He chills like a villain, man!'

Older Mrs Wells leaned forward and, with a flourish of her hands, said, 'Ah, villains are quickly undone, / they shine like blades anon, / but wear a smudge of brown, / that ends beneath their crown.'

The Psychologist was becoming quite agitated. 'Those two,' he said, pointing at Daniel and Older Mrs Wells, 'I would dearly like to perform some invasive medical experiments on them. But first, young lady Urchin, I have to ask, could I join The Secret Five? I could be your Resident Medical Man, on call, day and night, limb amputation my speciality, even when not needed, although on reflection I did fail that part of the entrance exam.'

Betty shook her head. 'In truth,' she said, 'I don't think we need a medical man. Do we, Daniel?'

'Yo! On de boss, Captain Obvious!' Daniel said to Betty, slopping some more red wine into his glass. 'Dis am crunk! Innit!'

Betty scowled at him. 'Sorry, Daniel,' she said.

Daniel looked bewildered and a teeny bit drunk. 'Hey, sis,' he said, waving his glass of wine at her. 'Why de polo pony, innit?'

Betty smiled and slapped him rather hard. Daniel put his wine down and rubbed his face.

'Is it my turn now?' asked the Magistrate, eagerly rolling up his sleeve.

'Gosh!' said Daniel, his eyes crossing as he tried to focus. 'Where am I?'

'You are indeed with friends,' said the Psychologist rather too fervently for a man with his Victorian hairstyle. 'And, boy Urchin, if I may have a talk with you later about the possibility of certain invasive procedures . . .'

* * *

Under the table, Whatshisname lifted his head and sniffed the air. *Woof woof woof?* he thought. He got up, picked up his bone for safekeeping, padded over to the door and poked all of his nose out into the corridor. He could definitely smell smoke! He glanced back into the room. No-one else seemed to have noticed, not even the black poodle, which was probably good news as it meant that he could impress it even more. Black poodles like nothing better than a heroic spaniel.

But what was he to do? He'd once sneaked a look at a film called *Lassie Saves the Day Yet Again* while the children were watching it one lazy Saturday afternoon between adventures. *What would Lassie have done*, he thought very quietly and only to himself. He weighed up his options. He could: (s) run about frantically barking; (i) whine a bit; (t) clamp his jaws around Betty's wrist and drag her into the corridor; (a) save himself and run for his life. He was about to opt for a commonsense combination of (s) and (a) when he quite suddenly decided that he definitely needed to impress the black poodle. New option (y) sprang to his canine mind and back out again. Glancing back at the black poodle to make sure its eyes were still wide open and able to see the launch of his daring new plan, he raced out of the door and tore off down the corridor, the bone in his mouth and his nose twitching madly as it followed the smell of smoke.

All of a heroic sudden he stopped outside the Butler's Bedroom. The door was strangely ajar, and he could see strange smoke billowing about dangerously inside the room! Now that he was out of sight of the black poodle, options (s) and (a) once again became his definite favourite. But Whatshisname was quite inquisitive for a dog of his size, and decided to poke his head around the door for a quick peek (two words, incidentally, that conjured up hazy memories of a hastily-grabbed opportunity behind a tree in a park many many sticks ago).

He saw that the bedspread was on fire, and the flames were in danger of reaching the curtains! He dropped the bone in shock!

Not only was he in shock, but it was a perfect place for a chapter break!

And yet, a chapter break didn't materialise. So, with little heed for his own safety, Whatshisname raced out of the Butler's Bedroom and headed for the exit, pausing to cock his leg up an aspidistra in the corner in readiness for a very long-overdue canine wee, made even more urgent by the excitement of the promise of a chapter break. But a thought suddenly struck him as he did so, and the plucky dog lowered his leg and turned on his pads. He headed straight back into the Butler's Bedroom for, in his haste, he had forgotten his bone! Bones (and, for that matter, peanut butter) were extremely hard to come by in this story, he had found, and the last thing he wanted was for that bone to be wasted in a disastrous fire.

Carefully, and quite cautiously, he padded into the bedroom again. The bedspread was still smoking! He went to grab the bone but then some primeval instinct, or the fact that he was now very *very* desperate for a wee, made him cock his leg up again and wee for a very long time all over the bedspread! Heaven!

There was a hissing and spitting as the flames were extinguished. He looked on, leg cocked, as the flames disappeared! How strange!

Thanks to Whatshisname, the danger of a disastrous Victorian fire was over! He had saved the world!

Or had he?

Chapter Thirty Two

In which Whatshisname is disappointed, again, but takes advantage of a wine-spill to drown his canine sorrows; Daniel becomes uncommonly persuasive then kills the kangaroo as it makes a guest appearance; there is a mildly interesting discussion about dado rails, of all things.

Whatshisname trotted enthusiastically back to the Dining Room, his precious bone in his semi-precious mouth. In the doorway he paused to await the applause and, perhaps, the offer of a whole year's supply of peanut butter on the house. But, to his dismay, everyone was still talking and eating. They hadn't even noticed him return! He glanced at the stuffed black poodle on the hearth. Nothing! Not even a wink.

He heard Betty call his name. Full of hope, yet devoid of significant amounts of faith and charity, he trotted over to her. 'Where have you been?' she scolded. 'Sit in a servile manner at my feet! Naughty boy for going off like that!'

Whatshisname slumped down at her feet. That was positively the first and last time he would put his life in danger! Honestly! Humans! Natural selection had a lot to answer for. He'd teach them. He closed his eyes and, in the space of a few seconds, proved that flatulence can time-travel.

'So,' the Policeman said in a rather stern Policeman's voice, 'I could hardly believe my own Policeman's ears when you said that there would be a disastrous fire while we are banqueting here. I am hence, and possibly henceforth, keeping an eye on *that* Mrs Wells, should she leave the table on the pretext of, erm, excusing herself, and forthwith undertaking a serious bout of Arson under our very Victorian noses.'

'Weeeellll,' said Betty uncertainly, and wasting several letters e and l in the process, 'we do have reason to believe that the fire might not actually happen, but we don't know why it won't happen. It's just that we were actually in this house in the twenty-first century and so Daniel and I had an informal meeting and came to the conclusion that it couldn't have burned to the ground. Isn't that right, Daniel?'

'Yes,' said Daniel, in a totally inadequate effort to show everyone that he was English and Normal, which is a pretty rare condition. He took another quick swig of wine.

'Well, I know I am a mere Child, but I think that these two are true heroes,' offered Bertie. 'Obviously, were it not for Betty and Daniel's presence, the disastrous fire would surely have taken place.'

'Woof woof woof?' said Whatshisname quietly but hopefully.

Just then there was an unexpected commotion from outside the room. There was a meaningful pause as people waited to see who would speak first about the unexpected commotion.

'And what is all that unexpected commotion that I hear, yea verily?' the Parson eventually said. 'This is really testing our Victorian forbearance, patience, kindness and generosity to the limit. And yet, given the desperately simple plot structure, I am deeply surprised that there are any commotions at all.'

Everyone watched carefully as the cause of the commotion, Mrs Wells the Younger, came back into the Dining Room. She was followed closely by a tall handsome man of about thirty-two-and-a-half years of age, dressed very smartly in some clothes of his own choosing. They were chatting, which hardly counted as a commotion, but times were hard.

'Why, Squire de Lylow!' bellowed the Magistrate, throwing the Psychologist off his lap and rushing over to shake the tall handsome man's hand.

The tall handsome man looked around the table. His eyes, which looked quite tired after all the travelling, rested on Betty. 'Good Lord!' he said.

'Indeed,' said the Parson.

'Never mind those,' urged Mrs Wells the Younger. 'These two dear children are the time travellers I just told you about, the moment you returned from London, only a few minutes ago. I also begged your forgiveness for the audacity of arranging a banquet, which I have explained to you, about which you were in agreement entirely.' She smiled, happy that she had so succinctly completed her expositional task.

'Gosh!' said Betty, staring at the man. 'You must be Squire de Lylow. You're really handsome and charming, you know, for a Squire.'

'Yes, I know,' said the Squire, nodding his handsome charming head in agreement. 'But enough, for now, of my rugged good looks and my innate charm, for Mrs Wells the Younger here informs me that you have single-handedly prevented a disastrous fire at my House.'

'Ah! 'ere comes the Sire,' said the Older Mrs Wells as grandiloquently as she could through a mouthful of roasted pig's giblets, '/ through bright boroughs / and stippled attire, / with brow a'furrowed . . .'

The Policeman brandished his truncheon again at Older Mrs Wells. 'Stop all that unsolicited poetry!' he said sternly. She wrinkled her old brow, and stopped it. Appreciative poetry audiences were hard to come by, even in Victorian times.

The handsome Squire came over to the table as Daniel was busy filling his wine glass. 'This celebration banquet is surely well deserved,' he said to the children. 'Not that I believe in all this time travel nonsense, but Mrs Wells, my trusty Upper Housemaid, is one to be greatly humoured at all times, I find, due to her tendency to blackmail me over certain indiscretions which, of course, are unfounded yet are, interestingly, of a carnal nature. I mean, I hardly knew the ladies in question.'

'Erm, please sire,' said Daniel, now recovered from his relapse but showing signs of becoming even more inebriated. 'We – me and Betty – are from another planet – no, I mean from another time – hic – really we are! I can't remember for the life of me from where – but we are – I'm sure.'

'Yes, sir,' agreed Betty, aiming a silent frown in Daniel's direction. 'And we *do* know all about your disastrous fire, the one that now seems not to have happened.'

'What I find most confusing,' said the Squire, 'is why you are so concerned about this notion of a fire, of all things?'

Just then, Older Mrs Wells jumped up, causing all attention to be directed at her. 'Ah!' she cried in the same insufferably didactic poets' voice. 'Would I not be keen to wait and tarry, / But to pluck myself away from thee, / Alas there is a need to hurry, / I am bereft, I need to go and pee.' And with that she scurried out of the room, clutching her long black Victorian dress around her short white Victorian legs.

Betty was suddenly quite worried. 'I'm quite worried,' she confirmed to Daniel.

Daniel tried hard to focus his gaze on Betty. 'And me,' he replied, reassuringly. 'Because other people keep drinking the wine! S'not fair! It's rather scrummy, don't you think? A bit like Ribena with a kick. No more ginger beer for me from now on.' He leaned over and grabbed at a full bottle of wine from right under the nose of the Parson!

Betty was astonished at his unseemly behaviour! 'I am sorry for his conduct, Mr Parson, sir,' she said. 'Daniel!' She grabbed Daniel's arm but, as she did, the bottle toppled over! Red wine gurgled onto the table and dripped onto the floor.

'Sis! Huh! Look what you've done!' moaned Daniel, pointing at the wine spill.

'Urchins!' bellowed the Magistrate, aiming his bellow directly at them. 'Stop this unnecessary behaviour or I will have you back in my court before you can say final convulsion!'

But Daniel was far too busy scooping wine from the table into his glass.

'Sorry, sir,' said Betty. 'Please forgive my brother. He had a difficult birth, apparently, and the effects have lingered.'

'Fascinating,' said the Psychologist.

Betty looked around the room. Older Mrs Wells, the Poet / Arsonist, was still nowhere to be seen!

Bertie leaned towards Betty. 'I do not like to interfere with the operational tactics of The Secret Five, but should you not be vigilant and meticulous about the whereabouts of Older Mrs Wells? Or maybe you should have a meeting? I could take notes if you like.'

Betty frowned. She had to take immediate decisive action! Everyone looked at her, awaiting her immediate decisive decision. After a few minutes of looking, most people became quite bored and started to chat amongst themselves about the indecisiveness of Victorian Urchins.

Whatshisname, still lying at Betty's feet, opened an eye when he heard a *drip drip drip* sound. The open eye saw some sort of red liquid forming a puddle close to his head. He opened the other eye. He lifted his head. Was it blood? Had there been a massacre while he had dozed for a few sticks? Maybe he was the only living member of The Secret Five now! What an opportunity! He'd be able to redefine the constitution to introduce special rules, like increased rest and recuperation time, and more efficient logistics for the supply of peanut butter and bones.

Then again, no, a massacre was unlikely, as he always slept with his senses taut, coiled like a spring, ready to uncoil at a thousandth of a stick's notice. Could it be tomato sauce, then? He *liked* tomato sauce. A lot. Especially when it smothered a grilled Cumberland sausage. Carefully, yet diligently, he sniffed the growing red puddle. No, it didn't smell bloody or tomatoey at all. Hmmm, maybe slightly fruity with reticent overtones of warm tartan slippers. He stuck out his long pink tongue and, rather hesitantly, licked the puddle. Nope, he was wrong about the warm tartan slippers. Much less subtle, but with something that hit the palate with a discernable touch of sweet cherries, warm brioche, and overripe postman's ankle with a delicate nuance of Marks and Spencer 50% wool-mix sock and athlete's foot powder.

Above the table, Betty was still quite worried, and had been sitting patiently waiting for the Whatshisname narrative to finish.

'Right,' she said. 'Listen up. As a responsible founding member of The Secret Five, it is ordained that I have to follow Older Mrs Wells in case she is tasked to start a disastrous fire, at long last. Daniel, you explain to the Squire all about the notion of a disastrous fire, if you will.'

And with that, she jumped up and hurried out of the room. Constable Landscape, considering it his duty to perform undercover back-up duties, hurried after Betty, his Victorian truncheon at the ready.

But Daniel was far too busy replenishing his glass of wine to notice all this exciting activity that was happening around him. He sat humming a little tune to himself.

The Psychologist coughed. 'Oh,' Daniel said, looking up and trying to focus on all their staring faces. There now seemed to be twice the number of people in the room, far too many characters for an effective narrative, he thought.

He sensed that people were looking at him expectantly yet patiently. He stood up. He suddenly felt quite happy and very important! This was his moment! Daniel is the Man!

'Well . . . right, erm, Shquire,' he said, leaning on the table and still trying hard to focus both his eyes on the mass of fuzzy people. 'I have to exshplain a noshun, I think. So . . . we, led by me . . .' he glanced about him furtively yet stupidly, 'are the shparehead . . . er, shpearhead contenginshy of The Secret Five! Oh yes we are! We are on a MISHUN, to shave the world! *All* of it! And all becush *your* . . .' – he wagged his finger at the Squire – 'great-great-great . . . great . . . great grandshun Shamspon . . . Shammon? Anyway, he is doing shumthing rather naughty and wants to domino the world, or shumthing like that.' He took a big sip of yummy wine. 'Do you know, thinking about it, I can't actuary remember why we are here.

Shumthing about Spamsong de Nylon and the United Shtates of Amerigo . . . ah! yes! got it! Where *you* . . .' – he waved his wine glass in the Squire's direction – 'will move to after the *disastrush* fire! That's it!' He raised his glass and knocked it back in one go.

'America?' the Squire laughed. 'And, pray, why should I travel all the way over there just because of a little disastrous fire, tell me? It is far too preposterous for words!'

'Prepostrush? No no no! No! Americo is the Land of the *Free*!' announced Daniel. He slammed his glass down and staggered over to the Squire. He grabbed the Squire's handy lapels. 'Let me tell you, Shquire, that Americons will send men *sssshoot*ing into the shky and into shpaysh!' He stepped back and waved his arms in the general direction of space. Everyone looked up. It was silent for a few moments, except for a gentle lapping sound from under the table. 'They will float shlowly about in shpaysh and . . . and mend stuff,' Daniel continued, now waving his arms about in a floating manner. 'And Americons will have *great huge big* houshes and all the shtreets are paved with *reeeeal* goldy woldy stuff, absholute bucketfuls of it, all going shpare, and shopgirlies and farmers and *everyone* will have huge big monshter cars and there will be heaps of global warming and loadsh of cheerleaders in *very* short shkirts.' He performed a cute little cheerleaders routine in front of the Squire. 'Give ush an *esh*, give ush a *queue*, give ush a *you* . . .'

'Stop this at once!' said the Squire, holding up his Squire's hand to stop it at once. 'Did you say *gold*? I must now confess to being mildly interested. Cheerleaders? Short skirts, eh? But wait, have I not so much more to keep me here in jolly old England?'

'I would say so!' said the Parson. 'Bless my Victorian Parson's soul, our Britain has so much more to offer! Think of the string quartets. The Romantic Poets. The doe-eyed orphans begging on street corners . . .'

'Yes, the firm yet gentle line of English hill and dale,' suggested Bertie. 'The tranquillity of the deer parks and the splendour of the ancient oaks, hayricks on farms and great wooden barns, gaggling geese and diving ducks on sunlit village greens, shining threads of foaming rivers and gurgling brooks, the clatter and clink of silverware on broad stately tables . . .'

'And,' added the Magistrate brightly, 'the hangings. We must not forget the hangings.'

'And, to add a further bright note, do not forget all the rampant diseases,' said the Psychologist. 'Cholera, diphtheria, typhoid, spermatorrhoea. And echoing asylums full of lost souls!' He rubbed his Psychologist's hands together with relish. 'Lost souls waiting for me to polish up my proficiency in taxidermy.'

'What about Bird's Custard?' suggested Mrs Wells the Younger. 'These Victorian days, I understand, Bird's Blancmange is available in no fewer than fourteen flavours! And, gentlemen, do not forget the wallpaper in stylish two-dimensional floral designs. We do have lots of that. You would miss the wallpaper.'

'That is quite true, my dear Mrs Wells the Younger,' said the Magistrate. 'There is indeed a lot of rather nice floral wallpaper in Victorian England. *And* there are dado rails! It is my daring supposition that America has not one yard of dado rail. That said, when all is said and done, what have the Americans done for us? Hmmm?'

The Squire pondered upon their words, carefully and thoughtfully scratching his rugged yet charming backside as he pondered.

'But Americons – they have wallpaper as well!' exclaimed Daniel, suddenly coming to life after a long bout of staring at the ceiling. 'They have *lotsh* of it. On their walls. Flock!'

'What?' boomed the Magistrate.

'Flock wallpaper!' said Daniel, searching around the table for more wine. 'But ash far as I know . . . hic . . . from all the Dreamworks filmsh I've seen, *no* doday rails.'

'That is probably true,' said the Squire, thoughtfully sniffing his rugged but charming fingertips. 'And I have had a sudden yet interesting thought. Maybe I could go over there to America and introduce dado rails to their nation! I could be the dado rail magnate! I could sell it to the natives for their wigwams.'

'Good one, Shquire!' encouraged Daniel, grabbing an almost empty bottle and draining the dregs into his glass.

'Woof . . . woo . . . wo,' said Whatshisname from under the table.

Just then, there was yet another commotion as Betty and Constable Landscape returned. The Constable was holding onto Older Mrs Wells very tightly indeed.

'Hellooooo Betty!' yelled Daniel, waving his arm at her. 'Sish! Come and have a drinkiepoo! And you, Conshtubble.'

'Stop!' said the Squire quite loudly. 'I wish to make an announcement!' He held up one of his Squire's free hands.

'What is he doing?' Betty whispered to Bertie.

Bertie whispered to Betty, explaining Daniel's suggestion to the Squire about America.

'*What*?' said Betty, rather too loudly.

'I said, *I wish to make an announcement!*' shouted the Squire. 'Pay attention, as this is quite an important part of the story! I have decided that I am going to sell this house and move to America where I will set up a dado rail business, marry, and have many children, grandchildren and great-grandchildren who will be able to travel the world and see far-off places such as Salzburg near Austria! And it is thanks to this young man, Daniel, for giving me his business advice and persuading me to go! Let us raise our glasses! To Daniel!' He raised his wine glass.

There were cries of *to Daniel* from the assembled crowd. But Betty was not impressed!

'No!' she shouted. 'You can't emigrate! Think of the future of the world!'

'Too late,' said the Squire, sipping his wine. 'For a start, I do not believe that you are time travellers . . .'

'Neither do I,' added the Psychologist.

'And neither do I,' said Daniel, swaying slightly.

'Wooooo . . .' said Whatshisname.

'And,' continued the Squire, 'when I make up my mind, nothing can stop me. Mrs Wells, come help me to start packing, if you will. Then I will throw you out onto the streets with barely the clothes you stand up in, plus your blackmail money of course.' He turned on his very own Squire's heels and disappeared out of the Dining Room.

'What have you done?' exclaimed Betty to Daniel. 'This means that Bartle de Lylow will be born as an American tourist, and then Sampson de Lylow will also be born, and he will turn into an arch villain to threaten the modern world!'

Daniel, smiling in rather a silly fashion, looked at Betty. His eyes looked very glazed, almost doubly so. He seemed to be quite confused for a moment, but the confused expression suddenly disappeared completely as his eyes closed and he keeled over onto the floor! He had mysteriously succumbed to the first recorded case of Juvenile Binge Drinking.

Everyone gathered round and looked down at Daniel where he had fallen. Whatshisname appeared from under the table, stood shakily and looked around him for a moment. He winked at the black poodle then walked unsteadily over to Daniel, his wobbly legs becoming entangled as he did so. He reached Daniel, tried his best to focus on him, failed, licked Daniel's spectacles, then collapsed on top of him, becoming the first and only recorded case of Canine Binge Drinking.

Betty looked down, quite aghast at her brother and her faithful dog, who both began to snore loudly and dribble enthusiastically all over the Persian rug.

The Psychologist knelt down and studied Daniel closely. 'I don't suppose,' he said, 'anyone minds if I took him away for some invasive Victorian experiments? And maybe the dog as well, for a spot of taxidermy practice?'

'Please do,' said Betty as she stormed out of the room.

PART SIX

Chapter Thirty Three

In which Sampson has turned quite evil and says quite evil things; a cake slice becomes his weapon of choice; Ricky enjoys the buffet nibbles; Pam Ayres is mentioned, albeit in a thoroughly undeserved ironic manner.

It was supposed to be a very happy event, the after-The-Birthday-Party party in the gymnasium of the Stanley Gibbons School for the Fairly Gifted. It had been planned to celebrate the success of the play with copious soft drinks and an even more copious buffet. Everyone had been invited – teachers, pupils, audience. Even Ricky and Amy were there as guests of George. But everything had gone very wrong following the on-stage humiliation of Sampson. Well, maybe not everything, as the Toasted Dairylea and Angel Delight Goujons, and the Baguette with Goats' Cheese & Oven Roasted Scooby Doo Raisin Bran Topping were both proving to be very popular amongst the guests.

And yet, a major crisis had developed right under everyone's noses while everyone's backs were turned and everyone's teeth were sinking into the toasted goujons. Sampson had continued his theme of becoming very *very* evil after the utter humiliation during the performance, and had stamped about backstage, then stamped about off-stage, on-stage, backstage again, in the corridors, and briefly, disastrously, in the boys' toilets when the moment dictated.

Then, to anyone who would listen, he threatened to take hostages or make a rooftop protest along the whole length and breadth of the school roof, which he quickly retracted having remembered his morbid fear of heights, lengths and breadths, not to mention the dodgy guttering and scary gargoyles, which we now have so it's too late.

Now Sampson suddenly appeared in the gymnasium doorway, spoiling everyone's enjoyment and looking quite evil for a boy with mightily small ears and no talent for playing castanets. George was in the middle of trying to persuade Ricky to tour with *Bash!* when they were rudely interrupted by Sampson (although now they had been interrupted they couldn't have been in the middle, but let's move on.)

'Right then!' Sampson yelled as he stormed in. 'It's about time you all took my sudden and unexpected evilness seriously! Stop talking, persuading, eating, drinking, and please pay attention! I've turned evil, see? And no-one will believe me!'

He grabbed a shiny cake slice from the buffet table and pointed it at Amy, who had been secretly sulking by Ricky's side.

'You!' Sampson shouted at her. 'The secret sulky scaredy-cat girl. Come here! I want to grab you and hold this knife to your throat in a threatening manner and take you hostage until my demands, as yet undefined and not really thought through properly, are met in full!'

Amy, typically, didn't know what to do. 'What shall I do?' she whispered to Ricky, who was now tucking eagerly into a plateful of buffet nibbles. He shrugged and looked puzzled. 'I'm not sure,' he said, spitting flecks of delicious goujon onto Amy's cheek. 'I don't think we ever covered hostage situations in our Secret Five training.'

'Yes we did,' Amy said. 'You must have missed that meeting.'

Then, to add to Ricky's dismay, Sampson suddenly and deliberately reached out and grabbed Amy by her closest arm. His face was relatively grim and there was a gentle hint of madness in both of his eyes as he yanked her relentlessly towards him. He dragged her backwards towards the doorway, the cake slice at her throat! Amy started to scream rather too loudly.

This was, Ricky thought, the worst adventure of all, only made bearable by the splendid buffet spread which really took some beating. And yet, some sibling instinct made him carefully place his plate back on the table and advance on Sampson. George followed him, close behind.

'Put her down!' Ricky shouted firmly. 'She's family!'

'Come and get her,' taunted Sampson.

'What?' asked Ricky, stopping in his tracks, thoroughly confused by the unexpected invitation.

'Be careful,' George whispered carelessly. 'He looks a bit dangerous to me.'

'I said . . .' replied Sampson, a little louder. 'Hang on a minute – secret sulky scaredy-cat girl, scream quieter, please! They can't hear my threats.'

Amy's screaming went quite quiet, so everyone could hear themselves thinking, which was a very good trick.

'I said, come and get her,' said Sampson, backing out of the gym. 'If you're brave enough, that is!'

That was it! Someone else was doubting Ricky's bravery! This called for drastic action. He might not be *very* brave, but he could be *somewhat* brave where his family was concerned. Instantly, without heed for his own safety, he returned to the buffet table, picked up another Dairylea and Angel Delight Goujon, popped it into his mouth, chose another one, ate it, picked up a pink fondant fancy, ate it, took a swig of delicious blackcurrant and rhubarb cordial, licked his lips with his very own tongue, then carefully and urgently followed Amy's quiet screams down the corridor. All the other people looked on, encouragingly nibbling their nibbles and wondering if this was all part of the play. Some people even started to clap and shout *he's behind you!*

George stood watching Ricky, wondering if his own role was now over and if he'd actually done enough to attract the attention of an agent or record company who, in a moment of madness, might sign up *Bash!* for a multi-million pound recording contract and, hopefully, the inevitable professional slavery.

Out in the corridor, somewhat brave Ricky had unexpectedly come across an open door. It was the library! From within he could hear a commotion, very similar to those nineteenth century commotions but with a more modernistic and contemporary feel to them. Instinctively he knew that libraries don't usually have commotions of any sort. There was something very wrong here (although deep down he knew that it was quite wrong to preface *wrong* with a qualifier, as he knew that something is either wrong or right, and strictly speaking there were no gradations of wrongness). Shaking his head at this unfortunate episode of invasive literary ineptitude, he carefully, yet somewhat bravely, stepped into the library. He followed the sound of the contemporary commotion. It came from the direction of Poetry and Literary Criticism! Somewhat bravely he peeked around the corner of the bookshelves, noting with interest that they had several new copies of York Advanced Notes on The Life and Works of Pam Ayres. Puzzled, yet strangely satisfied, he took a quick look up the aisle. Amy was sitting on the floor, tied up and leaning against The Romantics! Sampson was standing over her threateningly.

Taking his hands into his life, Ricky suddenly leapt out and equally suddenly confronted Sampson. 'Untie my pathetic sister!' he yelled somewhat bravely. 'And get her away from The Romantics and their hideous rhymes and their ill-informed Platonism! Or else!'

Amy screamed as Sampson leapt towards Ricky, brandishing the cake slice with the breezy enthusiasm of Jamie Oliver on speed. 'Oh yes? Oh yes? Or else *what*, Ricko?' he sneered evilly. 'You're the one who helped to humiliate and disgrace me! Come here and join your precious sister. I'm going to kill you both! If you don't mind. Ha ha! I'm really enjoying this!'

Ricky was stunned. Kill? This was The Secret Five! No-one had ever killed anyone before, to his knowledge. People didn't die! It had suddenly become a world that he no longer recognised, a far cry from his world where ordinary decent Britons could live without fear of dying, of homophobia, of paedophilia or toilet-breaks. Oh how he badly needed a chapter break to recover from the shock and give him time to think of a plan!

Unfortunately, that was highly unlikely at this stage, and Ricky had only just over a line break to think of a plan, which was no time at all. Sampson lurched forward and grabbed him! Firmly yet tenderly he threw Ricky against the bookshelves, causing *The Rime of the Ancyent Marinere In Seven Partes* to fall from the top shelf and hit Ricky very hard on the head. Ricky collapsed onto the floor alongside Amy, who shrieked in a rather pathetic girly way.

'But tell me, tell me, speak again,' sneered Sampson as he trussed Ricky up like a trussed-up oven-ready chicken but, mercifully, without the stuffing. 'You said *or else*. Or else what, Ricko? Eh?'

But somewhat brave Ricky was unconscious! Although *The Rime of the Ancyent Marinere In Seven Partes* is usually quite a skinny book, the Introduction and Preface by Melvyn Bragg and Ken Dodd had expanded it from 35 to 850 pages, making it a tome capable of inflicting considerable damage on an unsuspecting head, not to mention the loss of the reader's will to live.

'Ricky!' squealed Amy, struggling to free herself from her bonds in order to soothe her brother's brow.

'Quiet!' Sampson sneered at Amy. 'This is a hostage situation, so you need to start to develop the Patti Hearst Syndrome, and you can't do that while squealing all the time. So shush and start developing, silly squeally girl.' He rubbed his hands together evilly. 'Now, I have to think of my evil demands. Ha!'

He definitely needed time to think even more evilly. A chapter break would be very welcome, he thought. Very welcome indeed.

Chapter Thirty Four

In which Sampson acquires a fluffy white cat; a familiar character makes an appearance, maybe; some shocking truths are revealed but then quickly covered up again; the kangaroo makes an important keynote speech about tax credits.

Ricky was particularly upset when he came to, partly because he was missing the splendid buffet, partly because when *he'd* suggested a chapter break none had been forthcoming, and partly because he found himself trussed up in the library alongside The Romantics and had woken with his cheek pressed against Percy Bysshe Shelley's spine.

'So, you're awake, Ricko,' sneered Sampson, who was standing over him. 'I've become *really* evil while you've been unconscious. I've tickled your sister's feet!' He threw his head back and laughed quite an evil laugh for a boy with his size of ears and his taste in soft furnishing.

'And he's got himself a cat!' squeaked Amy rather too squeakily.

Ricky looked up and saw that Sampson was holding and stroking a beautiful Persian cat, which by now had had the benefit of many chapters to learn a few useful English phrases, should the adventure story ever sink so low as introducing a talking cat.

'The fluffy white pussy makes me look quite evil, don't you think?' sneered Sampson, evilly stroking the cat, which looked very thoughtful and was probably conjugating English verbs quietly to itself. 'And, while you've been unconscious, Ricko, I gave them all my ransom demands.'

'Gosh,' said Ricky.

'You may well say gosh,' said Sampson. 'My demands were truly evil! A one million pound ransom plus VAT and optional service charge, a nice shiny red helicopter to fly me out of here, with Debbie Harry as the pilot if at all possible, and a sharper cake slice.'

'Gosh!' said Ricky again, but this time with feeling and an exclamation mark for effect.

'But they refused him!' squealed Amy triumphantly.

'So they did, the *fools*,' sneered Sampson sneeringly. 'But I'm not an unreasonably evil person. So I settled for a W H Smith gift token and an Adult Daysaver bus ticket, which is tremendously good value as it gives unlimited travel for twenty-four hours excluding Night Services, which is very confusing don't you think? But I still plan to kill you both, as I feel extremely evil at the moment and must take full advantage of it.'

Just then, as they were beginning to fear the worst, Ricky and Amy heard a very familiar cackle. 'Ha!' the very familiar cackle cackled.

'It's Old Hag!' Amy whispered to Ricky. 'Do you think she's come to rescue us?'

But Sampson had overheard her with his very own small ears. 'No chance!' he sneered. He turned to Old Hag, who had entered the library and was looking around for someone she could show her library ticket to. Unfortunately for everyone she was still dressed in her schoolgirl's outfit, her old hag's bosom straining against the waistband of the short grey skirt. Her various veins, much to Ricky's disgust, seemed to be developing nicely into a detailed road map of the environs of Worcester.

'Sampson!' Old Hag cackled. 'Have you killed them yet? It's hard to tell.'

'Please help us, Old Hag!' pleaded Amy, rather pathetically, yet quite sweetly.

'Ha!' sneered Old Hag snidely, sidling slowly up to Sampson's side. 'And *ha!* again for luck. I'm with *him* in this evil adventure, foolish children.' She rubbed the back of her hand gently across Sampson's cheek, then gently across his face. 'After all, he is my dear son. Or didn't you realise that? Hmmm? You both look shocked. Ha! First you believed my cunning yet insufferable Black Country dialect disguise, then you miss all the other equally cunning clues. You were so wrapped up with your silly adventure and those interminable visits to tea shops!'

Ricky could not believe his own ears again. 'Your son?' he gasped, shocked yet slightly enthralled by the revelation.

But Amy, bless her, was not quite as shocked, for she had heard Sampson call Old Hag *Mummy* on stage. At the time she had thought it was just very good acting indeed. It had slowly dawned on her (although it had taken until sunset) that Old Hag was not as she seemed. In fact, she was worse than she seemed, so that was incredibly bad for everyone.

'You two evil persons!' said Ricky, glaring firmly at them both as he struggled to free himself.

'But you don't look much like Old Hag,' said Amy to Sampson. 'I'd say you look more like Clarissa the stunt nun and, erm, tell me Ricky, who else does he remind you of? His mightily small ears seem so familiar.'

Ricky stopped struggling and studied him carefully. Amy was right, Sampson did look like someone they knew. 'Well,' he said, 'I suppose . . . hmmm, he does look a lot like Uncle Quagmire – the ears and the hair, and the eyes and the mouth, but that's plain silly. How could . . .'

Old Hag suddenly looked quite agitated! 'No!' she interrupted, dramatically waving her arms about in a fit of intense overacting. 'I was swept away by the magic of Salzburg! I was the innocent party! He forced himself on me! I was young!'

Ricky and Amy looked at each other and frowned a secret frown. This was impossible! They could never imagine Old Hag being young. Amy in particular wondered what she was on about. Salzburg? Magic? Party? But she didn't want to look even more stupid than was necessary at this stage, so she kept quite quiet.

'What?' Sampson moaned. He dropped the Persian cat, which slouched off murmuring in broken English about the offhand treatment of Middle Eastern immigrants. 'What are you saying?' Sampson continued. 'Mummy, tell them about Bartle de Lylow, my daddy, and how he was killed in some distant war when I was still suckling noisily at your breast . . .'

'Yeuk!' said Ricky. 'Too much information!'

'Suckling?' queried Amy.

'. . . and that he was an evil hero who shot people just for the fun of it,' Sampson continued. 'Tell them! And while you're at it, tell *me* why you look so very old all of a sudden.'

But Old Hag had had enough. 'Ha! I need to pee,' she said, mysteriously scuttling off and taking her various veins with her. She paused in the doorway. 'Sampson, my boy! Your evil future is at stake here so I want you to kill them by the time I get back. And that's an order from your dear old, erm, your dear young mummy!'

Sampson watched Old Hag disappear, then turned to look down at Ricky and Amy. He tried to sneer again but his sneer had become too floppy for it to be of any immediate use. In fact, he looked upset and rather confused for someone intent on dominating the world in thirty years' time.

'He does look very like Uncle Quagmire,' said Amy. 'How queer!'

'I'm *Bartle's* son!' Sampson spluttered. 'And proud of it! I love dado rails, so I must be his offspring! He always wanted me to be evil, Mummy told me so!'

'Then why do you look like our Uncle Quagmire?' asked Ricky. 'Actually, come to think of it, and this is not a good thought, we must have been there, nearby, when you were so hastily conceived. Earlier today, to put a time stamp on it.'

'I don't understand all this!' wailed Amy. 'Will someone please explain!'

'*You* don't understand?' said Sampson. 'What about me?

Mummy said I should try to be very *very* evil and set my objective to dominate the world, as the Careers Officer didn't think I'd make a good door-to-door milkman or Anglican priest due to my knobbly knees. I tried to resist being evil until *you* . . .' – he pointed his cake slice at Ricky – 'made me very angry indeed on stage. You played *my* castanet solo! I was ejected from *Bash!*! I was deeply and utterly humiliated! Now you have to die!'

Much to Ricky and Amy's intense disappointment, his sneer was returning.

'I wish Whatshisname was here, bursting through the door and mounting a daring rescue attempt without any regard for his own life,' cried Amy. 'Come to think of it, I do believe I can smell creosote and pineapple! This is so exciting! Rescue at last!'

Both Ricky and Sampson turned to look in the direction of the door. They sniffed the air. They waited for a minute or so before shrugging their respective shoulders and accepting that the daring rescue attempt without any regard for Whatshisname's own life might not be going to happen after all.

Sampson quickly returned to his threatening old ways. 'Okay, so no-one's going to rescue you. Now you have to die!'

But Ricky was getting fed up of it all, especially all the endless sneering, and suddenly became even more somewhat braver. 'Listen,' he said to Sampson. 'I'm becoming more somewhat braver, as well as getting really fed up of it all, especially your endless sneering, it seems. Untie us this instant! You aren't evil at all. Renounce evil. You are good! Jolly good! I don't believe that Old Hag is your real mother, or that Bartle was your father.'

'Ricky!' said Amy. 'Is this helping? And can you *please* go slower?'

But Ricky was on a roll. 'I think kindly Uncle Quagmire is your real father – which does beg a question about fidelity, by the way – and kindly Clarissa the stunt nun is your natural mother. I think Old Hag snatched you . . .'

'You've lost me,' moaned Amy.

' . . . and you are *not* really evil,' continued Ricky. 'Old Hag is just using you for her own evil ends.'

'So does that mean . . .' began Amy.

'Huh? Not evil?' asked Sampson, unsneeringly. 'How does that work?'

'Ricky, does that mean . . .' began Amy again.

'Yes, Sampson,' said Ricky. 'You're *not* evil! Think of the good you can bring to the world. Think Nobel prizes! Think Blue Peter badges! In fact, you could be like an unbodied joy whose race is just begun, like a bright starry thing of heaven in the broad daylight.'

Amy looked strangely at Ricky, not realising that being pressed against The Romantics was having a sublime effect on the embodiment that was her brother.

'Ricky!' she said. 'Very good speech, albeit it a bit flowery, but does all that about Uncle Quagmire mean that . . . does it mean that . . . what does it mean?'

'And why should I do good?' Sampson shouted. He bent down, waving the cake slice close to Ricky's face. 'Say your goodbye, Ricko, castanet solo stealer. You are going to be the first member of your precious Secret Five to die a death worse than fate itself!'

'No, Sampson!' shrieked Amy. 'Listen! I'm being rather clever for a change, so it'll be worth it. If Ricky is right, and our Uncle Quagmire *is* your father – although I don't understand at all how that can happen – that makes you some sort of relative to us, doesn't it? And, incidentally, I think it makes our Uncle Quagmire some sort of untrustworthy scoundrel.'

Sampson looked at Amy. He was obviously thinking quite hard, as his little ears were wiggling and waggling.

'You're right, Amy!' Ricky said, in a rather grasping-at-straws tone of voice. 'Sampson here would be our, erm, brother-in-law . . . no, wait, third cousin-in-law . . . no . . .'

Just then, before Ricky could grasp the simplest of situations, and just as Sampson looked as though he was about to renounce a bit of evil and ruin the promise of a cliffhanger, a chapter break appeared without a by-your-leave, startling them all!

Chapter Thirty Five

In which The Secret Five are reunited; Daniel gasps a bit; Ricky gets killed; no he doesn't; yes he does; stop this arguing; okay; Betty has had enough, and flips; things are bad; no, really they are, death and destruction stalk the pages like a big fat stalking thing.

Daniel didn't know what had happened. He had landed with a big bump in a handy deserted corner of a school library. How strange! He had a hint of a headache, and a hazy memory of a meal with some Victorian people, a conversation with a real squire and some nice wine and . . . 'Oh gosh!' he said, quite embarrassed as he recalled drinking at least one tiny glass of red wine. Of course! That might be the cause of his feeling a little under the weather, which was bright with an eighty percent chance of a badly-needed shower.

'Oh, oh, I think I had a little too much to drink,' he mumbled to himself. He felt really bad about that, as he had made a point of attending a special Secret Five seminar on The Perils Of Tonic Wine and Overdosing on Blue Smarties.

'Too right, Daniel!' said Betty, from where she had landed. 'Now will you just get off me? And move your hands! Boys! You're all the same!'

Daniel, quite embarrassed yet quite intrigued, slowly moved his hands. 'Sorry. But where are we? And where's Whatshisname and Uncle Quagmire?' He stood up on his own two feet and looked around him.

'Hopefully we're in 1980,' Betty said. 'Uncle Quagmire sent us here, remember? He said, rather peculiarly, that he had some unfinished business with Alice the mysterious Victorian maid and that, against the odds, he would somehow find his own way back. I don't know where Whatshisname is, though.' She looked around her. No Whatshisname! Had he become lost, wandering through time for eternity, never to appear in any more exciting adventures?

No chance. Unbeknown to the children, and quite secretly, our brave but ugly hero now looked dolefully down on Betty and Daniel from the top of some bookshelves, where he had landed. At first he thought he had died and had been granted a last look down at his pals before entering the tunnel with the light at the end and where there would be an endless supply of peanut butter treats and an immediate opportunity for a painless testicle re-installation operation followed by endless heavenly opportunities for frenzied canine copulation.

But then reality struck, and his trusty instincts clicked in. He recalled that one moment he had been happily slurping at some yummy red liquid under an ornate table somewhere, the next moment he had landed on top of Mind, Body & Spirit in a school library. Indeed, he had landed there after being carried unconscious into a typical Victorian wardrobe, tongue lolling out of his pink mouth, dribbling all over the sprouts, and forcibly time-travelled to 1980 with his two pals.

The time-travel landing on top of the bookshelves had jolted him awake. Hearing Betty and Daniel talking, he opened his mouth to say *woof woof woof*.

'   ,' he said, as nothing at all came out. He'd been struck dumb as well! Poor Whatshisname! Apart from the mental anguish caused by the fluffy pink collar, and the dumbness, and the endless flurry of exclamation marks, he was now suffering badly from quite a significant headache!

But, despite the headache, he dared to look down. Quite suddenly, and quite pathetically, he discovered that he was also afraid of heights! Or was he afraid of bookshelves? He wasn't sure. Whatever, he knew that the phobia symptoms would begin soon – excessive sweating, rapid breathing, rapid heartbeat, nausea, dizziness. It was so exciting! He looked forward to them all, especially the rapid breathing, which he hadn't experienced since well before the surprise outing to the vets.

He whimpered quietly to himself and started to crawl very slowly along the top, trying not to look down, hoping to find some handy library ladders in the DIY section. Below him Betty and Daniel were still talking, unaware of his dire canine predicament.

'Forget Whatshisname,' Betty told Daniel. 'He'll be lost in time somewhere with his dire canine predicament. Never mind, eh? Now hush! There's a commotion! It's coming from the direction of Poetry & Literary Criticism!'

Sneakily, the two of them sneaked round the bookshelves. They heard a voice that sent shudders through their very ankles and up to their very knees.

'Ha!' said the voice. 'Some evil son you are! I can't leave you to do anything. They're still alive!'

'That's Old Hag!' whispered Betty. 'I bet she's up to no good.'

'Are we allowed to bet?' asked Daniel.

'I don't know, do I?' she snapped back quietly yet effectively. 'But look! There's Amy and Ricky, they're tied up by The Romantics! They might catch something and become profoundly imaginative! How utterly ghastly for them!'

They saw that Amy and Ricky were indeed tied up and looking rather sorry for themselves. Daniel gasped and felt much better for it. They also saw a boy who looked moderately evil and slightly familiar.

'That must be Sampson!' whispered Betty. 'By the look of it, he has turned moderately evil, so Amy and Ricky have indeed failed. Unless we can stop him. Let's have a meeting. This might be the climax of our adventure, the bit before the resolution!'

'I don't think we actually have time for a meeting,' whispered Daniel. 'It looks as though Old Hag is going to kill Amy and Ricky! Cool!'

Betty glared a big glare at him. 'What do you mean, *cool*? Killing is bad, Daniel! Very bad! And they're family!'

'Well, I do find myself wondering,' wondered Daniel, 'if it isn't about time there was an unexpected violent death or two in the story. Just to liven it up a bit. Midsomer Murders is full of them, apparently, and look how successful that is.'

But just as Betty was about to say something quite interesting for a change, Old Hag spotted them!

'Ha!' she cackled. 'Well, if it isn't Dando and the one with the big things. How was 1880? Shame you got yourself back, but now you're here, you may as well suffer some cackling!' She pointed a random old hag finger vaguely in their direction. 'Just look at them! Ha! They're rubbish. And definitely not evil enough, Sampson. They will certainly spoil your plans for world domination if you don't stop them.'

But Old Hag had underestimated the children's bravery and the daring yet shrewd plan that Betty and Daniel were about to put into action without a moment's thought for their own safety.

'What plan?' whispered Daniel to Betty.

Betty shrugged both her shoulders. 'No idea,' she whispered thoughtfully. 'But look! Sampson has dragged Amy to her feet and has the cake slice at her throat! We're not used to this sort of violent behaviour. What shall we do? It's rather spoiling our super adventure. And isn't there a health and safety issue with that cake slice?'

'Help us!' shrieked Amy pathetically yet artistically.

'Yes, help us!' endorsed Ricky. 'There's a rather nice buffet going to waste!'

'Don't panic,' said Daniel, gently sweating. 'Stay calm, just like we are . . . gosh . . . I feel . . . I feel rather . . .wack . . . yo! Sis! Kotch for a mo! Diss am soooo A-heavy. Too grimy fo' me, f'sho'! Absofrickinlutely gah! Nim nim nim. Innit!'

'Daniel!' scolded Betty, kicking his ankle. 'This is not the time to lapse into street talk!'

'Sis! Don' be trippin' like a lava lamp!' Daniel said. 'Dis am

shew as bones de bes' time, woo-man, innit?' And with that he
sank to the floor and started humming excerpts from Eminen's
latest choral album.

Betty knew immediately that she would have to be the one to
save the world, but now she had had enough.

'I've had enough!' she shrieked, confirming what we already
knew but without the extra irritating *had*. She advanced on
Sampson, waving her arms in the air. 'ENOUGH! I've had
EEEEENOUOUOUOUGH!'

Sampson looked uncertainly at Betty and the flurry of capitals.
The cake slice wavered at Amy's throat. He marvelled at Betty's
bosom, which was approaching very quickly and threatened to
surround him. But instead of attacking him, Betty flopped down on
the floor alongside Ricky. 'Go on then, tie *me* up!' she yelled. 'I've
had *enough*! In italics! I'm fed up of being the sensible one, the
one that has to think and make the decisions, the one with the
bosom that everyone keeps staring at . . .'

'Now you mention it . . .' said Sampson, releasing Amy and
staring down at Betty's bosom.

'See what I mean?' growled Betty.

Amy sank to the floor. She and Ricky glanced at each other
twice, then again for luck, and knew that, if Betty flipped, the end
of The Secret Five was surely upon them. A swift yet slow death
would be a sweet relief compared to there being no Secret Five,
they thought, although that point was surely debateable.

'Never mind her!' yelled Old Hag, stamping her feet. 'Be evil,
son! Go on, tie her up as well!'

'No!' shouted Ricky. 'Sampson, you're family! Our half-
brother, if my mathematics are correct! You can't hurt family!'

'Ha!' yelled Old Hag. 'Don't listen to them. You're *my* flesh
and blood. You extruded yourself from my own uterus . . .'

'Yo! Cool bitch!' murmured Daniel.

'No she didn't,' said Ricky. 'Sampson's mummy and daddy
are Clarissa and Uncle Quagmire.'

'What?' exclaimed Betty.

'Yo!' murmured Daniel again, staring at his feet.

'What?' exclaimed Betty yet again.

But now Old Hag had had enough dilly dallying. 'Ha! And ha! again. I've dillied and dallied for long enough,' she confirmed, advancing on Sampson. 'If you won't kill them I will! And then blame you! You will be evil by proxy! You will be an outcast, cast out and . . . and . . . proxied!'

'But,' moaned Sampson, 'they keep saying you're not my mummy. And they are The Secret Five with a vast experience of such things, so they should know. And they never ever lie.'

Old Hag pushed Sampson aside and grabbed the cake slice. 'Ha! You're rubbish as well,' she cackled. 'Just keep an eye on that Betty girl to make sure she doesn't try any tricks.'

'Okay,' said Sampson, eagerly going one step further by keeping two eyes on Betty.

'Hey, that's unfair! I don't know any tricks!' moaned Betty.

'Say your prayers, Ricko!' Old Hag spat, and thrust the cake slice towards Ricky's throat. Ricko screamed as he saw the flash of metal and Old Hag's spit arching towards him.

'Ha!' cackled Old Hag as she paused in her thrusting, flashing and arching. 'Sorry about the spitting. And I forgot to ask you if you had a last wish. Or a last cigarette maybe? Hmmm?'

'Gosh,' said Ricky, cowering politely. 'No, but thanks for asking.'

Old Hag thrust the cake slice again towards Ricky's throat. Betty looked on helplessly, as Daniel hummed a rather silly little tune and Sampson looked inquisitively down Betty's top.

This was a crisis indeed! Would there be anyone to save these brave children from a gruesome death? Would there?

Chapter Thirty Six

In which Old Hag has a surprise; we learn a thing or two about line dancing and the Birmingham area; more truths are revealed although who knows if they are the truth or not; indeed, who cares; reinforcements arrive; stick with it, we're near the end now.

Unfortunately, some churlish souls might say, there was someone to save these brave children from a gruesome death. Ricky's eyes were squeezed tightly shut as he heard a whine, a huge thud and a loud old haggish scream. It was as if she had been flattened by some rather large and rather heavy something or other falling from the top of the bookshelves.

'Get me out of here!' Old Hag said in a squashed old haggish voice. 'I'm old and vulnerable! Where's care in the community when you need it?'

Ricky dared to open his eyes and saw that the truly faithful but truly hungover dog Whatshisname had fallen off the top of the bookshelf on top of Old Hag! The cake slice had flipped out of her hand as she had been flattened, and it now lay at Daniel's feet.

Daniel paused in his humming as the deadly weapon missed his toes by millimetres.

Betty leapt to her feet. 'Daniel! Pick it up!'

But Daniel just stared at the cake slice in a pathetic way.

'Get this smelly animal off me!' moaned Old Hag, who was showing an unseemly amount of various veins and big flannel knickers as her skinny arms and legs flailed from beneath the considerable weight of Whatshisname.

'Yo! Issa a cool blade!' said Daniel, leaning forwards and

inspecting the cake slice. 'Hevvvveeee, Dude! Da blade iss lush, innit!'

Betty gasped a medium-sized gasp as Sampson went to grab the weapon! Without any thought for the safety of her own knee, she raised that very same knee into his groin, which we shall call, for decency's sake and in the true innocent spirit of The Secret Five, his Birmingham area. (She had learned the technique accidentally during a Secret Five special training session on defensive line dancing, and had been fascinated by the result, although it had taken Ricky a very long time to be able to speak and even longer to sit cross-legged.)

'Aaaaaah!' Sampson groaned loudly as he crumpled to the floor, clutching his Birmingham area, where his bollocks (oops!) now felt as though they had been seared with a blowtorch. 'Aaaaah! Oooooh!' he moaned again for effect.

'Shhhhh!' Daniel shushed. Carefully, he reached out and picked up the cake slice. 'Nang nang! Cool!' he said, examining it closely.

'Daniel!' said Betty. 'Now give it to me. But first, it is my sisterly duty to slap you extremely hard.'

Dutifully, she slapped him extremely hard, as she didn't like to let him down, and wrenched the cake slice off him. Daniel looked stunned. 'What's happening?' he said, staring wide-eyed at the chaos around him. 'And why is Whatshisname on top of Old Hag?'

'Daniel!' said Betty. 'Get up and help me untie Ricky and Amy. And we need to stop Sampson's evilness while Old Hag is disabled.'

'Hmmm, complicated, isn't it?' noted Daniel. 'I can't recall such a knotty adventure before, can you? Oh, can I clean my spectacles before I untie you two? They're filthy, what with all the time travelling.'

'Oh for goodness' sake, untie us!' yelled Ricky.

On top of Old Hag, Whatshisname managed to open an eye. He still felt extremely poorly but was keen to know what all the noise was. It wasn't helping his banging head. What was happening? Oh, yes, of course, he'd fallen off the top of the bookshelf after he'd crept to the edge and looked down. It had made him feel quite giddy! It had been a good job Old Hag was there to cushion his fall. As he'd toppled over the edge, he had seen his canine life flash before his canine eyes – all those lost opportunities, those bones that he'd buried in forgotten places, all those puppies he'd never had the chance to father, those surprise visits to the vet's, the fluffy pink collar – hmmm, maybe there were some distinct advantages to dying after all.

For now, he just couldn't be bothered to move off Old Hag. He'd put his head down for a few sticks and have a snooze. No more slurping unidentified red liquids . . . no more . . . zzzzzz.

'Get this dozy mutt off me!' screamed Old Hag. 'And can someone stop her dribbling?'

'Ur,' groaned Sampson, still clutching his Birmingham area.

'Do you think Sampson will be all right?' Amy asked. 'And why is he holding his . . . his . . .'

'We're calling it his Birmingham area,' Betty whispered to her. 'And it was me that hurt him.'

'Oh, gosh!' said Amy, unable to grasp the concept of hurting someone.

Betty and Daniel untied the ropes – the rather flimsy pathetic ropes that a child of three could probably have snapped with one finger – that had bound Ricky and Amy. 'I wasn't actually afraid,' Ricky said bravely as he stood up. 'It was all under my control.'

'Yes, right,' said Betty, with unprecedented but totally wasted irony.

'I'm glad you agree. At least I didn't wave my arms about shouting *enough enough*!' said Ricky.

'Well,' chipped in Amy, '*I* would have saved the day if you could all have waited a minute!'

'Huh!' said Daniel. '*I* was biding my time to strike. Another minute and you'd have all been free!'

'I don't think so,' said Ricky. 'You were in a street-talk coma.'

'To be honest,' Betty said, rather sensibly, 'Whatshisname rescued us all, and he's my dog and I trained him in the art of self defiance, so there!'

Just then, unexpectedly, Sampson spoke up. 'Er, I say, Mummy,' he said to Old Hag. 'I *am* in considerable pain . . . oooh . . . from that girl's knee thrust into my testicles.'

'Isn't that our secret password?' Amy whispered to Betty. 'How does he know it?'

'But, oooh,' Sampson continued, 'I'd really like you to tell me the truth before I decide whether to be evil or not. It's a difficult choice and an uninformed decision . . . oooh . . . aaah . . . wouldn't be right. I don't want to dominate the world under false pretences.'

'Will you get this mutt off me if I tell?' said Old Hag, her face pressed to the floor and her various veins bulging to bursting point.

The children gathered around and agreed that they would rescue her, although they had not really thought it through, in particular how they might move Whatshisname.

'Ha!' squeaked Old Hag. 'You want the truth? The truth is that I'm really your mummy!'

'No you're not!' said the children, not quite together, so it sounded more like 'No you're no not you're no not you're you're not not.'

'Ha!' cackled Old Hag. 'You're all too clever for your own good! All right, I'll make this easy for you. Sampson. I'm not your mummy!'

'Oh! What?' groaned Sampson.

'But I loved you as your real mummy would, after I snatched you from the cradle at Clarissa's posh house for my own evil ends,' continued Old Hag. 'I had a compulsive disorder, a compulsion to change nappies, you see. It was the smell of ammonia. Lovely. It was out of my control.'

'Told you!' smirked Ricky.

Amy looked quite confused. 'I am very confused,' she said, going one qualifier further, which was not good for her literary future. 'You said that our very own Uncle Quagmire is Sampson's father. How . . . what . . . where . . . why . . .'

'Ha! She's off again with her adverbs!' muttered Old Hag from her privileged position under a big fat snoring dribbling dog. 'And, despite her youthful exuberance, she's not going to understand all this, is she? What a waste of a character . . . will *someone* stop this dog dribbling on me!'

'But we're The Secret Five!' Amy whined. 'How can such things happen? Our mother Aunt Trinny is our father Uncle Quagmire's wife and surely it's just not physically possible!'

'Excuse me, Thick Annie,' interrupted Old Hag. 'I'm really getting tired of being under this fat dribbly dog. And the collar! Yeuk! It's blinding me. But now can I finish my evil speech?'

'Shall we let her?' Betty asked the others.

'Ooooh,' moaned Sampson.

'Let's hear what she has to say,' said Daniel.

'Thank you. Ahem. I did nothing wrong,' Old Hag said in a little voice that she'd recently stolen from a little person. 'I was young, misguided . . .'

'Enough!' said Ricky in rather a manful way for a boy with his taste in socks. 'I think we all know that you stole Sampson for your own highly evil ends, and that goes against all the teachings and beliefs of The Secret Five, at least those I can remember from the meetings I managed to attend.' He pointed a manly finger at Old Hag. 'We, The Secret Five, declare you as officially evil, Old Hag!'

'Well said,' whispered Betty, somewhat afraid that her senior position was being undermined. 'But isn't that my role, to declare people evil?'

Ricky looked mildly embarrassed but was very keen to continue his maiden speech. 'And you, haggish Old Hag, tried all ways to turn Sampson into an equally evil monster and it hasn't worked!

Because of our intervention, our careful strategic planning, our relentless time travel, Uncle Quagmire's libido and, of course, our daring individual bravery, especially me, Sampson is now the offspring not of Bartle but of the kindly, if a trifle unfaithful, Uncle Quagmire, and is therefore basically *good!*'

'Ha!' Old Hag cackled. 'I was doing all right until you interfering kids came along. With the right training and an effective appraisal system, Sampson here could have been the most reviled person in modern times, after certain British prime ministers, all members of parliament, and disgraced TV game show hosts, and he'd have made me the most famous old hag in history!' She looked up at Sampson. 'You were doing rubbish at it, though. The castanet solo was my last chance to turn you!'

Carefully, Sampson stood up, grimacing from the effects of the raging furnace in the central Birmingham area, now spreading to the suburbs as far as Erdington and Edgbaston. 'You . . . you evil, nasty, unmotherly person!' he cried. 'You lied to me! I *never* suckled at your breast . . .'

'Oh, please!' moaned Amy.

'. . . but,' continued Sampson, still grimacing but now frowning as well, 'I don't understand how I was Clarissa and Bartle's child until The Secret Five came along and now I'm Clarissa and Uncle Quagmire's child. How could that be?'

Betty glanced at Daniel, Ricky glanced at Amy, Whatshisname opened one eye, couldn't see anyone to glance at, so fell asleep again, back into the dream about the fit black poodle and the bondage game with the leash.

'It's best not to ask,' Betty said to Sampson. 'It's the rather complex nature of the narrative, you see.'

'And the inbuilt plot holes,' added Ricky brightly. 'It's part of our unfailing charm. Apparently.'

'And all this time travel can make it all so very complicated,' said Daniel.

'Why?' asked Amy.

Just then, to everyone's surprise, they heard the library door being opened rather suddenly! They all turned and looked at the door, fully expecting to be astonished to see George swarm in with a policeman who looked very much like Constable Landscape but in a modern day policeman's uniform.

They weren't disappointed.

'Thank God![1] You're both safe!' sighed George after he had finished swarming in with the policeman. George stood with his feet apart, wiggled his hips and ran his very own fingers through his very own hair, yet again. 'We heard all the contemporary commotion and the story climax dialogue so I called the police, after we had polished off the splendid buffet of course. Yeah!' He pointed a finger dramatically at the policeman. 'I have the utmost respect for the police, and always will have, yeah. Constable Simon Country here rushed over in his 1980 Series 3 Austin Allegro panda car to arrest and detain the evil ones, and the flying squad back-up are on their way in their Ford Granada GT . . .' He stopped with a start. 'Blimey! Jesus to a child[2]! Who *is* the girl with the big knockers? And who on earth is McFly?'

'Erm, thank you, George,' said Ricky. He pointed at Old Hag. 'Constable Country, if you please, the evil moaning woman under the fat ugly dog with the pink fluffy collar is the one you want to arrest. She is the evil rogue behind the plot to nurture Sampson to dominate the world.'

Betty nudged Daniel. 'Is that who I think it is?' she whispered, nodding in George's direction.

Daniel shrugged. 'He could be,' he whispered back. 'Why, do you fancy him?'

'Best not to,' Betty replied.

---

[1] *Other objects of worship are available.*

[2] *Other divine prophets are also available.*

Just then (which, for clarity's sake, was a different just then from the previous one) a scruffy plain-clothes man in flared trousers swooped into the library, his tie undone and a cigarette hanging rather dangerously from his lips.

'Ah,' said the constable in a timely effort to explain the sudden appearance of yet another peripheral character. 'The Flying Squad. Reinforcements at last.' He raised his constable's arm. 'Over here, sir.'

The scruffy reinforcement approached and glared at them all. 'You can all call me The Guvnor,' he growled. 'Capital T, capital G, capital N, if you please.' He glared again, causing Amy to hide behind George.

The GuvNor pointed at Daniel. 'You!' he said. 'Despite the pathetic attempt to disguise yourself with those naff spectacles, I sense that I must have seen your ugly mug before. You look well bad, you do, so I must have done.' He walked up to Daniel, removed the cigarette from his very own lips, and pressed his face close to Daniel's. 'I'm The GuvNor, and I haven't had my dinner yet, so unless you want a good kicking, you'd better come quietly, son.'

Daniel opened his mouth to protest, but only a feeble mewing came out. Betty tutted at Daniel.

The constable pointed at Old Hag. 'But Guvnor . . . sorry, I mean GuvNor . . .'

'Shut it, Constable!' said The GuvNor. 'I can always tell the criminal element, soon as I walk into a room. And this blagger is it.' He breathed on Daniel's spectacle lenses. 'What's your name, son?'

'Dur . . . dur . . .' stammered Daniel.

'Well, Durdur,' said The GuvNor, backing away from Daniel. 'Get your trousers on, son. You're well and truly nicked!'

Daniel looked down to check that he still had his trousers on. He mewed again, then removed his spectacles. He twitched, then pointed a spectacle arm at The GuvNor. 'Yo, get right, dude! Love dis pig's hexa screensava! Yo me homeboy! Like, whoa, man! Cool! Innit?'

'Oh no!' Betty said. 'Not again! Look what he's done to Daniel now!'

'He'll have to stay like that,' urged Ricky. 'I'm fed up of us having to slap him out of it.'

'Erm, GuvNor,' Constable Country said, pointing again to Old Hag. 'Over here. This one's the criminal element.'

The GuvNor looked at Daniel, then at Old Hag, then back at Daniel. 'You sure?' he said to Constable Country. 'But what about Durdur here?'

'I'm sure,' said the constable, quite assertively for a man with his taste in truncheons. 'She's under this rather large dribbling dog with the fluffy pink collar.'

Looking quite unconvinced, The GuvNor glared and pointed his finger at Daniel. 'I'll deal with you later, Durdur.' He then stepped over to where Old Hag lay squashed under Whatshisname. He bent over and peered down at them.

'Hello hello hello!' he said. 'She *is* a big doggy, isn't she? Better phone through for an industrial winch.'

Whatshisname suddenly and unexpectedly opened his eyes! He was keen to protest at being called a she and to avoid being winched anywhere. He noticed that everyone was looking at him. He lifted his head, which felt quite heavy compared to its normal unladen weight, and it was pounding very hard indeed. 'Woof woof woof?' he said weakly, slightly relieved that his dumbness had only lasted for a few sticks.

Betty bent down to stroke him. 'Silly doggy!' she said. Gently, yet roughly, she took hold of his collar. Ricky and Amy grabbed an ear each and, pulling with all their pathetic might, dragged Whatshisname off Old Hag, leaving a long trail of translucent dribble.

Old Hag struggled to her feet, showing an unseemly amount of scrawny leg and bulging various veins in the process. 'Ha!' she cackled as Constable Country handcuffed her. 'I'm old, you know. But I will be back!'

'I think not,' said The GuvNor. 'You're well and truly nicked. Anything you say will be ignored and treated with the utmost disdain. You are not obliged to say anything other than *ouch stop it* as I bludgeon you with a pick-axe handle. Constable, fetch it from the back of the Seventies motor, if you please.'

'But GuvNor!' whispered the constable. 'The witnesses!'

'What? Oh, all right. Maybe later,' sighed The GuvNor. He pointed a trained Flying Squad finger at Old Hag. 'Lady, you're going to be locked up for a very long time. Unless, that is, you can overpower the constable, and engineer a daring escape when his Allegro[3] breaks down as he drives you to the nearest police station.'

Sampson stepped forward to block their path as the constable led Old Hag away. 'Stop! I feel the need to give some sort of lengthy monologue at this point to you, my non-mother,' he said, glaring at Old Hag. 'About your cruelty and your lying and the way you used me to fulfil your own evil ambition. About how you betrayed me for . . .'

'Hey! Sampson, do you want to rejoin *Bash!*?' George suddenly interrupted, throwing a spare arm around both of Sampson's spare shoulders. 'You could perfect your castanet solo on our latest song. One day we'll be famous, you, me, and perhaps Andrew.'

Sampson looked very pleased with himself, almost forgetting all about his silly old aching testicles. 'Gosh!' he said. 'But to be honest, I was hoping to be invited to join The Secret Five.'

'He can do that as well,' Ricky said. 'Can't he Betty? Now that Old Hag is no longer a member.'

---

[3] Many other makes of highly unreliable British cars were available at the time

'Hey!' cackled Old Hag. 'Why am I no longer a member?'

'Because,' said Betty, who knew all about these things, 'if you have a criminal conviction you aren't allowed in. That's the constitution, you see. Can't change it, sorry.'

'Ha!' said Old Hag, ruthlessly glaring her very best glare at the children. 'Torture me, hang me, beat me, but renounce my associate membership of The Secret Five? Never! You've made a big mistake! I won't forget it! Anyway, think about it, I'll be incarcerated in 1980, which will probably mean I won't be around in 2010, which will mean that this adventure will never take place! Ha! Let that be a lesson to you, interfering children!'

The children looked at each other and frowned as the two policemen dragged Old Hag unceremoniously, yet daintily, out of the library.

'What did she mean?' asked Amy.

'It's probably best not to think about it too much,' said Betty. 'But Sampson, you can still be a Secret Five member *and* be in *Bash!*, just as long as you don't turn evil.'

Sampson smiled a big smile for someone with a heat wave in the Birmingham area and his dubious talent in castanet playing. 'Despite my premature smile,' he said, 'I'm worried that Mummy – sorry, Old Hag – will come back to intimidate me and make me cry a bit.'

'Oh, we've got that covered,' said Betty reassuringly. 'The Secret Five Witness Protection Programme will make sure you're safe.'

Sampson looked relieved. George, without asking, took his arm. 'Let's go outside,' he said to Sampson as he led him out of the library. The children watched them walk off into the sunset, which had appeared without warning but was well overdue in the narrative.

'Did you see how happy and unevil Sampson was?' Betty said. 'Doesn't that make you happy too? All I know is that we saved the world! I'm so glad that our work here is done.'

Daniel was also glad, and so was Ricky and Amy. In fact, everyone was glad, even Whatshisname, who was glad twice but no-one noticed because the first glad stopped after the second one started.

'Isn't this the point where we all tell each other we don't want another scary adventure like that one, give a happy sigh and finish the story here and now?' suggested Ricky. 'Then someone says Good Luck Secret Five, and may you have lots more adventures!'

They murmured agreement, except Daniel who murmured something that sounded like 'Iss all sooo like a'gravy, man. Innit?'

Then Betty spoke. 'Actually, first, we do need to get back home, sprouts and portals permitting, and preferably without having to carry Whatshisname on our backs. You see, we need to have an on-site meeting to review our performances.'

'What?' squeaked Ricky.

'She's right. Don't you remember?' Amy said. 'We all agreed at a meeting that we should have performance reviews after each adventure. Betty said we are to be results-oriented, and have to stretch the boundaries of Best Practice and discuss New Ways of Working. Or did you miss that meeting, Ricky?'

Ricky looked very miserable indeed.

'Anyway,' said Betty. 'We'll need to know if Uncle Quagmire made it home safely, as surely that will measure the success of the adventure.'

'Yo, woo-man,' said Daniel. 'Tha's hellza key! Boomshakalaka! Innit?'

'Can't we leave Daniel behind?' suggested Amy hopefully.

They all laughed, except Daniel of course. And Betty and Ricky. And Whatshisname.

Chapter Thirty Seven

In which Betty becomes bossy again; Daniel yells at the author, who gets a bit upset and tries not to show it too much but it really hurt; you have an opportunity to get a refund on this book as long as you haven't dog-eared or bitten or annotated the pages; I mean, why on earth should you want to annotate the pages anyway; and finally, what was I thinking.

The children were so excited at being home again and could hardly contain themselves as they walked up to the front door of Guantanamo Cottage. Whatshisname had quite recovered from his ordeal with the wine, thanks mainly to a couple of bouts of hearty vomiting over the Fiction A-D section, predominantly over Jeffrey Archer. Now, he was back to his old self, making sure that he had the chance for a last trot and patter as he followed his chums up the path. All he had to do now was to try and get rid of the stupid pink fluffy collar. But he was safe at last!

And yet, looking back, their final time travel trip from 1980 had almost gone very badly wrong when Whatshisname had been sick all over the Brussels sprouts which, as everyone knows, could have affected the dithiolthiones and consequently the quantum object's timeline resistance which in turn might have dramatically reduced the effect of the spatial vortex . . .

'Oh, for goodness' sake!' moaned Daniel, whose bout of street-talk had mercifully ended as they had climbed into the school's handy portal wardrobe with their vomit-glazed sprouts. He glared upwards, ripped his spectacles off and pointed them into the sky. 'How much more of this can we take? GO AWAY! LEAVE US ALONE!!'

Amy glanced at the sky and frowned an extremely large award-winning frown. 'He's doing it again! Who is he talking to?'

'Daniel!' scolded Betty. 'Calm down, put your nice spectacles back on, you're confusing Amy. We're home. We've saved the world!'

'No thanks to *him*!' moaned Daniel, pointing upwards. 'And why were we made to take this fat ugly dog? He was a burden. We'd have saved the world much quicker if he hadn't been there. I think we should change The Secret Five constitution to bar dogs. And cats. And hamsters, I've never liked hamsters.'

'Woof woof woof?' said Whatshisname mournfully.

'I'll add it to the agenda for the next meeting,' said Betty. 'Now, let's get inside.'

'Well well well,' Aunt Trinny said as the five of them trooped or trotted through the front door. 'Where have you all been? I was planning on being worried sick about you all very soon. Uncle Quagmire arrived back just a few minutes ago, and is upstairs putting his socks back on. I did miss him so. Not so much you children, though. Now, I'll just pop and make sure that there's enough lukewarm water for baths and some moderately clean clothes for you all. You'll probably want to have an extraordinary meeting while I'm gone, won't you now?'

They nodded their rather tired heads and gathered round the typical kitchen table for the meeting, Whatshisname flopping down at Betty's feet.

'Right,' said Betty slightly seriously and rather importantly. 'I declare the extraordinary meeting of the founder members of The Secret . . . Palpable . . . Three Hundred and Fifteen open. Let's have the password from you all and we can begin the meeting.'

'Can't we skip the password bit?' Amy pleaded. 'I can never remember it and we *do* know each other.'

Betty gave Amy one of her biggest frowns, which she'd been saving up for several chapters. 'That's not the point,' she scolded. 'We've been through all this. Passwords are important.'

'Is it testicle?' Ricky offered.

Betty stamped her foot. Whatshisname yelped. 'Honestly!' she said. 'We go on a fantastic adventure and all the rules are forgotten.'

'I agree that we should forget passwords,' said Daniel. 'I'm tired.'

'And I'm hungry,' said Ricky.

Just then, without any warning whatsoever, the door opened and in walked Uncle Quagmire.

'My, my, my,' he said, rather selfishly. 'You all look as though you're having an official meeting. Very splendivenient. Can I join in?'

They all said *no*, but Uncle Quagmire sat down and spoke. 'What heroes you all are! You certainly restored the faith in my lack of faith in you, to be sure. I'd like to thank you for saving the world from the evil mastermind that was Sampson. I missed the actual saving bit, as I was somewhat detained in Victorian times . . .'

'With Alice?' Betty said.

Uncle Quagmire wiggled and waggled his ears and looked slightly embarrassed. 'Not exactly,' he said. 'At least, not just with Alice. I was, well, talking to both Mrs Wells as well.'

'That was nice of you,' said Amy.

'So, Uncle Quagmire,' said Daniel, 'if I may ask a question about you being Sampson's father?'

'I told you,' said Amy. 'That can't be so!'

'Indeed, it can't be so,' said Uncle Quagmire rather hurriedly. He looked down mournfully. 'But, children, maybe I'm not the man you all thought I was.'

'That's good news, isn't it?' said Betty. Everyone nodded their heads in agreement.

'Ahem,' said Uncle Quagmire. 'It's all best forgotten, eh? Look, I think I'll leave you to it after all. All this incisive questigating is too much for me. Anyway, I have another super invention to invent in my shed. I've been working on a combined toaster and wrist watch, you see. I just have to overcome a few hitches and it's there.' He stood up. 'So, I will see you anon, Secret Five. And don't forget to have a bath. You all smell quite disgusting. Especially that dog.'

'Woof woof woof!' agreed Whatshisname.

'Now, let's get down to the agenda,' said Betty, after Uncle Quagmire had left the room. 'About the adventure. I think it went rather well. A few issues, though. Amy, I thought, needed more blue-sky thinking outside the box, and we'll be arranging more training sessions with some blue sky, several boxes and a bit more thinking for her. Secondly, I sensed that Ricky's moodiness was a constant threat to our teamwork . . .'

'It wasn't moodiness, it was hunger!' wailed Ricky.

'Be that as it be,' said Betty. 'As for Daniel, I thought you should have stretched the envelope a little more at times, so we'll be sorting out some training and some envelopes for you to stretch. Also, I thought that your repeated bouts of street-talk threatened our very success at all times.'

'What street-talk?' asked Daniel. 'And what size envelopes?'

'So, overall,' said Betty, ignoring the questions from the floor, 'I think we stepped up to the plate and got all our ducks in a line.'

Ricky put his hand up. 'Betty, I'm really glad about the lined-up ducks, although I must have missed them in the excitement, and I've no idea where that plate was that I stepped up to, but can we discuss all those privileges I missed out on?'

'No,' said Betty quite firmly. 'But I did wonder if we should have some adventure awards handed out. I wondered if there could be an award for Best Dog in a Supporting Role . . .'

Lying at Betty's feet, Whatshisname opened one eye. This sounded promising, although now he was slightly worried that the only spontaneously prepared speech he had ready was *woof woof woof.*

'. . . but,' butted Betty, 'on second thoughts, I think we should skip that award and move on to Best Character for Use of Superlatives.'

The others frowned.

'Don't you think that would be sumptuously uplifting?' Betty asked. 'And wonderfully enormously exquisite?'

Under the table, Whatshisname sighed. He had become quite bored with the meeting. He stood up and padded over to the window. He put his front paws onto the windowsill and peered out, squinting as his fluffy pink collar reflected in the glass. He could see the typical village postman gingerly riding his squeaky bike towards the cottage.

He watched as the typical village postman leapt off his bike, took a letter from his bag, looked at the long long path that led to the front door, and then threw the letter over the gate into the compost heap. Without a thought for his own safety, Whatshisname trotted outside, ran down the path, past the kangaroo that was asleep on the lawn, and carefully picked up the letter in his mouth. He chewed and chewed the letter until it was mush, then swallowed it with a big gulp. He trotted onto the lawn and flopped down by the sleeping kangaroo. He wondered if this was Pavlov's kangaroo. Maybe, maybe not. He still hadn't made any inroads into the philosophical argument about whether animals think, and whether Dog exists. Ho hum. Honing of his personal philosophical system would have to wait. He sighed and closed his eyes. After *that* adventure, he knew that he deserved a peaceful nap. He'd just settle down and doze for a few sticks . . . zzzzzzzz.

Inside the cottage, Daniel was reverting to his strange habit of looking up and shaking his fist. 'I've already warned you!' he yelled. 'Go away! Leave us alo

The Very End

Reading Groups –
suggested discussion points

Stupidity is the re-occurring theme of the novel. At what point in the novel did you realise this and did Amy have any influence on your will to carry on living?

While you were reading the novel, did you at any time want to accidentally drop it in a bucket of sulphuric acid? If so, why do you think that is?

Do you think that the characters' fractious relationship with the author is purely down to the characters' jealousy of his innate talent and charm? Or not?

When Whatshisname ponders on the question 'do animals think?', do you think that he really thinks that or is it that the author thinks that he doesn't think but thinks that making him wonder if he thinks or not thinks actually makes the reader think a lot about whether animals think or don't think? What do you think?

How did you feel when Ricky left the book in chapter eight – or was it nine – anyway, how did you feel? Apart from empathy and envy, that is.

Do you think that the predominance of irony as a device in the book, yeah right, is due to the incongruity between the reader's expectations and the immensely powerful and complex characters, lol?

Did the fact that all the characters are anti-heroes and utter failures have an influence on your decision to skip-read the book after page ten?

Food is an important motif in the book. Do you think that Ricky's obsession with teashops is healthy? Or not? Or don't you care that much?

What about Old Hag's support for West Bromwich Albion? Do you think that it epitomises the frailty of the human condition and the futility of life itself, or the fact that she has always liked the centre-back's tight shorts and sturdy thighs?

How did you cope with the lack of a phallic symbol in the book? Did it matter that the lack of an object that symbolises regenerative power, and that might have acted as an aid to interpretation of the psychological condition of the characters, caused you to occasionally hanker for the mention of a banana?

Should Daniel have taken to wearing spectacles halfway through the book? Or did you already think that he wore spectacles anyway? To satisfy all readers, should the narrative have been multi-choice from then on (e.g, *1. Daniel looked up and took off his spectacles. 2. Daniel looked up and didn't take off his spectacles because he didn't wear any).* Or should Daniel have been killed off in chapter one to avoid all this confusion about spectacles?

What kind of man is Uncle Quagmire? Do you think his moral compass was a bit wonky and always pointing south? Did he really have rumpy-pumpy with a stunt nun? If you think yes, did you yearn for a pull-out graphic sex scene complete with illustrations? If so, are the others in your reading group looking at you in a different way now? Serves you right, weirdo.

One reviewer said that the novel reminded him of Dickens' early works. Discuss what sort of illegal substances that reviewer may have taken before reading the book.

The kangaroo played a central role in the novel. Do you think that this animal is of metaphorical significance and symbolises abandonment, anxiety amongst immigrants, unfulfilled symbiosis, or hearty meals for an Australian family of four for a week?

Now you've reached the end, discuss what you'd really like to do with this book.

Want more? Crikey! Oh well, see:
www.thesecretfive.com

Credits

My thanks go to:

Those readers of the draft manuscripts who were inspirational in their feedback, in particular my ex-uni writing group, Twisted Scribblers, who had to suffer the monthly onslaught of chapters and worried constantly about my sanity.

My wife Elizabeth for her patience and support, and for suppressing the instinct to call in psychiatric help when she used to catch sight of the draft text.

George Long for his embodiment of Whatshisname in the initial artwork, and Mark Pettifer for his help in developing that artwork and other arty stuff.

The wonderful and patient people at Troubador Publishing.

And, of course, Enid Blyton and her contemporaries for providing me with the stories that enthralled and captivated me as a child.

The great Herbert George Wells, whose childhood in this narrative is mostly imagined.

Harold Pinter for his admirable ability to perplex and inspire.

The makers of The Sound of Music for . . . well, The Sound of Music, albeit without stunt nuns.

Wham! It's heartwarming to think that Ricky and Amy were the inspiration for their lyrics and their name.

All the other 'names' in the book for (hopefully) being such good sports.

And, the host of philosophers throughout the ages for giving Whatshisname his sense of purpose.